Honore de Balzac

The Lesser Bourgeoisie

outlook

Honore de Balzac

The Lesser Bourgeoisie

1st Edition | ISBN: 978-3-73408-389-1

Place of Publication: Frankfurt am Main, Germany

Year of Publication: 2019

Outlook Verlag GmbH, Germany.

THE LESSER BOURGEOISIE
(The Middle Classes)

By Honore De Balzac

Translated by Katharine Prescott Wormeley

———————————————————————

DEDICATION

To Constance-Victoire.

Here, madame, is one of those books which come into the mind,
whence no one knows, giving pleasure to the author before he can
foresee what reception the public, our great ·present judge, will
accord to it. Feeling almost certain of your sympathy in my
pleasure, I dedicate the book to you. Ought it not to belong to
you as the tithe formerly belonged to the Church in memory of God,
who makes all things bud and fruit in the fields and in the
intellect?

A few lumps of clay, left by Moliere at the feet of his colossal
statue of Tartuffe, have here been kneaded by a hand more daring
than able; but, at whatever distance I may be from the greatest of
comic writers, I shall still be glad to have used these crumbs in
showing the modern Hypocrite in action. The chief encouragement
that I have had in this difficult undertaking was in finding it
apart from all religious questions,—questions which ought to be
kept out of it for the sake of one so pious as yourself; and also
because of what a great writer has lately called our present
"indifference in matters of religion."

May the double signification of your names be for my book a
prophecy! Deign to find here the respectful gratitude of him who
ventures to call himself the most devoted of your servants.

De Balzac.

———————————————————————

THE LESSER BOURGEOISIE

(The Middle Classes)

PART I. THE LESSER BOURGEOIS OF PARIS

CHAPTER I. DEPARTING PARIS

The tourniquet Saint-Jean, the narrow passage entered through a turnstile, a description of which was said to be so wearisome in the study entitled "A Double Life" (Scenes from Private Life), that naive relic of old Paris, has at the present moment no existence except in our said typography. The building of the Hotel-de-Ville, such as we now see it, swept away a whole section of the city.

In 1830, passers along the street could still see the turnstile painted on the sign of a wine-merchant, but even that house, its last asylum, has been demolished. Alas! old Paris is disappearing with frightful rapidity. Here and there, in the course of this history of Parisian life, will be found preserved, sometimes the type of the dwellings of the middle ages, like that described in "Fame and Sorrow" (Scenes from Private Life), one or two specimens of which exist to the present day; sometimes a house like that of Judge Popinot, rue du Fouarre, a specimen of the former bourgeoisie; here, the remains of Fulbert's house; there, the old dock of the Seine as it was under Charles IX. Why should not the historian of French society, a new Old Mortality, endeavor to save these curious expressions of the past, as Walter Scott's old man rubbed up the tombstones? Certainly, for the last ten years the outcries of literature in this direction have not been superfluous; art is beginning to disguise beneath its floriated ornaments those ignoble facades of what are called in Paris "houses of product," which one of our poets has jocosely compared to chests of drawers.

Let us remark here, that the creation of the municipal commission "del ornamento" which superintends at Milan the architecture of street facades, and to which every house owner is compelled to subject his plan, dates from the seventeenth century. Consequently, we see in that charming capital the effects of this public spirit on the part of nobles and burghers, while we admire their buildings so full of character and originality. Hideous, unrestrained speculation which, year after year, changes the uniform level of storeys, compresses a whole apartment into the space of what used to be a salon, and wages war upon gardens, will infallibly react on Parisian manners and morals. We shall soon be forced to live more without than within. Our sacred private life, the freedom and liberty of home, where will they be?— reserved for those who can muster fifty thousand francs a year! In fact, few millionaires now allow themselves the luxury of a house to themselves, guarded by a courtyard on a street and protected from public curiosity by a shady garden at the back.

3

By levelling fortunes, that section of the Code which regulates testamentary bequests, has produced these huge stone phalansteries, in which thirty families are often lodged, returning a rental of a hundred thousand francs a year. Fifty years hence we shall be able to count on our fingers the few remaining houses which resemble that occupied, at the moment our narrative begins, by the Thuillier family,—a really curious house which deserves the honor of an exact description, if only to compare the life of the bourgeoisie of former times with that of to-day.

The situation and the aspect of this house, the frame of our present Scene of manners and morals, has, moreover, a flavor, a perfume of the lesser bourgeoisie, which may attract or repel attention according to the taste of each reader.

In the first place, the Thuillier house did not belong to either Monsieur or Madame Thuillier, but to Mademoiselle Thuillier, the sister of Monsieur Thuillier.

This house, bought during the first six months which followed the revolution of July by Mademoiselle Marie-Jeanne-Brigitte Thuillier, a spinster of full age, stands about the middle of the rue Saint-Dominique d'Enfer, to the right as you enter by the rue d'Enfer, so that the main building occupied by Monsieur Thuillier faces south.

The progressive movement which is carrying the Parisian population to the heights along the right bank of the Seine had long injured the sale of property in what is called the "Latin quarter," when reasons, which will be given when we come to treat of the character and habits of Monsieur Thuillier, determined his sister to the purchase of real estate. She obtained this property for the small sum of forty-six thousand francs; certain extras amounted to six thousand more; in all, the price paid was fifty-two thousand francs. A description of the property given in the style of an advertisement, and the results obtained by Monsieur Thuillier's exertions, will explain by what means so many fortunes increased enormously after July, 1830, while so many others sank.

Toward the street the house presents a facade of rough stone covered with plaster, cracked by weather and lined by the mason's instrument into a semblance of blocks of cut stone. This frontage is so common in Paris and so ugly that the city ought to offer premiums to house-owners who would build their facades of cut-stone blocks. Seven windows lighted the gray front of this house which was raised three storeys, ending in a mansard roof covered with slate. The porte-cochere, heavy and solid, showed by its workmanship and style that the front building on the street had been erected in the days of the Empire, to utilize a part of the courtyard of the vast old mansion, built at an epoch when the quarter d'Enfer enjoyed a certain vogue.

On one side was the porter's lodge; on the other the staircase of the front building. Two wings, built against the adjoining houses, had formerly served as stables, coach-house, kitchen and offices to the rear dwelling; but since 1830, they had been converted into warerooms. The one on the right was let to a certain M. Metivier, jr., wholesale dealer in paper; that on the left to a bookseller named Barbet. The offices of each were above the warerooms; the bookseller occupying the first storey, and the paper-dealer the second storey of the house on the street. Metivier, jr., who was more of a commission merchant in paper than a regular dealer, and Barbet, much more of a money lender and discounter than a bookseller, kept these vast warerooms for the purpose of storing,—one, his stacks of paper, bought of needy manufacturers, the other, editions of books given as security for loans.

The shark of bookselling and the pike of paper-dealing lived on the best of terms, and their mutual operations, exempt from the turmoil of retail business, brought so few carriages into that tranquil courtyard that the concierge was obliged to pull up the grass between the paving stones. Messrs. Barbet and Metivier paid a few rare visits to their landlords, and the punctuality with which they paid their rent classed them as good tenants; in fact, they were looked upon as very honest men by the Thuillier circle.

As for the third floor on the street, it was made into two apartments; one of which was occupied by M. Dutocq, clerk of the justice of peace, a retired government employee, and a frequenter of the Thuillier salon; the other by the hero of this Scene, about whom we must content ourselves at the present moment by fixing the amount of his rent,—namely, seven hundred francs a year,—and the location he had chosen in the heart of this well-filled building, exactly three years before the curtain rises on the present domestic drama.

The clerk, a bachelor of fifty, occupied the larger of the two apartments on the third floor. He kept a cook, and the rent of the rooms was a thousand francs a year. Within two years of the time of her purchase, Mademoiselle Thuillier was receiving seven thousand two hundred francs in rentals, for a house which the late proprietor had supplied with outside blinds, renovated within, and adorned with mirrors, without being able to sell or let it. Moreover, the Thuilliers themselves, nobly lodged, as we shall see, enjoyed also a fine garden,—one of the finest in that quarter,—the trees of which shaded the lonely little street named the rue Neuve-Saint-Catherine.

Standing between the courtyard and the garden, the main building, which they inhabited, seems to have been the caprice of some enriched bourgeois in the reign of Louis XIV.; the dwelling, perhaps, of a president of the parliament, or that of a tranquil savant. Its noble free-stone blocks, damaged by time, have a certain air of Louis-the-Fourteenth grandeur; the courses of the facade define the storeys; panels of red brick recall the appearance of the stables at Versailles; the windows have masks carved as ornaments in the centre of their arches and below their sills. The door, of small panels in the upper half and plain below, through which, when open, the garden can be seen, is of that honest, unassuming style which was often employed in former days for the porter's lodges of the royal chateaux.

This building, with five windows to each course, rises two storeys above the ground-floor, and is particularly noticeable for a roof of four sides ending in a weather-vane, and broken here and there by tall, handsome chimneys, and oval windows. Perhaps this structure is the remains of some great mansion; but after examining all the existing old maps of Paris, we find nothing which bears out this conjecture. Moreover, the title-deeds of property under Louis XIV. was Petitot, the celebrated painter in miniature, who obtained it originally from President Lecamus. We may therefore believe that Lecamus lived in this building while he was erecting his more famous mansion in the rue de Thorigny.

So Art and the legal robe have passed this way in turn. How many instigations of needs and pleasures have led to the interior arrangement of the dwelling! To right, as we enter a square hall forming a closed vestibule, rises a stone staircase with two windows looking on the garden. Beneath the staircase opens a door to the cellar. From this vestibule we enter the dining-room, lighted from the courtyard, and the dining-room communicates at its side with the kitchen, which forms a continuation of the wing in which are the warerooms of Metivier and Barbet. Behind the staircase extends, on the garden side, a fine study or office with two large windows. The first and second floor form two complete apartments, and the servants' quarters are shown by the oval windows in the four-sided roof.

A large porcelain stove heats the square vestibule, the two glass doors of which, placed opposite to each other, light it. This room, paved in black and white marble, is especially noticeable for a ceiling of beams formerly painted and gilt, but which had since received, probably under the Empire, a coat of plain white paint. The three doors of the study, salon and dining-room, surmounted by oval panels, are awaiting a restoration that is more than needed. The wood-work is heavy, but the ornamentation is not without merit. The salon, panelled throughout, recalls the great century by its tall mantelpiece of Languedoc marble, its ceiling decorated at the corners, and by the style of its windows, which still retain their little panes. The dining-room, communicating with the salon by a double door, is floored with stone; the wood-work is oak, unpainted, and an atrocious modern wall-paper has been substituted for the tapestries of the olden time. The ceiling is of chestnut; and the study, modernized by Thuillier, adds its quota to these discordances.

The white and gold mouldings of the salon are so effaced that nothing remains of the gilding but reddish lines, while the white enamelling is yellow, cracked, and peeling off. Never did the Latin saying "Otium cum dignitate" have a greater commentary to the mind of a poet than in this noble building. The iron-work of the staircase baluster is worthy of the artist and the magistrate; but to find other traces of their taste to-day in this majestic relic, the eyes of an artistic observer are needed.

The Thuilliers and their predecessors have frequently degraded this jewel of the upper bourgeoisie by the habits and inventions of the lesser bourgeoisie. Look at those walnut chairs covered with horse-hair, that mahogany table with its oilcloth cover, that sideboard, also of mahogany, that carpet, bought at a bargain, beneath the table, those metal lamps, that wretched paper with its red border, those execrable engravings, and the calico curtains with red fringes, in a dining-room, where the friends of Petitot once feasted! Do you notice the effect produced in the salon by those portraits of Monsieur and Madame and Mademoiselle Thuillier by Pierre Grassou, the artist par excellence of the modern bourgeoisie. Have you remarked the card-tables and the consoles of the Empire, the tea-table supported by a lyre, and that species of sofa, of gnarled mahogany, covered in painted velvet of a chocolate tone? On the chimney-piece, with the clock (representing the Bellona of the Empire), are candelabra with fluted columns. Curtains of woollen damask, with under-curtains of embroidered muslin held back by stamped brass holders, drape the windows. On the floor a cheap carpet. The handsome vestibule has wooden benches, covered with velvet, and the panelled walls with their fine carvings are mostly hidden by wardrobes, brought there from time to time from the bedrooms occupied by the Thuilliers. Fear, that hideous divinity, has caused the family to add sheet-iron doors on the garden side and on the courtyard side, which are folded back against the walls in the daytime, and are closed at night.

It is easy to explain the deplorable profanation practised on this monument of the private life of the bourgeoisie of the seventeenth century, by the private life of the bourgeoisie of the nineteenth. At the beginning of the Consulate, let us say, some master-mason having bought the ancient building, took the idea of turning to account the ground which lay between it and the street. He probably pulled down the fine porte-cochere or entrance gate, flanked by little lodges which guarded the charming "sejour" (to use a word of the olden time), and proceeded, with the industry of a Parisian proprietor, to impress his withering mark on the elegance of the old building. What a curious study might be made of the successive title-deeds of property in Paris! A private lunatic asylum performs its functions in the rue des Batailles in the former dwelling of the Chevalier Pierre Bayard du Terrail, once without fear and without reproach; a street has now been built by the present bourgeois administration through the site of the hotel Necker. Old Paris is departing, following its kings who abandoned it. For one masterpiece of architecture saved from destruction by a Polish princess (the hotel Lambert, Ile Saint-Louis, bought and occupied by the Princess Czartoriska) how many little palaces have fallen, like this dwelling of Petitot, into the hands of such as Thuillier.

Here follows the causes which made Mademoiselle Thuillier the owner of the house.

CHAPTER II. THE HISTORY OF A TYRANNY

At the fall of the Villele ministry, Monsieur Louis-Jerome Thuillier, who had then seen twenty-six years' service as a clerk in the ministry of finance, became sub-director of a department thereof; but scarcely had he enjoyed the subaltern authority of a position formerly his lowest hope, when the events of July, 1830, forced him to resign it. He calculated, shrewdly enough, that his pension would be honorably and readily given by the new-comers, glad to have another office at their disposal. He was right; for a pension of seventeen hundred francs was paid to him immediately.

When the prudent sub-director first talked of resigning, his sister, who was far more the companion of his life than his wife, trembled for his future.

"What will become of Thuillier?" was a question which Madame and Mademoiselle Thuillier put to each other with mutual terror in their little lodging on a third floor of the rue d'Argenteuil.

"Securing his pension will occupy him for a time," Mademoiselle Thuillier said one day; "but I am thinking of investing my savings in a way that will cut out work for him. Yes; it will be something like administrating the finances to manage a piece of property."

"Oh, sister! you will save his life," cried Madame Thuillier.

"I have always looked for a crisis of this kind in Jerome's life," replied the old maid, with a protecting air.

Mademoiselle Thuillier had too often heard her brother remark: "Such a one is dead; he only survived his retirement two years"; she had too often heard Colleville, her brother's intimate friend, a government employee like himself, say, jesting on this climacteric of bureaucrats, "We shall all come to it, ourselves," not to appreciate the danger her brother was running. The change from activity to leisure is, in truth, the critical period for government employees of all kinds.

Those of them who know not how to substitute, or perhaps cannot substitute other occupations for the work to which they have been accustomed, change in a singular manner; some die outright; others take to fishing, the vacancy of that amusement resembling that of their late employment under government; others, who are smarter men, dabble in stocks, lose their savings, and are thankful to obtain a place in some enterprise that is likely to succeed, after a first disaster and liquidation, in the hands of an abler management. The late clerk then rubs his hands, now empty, and says to himself, "I always did foresee the success of the business." But nearly all these retired bureaucrats have to fight against their former habits.

"Some," Colleville used to say, "are victims to a sort of 'spleen' peculiar to the government clerk; they die of a checked circulation; a red-tapeworm is in their vitals. That little Poiret couldn't see the well-known white carton without changing color at the beloved sight; he used to turn from green to yellow."

Mademoiselle Thuillier was considered the moving spirit of her brother's household; she was not without decision and force of character, as the following history will show. This superiority over those who immediately surrounded her enabled her to judge her brother, although she adored him. After witnessing the failure of the hopes she had set upon her idol, she had too much real maternity in her feeling for him to let herself be mistaken as to his social value.

Thuillier and his sister were children of the head porter at the ministry of finance. Jerome had escaped, thanks to his near-sightedness, all drafts and conscriptions. The father's ambition was to make his son a government clerk. At the beginning of this century the army presented too many posts not to leave various vacancies in the government offices. A deficiency of minor officials enabled old Pere Thuillier to hoist his son upon the lowest step of the bureaucratic hierarchy. The old man died in 1814, leaving Jerome on the point of becoming sub-director, but with no other fortune than that prospect. The worthy Thuillier and his wife (who died in 1810) had retired from active service in 1806, with a pension as their only means of support; having spent what property they had in giving Jerome the education required in these days, and in supporting both him and his sister.

The influence of the Restoration on the bureaucracy is well known. From the forty and one suppressed departments a crowd of honorable employees returned to Paris with nothing to do, and clamorous for places inferior to those they had lately occupied. To these acquired rights were added those of exiled families ruined by the Revolution. Pressed between the two floods, Jerome thought himself lucky not to have been dismissed under some frivolous pretext. He trembled until the day when, becoming by mere chance sub-director, he saw himself secure of a retiring pension. This cursory view of matters will serve to explain Monsieur Thuillier's very limited scope and knowledge. He had learned the Latin, mathematics, history, and geography that are taught in schools, but he never got beyond what is called the second class; his father having preferred to take advantage of a sudden opportunity to place him at the ministry. So, while the young Thuillier was making his first records on the Grand-Livre, he ought to have been studying his rhetoric and philosophy.

While grinding the ministerial machine, he had no leisure to cultivate letters, still less the arts; but he acquired a routine knowledge of his business, and when he had an opportunity to rise, under the Empire, to the sphere of superior employees, he assumed a superficial air of competence which concealed the son of a porter, though none of it rubbed into his mind. His ignorance, however, taught him to keep silence, and silence served him well. He accustomed himself to practise, under the imperial regime, a passive obedience which pleased his superiors; and it was to this quality that he owed at a later period his promotion to the rank of sub-director. His routine habits then became great experience; his manners and his silence concealed his lack of education, and his absolute nullity was a recommendation, for a cipher was needed. The government was afraid of displeasing both parties in the Chamber by selecting a man from either side; it therefore got out of the difficulty by resorting to the rule of seniority. That is how Thuillier became sub-director. Mademoiselle Thuillier, knowing that her brother abhorred reading, and could substitute no business for the bustle of a public office, had wisely resolved to plunge him into the cares of property, into the culture of a garden, in short, into all the infinitely petty concerns and neighborhood intrigues which make up the life of the bourgeoisie.

The transplanting of the Thuillier household from the rue d'Argenteuil to the rue Saint-Dominique d'Enfer, the business of making the purchase, of finding a suitable porter, and then of obtaining tenants occupied Thuillier from 1831 to 1832. When the phenomenon of the change was accomplished, and the sister saw that Jerome had borne it fairly well, she found him other cares and occupations (about which we shall hear later), all based upon the character of the man himself, as to which it will now be useful to give information.

Though the son of a ministerial porter, Thuillier was what is called a fine man, slender in figure, above middle height, and possessing a face that was rather agreeable if wearing his spectacles, but frightful without them; which is frequently the case with near-sighted persons; for the habit of looking through glasses has covered the pupils of his eyes with a sort of film.

Between the ages of eighteen and thirty, young Thuillier had much success among women, in a sphere which began with the lesser bourgeois and ended in that of the heads of departments. Under the Empire, war left Parisian society rather denuded of men of energy, who were mostly on the battlefield; and perhaps, as a great physician has suggested, this may account for the flabbiness of the generation which occupies the middle of the nineteenth century.

Thuillier, forced to make himself noticeable by other charms than those of mind, learned to dance and to waltz in a way to be cited; he was called "that handsome Thuillier"; he played billiards to perfection; he knew how to cut out likenesses in black paper, and his friend Colleville coached him so well that he was able to sing all the ballads of the day. These various small accomplishments resulted in that appearance of success which deceives youth and befogs it about the future. Mademoiselle Thuillier, from 1806 to 1814, believed in her brother as Mademoiselle d'Orleans believed in Louis-Philippe. She was proud of Jerome; she expected to see him the director-general of his department of the ministry, thanks to his successes in certain salons, where, undoubtedly, he would never have been admitted but for the circumstances which made society under the Empire a medley.

But the successes of "that handsome Thuillier" were usually of short duration; women did not care to keep his devotion any more than he desired to make his devotion eternal. He was really an unwilling Don Juan; the career of a "beau" wearied him to the point of aging him; his face, covered with lines like that of an old coquette, looked a dozen years older than the registers made him. There remained to him of all his successes in gallantry, a habit of looking at himself in mirrors, of buttoning his coat to define his waist, and of posing in various dancing attitudes; all of which prolonged, beyond the period of enjoying his advantages, the sort of lease that he held on his cognomen, "that handsome Thuillier."

The truth of 1806 has, however, become a fable, in 1826. He retains a few vestiges of the former costume of the beaux of the Empire, which are not unbecoming to the dignity of a former sub-director. He still wears the white cravat with innumerable folds, wherein his chin is buried, and the coquettish bow, formerly tied by the hands of beauty, the two ends of which threaten danger to the passers to right and left. He follows the fashions of former days, adapting them to his present needs; he tips his hat on the back of his head, and wears shoes and thread stockings in summer; his long-tailed coats remind one of the well-known "surtouts" of the Empire; he has not yet abandoned his frilled shirts and his white waistcoats; he still plays with his Empire switch, and holds himself so erect that his back bends in. No one, seeing Thuillier promenading on the boulevards, would take him for the son of a man who cooked the breakfasts of the clerks at a ministry and wore the livery of Louis XVI.; he resembles an imperial diplomatist or a sub-prefect. Now, not only did Mademoiselle Thuillier very innocently work upon her brother's weak spot by encouraging in him an excessive care of his person, which, in her, was simply a continuation of her worship, but she also provided him with family joys, by transplanting to their midst a household which had hitherto been quasi-collateral to them.

It was that of Monsieur Colleville, an intimate friend of Thuillier. But before we proceed to describe Pylades let us finish with Orestes, and explain why Thuillier—that handsome Thuillier—was left without a family of his own—for the family, be it said, is non-existent without children. Herein appears one of those deep mysteries which lie buried in the arena of private life, a few shreds of which rise to the surface at moments when the pain of a concealed situation grows poignant. This concerns the life of Madame and Mademoiselle Thuillier; so far, we have seen only the life (and we may call it the public life) of Jerome Thuillier.

Marie-Jeanne-Brigitte Thuillier, four years older than her brother, had been utterly sacrificed to him; it was easier to give a career to one than a "dot" to the other. Misfortune to some natures is a pharos, which illumines to their eyes the dark low corners of social existence. Superior to her brother both in mind and energy, Brigitte had one of those natures which, under the hammer of persecution, gather themselves together, become compact and powerfully resistant, not to say inflexible. Jealous of her independence, she kept aloof from the life of the household; choosing to make herself the sole arbiter of her own fate. At fourteen years of age, she went to live alone in a garret, not far from the ministry of finance, which was then in the rue Vivienne, and also not far from the Bank of France, then, and now, in the rue de la Vrilliere. There she bravely gave herself up to a form of industry little known and the perquisite of a few persons, which she obtained, thanks to the patrons of her father. It consisted in making bags to hold coin for the Bank, the Treasury, and the great financial houses. At the end of three years she employed two workwomen. By investing her savings on the Grand-Livre, she found herself, in 1814, the mistress of three thousand six hundred francs a year, earned in fifteen years. As she spent little, and dined with her father as long as he lived, and, as government securities were very low during the last convulsions of the Empire, this result, which seems at first sight exaggerated, explains itself.

On the death of their father, Brigitte and Jerome, the former being twenty-seven, the latter twenty-three, united their existence. Brother and sister were bound together by an extreme affection. If Jerome, then at the height of his success, was pinched for money, his sister, clothed in serge, and her fingers roughened by the coarse thread with which she sewed her bags, would give him a few louis. In Brigitte's eyes Jerome was the handsomest and most charming man in the whole French Empire. To keep house for this cherished brother, to be initiated into the secrets of Lindor and Don Juan, to be his handmaiden, his spaniel, was Brigitte's dream. She immolated herself lovingly to an idol whose selfishness, always great, was enormously increased by her self-sacrifice. She sold her business to her fore-woman for fifteen thousand francs and came to live with Thuillier in the rue d'Argenteuil, where she made herself the mother, protectress, and servant of this spoiled child of women. Brigitte, with the natural caution of a girl who owed everything to her own discretion and her own labor, concealed the amount of her savings from Jerome,—fearing, no doubt, the extravagance of a man of gallantry. She merely paid a quota of six hundred francs a year to the expenses of the household, and this, with her brother's eighteen hundred, enabled her to make both ends meet at the end of the year.

From the first days of their coming together, Thuillier listened to his sister as to an oracle; he consulted her in his trifling affairs, kept none of his secrets from her, and thus made her taste the fruit of despotism which was, in truth, the one little sin of her nature. But the sister had sacrificed everything to the brother; she had staked her all upon his heart; she lived by him only. Brigitte's ascendancy over Jerome was singularly proved by the marriage which she procured for him about the year 1814.

Seeing the tendency to enforced reduction which the new-comers to power under the Restoration were beginning to bring about in the government offices, and particularly since the return of the old society which sought to ride over the bourgeoisie, Brigitte understood, far better than her brother could explain it to her, the social crisis which presently extinguished their common hopes. No more successes for that handsome Thuillier in the salons of the nobles who now succeeded the plebeians of the Empire!

Thuillier was not enough of a person to take up a politic opinion and choose a party; he felt, as his sister did for him, the necessity of profiting by the remains of his youth to make a settlement. In such a situation, a sister as jealous of her power as Brigitte naturally would, and ought, to marry her brother, to suit herself as well as to suit him; for she alone could make him really happy, Madame Thuillier being only an indispensable accessory to the obtaining of two or three children. If Brigitte did not have an intellect quite the equal of her will, at least she had the instinct of her despotism; without, it is true, education, she marched straight before her, with the headstrong determination of a nature accustomed to succeed. She had the genius of housekeeping, a faculty for economy, a thorough understanding of how to live, and a love for work. She saw plainly that she could never succeed in marrying Jerome into a sphere above their own, where parents might inquire into their domestic life and feel uneasy at finding a mistress already reigning in the home. She therefore sought in a lower grade for persons to dazzle, and found, almost beside her, a suitable match.

The oldest usher at the Bank, a man named Lemprun, had an only daughter, called Celeste. Mademoiselle Celeste Lemprun would inherit the fortune of her mother, the only daughter of a rich farmer. This fortune consisted of some acres of land in the environs of Paris, which the old father still worked; besides this, she would have the property of Lemprun himself, a man who had left the firms of Thelusson and of Keller to enter the service of the Bank of France. Lemprun, now the head of that service, enjoyed the respect and consideration of the governors and auditors.

The Bank council, on hearing of the probable marriage of Celeste to an honorable employee at the ministry of finance, promised a wedding present of six thousand francs. This gift, added to twelve thousand given by Pere Lemprun, and twelve thousand more from the maternal grandfather, Sieur Galard, market-gardener at Auteuil, brought up the dowry to thirty thousand francs. Old Galard and Monsieur and Madame Lemprun were delighted with the marriage. Lemprun himself knew Mademoiselle Thuillier, and considered her one of the worthiest and most conscientious women in Paris. Brigitte then, for the first time, allowed her investments on the Grand-Livre to shine forth, assuring Lemprun that she should never marry; consequently, neither he nor his wife, persons devoted to the main chance, would ever allow themselves to find fault with Brigitte. Above all, they were greatly struck by the splendid prospects of the handsome Thuillier, and the marriage took place, as the conventional saying is, to the general satisfaction.

The governor of the Bank and the secretary were the bride's witnesses; Monsieur de la Billardiere, director of Thuillier's department, and Monsieur Rabourdin, head of the office, being those of the groom. Six days after the marriage old Lemprun was the victim of a daring robbery which made a great noise in the newspapers of the day, though it was quickly forgotten during the events of 1815. The guilty parties having escaped detection, Lemprun wished to make up the loss; but the Bank agreed to carry the deficit to its profit and loss account; nevertheless, the poor old man actually died of the grief this affair had caused him. He regarded it as an attack upon his aged honor.

Madame Lemprun then resigned all her property to her daughter, Madame Thuillier, and went to live with her father at Auteuil until he died from an accident in 1817. Alarmed at the prospect of having to manage or lease the market-garden and the farm of her father, Madame Lemprun entreated Brigitte, whose honesty and capacity astonished her, to wind up old Galard's affairs, and to settle the property in such a way that her daughter should take possession of everything, securing to her mother fifteen hundred francs a year and the house at Auteuil. The landed property of the old farmer was sold in lots, and brought in thirty thousand francs. Lemprun's estate had given as much more, so that Madame Thuillier's fortune, including her "dot," amounted in 1818 to ninety thousand francs. Joining the revenue of this property to that of the brother and sister, the Thuillier household had an income, in 1818, amounting to eleven thousand francs, managed by Brigitte alone on her sole responsibility. It is necessary to begin by stating this financial position, not only to prevent objections but to rid the drama of difficulties.

Brigitte began, from the first, by allowing her brother five hundred francs a month, and by sailing the household boat at the rate of five thousand francs a year. She granted to her sister-in-law fifty francs a month, explaining to her carefully that she herself was satisfied with forty. To strengthen her despotism by the power of money, Brigitte laid by the surplus of her own funds. She made, so it was said in business offices, usurious loans by means of her brother, who appeared as a money-lender. If, between the years 1813 and 1830, Brigitte had capitalized sixty thousand francs, that sum can be explained by the rise in the Funds, and there is no need to have recourse to accusations more or less well founded, which have nothing to do with our present history.

From the first days of the marriage, Brigitte subdued the unfortunate Madame Thuillier with a touch of the spur and a jerk of the bit, both of which she made her feel severely. A further display of tyranny was useless; the victim resigned herself at once. Celeste, thoroughly understood by Brigitte, a girl without mind or education, accustomed to a sedentary life and a tranquil atmosphere, was extremely gentle by nature; she was pious in the fullest acceptation of the word; she would willingly have expiated by the hardest punishments the involuntary wrong of giving pain to her neighbor. She was utterly ignorant of life; accustomed to be waited on by her mother, who did the whole service of the house, for Celeste was unable to make much exertion, owing to a lymphatic constitution which the least toil wearied. She was truly a daughter of the people of Paris, where children, seldom handsome, and of no vigor, the product of poverty and toil, of homes without fresh air, without freedom of action, without any of the conveniences of life, meet us at every turn.

At the time of the marriage, Celeste was seen to be a little woman, fair and faded almost to sickliness, fat, slow, and silly in the countenance. Her forehead, much too large and too prominent, suggested water on the brain, and beneath that waxen cupola her face, noticeably too small and ending in a point like the nose of a mouse, made some people fear she would become, sooner or later, imbecile. Her eyes, which were light blue, and her lips, always fixed in a smile, did not contradict that idea. On the solemn occasion of her marriage she had the manner, air, and attitude of a person condemned to death, whose only desire is that it might all be over speedily.

"She is rather round," said Colleville to Thuillier.

Brigitte was just the knife to cut into such a nature, to which her own formed the strongest contrast. Mademoiselle Thuillier was remarkable for her regular and correct beauty, but a beauty injured by toil which, from her very childhood, had bent her down to painful, thankless tasks, and by the secret privations she imposed upon herself in order to amass her little property. Her complexion, early discolored, had something the tint of steel. Her brown eyes were framed in brown; on the upper lip was a brown floss like a sort of smoke. Her lips were thin, and her imperious forehead was surmounted by hair once black, now turning to chinchilla. She held herself as straight as the fairest beauty; but all things else about her showed the hardiness of her life, the deadening of her natural fire, the cost of what she was!

To Brigitte, Celeste was simply a fortune to lay hold of, a future mother to rule, one more subject in her empire. She soon reproached her for being *weak*, a constant word in her vocabulary, and the jealous old maid, who would strongly have resented any signs of activity in her sister-in-law, now took a savage pleasure in prodding the languid inertness of the feeble creature. Celeste, ashamed to see her sister-in-law displaying such energy in household work, endeavored to help her, and fell ill in consequence. Instantly, Brigitte was devoted to her, nursed her like a beloved sister, and would say, in presence of Thuillier: "You haven't any strength, my child; you must never do anything again." She showed up Celeste's incapacity by that display of sympathy with which strength, seeming to pity weakness, finds means to boast of its own powers.

But, as all despotic natures liking to exercise their strength are full of tenderness for physical sufferings, Brigitte took such real care of her sister-in-law as to satisfy Celeste's mother when she came to see her daughter. After Madame Thuillier recovered, however, she called her, in Celeste's hearing, "a helpless creature, good for nothing!" which sent the poor thing crying to her room. When Thuillier found her there, drying her eyes, he excused her sister, saying:—

"She is an excellent woman, but rather hasty; she loves you in her own way; she behaves just so with me."

Celeste, remembering the maternal care of her sister-in-law during her illness, forgave the wound. Brigitte always treated her brother as the king of the family; she exalted him to Celeste, and made him out an autocrat, a Ladislas, an infallible pope. Madame Thuillier having lost her father and grandfather, and being well-nigh deserted by her mother, who came to see her on Thursdays only (she herself spending Sundays at Auteuil in summer), had no one left to love except her husband, and she did love him,—in the first place, because he was her husband, and secondly, because he still remained to her "that handsome Thuillier." Besides, he sometimes treated her like a wife, and all these reasons together made her adore him. He seemed to her all the more perfect because he often took up her defence and scolded his sister, not from any real interest in his wife, but for pure selfishness, and in order to have peace in the household during the very few moments that he stayed there.

In fact, that handsome Thuillier was never at home except at dinner, after which meal he went out, returning very late at night. He went to balls and other social festivities by himself, precisely as if he were still a bachelor. Thus the two women were always alone together. Celeste insensibly fell into a passive attitude, and became what Brigitte wanted her,—a helot. The Queen Elizabeth of the household then passed from despotism to a sort of pity for the poor victim who was always sacrificed. She ended by softening her haughty ways, her cutting speech, her contemptuous tones, as soon as she was certain that her sister-in-law was completely under the yoke. When she saw the wounds it made on the neck of her victim, she took care of her as a thing of her own, and Celeste entered upon happier days. Comparing the end with the beginning, she even felt a sort of love for her torturer. To gain some power of self-defence, to become something less a cipher in the household, supported, unknown to herself, by her own means, the poor helot had but a single chance, and that chance never came to her.

Celeste had no child. This barrenness, which, from month to month, brought floods of tears from her eyes, was long the cause of Brigitte's scorn; she reproached the poor woman bitterly for being fit for nothing, not even to bear children. The old maid, who had longed to love her brother's child as if it were her own, was unable, for years, to reconcile herself to this irremediable sterility.

At the time when our history begins, namely, in 1840, Celeste, then forty-six years old, had ceased to weep; she now had the certainty of never being a mother. And here is a strange thing. After twenty-five years of this life, in which victory had ended by first dulling and then breaking its own knife, Brigitte loved Celeste as much as Celeste loved Brigitte. Time, ease, and the perpetual rubbing of domestic life, had worn off the angles and smoothed the asperities; Celeste's resignation and lamb-like gentleness had brought, at last, a serene and peaceful autumn. The two women were still further united by the one sentiment that lay within them, namely, their adoration for the lucky and selfish Thuillier.

Moreover, these two women, both childless, had each, like all women who have vainly desired children, fallen in love with a child. This fictitious motherhood, equal in strength to a real motherhood, needs an explanation which will carry us to the very heart of our drama, and will show the reason of the new occupation which Mademoiselle Thuillier provided for her brother.

CHAPTER III. COLLEVILLE

Thuillier had entered the ministry of finance as supernumerary at the same time as Colleville, who has been mentioned already as his intimate friend. In opposition to the well-regulated, gloomy household of Thuillier, social nature had provided that of Colleville; and if it is impossible not to remark that this fortuitous contrast was scarcely moral, we must add that, before deciding that point, it would be well to wait for the end of this drama, unfortunately too true, for which the present historian is not responsible.

Colleville was the only son of a talented musician, formerly first violin at the Opera under Francoeur and Rebel, who related, at least six times a month during his lifetime, anecdotes concerning the representations of the "Village Seer"; and mimicked Jean-Jacques Rousseau, taking him off to perfection. Colleville and Thuillier were inseparable friends; they had no secrets from each other, and their friendship, begun at fifteen years of age, had never known a cloud up to the year 1839. The former was one of those employees who are called, in the government offices, pluralists. These clerks are remarkable for their industry. Colleville, a good musician, owed to the name and influence of his father a situation as first clarionet at the Opera-Comique, and so long as he was a bachelor, Colleville, who was rather richer than Thuillier, shared his means with his friend. But, unlike Thuillier, Colleville married for love a Mademoiselle Flavie, the natural daughter of a celebrated danseuse at the Opera; her reputed father being a certain du Bourguier, one of the richest contractors of the day. In style and origin, Flavie was apparently destined for a melancholy career, when Colleville, often sent to her mother's apartments, fell in love with her and married her. Prince Galathionne, who at that time was "protecting" the danseuse, then approaching the end of her brilliant career, gave Flavie a "dot" of twenty thousand francs, to which her mother added a magnificent trousseau. Other friends and opera-comrades sent jewels and silver-ware, so that the Colleville household was far richer in superfluities than in capital. Flavie, brought up in opulence, began her married life in a charming apartment, furnished by her mother's upholsterer, where the young wife, who was full of taste for art and for artists, and possessed a certain elegance, ruled, a queen.

Madame Colleville was pretty and piquant, clever, gay, and graceful; to express her in one sentence,—a charming creature. Her mother, the danseuse, now forty-three years old, retired from the stage and went to live in the country,—thus depriving her daughter of the resources derived from her wasteful extravagance. Madame Colleville kept a very agreeable but extremely free and easy household. From 1816 to 1826 she had five children. Colleville, a musician in the evening, kept the books of a merchant from seven to nine in the morning, and by ten o'clock he was at his ministry. Thus, by blowing into a bit of wood by night, and writing double-entry accounts in the early morning, he managed to eke out his earnings to seven or eight thousand francs a year.

Madame Colleville played the part of a "comme il faut" woman; she received on Wednesdays, gave a concert once a month and a dinner every fortnight. She never saw Colleville except at dinner and at night, when he returned about twelve o'clock, at which hour she was frequently not at home herself. She went to the theatres, where boxes were sometimes given to her; and she would send word to Colleville to come and fetch her from such or such a house, where she was supping and dancing. At her own house, guests found excellent cheer, and her society, though rather mixed, was very amusing; she received and welcomed actresses, artists, men of letters, and a few rich men. Madame Colleville's elegance was on a par with that of Tullia, the leading prima-donna, with whom she was intimate; but though the Collevilles encroached on their capital and were often in difficulty by the end of the month, Flavie was never in debt.

Colleville was very happy; he still loved his wife, and he made himself her best friend. Always received by her with affectionate smiles and sympathetic pleasure, he yielded readily to the irresistible grace of her manners. The vehement activity with which he pursued his three avocations was a part of his natural character and temperament. He was a fine stout man, ruddy, jovial, extravagant, and full of ideas. In ten years there was never a quarrel in his household. Among business men he was looked upon, in common with all artists, as a scatter-brained fellow; and superficial persons thought that the constant hurry of this hard worker was only the restless coming and going of a busybody.

Colleville had the sense to seem stupid; he boasted of his family happiness, and gave himself unheard-of trouble in making anagrams, in order at times to seem absorbed in that passion. The government clerks of his division at the ministry, the office directors, and even the heads of divisions came to his concerts; now and then he quietly bestowed upon them opera tickets, when he needed some extra indulgence on account of his frequent absence. Rehearsals took half the time that he ought to have been at his desk; but the musical knowledge his father had bequeathed to him was sufficiently genuine and well-grounded to excuse him from all but final rehearsals. Thanks to Madame Colleville's intimacies, both the theatre and the ministry lent themselves kindly to the needs of this industrious pluralist, who, moreover, was bringing up, with great care, a youth, warmly recommended to him by his wife, a future great musician, who sometimes took his place in the orchestra with a promise of eventually succeeding him. In fact, about the year 1827 this young man became the first clarionet when Colleville resigned his position.

The usual comment on Flavie was, "That little slip of a coquette, Madame Colleville." The eldest of the Colleville children, born in 1816, was the living image of Colleville himself. In 1818, Madame Colleville held the cavalry in high estimation, above even art; and she distinguished more particularly a sub-lieutenant in the dragoons of Saint-Chamans, the young and rich Charles de Gondreville, who afterwards died in the Spanish campaign. By that time Flavie had had a second son, whom she henceforth dedicated to a military career. In 1820 she considered banking the nursing mother of trade, the supporter of Nations, and she made the great Keller, that famous banker and orator, her idol. She then had another son, whom she named Francois, resolving to make him a merchant,—feeling sure that Keller's influence would never fail him. About the close of the year 1820, Thuillier, the intimate friend of Monsieur and Madame Colleville, felt the need of pouring his sorrows into the bosom of this excellent woman, and to her he related his conjugal miseries. For six years he had longed to have children, but God did not bless him; although that poor Madame Thuillier had made novenas, and had even gone, uselessly, to Notra-Dame de Liesse! He depicted Celeste in various lights, which brought the words "Poor Thuillier!" from Flavie's lips. She herself was rather sad, having at the moment no dominant opinion. She poured her own griefs into Thuillier's bosom. The great Keller, that hero of the Left, was, in reality, extremely petty; she had learned to know the other side of public fame, the follies of banking, the emptiness of eloquence! The orator only spoke for show; to her he had behaved extremely ill. Thuillier was indignant. "None but stupid fellows know how to love," he said; "take me!" That handsome Thuillier was henceforth supposed to be paying court to Madame Colleville, and was rated as one of her "attentives,"—a word in vogue during the Empire.

"Ha! you are after my wife," said Colleville, laughing. "Take care; she'll leave you in the lurch, like all the rest."

A rather clever speech, by which Colleville saved his marital dignity. From 1820 to 1821, Thuillier, in virtue of his title as friend of the family, helped Colleville, who had formerly helped him; so much so, that in eighteen months he had lent nearly ten thousand francs to the Colleville establishment, with no intention of ever claiming them. In the spring of 1821, Madame Colleville gave birth to a charming little girl, to whom Monsieur and Madame Thuillier were godfather and godmother. The child was baptized Celeste-Louise-

Caroline-Brigitte; Mademoiselle Thuillier wishing that her name should be given among others to the little angel. The name of Caroline was a graceful attention paid to Colleville. Old mother Lemprun assumed the care of putting the baby to nurse under her own eyes at Auteuil, where Celeste and her sister-in-law Brigitte, paid it regularly a semi-weekly visit.

As soon as Madame Colleville recovered she said to Thuillier, frankly, in a very serious tone:—

"My dear friend, if we are all to remain good friends, you must be our friend only. Colleville is attached to you; well, that's enough for you in this household."

"Explain to me," said the handsome Thuillier to Tullia after this remark, "why women are never attached to me. I am not the Apollo Belvidere, but for all that I'm not a Vulcan; I am passably good-looking, I have sense, I am faithful—"

"Do you want me to tell you the truth?" replied Tullia.

"Yes," said Thuillier.

"Well, though we can, sometimes, love a stupid fellow, we never love a silly one."

Those words killed Thuillier; he never got over them; henceforth he was a prey to melancholy and accused all women of caprice.

The secretary-general of the ministry, des Lupeaulx, whose influence Madame Colleville thought greater than it was, and of whom she said, later, "That was one of my mistakes," became for a time the great man of the Colleville salon; but as Flavie found he had no power to promote Colleville into the upper division, she had the good sense to resent des Lupeaulx's attentions to Madame Rabourdin (whom she called a minx), to whose house she had never been invited, and who had twice had the impertinence not to come to the Colleville concerts.

Madame Colleville was deeply affected by the death of young Gondreville; she felt, she said, the finger of God. In 1824 she turned over a new leaf, talked of economy, stopped her receptions, busied herself with her children, determined to become a good mother of a family; no favorite friend was seen at her house. She went to church, reformed her dress, wore gray, and talked Catholicism, mysticism, and so forth. All this produced, in 1825, another little son, whom she named Theodore. Soon after, in 1826, Colleville was appointed sub-director of the Clergeot division, and later, in 1828, collector of taxes in a Paris arrondissement. He also received the cross of the Legion of honor, to enable him to put his daughter at the royal school of Saint-Denis.

The half-scholarship obtained by Keller for the eldest boy, Charles, was transferred to the second in 1830, when Charles entered the school of Saint-Louis on a full scholarship. The third son, taken under the protection of Madame la Dauphine, was provided with a three-quarter scholarship in the Henri IV. school.

In 1830 Colleville, who had the good fortune not to lose a child, was obliged, owing to his well-known attachment to the fallen royal family, to send in his resignation; but he was clever enough to make a bargain for it,— obtaining in exchange a pension of two thousand four hundred francs, based on his period of service, and ten thousand francs indemnity paid by his successor; he also received the rank of officer of the Legion of honor. Nevertheless, he found himself in rather a cramped condition when Mademoiselle Thuillier, in 1832, advised him to come and live near them; pointing out to him the possibility of obtaining some position in the mayor's office, which, in fact, he did obtain a few weeks later, at a salary of three thousand francs. Thus Thuillier and Colleville were destined to end their days together. In 1833 Madame Colleville, then thirty-five years old, settled herself in the rue d'Enfer, at the corner of the rue des Deux-Eglises with Celeste and little Theodore, the other boys being at their several schools. Colleville was equidistant between the mayor's office and the rue Saint-Dominique d'Enfer. Thus the household, after a brilliant, gay, headlong, reformed, and calmed existence, subsided finally into bourgeois obscurity with five thousand four hundred francs a year for its sole dependence.

Celeste was by this time twelve years of age, and she promised to be pretty. She needed masters, and her education ought to cost not less than two thousand francs a year. The mother felt the necessity of keeping her under the eye of her godfather and godmother. She therefore very willingly adopted the proposal of Mademoiselle Thuillier, who, without committing herself to any engagement, allowed Madame Colleville to understand that the fortunes of her brother, his wife, and herself would go, ultimately, to the little Celeste. The child had been left at Auteuil until she was seven years of age, adored by the good old Madame Lemprun, who died in 1829, leaving twenty thousand francs, and a house which was sold for the enormous sum of twenty-eight thousand. The lively little girl had seen very little of her mother, but very much of Mademoiselle and Madame Thuillier when she first returned to the paternal mansion in 1829; but in 1833 she fell under the dominion of Flavie, who was then, as we have said, endeavoring to do her duty, which, like other women instigated by remorse, she exaggerated. Without being an unkind mother, Flavie was very stern with her daughter. She remembered her own bringing-up, and swore within herself to make Celeste a virtuous woman. She took her to mass, and had her prepared for her first communion by a rector who has since become a bishop. Celeste was all the more readily pious, because her godmother, Madame Thuillier, was a saint, and the child adored her; she felt that the poor neglected woman loved her better than her own mother.

From 1833 to 1840 she received a brilliant education according to the ideas of the bourgeoisie. The best music-masters made her a fair musician; she could paint a water-color properly; she danced extremely well; and she had studied the French language, history, geography, English, Italian,—in short, all that constitutes the education of a well-brought-up young lady. Of medium height, rather plump, unfortunately near-sighted, she was neither plain nor pretty; not without delicacy or even brilliancy of complexion, it is true, but totally devoid of all distinction of manner. She had a great fund of reserved sensibility, and her godfather and godmother, Mademoiselle Thuillier and Colleville, were unanimous on one point,—the great resource of mothers— namely, that Celeste was capable of attachment. One of her beauties was a magnificent head of very fine blond hair; but her hands and feet showed her bourgeois origin.

Celeste endeared herself by precious qualities; she was kind, simple, without gall of any kind; she loved her father and mother, and would willingly sacrifice herself for their sake. Brought up to the deepest admiration for her godfather by Brigitte (who taught her to say "Aunt Brigitte"), and by Madame Thuillier and her own mother, Celeste imbibed the highest idea of the ex-beau of the Empire. The house in the rue Saint-Dominique d'Enfer produced upon her very much the effect of the Chateau des Tuileries on a courtier of the new dynasty.

Thuillier had not escaped the action of the administrative rolling-pin which thins the mind as it spreads it out. Exhausted by irksome toil, as much as by his life of gallantry, the ex-sub-director had well-nigh lost all his faculties by the time he came to live in the rue Saint-Dominique. But his weary face, on which there still reigned an air of imperial haughtiness, mingled with a certain contentment, the conceit of an upper official, made a deep impression upon Celeste. She alone adored that haggard face. The girl, moreover, felt herself to be the happiness of the Thuillier household.

CHAPTER IV. THE CIRCLE OF MONSIEUR AND MADAME THUILLIER

The Collevilles and their children became, naturally, the nucleus of the circle which Mademoiselle Thuillier had the ambition to group around her brother. A former clerk in the Billardiere division of the ministry, named Phellion, had lived for the last thirty years in their present quarter. He was promptly greeted by Colleville and Thuillier at the first review. Phellion proved to be one of the most respected men in the arrondissement. He had one daughter, now married to a school-teacher in the rue Saint-Hyacinthe, a Monsieur Barniol. Phellion's eldest son was a professor of mathematics in a royal college; he gave lectures and private lessons, being devoted, so his father was wont to say, to pure mathematics. A second son was in the government School of Engineering. Phellion had a pension of nine hundred francs, and he possessed a little property of nine thousand and a few odd hundred francs; the fruit of his economy and that of his wife during thirty years of toil and privation. He was, moreover, the owner of a little house and garden where he lived in the "impasse" des Feuillantines,—in thirty years he had never used the old-fashioned word "cul-de-sac"!

Dutocq, the clerk of the justice of peace, was also a former employee at the ministry of finance. Sacrificed, in former days, to one of those necessities which are always met with in representative government, he had accepted the position of scapegoat, receiving, privately, a round sum of money and the opportunity to buy his present post of clerk in the arrondissement. This man, not very honorable, and known to be a spy in the government offices, was never welcomed as he thought he ought to be by the Thuilliers; but the coldness of his landlords only made him the more persistent in going to see them. He was a bachelor and had various vices; he therefore concealed his life carefully, knowing well how to maintain his position by flattering his superiors. The justice of peace was much attached to Dutocq. This man, base as he was, managed, in the end, to make himself tolerated by the Thuilliers, chiefly by coarse and cringing adulation. He knew the facts of Thuillier's whole life, his relations with Colleville, and, above all, with Madame Colleville. One and all they feared his tongue, and the Thuilliers, without admitting him to any intimacy, endured his visits.

The family which became the flower of the Thuillier salon was that of a former ministerial clerk, once an object of pity in the government offices, who, driven by poverty, left the public service, in 1827, to fling himself into a business enterprise, having, as he thought, an idea. Minard (that was his name) foresaw a fortune in one of those wicked conceptions which reflect such discredit on French commerce, but which, in the year 1827, had not yet been exposed and blasted by publicity. Minard bought tea and mixed it with tea-leaves already used; also he adulterated the elements of chocolate in a manner which enabled him to sell the chocolate itself very cheaply. This trade in colonial products, begun in the quartier Saint-Marcel, made a merchant of Minard. He started a factory, and through these early connections he was able to reach the sources of raw material. He then did honorably, and on a large scale, a business begun in the first instance dishonorably. He became a distiller, worked upon untold quantities of products, and, by the year 1835, was considered the richest merchant in the region of the Place Maubert. By that time he had bought a handsome house in the rue des Macons-Sorbonne; he had been assistant mayor, and in 1839 became mayor of his arrondissement and judge in the Court of Commerce. He kept a carriage, had a country-place near Lagny; his wife wore diamonds at the court balls, and he prided himself on the rosette of an officer of the Legion of honor in his buttonhole.

Minard and his wife were exceedingly benevolent. Perhaps he wished to return in retail to the poor the sums he had mulcted from the public by the wholesale. Phellion, Colleville, and Thuillier met their old comrade, Minard, at election, and an intimacy followed; all the closer with the Thuilliers and Collevilles because Madame Minard seemed enchanted to make an acquaintance for her daughter in Celeste Colleville. It was at a grand ball given by the Minards that Celeste made her first appearance in society (being at that time sixteen and a half years old), dressed as her Christian named demanded, which seemed to be prophetic of her coming life. Delighted to be friendly with Mademoiselle Minard, her elder by four years, she persuaded her father and godfather to cultivate the Minard establishment, with its gilded salons and great opulence, where many political celebrities of the "juste milieu" were wont to congregate, such as Monsieur Popinot, who became, after a time, minister of commerce; Cochin, since made Baron Cochin, a former employee at the ministry of finance, who, having a large interest in the drug business, was now the oracle of the Lombard and Bourdonnais quarters, conjointly with Monsieur Anselme Popinot. Minard's eldest son, a lawyer, aiming to succeed those barristers who were turned down from the Palais for political reasons in 1830, was the genius of the household, and his mother, even more than his father, aspired to marry him well. Zelie Minard, formerly a flower-maker, felt an ardent passion for the upper social spheres, and desired to enter them through the marriages of her son and daughter; whereas Minard, wiser than she, and imbued with the vigor of the middle classes, which the revolution of July had infiltrated into the fibres of government, thought only of wealth and fortune.

He frequented the Thuillier salon to gain information as to Celeste's probable inheritance. He knew, like Dutocq and Phellion, the reports occasioned by Thuillier's former intimacy with Flavie, and he saw at a glance the idolatry of the Thuilliers for their godchild. Dutocq, to gain admittance to Minard's house, fawned upon him grossly. When Minard, the Rothschild of the arrondissement, appeared at the Thuilliers', he compared him cleverly to Napoleon, finding him stout, fat, and blooming, having left him at the ministry thin, pale, and puny.

"You looked, in the division Billardiere," he said, "like Napoleon before the 18th Brumaire, and I behold you now the Napoleon of the Empire."

Notwithstanding which flattery, Minard received Dutocq very coldly and did not invite him to his house; consequently, he made a mortal enemy of the former clerk.

Monsieur and Madame Phellion, worthy as they were, could not keep themselves from making calculations and cherishing hopes; they thought that Celeste would be the very wife for their son the professor; therefore, to have, as it were, a watcher in the Thuillier salon, they introduced their son-in-law, Monsieur Barniol, a man much respected in the faubourg Saint-Jacques, and also an old employee at the mayor's office, an intimate friend of theirs, named Laudigeois. Thus the Phellions formed a phalanx of seven persons; the Collevilles were not less numerous; so that on Sundays it often appeared that thirty persons were assembled in the Thuillier salon. Thuillier renewed acquaintance with the Saillards, Baudoyers, and Falleixs,—all persons of respectability in the quarter of the Palais-Royal, whom they often invited to dinner.

Madame Colleville was, as a woman, the most distinguished member of this society, just as Minard junior and Professor Phellion were superior among the men. All the others, without ideas or education, and issuing from the lower ranks, presented the types and the absurdities of the lesser bourgeoisie. Though all success, especially if won from distant sources, seems to presuppose some genuine merit, Minard was really an inflated balloon. Expressing himself in empty phrases, mistaking sycophancy for politeness, and wordiness for wit, he uttered his commonplaces with a brisk assurance that passed for eloquence. Certain words which said nothing but answered all things,—progress, steam, bitumen, National guard, order, democratic element, spirit of association, legality, movement, resistance,—seemed, as each political phase developed, to have been actually made for Minard, whose talk was a paraphrase on the ideas of his newspaper. Julien Minard, the young lawyer, suffered from his father as much as his father suffered from his wife.

Zelie had grown pretentious with wealth, without, at the same time, learning to speak French. She was now very fat, and gave the idea, in her rich surroundings, of a cook married to her master.

Phellion, that type and model of the petty bourgeois, exhibited as many virtues as he did absurdities. Accustomed to subordination during his bureaucratic life, he respected all social superiority. He was therefore silent before Minard. During the critical period of retirement from office, he had held his own admirably, for the following reason. Never until now had that worthy and excellent man been able to indulge his own tastes. He loved the city of Paris; he was interested in its embellishment, in the laying out of its streets; he was capable of standing for hours to watch the demolition of houses. He might now have been observed, stolidly planted on his legs, his nose in the air, watching for the fall of a stone which some mason was loosening at the top of a wall, and never moving till the stone fell; when it had fallen he went away as happy as an academician at the fall of a romantic drama. Veritable supernumeraries of the social comedy, Phellion, Laudigeois, and their kind, fulfilled the functions of the antique chorus. They wept when weeping was in order, laughed when they should laugh, and sang in parts the public joys and sorrows; they triumphed in their corner with the triumphs of Algiers, of Constantine, of Lisbon, of Sainte-Jean d'Ulloa; they deplored the death of Napoleon and the fatal catastrophes of the Saint-Merri and the rue Transnonnain, grieving over celebrated men who were utterly unknown to them. Phellion alone presents a double side: he divides himself conscientiously between the reasons of the opposition and those of the government. When fighting went on in the streets, Phellion had the courage to declare himself before his neighbors; he went to the Place Saint-Michel, the place where his battalion assembled; he felt for the government and did his duty. Before and during the riot, he supported the dynasty, the product of July; but, as soon as the political trials began, he stood by the accused. This innocent "weather-cockism" prevails in his political opinions; he produces, in reply to all arguments, the "colossus of the North." England is, to his thinking, as to that of the old "Constitutionnel," a crone with two faces,— Machiavellian Albion, and the model nation: Machiavellian, when the interests of France and of Napoleon are concerned; the model nation when the faults of the government are in question. He admits, with his chosen paper, the democratic element, but refuses in conversation all compact with the republican spirit. The republican spirit to him means 1793, rioting, the Terror, and agrarian law. The democratic element is the development of the lesser bourgeoisie, the reign of Phellions.

The worthy old man is always dignified; dignity serves to explain his life. He has brought up his children with dignity; he has kept himself a father in their eyes; he insists on being honored in his home, just as he himself honors power and his superiors. He has never made debts. As a juryman his conscience obliges him to sweat blood and water in the effort to follow the debates of a trial; he never laughs, not even if the judge, and audience, and all the officials laugh. Eminently useful, he gives his services, his time, everything—except his money. Felix Phellion, his son, the professor, is his idol; he thinks him capable of attaining to the Academy of Sciences. Thuillier, between the audacious nullity of Minard, and the solid silliness of Phellion, was a neutral substance, but connected with both through his dismal experience. He managed to conceal the emptiness of his brain by commonplace talk, just as he covered the yellow skin of his bald pate with thready locks of his gray hair, brought from the back of his head with infinite art by the comb of his hairdresser.

"In any other career," he was wont to say, speaking of the government employ, "I should have made a very different fortune."

He had seen the *right*, which is possible in theory and impossible in practice,—results proving contrary to premises,—and he related the intrigues and the injustices of the Rabourdin affair.

"After that, one can believe all, and believe nothing," he would say. "Ah! it is a queer thing, government! I'm very glad not to have a son, and never to see him in the career of a place-hunter."

Colleville, ever gay, rotund, and good-humored, a sayer of "quodlibets," a maker of anagrams, always busy, represented the capable and bantering bourgeois, with faculty without success, obstinate toil without result; he was also the embodiment of jovial resignation, mind without object, art with usefulness, for, excellent musician that he was, he never played now except for his daughter.

The Thuillier salon was in some sort a provincial salon, lighted, however, by continual flashes from the Parisian conflagration; its mediocrity and its platitudes followed the current of the times. The popular saying and thing (for in Paris the thing and its saying are like the horse and its rider) ricochetted, so to speak, to this company. Monsieur Minard was always impatiently expected, for he was certain to know the truth of important circumstances. The women of the Thuillier salon held by the Jesuits; the men defended the University; and, as a general thing, the women listened. A man of intelligence (could he have borne the dulness of these evenings) would have laughed, as he would at a comedy of Moliere, on hearing, amid endless discussion, such remarks as the following:—

"How could the Revolution of 1789 have been avoided? The loans of Louis

XIV. prepared the way for it. Louis XV., an egotist, a man of narrow mind (didn't he say, 'If I were lieutenant of police I would suppress cabriolets'?), that dissolute king—you remember his Parc aux Cerfs?—did much to open the abyss of revolution. Monsieur de Necker, an evil-minded Genovese, set the thing a-going. Foreigners have always tried to injure France. The maximum did great harm to the Revolution. Legally Louis XVI. should never have been condemned; a jury would have acquitted him. Why did Charles X. fall? Napoleon was a great man, and the facts that prove his genius are anecdotal: he took five pinches of snuff a minute out of a pocket lined with leather made in his waistcoat. He looked into all his tradesmen's accounts; he went to Saint-Denis to judge for himself the prices of things. Talma was his friend; Talma taught him his gestures; nevertheless, he always refused to give Talma the Legion of honor! The emperor mounted guard for a sentinel who went to sleep, to save him from being shot. Those were the things that made his soldiers adore him. Louis XVIII., who certainly had some sense, was very unjust in calling him Monsieur de Buonaparte. The defect of the present government is in letting itself be led instead of leading. It holds itself too low. It is afraid of men of energy. It ought to have torn up all the treaties of 1815 and demanded the Rhine. They keep the same men too long in the ministry"; etc., etc.

"Come, you've exerted your minds long enough," said Mademoiselle Thuillier, interrupting one of these luminous talks; "the altar is dressed; begin your little game."

If these anterior facts and all these generalities were not placed here as the frame of the present Scene, to give an idea of the spirit of this society, the following drama would certainly have suffered greatly. Moreover, this sketch is historically faithful; it shows a social stratum of importance in any portrayal of manners and morals, especially when we reflect that the political system of the Younger branch rests almost wholly upon it.

The winter of the year 1839 was, it may be said, the period when the Thuillier salon was in its greatest glory. The Minards came nearly every Sunday, and began their evening by spending an hour there, if they had other engagements elsewhere. Often Minard would leave his wife at the Thuilliers and take his son and daughter to other houses. This assiduity on the part of the Minards was brought about by a somewhat tardy meeting between Messieurs Metivier, Barbet, and Minard on an evening when the two former, being tenants of Mademoiselle Thuillier, remained rather longer than usual in discussing business with her. From Barbet, Minard learned that the old maid had money transactions with himself and Metivier to the amount of sixty thousand francs, besides having a large deposit in the Bank.

"Has she an account at the Bank?" asked Minard.

"I believe so," replied Barbet. "I give her at least eighty thousand francs there."

Being on intimate terms with a governor of the Bank, Minard ascertained that Mademoiselle Thuillier had, in point of fact, an account of over two hundred thousand francs, the result of her quarterly deposits for many years. Besides this, she owned the house they lived in, which was not mortgaged, and was worth at least one hundred thousand francs, if not more.

"Why should Mademoiselle Thuillier work in this way?" said Minard to Metivier. "She'd be a good match for you," he added.

"I? oh, no," replied Metivier. "I shall do better by marrying a cousin; my uncle Metivier has given me the succession to his business; he has a hundred thousand francs a year and only two daughters."

However secretive Mademoiselle Thuillier might be,—and she said nothing of her investments to any one, not even to her brother, although a large amount of Madame Thuillier's fortune went to swell the amount of her own savings,—it was difficult to prevent some ray of light from gliding under the bushel which covered her treasure.

Dutocq, who frequented Barbet, with whom he had some resemblance in character and countenance, had appraised, even more correctly than Minard, the Thuillier finances. He knew that their savings amounted, in 1838, to one hundred and fifty thousand francs, and he followed their progress secretly, calculating profits by the help of that all-wise money-lender, Barbet.

"Celeste will have from my brother and myself two hundred thousand francs in ready money," the old maid had said to Barbet in confidence, "and Madame Thuillier wishes to secure to her by the marriage contract the ultimate possession of her own fortune. As for me, my will is made. My brother will have everything during his lifetime, and Celeste will be my heiress with that reservation. Monsieur Cardot, the notary, is my executor."

Mademoiselle Thuillier now instigated her brother to renew his former relations with the Saillards, Baudoyers, and others, who held a position similar to that of the Thuilliers in the quartier Saint-Antoine, of which Monsieur Saillard was mayor. Cardot, the notary, had produced his aspirant for Celeste's hand in the person of Monsieur Godeschal, attorney and successor to Derville; an able man, thirty-six years of age, who had paid one hundred thousand francs for his practice, which the two hundred thousand of the "dot" would doubly clear off. Minard, however, got rid of Godeschal by informing Mademoiselle Thuillier that Celeste's sister-in-law would be the famous Mariette of the Opera.

"She came from the stage," said Colleville, alluding to his wife, "and there's no need she should return to it."

"Besides, Monsieur Godeschal is too old for Celeste," remarked Brigitte.

"And ought we not," added Madame Thuillier, timidly, "to let her marry according to her own taste, so as to be happy?"

The poor woman had detected in Felix Phellion a true love for Celeste; the love that a woman crushed by Brigitte and wounded by her husband's indifference (for Thuillier cared less for his wife than he did for a servant) had dreamed that love might be,—bold in heart, timid externally, sure of itself, reserved, hidden from others, but expanding toward heaven. At twenty-three years of age, Felix Phellion was a gentle, pure-minded young man, like all true scholars who cultivate knowledge for knowledge's sake. He had been sacredly brought up by his father, who, viewing all things seriously, had given him none but good examples accompanied by trivial maxims. He was a young man of medium height, with light chestnut hair, gray eyes, and a skin full of freckles; gifted with a charming voice, a tranquil manner; making few gestures; thoughtful, saying little, and that little sensible; contradicting no one, and quite incapable of a sordid thought or a selfish calculation.

"That," thought Madame Thuillier, "is what I should have liked my husband to be."

One evening, in the month of February, 1840, the Thuillier salon contained the various personages whose silhouettes we have just traced out, together with some others. It was nearly the end of the month. Barbet and Metivier having business with mademoiselle Brigitte, were playing whist with Minard and Phellion. At another table were Julien the advocate (a nickname given by Colleville to young Minard), Madame Colleville, Monsieur Barniol, and Madame Phellion. "Bouillotte," at five sous a stake, occupied Madame Minard, who knew no other game, Colleville, old Monsieur Saillard, and Bandoze, his son-in-law. The substitutes were Laudigeois and Dutocq. Mesdames Falleix, Baudoyer, Barniol, and Mademoiselle Minard were playing boston, and Celeste was sitting beside Prudence Minard. Young Phellion was listening to Madame Thuillier and looking at Celeste.

At a corner of the fireplace sat enthroned on a sofa the Queen Elizabeth of the family, as simply dressed as she had been for the last thirty years; for no prosperity could have made her change her habits. She wore on her chinchilla hair a black gauze cap, adorned with the geranium called Charles X.; her gown, of plum-colored stuff, made with a yoke, cost fifteen francs, her embroidered collarette was worth six, and it ill disguised the deep wrinkle produced by the two muscles which fastened the head to the vertebral column. The actor, Monvel, playing Augustus Caesar in his old age, did not present a harder and sterner profile than that of this female autocrat, knitting socks for her brother. Before the fireplace stood Thuillier in an attitude, ready to go forward and meet the arriving guests; near him was a young man whose entrance had produced a great effect, when the porter (who on Sundays wore his best clothes and waited on the company) announced Monsieur Olivier Vinet.

A private communication made by Cardot to the celebrated "procureur-general," father of this young man, was the cause of his visit. Olivier Vinet had just been promoted from the court of Arcis-sur-Aube to that of the Seine, where he now held the post of substitute "procureur-de-roi." Cardot had already invited Thuillier and the elder Vinet, who was likely to become minister of justice, with his son, to dine with him. The notary estimated the fortunes which would eventually fall to Celeste at seven hundred thousand francs. Vinet junior appeared charmed to obtain the right to visit the Thuilliers on Sundays. Great dowries make men commit great and unbecoming follies without reserve or decency in these days.

Ten minutes later another young man, who had been talking with Thuillier before the arrival of Olivier Vinet, raised his voice eagerly, in a political discussion, and forced the young magistrate to follow his example in the vivacious argument which now ensued. The matter related to the vote by which the Chamber of Deputies had just overthrown the ministry of the 12th of May, refusing the allowance demanded for the Duc de Nemours.

"Assuredly," said the young man, "I am far from belonging to the dynastic party; I am very far from approving of the rise of the bourgeoisie to power. The bourgeoisie ought not, any more than the aristocracy of other days, to assume to be the whole nation. But the French bourgeoisie has now taken upon itself to create a new dynasty, a royalty of its own, and behold how it treats it! When the people allowed Napoleon to rise to power, it created with him a splendid and monumental state of things; it was proud of his grandeur; and it nobly gave its blood and sweat in building up the edifice of the Empire. Between the magnificence of the aristocratic throne and those of the imperial purple, between the great of the earth and the People, the bourgeoisie is proving itself petty; it degrades power to its own level instead of rising up to it. The saving of candle-ends it has so long practised behind its counters, it now seeks to impose on its princes. What may perhaps have been virtue in its shops is a blunder and a crime higher up. I myself have wanted many things for the people, but I never should have begun by lopping off ten millions of francs from the new civil list. In becoming, as it were, nearly the whole of

France, the bourgeoisie owed to us the prosperity of the people, splendor without ostentation, grandeur without privilege."

The father of Olivier Vinet was just now sulking with the government. The robe of Keeper of the Seals, which had been his dream, was slow in coming to him. The young substitute did not, therefore, know exactly how to answer this speech; he thought it wise to enlarge on one of its side issues.

"You are right, monsieur," said Olivier Vinet. "But, before manifesting itself magnificently, the bourgeoisie has other duties to fulfil towards France. The luxury you speak of should come after duty. That which seems to you so blameable is the necessity of the moment. The Chamber is far from having its full share in public affairs; the ministers are less for France than they are for the crown, and parliament has determined that the administration shall have, as in England, a strength and power of its own, and not a mere borrowed power. The day on which the administration can act for itself, and represent the Chamber as the Chamber represents the country, parliament will be found very liberal toward the crown. The whole question is there. I state it without expressing my own opinion, for the duties of my post demand, in politics, a certain fealty to the crown."

"Setting aside the political question," replied the young man, whose voice and accent were those of a native of Provence, "it is certainly true that the bourgeoisie has ill understood its mission. We can see, any day, the great law officers, attorney-generals, peers of France in omnibuses, judges who live on their salaries, prefects without fortunes, ministers in debt! Whereas the bourgeoisie, who have seized upon those offices, ought to dignify them, as in the olden time when aristocracy dignified them, and not occupy such posts solely for the purpose of making their fortune, as scandalous disclosures have proved."

"Who is this young man?" thought Olivier Vinet. "Is he a relative? Cardot ought to have come with me on this first visit."

"Who is that little monsieur?" asked Minard of Barbet. "I have seen him here several times."

"He is a tenant," replied Metivier, shuffling the cards.

"A lawyer," added Barbet, in a low voice, "who occupies a small apartment on the third floor front. Oh! *He* doesn't amount to much; he has nothing."

"What is the name of that young man?" said Olivier Vinet to Thuillier.

"Theodose de la Peyrade; he is a barrister," replied Thuillier, in a whisper.

At that moment the women present, as well as the men, looked at the two young fellows, and Madame Minard remarked to Colleville:—

"He is rather good-looking, that stranger."

"I have made his anagram," replied Colleville, "and his name, Charles-Marie-Theodose de la Peyrade, prophecies: 'Eh! monsieur payera, de la dot, des oies et le char.' Therefore, my dear Mamma Minard, be sure you don't give him your daughter."

"They say that young man is better-looking than my son," said Madame Phellion to Madame Colleville. "What do you think about it?"

"Oh! in the matter of physical beauty a woman might hesitate before choosing," replied Madame Colleville.

At that moment it occurred to young Vinet as he looked round the salon, so full of the lesser bourgeoisie, that it might be a shrewd thing to magnify that particular class; and he thereupon enlarged upon the meaning of the young Provencal barrister, declaring that men so honored by the confidence of the government should imitate royalty and encourage a magnificence surpassing that of the former court. It was folly, he said, to lay by the emoluments of an office. Besides, could it be done, in Paris especially, where costs of living had trebled,—the apartment of a magistrate, for instance, costing three thousand francs a year?

"My father," he said in conclusion, "allows me three thousand francs a year, and that, with my salary, barely allows me to maintain my rank."

When the young substitute rode boldly into this bog-hole, the Provencal, who had slyly enticed him there, exchanged, without being observed, a wink with Dutocq, who was just then waiting for the place of a player at bouillotte.

"There is such a demand for offices," remarked the latter, "that they talk of creating two justices of the peace to each arrondissement in order to make a dozen new clerkships. As if they could interfere with our rights and our salaries, which already require an exhorbitant tax!"

"I have not yet had the pleasure of hearing you at the Palais," said Vinet to Monsieur de la Peyrade.

"I am advocate for the poor, and I plead only before the justice of peace," replied la Peyrade.

Mademoiselle Thuillier, as she listened to young Vinet's theory of the necessity of spending an income, assumed a distant air and manner, the significance of which was well understood by Dutocq and the young Provencal. Vinet left the house in company with Minard and Julien the advocate, so that the battle-field before the fire-place was abandoned to la

Peyrade and Dutocq.

"The upper bourgeoisie," said Dutocq to Thuillier, "will behave, in future, exactly like the old aristocracy. The nobility wanted girls with money to manure their lands, and the parvenus of to-day want the same to feather their nests."

"That's exactly what Monsieur Thuillier was saying to me this morning," remarked la Peyrade, boldly.

"Vinet's father," said Dutocq, "married a Demoiselle de Chargeboeuf and has caught the opinions of the nobility; he wants a fortune at any price; his wife spends money regally."

"Oh!" said Thuillier, in whom the jealousy between the two classes of the bourgeoisie was fully roused, "take offices away from those fellows and they'd fall back where they came."

Mademoiselle was knitting with such precipitous haste that she seemed to be propelled by a steam-engine.

"Take my place, Monsieur Dutocq," said Madame Minard, rising. "My feet are cold," she added, going to the fire, where the golden ornaments of her turban made fireworks in the light of the Saint-Aurora wax-candles that were struggling vainly to light the vast salon.

"He is very small fry, that young substitute," said Madame Minard, glancing at Mademoiselle Thuillier.

"Small fry!" cried la Peyrade. "Ah, madame! how witty!"

"But madame has so long accustomed us to that sort of thing," said the handsome Thuillier.

Madame Colleville was examining la Peyrade and comparing him with young Phellion, who was just then talking to Celeste, neither of them paying any heed to what was going on around them. This is, certainly, the right moment to depict the singular personage who was destined to play a signal part in the Thuillier household, and who fully deserves the appellation of a great artist.

CHAPTER V. A PRINCIPAL PERSONAGE

There exists in Provence, especially about Avignon, a race of men with blond or chestnut hair, fair skin, and eyes that are almost tender, their pupils calm, feeble, or languishing, rather than keen, ardent, or profound, as they usually are in the eyes of Southerners. Let us remark, in passing, that among Corsicans, a race subject to fits of anger and dangerous irascibility, we often meet with fair skins and physical natures of the same apparent tranquillity. These pale men, rather stout, with somewhat dim and hazy eyes either green or blue, are the worst species of humanity in Provence; and Charles-Marie-Theodose de la Peyrade presents a fine type of that race, the constitution of which deserves careful examination on the part of medical science and philosophical physiology. There rises, at times, within such men, a species of bile,—a bitter gall, which flies to their head and makes them capable of ferocious actions, done, apparently, in cold blood. Being the result of an inward intoxication, this sort of dumb violence seems to be irreconcilable with their quasi-lymphatic outward man, and the tranquillity of their benignant glance.

Born in the neighborhood of Avignon, the young Provencal whose name we have just mentioned was of middle height, well-proportioned, and rather stout; the tone of his skin had no brilliancy; it was neither livid nor dead-white, nor colored, but gelatinous,—that word can alone give a true idea of the flabby, hueless envelope, beneath which were concealed nerves that were less vigorous than capable of enormous resistance at certain given moments. His eyes, of a pale cold blue, expressed in their ordinary condition a species of deceptive sadness, which must have had great charms for women. The forehead, finely cut, was not without dignity, and it harmonized well with the soft, light chestnut hair curling naturally, but slightly, at its tips. The nose, precisely like that of a hunting dog, flat and furrowed at the tip, inquisitive, intelligent, searching, always on the scent, instead of expressing good-humor, was ironical and mocking; but this particular aspect of his nature never showed itself openly; the young man must have ceased to watch himself, he must have flown into fury before the power came to him to flash out the sarcasm and the wit which embittered, tenfold, his infernal humor. The mouth, the curving lines and pomegranate-colored lips of which were very pleasing, seemed the admirable instrument of an organ that was almost sweet in its middle tones, where its owner usually kept it, but which, in its higher key, vibrated on the ear like the sound of a gong. This falsetto was the voice of his nerves and his anger. His face, kept expressionless by an inward command, was oval in form. His manners, in harmony with the sacerdotal calmness of the face, were reserved and conventional; but he had supple, pliant ways which, though they never descended to wheedling, were not lacking in seduction; although as soon as his back was turned their charm seemed inexplicable. Charm, when it takes its rise in the heart, leaves deep and lasting traces; that which is merely a product of art, or of eloquence, has only a passing power; it produces its immediate effect, and that is all. But how many philosophers are there in life who are able to distinguish the difference? Almost always the trick is played (to use a popular expression) before the ordinary run of men have perceived its methods.

Everything about this young man of twenty-seven was in harmony with his character; he obeyed his vocation by cultivating philanthropy,—the only expression which explains the philanthropist. Theodose loved the People, for he limited his love for humanity. Like the horticulturist who devotes himself to roses, or dahlias, or heart's-ease, or geraniums, and pays no attention to the plants his fancy has not selected, so this young La Rochefoucault-Liancourt gave himself to the workingmen, the proletariat and the paupers of the faubourgs Saint-Jacques and Saint-Marceau. The strong man, the man of genius at bay, the worthy poor of the bourgeois class, he cut them off from the bosom of his charity. The heart of all persons with a mania is like those boxes with compartments, in which sugarplums are kept in sorts: "suum cuique tribuere" is their motto; they measure to each duty its dose. There are some philanthropists who pity nothing but the man condemned to death. Vanity is certainly the basis of philanthropy; but in the case of this Provencal it was calculation, a predetermined course, a "liberal" and democratic hypocrisy, played with a perfection that no other actor will ever attain.

Theodose did not attack the rich; he contented himself with not understanding them; he endured them; every one, in his opinion, ought to enjoy the fruits of his labor. He had been, he said, a fervent disciple of Saint-Simon, but that mistake must be attributed to his youth: modern society could have no other basis than heredity. An ardent Catholic, like all men from the Comtat, he went to the earliest morning masses, and thus concealed his piety. Like other philanthropists, he practised a sordid economy, and gave to the poor his time, his legal advice, his eloquence, and such money as he extracted for them from the rich. His clothes, always of black cloth, were worn until the seams became white. Nature had done a great deal for Theodose in not giving him that fine manly Southern beauty which creates in others an imaginary expectation, to which it is more than difficult for a man to respond. As it was, he could be what suited him at the moment,—an agreeable man or a very ordinary one. Never, since his admission to the Thuilliers', had he ventured, till this evening, to raise his voice and speak as dogmatically as he had risked doing to Olivier Vinet; but perhaps Theodose de la Peyrade was not sorry to seize the opportunity to come out from the shade in which he had hitherto kept himself. Besides, it was necessary to get rid of the young substitute, just as the Minards had previously ruined the hopes of Monsieur Godeschal. Like all superior men (for he certainly had some superiority), Vinet had never lowered himself to the point where the threads of these bourgeois spider-webs became visible to him, and he had therefore plunged, like a fly, headforemost, into the almost invisible trap to which Theodose inveigled him.

To complete this portrait of the poor man's lawyer we must here relate the circumstances of his first arrival at the Thuilliers'.

Theodose came to lodge in Mademoiselle Thuillier's house toward the close of the year 1837. He had taken his degree about five years earlier, and had kept the proper number of terms to become a barrister. Circumstances, however, about which he said nothing, had interfered to prevent his being called to the bar; he was, therefore, still a licentiate. But soon after he was installed in the little apartment on the third floor, with the furniture rigorously required by all members of his noble profession,—for the guild of barristers admits no brother unless he has a suitable study, a legal library, and can thus, as it were, verify his claims,—Theodose de la Peyrade began to practise as a barrister before the Royal Court of Paris.

The whole of the year 1838 was employed in making this change in his condition, and he led a most regular life. He studied at home in the mornings till dinner-time, going sometimes to the Palais for important cases. Having become very intimate with Dutocq (so Dutocq said), he did certain services to the poor of the faubourg Saint-Jacques who were brought to his notice by that official. He pleaded their cases before the court, after bringing them to the notice of the attorneys, who, according to the statutes of their order, are obliged to take turns in doing business for the poor. As Theodose was careful to plead only safe cases, he won them all. Those persons whom he thus obliged expressed their gratitude and their admiration, in spite of the young lawyer's admonitions, among their own class, and to the porters of private houses, through whom many anecdotes rose to the ears of the proprietors. Delighted to have in their house a tenant so worthy and so charitable, the Thuilliers wished to attract him to their salon, and they questioned Dutocq about him. The mayor's clerk replied as the envious reply; while doing justice to the young man he dwelt on his remarkable avarice, which might, however, be the effect of poverty.

"I have had other information about him. He belongs to the Peyrades, an old family of the 'comtat' of Avignon; he came here toward the end of 1829, to inquire about an uncle whose fortune was said to be considerable; he discovered the address of the old man only three days before his death; and the furniture of the deceased merely sufficed to bury him and pay his debts. A friend of this useless uncle gave a couple of hundred louis to the poor fortune-hunter, advising him to finish his legal studies and enter the judiciary career. Those two hundred louis supported him for three years in Paris, where he lived like an anchorite. But being unable to discover his unknown friend and benefactor, the poor student was in abject distress in 1833. He worked then, like so many other licentiates, in politics and literature, by which he kept himself for a time above want—for he had nothing to expect from his family. His father, the youngest brother of the dead uncle, has eleven other children, who live on a small estate called Les Canquoelles. He finally obtained a place on a ministerial newspaper, the manager of which was the famous Cerizet, so celebrated for the persecutions he met with, under the Restoration, on account of his attachment to the liberals,—a man whom the new Left will never forgive for having made his paper ministerial. As the government of these days does very little to protect even its most devoted servants (witness the Gisquet affair), the republicans have ended by ruining Cerizet. I tell you this to explain how it is that Cerizet is now a copying clerk in my office. Well, in the days when he flourished as managing editor of a paper directed by the Perier ministry against the incendiary journals, the 'Tribune' and others, Cerizet, who is a worthy fellow after all, though he is too fond of women, pleasure, and good living, was very useful to Theodose, who edited the political department of the paper; and if it hadn't been for the death of Casimir Perier that young man would certainly have received an appointment as substitute judge in Paris. As it was, he dropped back in 1834-35, in spite of his talent; for his connection with a ministerial journal of course did him harm. 'If it had not been for my religious principles,' he said to me, 'I should have thrown myself into the Seine.' However, it seems that the friend of his uncle must have heard of his distress, for again he sent him a sum of money; enough to complete his terms for the bar; but, strange to say, he has never known the name or the address of this mysterious benefactor. After all, perhaps, under such circumstances, his economy is excusable, and he must have great strength of mind to refuse what the poor devils whose cases he wins by his devotion offer him. He is indignant at the way other lawyers speculate on the possibility or impossibility of poor creatures, unjustly sued, paying for the costs of their defence. Oh! he'll succeed in the end. I shouldn't be surprised to see that fellow in some very brilliant position; he has tenacity, honesty, and courage. He studies, he delves."

Notwithstanding the favor with which he was greeted, la Peyrade went discreetly to the Thuilliers'. When reproached for this reserve he went oftener, and ended by appearing every Sunday; he was invited to all dinner-parties, and became at last so familiar in the house that whenever he came to see Thuillier about four o'clock he was always requested to take "pot-luck" without ceremony. Mademoiselle Thuillier used to say:—

"Then we know that he will get a good dinner, poor fellow!"

A social phenomenon which has certainly been observed, but never, as yet, formulated, or, if you like it better, published, though it fully deserves to be recorded, is the return of habits, mind, and manners to primitive conditions in certain persons who, between youth and old age, have raised themselves above their first estate. Thus Thuillier had become, once more, morally speaking, the son of a concierge. He now made use of many of his father's jokes, and a little of the slime of early days was beginning to appear on the surface of his declining life. About five or six times a month, when the soup was rich and good he would deposit his spoon in his empty plate and say, as if the proposition were entirely novel:—

"That's better than a kick on the shin-bone!"

On hearing that witticism for the first time Theodose, to whom it was really new, laughed so heartily that the handsome Thuillier was tickled in his vanity as he had never been before. After that, Theodose greeted the same speech with a knowing little smile. This slight detail will explain how it was that on the morning of the day when Theodose had his passage at arms with Vinet he had said to Thuillier, as they were walking in the garden to see the effect of a frost:—

"You have much more wit than you give yourself credit for."

To which he received this answer:—

"In any other career, my dear Theodose, I should have made my way nobly; but the fall of the Emperor broke my neck."

"There is still time," said the young lawyer. "In the first place, what did that mountebank, Colleville, ever do to get the cross?"

There la Peyrade laid his finger on a sore wound which Thuillier hid from every eye so carefully that even his sister did not know of it; but the young man, interested in studying these bourgeois, had divined the secret envy that gnawed at the heart of the ex-official.

"If you, experienced as you are, will do the honor to follow my advice," added the philanthropist, "and, above all, not mention our compact to any one, I will undertake to have you decorated with the Legion of honor, to the applause of the whole quarter."

"Oh! if we succeed in that," cried Thuillier, "you don't know what I would do for you."

This explains why Thuillier carried his head high when Theodose had the audacity that evening to put opinions into his mouth.

In art—and perhaps Moliere had placed hypocrisy in the rank of art by classing Tartuffe forever among comedians—there exists a point of perfection to which genius alone attains; mere talent falls below it. There is so little difference between a work of genius and a work of talent, that only men of genius can appreciate the distance that separates Raffaelle from Correggio, Titian from Rubens. More than that; common minds are easily deceived on this point. The sign of genius is a certain appearance of facility. In fact, its work must appear, at first sight, ordinary, so natural is it, even on the highest subjects. Many peasant-women hold their children as the famous Madonna in the Dresden gallery holds hers. Well, the height of art in a man of la Peyrade's force was to oblige others to say of him later: "Everybody would have been taken in by him."

Now, in the salon Thuillier, he noted a dawning opposition; he perceived in Colleville the somewhat clear-sighted and criticising nature of an artist who has missed his vocation. The barrister felt himself displeasing to Colleville, who (as the result of circumstances not necessary to here report) considered himself justified in believing in the science of anagrams. None of this anagrams had ever failed. The clerks in the government office had laughed at him when, demanding an anagram on the name of the poor helpless Auguste-Jean-Francois Minard, he had produced, "J'amassai une si grande fortune"; and the event had justified him after the lapse of ten years! Theodose, on several occasions, had made advances to the jovial secretary of the mayor's office, and had felt himself rebuffed by a coldness which was not natural in so sociable a man. When the game of bouillotte came to an end, Colleville seized the moment to draw Thuillier into the recess of a window and say to him:—

"You are letting that lawyer get too much foothold in your house; he kept the ball in his own hands all the evening."

"Thank you, my friend; forewarned is forearmed," replied Thuillier, inwardly scoffing at Colleville.

Theodose, who was talking at the moment to Madame Colleville, had his eye on the two men, and, with the same prescience by which women know when and how they are spoken of, he perceived that Colleville was trying to injure him in the mind of the weak and silly Thuillier. "Madame," he said in Flavie's ear, "if any one here is capable of appreciating you it is certainly I. You seem to me a pearl dropped into the mire. You say you are forty-two, but a woman is no older than she looks, and many women of thirty would be thankful to have your figure and that noble countenance, where love has passed without ever filling the void in your heart. You have given yourself to

God, I know, and I have too much religion myself to regret it, but I also know that you have done so because no human being has proved worthy of you. You have been loved, but you have never been adored—I have divined that. There is your husband, who has not known how to please you in a position in keeping with your deserts. He dislikes me, as if he thought I loved you; and he prevents me from telling you of a way that I think I have found to place you in the sphere for which you were destined. No, madame," he continued, rising, "the Abbe Gondrin will not preach this year through Lent at our humble Saint-Jacques du Haut-Pas; the preacher will be Monsieur d'Estival, a compatriot of mine, and you will hear in him one of the most impressive speakers that I have ever known,—a priest whose outward appearance is not agreeable, but, oh! what a soul!"

"Then my desire will be gratified," said poor Madame Thuillier. "I have never yet been able to understand a famous preacher."

A smile flickered on the lips of Mademoiselle Thuillier and several others who heard the remark.

"They devote themselves too much to theological demonstration," said Theodose. "I have long thought so myself—but I never talk religion; if it had not been for Madame *de* Colleville, I—"

"Are there demonstrations in theology?" asked the professor of mathematics, naively, plunging headlong into the conversation.

"I think, monsieur," replied Theodose, looking straight at Felix Phellion, "that you cannot be serious in asking me such a question."

"Felix," said old Phellion, coming heavily to the rescue of his son, and catching a distressed look on the pale face of Madame Thuillier,—"Felix separates religion into two categories; he considers it from the human point of view and the divine point of view,—tradition and reason."

"That is heresy, monsieur," replied Theodose. "Religion is one; it requires, above all things, faith."

Old Phellion, nonplussed by that remark, nodded to his wife:—

"It is getting late, my dear," and he pointed to the clock.

"Oh, Monsieur Felix," said Celeste in a whisper to the candid mathematician, "Couldn't you be, like Pascal and Bossuet, learned and pious both?"

The Phellions, on departing, carried the Collevilles with them. Soon no one remained in the salon but Dutocq, Theodose, and the Thuilliers.

The flattery administered by Theodose to Flavie seems at the first sight coarsely commonplace, but we must here remark, in the interests of this history, that the barrister was keeping himself as close as possible to these vulgar minds; he was navigating their waters; he spoke their language. His painter was Pierre Grassou, and not Joseph Bridau; his book was "Paul and Virginia." The greatest living poet for him was Casimire de la Vigne; to his eyes the mission of art was, above all things, utility. Parmentier, the discoverer of the potato, was greater to him that thirty Raffaelles; the man in the blue cloak seemed to him a sister of charity. These were Thuillier's expressions, and Theodose remembered them all—on occasion.

"That young Felix Phellion," he now remarked, "is precisely the academical man of our day; the product of knowledge which sends God to the rear. Heavens, what are we coming to? Religion alone can save France; nothing but the fear of hell will preserve us from domestic robbery, which is going on at all hours in the bosom of families, and eating into the surest fortunes. All of you have a secret warfare in your homes."

After this shrewd tirade, which made a great impression upon Brigitte, he retired, followed by Dutocq, after wishing good evening to the three Thuilliers.

"That young man has great capacity," said Thuillier, sententiously.

"Yes, that he has," replied Brigitte, extinguishing the lamps.

"He has religion," said Madame Thuillier, as she left the room.

"Monsieur," Phellion was saying to Colleville as they came abreast of the Ecole de Mines, looking about him to see that no one was near, "it is usually my custom to submit my insight to that of others, but it is impossible for me not to think that that young lawyer plays the master at our friend Thuillier's."

"My own opinion," said Colleville, who was walking with Phellion behind his wife, Madame Phellion, and Celeste, "is that he's a Jesuit; and I don't like Jesuits; the best of them are no good. To my mind a Jesuit means knavery, and knavery for knavery's sake; they deceive for the pleasure of deceiving, and, as the saying is, to keep their hand in. That's my opinion, and I don't mince it."

"I understand you, monsieur," said Phellion, who was arm-in-arm with Colleville.

"No, Monsieur Phellion," remarked Flavie in a shrill voice, "you don't understand Colleville; but I know what he means, and I think he had better stop saying it. Such subjects are not to be talked of in the street, at eleven o'clock at night, and before a young lady."

"You are right, wife," said Colleville.

49

When they reached the rue des Deux-Eglises, which Phellion was to take, they all stopped to say good-night, and Felix Phellion, who was bring up the rear, said to Colleville:—

"Monsieur, your son Francois could enter the Ecole Polytechnique if he were well-coached; I propose to you to fit him to pass the examinations this year."

"That's an offer not to be refused! Thank you, my friend," said Colleville. "We'll see about it."

"Good!" said Phellion to his son, as they walked on.

"Not a bad stroke!" said the mother.

"What do you mean by that?" asked Felix.

"You are very cleverly paying court to Celeste's parents."

"May I never find the solution of my problem if I even thought of it!" cried the young professor. "I discovered, when talking with the little Collevilles, that Francois has a strong turn for mathematics, and I thought I ought to enlighten his father."

"Good, my son!" repeated Phellion. "I wouldn't have you otherwise. My prayers are granted! I have a son whose honor, probity, and private and civic virtues are all that I could wish."

Madame Colleville, as soon as Celeste had gone to bed, said to her husband:—

"Colleville, don't utter those blunt opinions about people without knowing something about them. When you talk of Jesuits I know you mean priests; and I wish you would do me the kindness to keep your opinions on religion to yourself when you are in company with your daughter. We may sacrifice our own souls, but not the souls of our children. You don't want Celeste to be a creature without religion? And remember, my dear, that we are at the mercy of others; we have four children to provide for; and how do you know that, some day or other, you may not need the services of this one or that one? Therefore don't make enemies. You haven't any now, for you are a good-natured fellow; and, thanks to that quality, which amounts in you to a charm, we have got along pretty well in life, so far."

"That's enough!" said Colleville, flinging his coat on a chair and pulling off his cravat. "I'm wrong, and you are right, my beautiful Flavie."

"And on the next occasion, my dear old sheep," said the sly creature, tapping her husband's cheek, "you must try to be polite to that young lawyer; he is a schemer and we had better have him on our side. He is playing comedy

—well! play comedy with him; be his dupe apparently; if he proves to have talent, if he has a future before him, make a friend of him. Do you think I want to see you forever in the mayor's office?"

"Come, wife Colleville," said the former clarionet, tapping his knee to indicate the place he wished his wife to take. "Let us warm our toes and talk. —When I look at you I am more than ever convinced that the youth of women is in their figure."

"And in their heart."

"Well, both," assented Colleville; "waist slender, heart solid—"

"No, you old stupid, deep."

"What is good about you is that you have kept your fairness without growing fat. But the fact is, you have such tiny bones. Flavie, it is a fact that if I had life to live over again I shouldn't wish for any other wife than you."

"You know very well I have always preferred you to *others*. How unlucky that monseigneur is dead! Do you know what I covet for you?"

"No; what?"

"Some office at the Hotel de Ville,—an office worth twelve thousand francs a year; cashier, or something of that kind; either there, or at Poissy, in the municipal department; or else as manufacturer of musical instruments—"

"Any one of them would suit me."

"Well, then! if that queer barrister has power, and he certainly has plenty of intrigue, let us manage him. I'll sound him; leave me to do the thing—and, above all, don't thwart his game at the Thuilliers'."

Theodose had laid a finger on a sore sport in Flavie Colleville's heart; and this requires an explanation, which may, perhaps, have the value of a synthetic glance at women's life.

At forty years of age a woman, above all, if she has tasted the poisoned apple of passion, undergoes a solemn shock; she sees two deaths before her: that of the body and that of the heart. Dividing women into two great categories which respond to the common ideas, and calling them either virtuous or guilty, it is allowable to say that after that fatal period they both suffer pangs of terrible intensity. If virtuous, and disappointed in the deepest hopes of their nature—whether they have had the courage to submit, whether they have buried their revolt in their hearts or at the foot of the altar—they never admit to themselves that all is over for them without horror. That thought has such strange and diabolical depths that in it lies the reason of some of those apostasies which have, at times, amazed the world and

51

horrified it. If guilty, women of that age fall into one of several delirious conditions which often turn, alas! to madness, or end in suicide, or terminate in some with passion greater than the situation itself.

The following is the "dilemmatic" meaning of this crisis. Either they have known happiness, known it in a virtuous life, and are unable to breathe in any air but that surcharged with incense, or act in any but a balmy atmosphere of flattery and worship,—if so, how is it possible to renounce it?—or, by a phenomenon less rare than singular, they have found only wearying pleasures while seeking for the happiness that escaped them—sustained in that eager chase by the irritating satisfactions of vanity, clinging to the game like a gambler to his double or quits; for to them these last days of beauty are their last stake against despair.

"You have been loved, but never adored."

That speech of Theodose, accompanied by a look which read, not into her heart, but into her life, was the key-note to her enigma, and Flavie felt herself divined.

The lawyer had merely repeated ideas which literature has rendered trivial; but what matter where the whip comes from, or how it is made, if it touches the sensitive spot of a horse's hide? The emotion was in Flavie, not in the speech, just as the noise is not in the avalanche, though it produces it.

A young officer, two fops, a banker, a clumsy youth, and Colleville, were poor attempts at happiness. Once in her life Madame Colleville had dreamed of it, but never attained it. Death had hastened to put an end to the only passion in which she had found a charm. For the last two years she had listened to the voice of religion, which told her that neither the Church, nor its votaries, should talk of love or happiness, but of duty and resignation; that the only happiness lay in the satisfaction of fulfilling painful and costly duties, the rewards for which were not in this world. All the same, however, she was conscious of another clamoring voice; but, inasmuch as her religion was only a mask which it suited her to wear, and not a conversion, she did not lay it aside, thinking it a resource. Believing also that piety, false or true, was a becoming manner in which to meet her future, she continued in the Church, as though it were the cross-roads of a forest, where, seated on a bench, she read the sign-posts, and waited for some lucky chance; feeling all the while that night was coming on.

Thus it happened that her interest was keenly excited when Theodose put her secret condition of mind into words, seeming to promise her the realization of her castle in the air, already built and overthrown some six or eight times.

From the beginning of the winter she had noticed that Theodose was examining and studying her, though cautiously and secretly. More than once, she had put on her gray moire silk with its black lace, and her headdress of Mechlin with a few flowers, in order to appear to her best advantage; and men know very well when a toilet has been made to please them. The old beau of the Empire, that handsome Thuillier, overwhelmed her with compliments, assuring her she was queen of the salon, but la Peyrade said infinitely more to the purpose by a look.

Flavie had expected, Sunday after Sunday, a declaration, saying to herself at times:—

"He knows I am ruined and haven't a sou. Perhaps he is really pious."

Theodose did nothing rashly; like a wise musician, he had marked the place in his symphony where he intended to tap his drum. When he saw Colleville attempting to warn Thuillier against him, he fired his broadside, cleverly prepared during the three or four months in which he had been studying Flavie; he now succeeded with her as he had, earlier in the day, succeeded with Thuillier.

While getting into bed, Theodose said to himself:—

"The wife is on my side; the husband can't endure me; they are now quarrelling; and I shall get the better of it, for she does what she likes with that man."

The lawyer was mistaken in one thing: there was no dispute whatever, and Colleville was sleeping peacefully beside his dear little Flavie, while she was saying to herself:—

"Certainly Theodose must be a superior man."

Many men, like la Peyrade, derive their superiority from the audacity, or the difficulty, of an enterprise; the strength they display increases their muscular power, and they spend it freely. Then when success is won, or defeat is met, the public is astonished to find how small, exhausted, and puny those men really are. After casting into the minds of the two persons on whom Celeste's fate chiefly depended, an interest and curiosity that were almost feverish, Theodose pretended to be a very busy man; for five or six days he was out of the house from morning till night, in order not to meet Flavie until the time when her interest should increase to the point of overstepping conventionality, and also in order to force the handsome Thuillier to come and fetch him.

The following Sunday he felt certain he should find Madame Colleville at church; he was not mistaken, for they came out, each of them, at the same moment, and met at the corner of the rue des Deux-Eglises. Theodose offered his arm, which Flavie accepted, leaving her daughter to walk in front with her brother Anatole. This youngest child, then about twelve years old, being destined for the seminary, was now at the Barniol institute, where he obtained an elementary education; Barniol, the son-in-law of the Phellions, was naturally making the tuition fees light, with a view to the hoped-for alliance between Felix and Celeste.

"Have you done me the honor and favor of thinking over what I said to you so badly the other day?" asked the lawyer, in a caressing tone, pressing the lady's arm to his heart with a movement both soft and strong; for he seemed to wish to restrain himself and appear respectful, in spite of his evident eagerness. "Do not misunderstand my intentions," he continued, after receiving from Madame Colleville one of those looks which women trained to the management of passion know how to give,—a look that, by mere expression, can convey both severe rebuke and secret community of sentiment. "I love you as we love a noble nature struggling against misfortune; Christian charity enfolds both the strong and the weak; its treasure belongs to both. Refined, graceful, elegant as you are, made to be an ornament of the highest society, what man could see you without feeling an immense compassion in his heart—buried here among these odious bourgeois, who know nothing of you, not even the aristocratic value of a single one of your attitudes, or those enchanting inflections of your voice! Ah! if I were only rich! if I had power! your husband, who is certainly a good fellow, should be made receiver-general, and you yourself could get him elected deputy. But, alas! poor ambitious man, my first duty is to silence my ambition. Knowing myself at the bottom of the bag like the last number in a family lottery, I can only offer you my arm and not my heart. I hope all from a good marriage, and, believe me, I shall make my wife not only happy, but I shall make her one of the first in the land, receiving from her the means of success. It is so fine a day, will you not take a turn in the Luxembourg?" he added, as they reached the rue d'Enfer at the corner of Colleville's house, opposite to which was a passage leading to the gardens by the stairway of a little building, the last remains of the famous convent of the Chartreux.

The soft yielding of the arm within his own, indicated a tacit consent to this proposal, and as Flavie deserved the honor of a sort of enthusiasm, he drew her vehemently along, exclaiming:—

"Come! we may never have so good a moment—But see!" he added, "there is your husband at the window looking at us; let us walk slowly."

"You have nothing to fear from Monsieur Colleville," said Flavie, smiling; "he leaves me mistress of my own actions."

"Ah! here, indeed, is the woman I have dreamed of," cried the Provencal, with that ecstasy that inflames the soul only, and in tones that issue only from Southern lips. "Pardon me, madame," he said, recovering himself, and returning from an upper sphere to the exiled angel whom he looked at piously, —"pardon me, I abandon what I was saying; but how can a man help feeling for the sorrows he has known himself when he sees them the lot of a being to whom life should bring only joy and happiness? Your sufferings are mine; I am no more in my right place than you are in yours; the same misfortune has made us brother and sister. Ah! dear Flavie, the first day it was granted to me to see you—the last Sunday in September, 1838—you were very beautiful; I shall often recall you to memory in that pretty little gown of mousseline-de-laine of the color of some Scottish tartan! That day I said to myself: 'Why is that woman so often at the Thuilliers'; above all, why did she ever have intimate relations with Thuillier himself?—'"

"Monsieur!" said Flavie, alarmed at the singular course la Peyrade was giving to the conversation.

"Eh! I know all," he cried, accompanying the words with a shrug of his shoulders. "I explain it all to my own mind, and I do not respect you less. You now have to gather the fruits of your sin, and I will help you. Celeste will be very rich, and in that lies your own future. You can have only one son-in-law; chose him wisely. An ambitious man might become a minister, but you would humble your daughter and make her miserable; and if such a man lost his place and fortune he could never recover it. Yes, I love you," he continued. "I love you with an unlimited affection; you are far above the mass of petty considerations in which silly women entangle themselves. Let us understand each other."

Flavie was bewildered; she was, however, awake to the extreme frankness of such language, and she said to herself, "He is not a secret manoeuvrer, certainly." Moreover, she admitted to her own mind that no one had ever so deeply stirred and excited her as this young man.

"Monsieur," she said, "I do not know who could have put into your mind so great an error as to my life, nor by what right you—"

"Ah! pardon me, madame," interrupted the Provencal with a coolness that smacked of contempt. "I must have dreamed it. I said to myself, 'She is all that!' But I see I was judging from the outside. I know now why you are living and will always live on a fourth floor in the rue d'Enfer."

And he pointed his speech with an energetic gesture toward the Colleville windows, which could be seen through the passage from the alley of the Luxembourg, where they were walking alone, in that immense tract trodden by so many and various young ambitions.

"I have been frank, and I expected reciprocity," resumed Theodose. "I myself have had days without food, madame; I have managed to live, pursue my studies, obtain my degree, with two thousand francs for my sole dependence; and I entered Paris through the Barriere d'Italie, with five hundred francs in my pocket, firmly resolved, like one of my compatriots, to become, some day, one of the foremost men of our country. The man who has often picked his food from baskets of scraps where the restaurateurs put their refuse, which are emptied at six o'clock every morning—that man is not likely to recoil before any means,—avowable, of course. Well, do you think me the friend of the people?" he said, smiling. "One has to have a speaking-trumpet to reach the ear of Fame; she doesn't listen if you speak with your lips; and without fame of what use is talent? The poor man's advocate means to be some day the advocate of the rich. Is that plain speaking? Don't I open my inmost being to you? Then open your heart to me. Say to me, 'Let us be friends,' and the day will come when we shall both be happy."

"Good heavens! why did I ever come here? Why did I ever take your arm?" cried Flavie.

"Because it is in your destiny," he replied. "Ah! my dear, beloved Flavie," he added, again pressing her arm upon his heart, "did you expect to hear the vulgarities of love from me? We are brother and sister; that is all."

And he led her towards the passage to return to the rue d'Enfer.

Flavie felt a sort of terror in the depths of the contentment which all women find in violent emotions; and she took that terror for the sort of fear which a new passion always excites; but for all that, she felt she was fascinated, and she walked along in absolute silence.

"What are you thinking of?" asked Theodose, when they reached the middle of the passage.

"Of what you have just said to me," she answered.

"At our age," he said, "it is best to suppress preliminaries; we are not children; we both belong to a sphere in which we should understand each other. Remember this," he added, as they reached the rue d'Enfer.—"I am wholly yours."

So saying, he bowed low to her.

"The iron's in the fire now!" he thought to himself as he watched his giddy prey on her way home.

CHAPTER VI. A KEYNOTE

When Theodose reached home he found, waiting for him on the landing, a personage who is, as it were, the submarine current of this history; he will be found within it like some buried church on which has risen the facade of a palace. The sight of this man, who, after vainly ringing at la Peyrade's door, was now trying that of Dutocq, made the Provencal barrister tremble—but secretly, within himself, not betraying externally his inward emotion. This man was Cerizet, whom Dutocq had mentioned to Thuillier as his copying-clerk.

Cerizet was only thirty-eight years old, but he looked a man of fifty, so aged had he become from causes which age all men. His hairless head had a yellow skull, ill-covered by a rusty, discolored wig; the mask of his face, pale, flabby, and unnaturally rough, seemed the more horrible because the nose was eaten away, though not sufficiently to admit of its being replaced by a false one. From the spring of this nose at the forehead, down to the nostrils, it remained as nature had made it; but disease, after gnawing away the sides near the extremities, had left two holes of fantastic shape, which vitiated pronunciation and hampered speech. The eyes, originally handsome, but weakened by misery of all kinds and by sleepless nights, were red around the edges, and deeply sunken; the glance of those eyes, when the soul sent into them an expression of malignancy, would have frightened both judges and criminals, or any others whom nothing usually affrights.

The mouth, toothless except for a few black fangs, was threatening; the saliva made a foam within it, which did not, however, pass the pale thin lips. Cerizet, a short man, less spare than shrunken, endeavored to remedy the defects of his person by his clothes, and although his garments were not those of opulence, he kept them in a condition of neatness which may even have increased his forlorn appearance. Everything about him seemed dubious; his age, his nose, his glance inspired doubt. It was impossible to know if he were thirty-eight or sixty; if his faded blue trousers, which fitted him well, were of a coming or a past fashion. His boots, worn at the heels, but scrupulously blacked, resoled for the third time, and very choice, originally, may have trodden in their day a ministerial carpet. The frock coat, soaked by many a down-pour, with its brandebourgs, the frogs of which were indiscreet enough to show their skeletons, testified by its cut to departed elegance. The satin stock-cravat fortunately concealed the shirt, but the tongue of the buckle behind the neck had frayed the satin, which was re-satined, that is, re-polished, by a species of oil distilled from the wig. In the days of its youth the waistcoat was not, of course, without freshness, but it was one of those waistcoats, bought for four francs, which come from the hooks of the ready-made clothing dealer. All these things were carefully brushed, and so was the shiny and misshapen hat. They harmonized with each other, even to the black gloves which covered the hands of this subaltern Mephistopheles, whose whole anterior life may be summed up in a single phrase:—

He was an artist in evil, with whom, from the first, evil had succeeded; a man misled by these early successes to continue the plotting of infamous deeds within the lines of strict legality. Becoming the head of a printing-office by betraying his master [see "Lost Illusions"], he had afterwards been condemned to imprisonment as editor of a liberal newspaper. In the provinces, under the Restoration, he became the bete noire of the government, and was called "that unfortunate Cerizet" by some, as people spoke of "the unfortunate Chauvet" and "the heroic Mercier." He owed to this reputation of persecuted patriotism a place as sub-prefect in 1830. Six months later he was dismissed; but he insisted that he was judged without being heard; and he made so much talk about it that, under the ministry of Casimir Perier, he became the editor of an anti-republican newspaper in the pay of the government. He left that position to go into business, one phase of which was the most nefarious stock-company that ever fell into the hands of the correctional police. Cerizet proudly accepted the severe sentence he received; declaring it to be a revengeful plot on the part of the republicans, who, he said, would never forgive him for the hard blows he had dealt them in his journal. He spent the time of his imprisonment in a hospital. The government by this time were ashamed of a man whose almost infamous habits and shameful business transactions, carried on in company with a former banker, named Claparon, led him at last into well-deserved public contempt.

Cerizet, thus fallen, step by step, to the lowest rung of the social ladder, had recourse to pity in order to obtain the place of copying clerk in Dutocq's office. In the depths of his wretchedness the man still dreamed of revenge, and, as he had nothing to lose, he employed all means to that end. Dutocq and himself were bound together in depravity. Cerizet was to Dutocq what the hound is the huntsman. Knowing himself the necessities of poverty and wretchedness, he set up that business of gutter usury called, in popular parlance, "the loan by the little week." He began this at first by help of Dutocq, who shared the profits; but, at the present moment this man of many legal crimes, now the banker of fishwives, the money-lender of costermongers, was the gnawing rodent of the whole faubourg.

"Well," said Cerizet as Dutocq opened his door, "Theodose has just come in; let us go to his room."

The advocate of the poor was fain to allow the two men to pass before him.

All three crossed a little room, the tiled floor of which, covered with a coating of red encaustic, shone in the light; thence into a little salon with crimson curtains and mahogany furniture, covered with red Utrecht velvet; the wall opposite the window being occupied by book-shelves containing a legal library. The chimney-piece was covered with vulgar ornaments, a clock with four columns in mahogany, and candelabra under glass shades. The study, where the three men seated themselves before a soft-coal fire, was the study of a lawyer just beginning to practise. The furniture consisted of a desk, an armchair, little curtains of green silk at the windows, a green carpet, shelves for lawyer's boxes, and a couch, above which hung an ivory Christ on a velvet background. The bedroom, kitchen, and rest of the apartment looked out upon the courtyard.

"Well," said Cerizet, "how are things going? Are we getting on?"

"Yes," replied Theodose.

"You must admit," cried Dutocq, "that my idea was a famous one, in laying hold of that imbecile of a Thuillier?"

"Yes, but I'm not behindhand either," exclaimed Cerizet. "I have come now to show you a way to put the thumbscrews on the old maid and make her spin like a teetotum. We mustn't deceive ourselves; Mademoiselle Thuillier is the head and front of everything in this affair; if we get her on our side the town is won. Let us say little, but that little to the point, as becomes strong men with each other. Claparon, you know, is a fool; he'll be all his life what he always was,—a cat's-paw. Just now he is lending his name to a notary in Paris, who is concerned with a lot of contractors, and they are all—notary and masons—on the point of ruin. Claparon is going headlong into it. He never yet was bankrupt; but there's a first time for everything. He is hidden now in my hovel in the rue des Poules, where no one will ever find him. He is desperate, and he hasn't a penny. Now, among the five or six houses built by these contractors, which have to be sold, there's a jewel of a house, built of freestone, in the neighborhood of the Madeleine,—a frontage laced like a melon, with beautiful carvings,—but not being finished, it will have to be sold for what it will bring; certainly not more than a hundred thousand francs. By spending twenty-five thousand francs upon it it could be let, undoubtedly, for ten thousand. Make Mademoiselle Thuillier the proprietor of that house and you'll win her love; she'll believe that you can put such chances in her way every year. There are two ways of getting hold of vain people: flatter their vanity, *or* threaten them; and there are also two ways of managing misers: fill their purse, or else attack it. Now, this stroke of business, while it does good to Mademoiselle Thuillier, does good to us as well, and it would be a pity not to profit by the chance."

"But why does the notary let it slip through his fingers?" asked Dutocq.

"The notary, my dear fellow! Why, he's the very one who saves us. Forced to sell his practice, and utterly ruined besides, he reserved for himself this crumb of the cake. Believing in the honesty of that idiot Claparon, he has asked him to find a dummy purchaser. We'll let him suppose that Mademoiselle Thuillier is a worthy soul who allows Claparon to use her name; they'll both be fooled, Claparon and the notary too. I owe this little trick to my friend Claparon, who left me to bear the whole weight of the trouble about his stock-company, in which we were tricked by Conture, and I hope you may never be in that man's skin!" he added, infernal hatred flashing from his worn and withered eyes. "Now, I've said my say, gentlemen," he continued, sending out his voice through his nasal holes, and taking a dramatic attitude; for once, at a moment of extreme penury, he had gone upon the stage.

As he finished making his proposition some one rang at the outer door, and la Peyrade rose to go and open it. As soon as his back was turned, Cerizet said, hastily, to Dutocq:—

"Are you sure of him? I see a sort of air about him—And I'm a good judge of treachery."

"He is so completely in our power," said Dutocq, "that I don't trouble myself to watch; but, between ourselves, I didn't think him as strong as he proves to be. The fact is, we thought we were putting a barb between the legs of a man who didn't know how to ride, and the rogue is an old jockey!"

"Let him take care," growled Cerizet. "I can blow him down like a house of cards any day. As for you, papa Dutocq, you are able to see him at work all the time; watch him carefully. Besides, I'll feel his pulse by getting Claparon to propose to him to get rid of us; that will help us to judge him."

"Pretty good, that!" said Dutocq. "You are daring, anyhow."

"I've got my hand in, that's all," replied Cerizet.

These words were exchanged in a low voice during the time that it took Theodose to go to the outer door and return. Cerizet was looking at the books when the lawyer re-entered the room.

"It is Thuillier," said Theodose. "I thought he'd come; he is in the salon. He mustn't see Cerizet's frock-coat; those frogs would frighten him."

"Pooh! you receive the poor in your office, don't you? That's in your role. Do you want any money?" added Cerizet, pulling a hundred francs out of his trousers' pocket. "There it is; it won't look amiss."

And he laid the pile on the chimney-piece.

"And now," said Dutocq, "we had better get out through the bedroom."

"Well, good-bye," said Theodose, opening a hidden door which communicated from the study to the bedroom. "Come in, Monsieur Thuillier," he called out to the beau of the Empire.

When he saw him safely in the study he went to let out his two associates through the bedroom and kitchen into the courtyard.

"In six months," said Cerizet, "you'll have married Celeste and got your foot into the stirrup. You are lucky, you are, not to have sat, like me, in the prisoners' dock. I've been there twice: once in 1825, for 'subversive articles' which I never wrote, and the second time for receiving the profits of a joint-stock company which had slipped through my fingers! Come, let's warm this thing up! Sac-a-papier! Dutocq and I are sorely in need of that twenty-five thousand francs. Good courage, old fellow!" he added, holding out his hand to Theodose, and making the grasp a test of faithfulness.

The Provencal gave Cerizet his right hand, pressing the other's hand warmly:—

"My good fellow," he said, "be very sure that in whatever position I may find myself I shall never forget that from which you have drawn me by putting me in the saddle here. I'm simply your bait; but you are giving me the best part of the catch, and I should be more infamous than a galley-slave who turns policeman if I didn't play fair."

As soon as the door was closed, Cerizet peeped through the key-hole, trying to catch sight of la Peyrade's face. But the Provencal had turned back to meet Thuillier, and his distrustful associate could not detect the expression of his countenance.

That expression was neither disgust nor annoyance, it was simply joy, appearing on a face that now seemed freed. Theodose saw the means of success approaching him, and he flattered himself that the day would come when he might get rid of his ignoble associates, to whom he owed everything. Poverty has unfathomable depths, especially in Paris, slimy bottoms, from which, when a drowned man rises to the surface of the water, he brings with him filth and impurity clinging to his clothes, or to his person. Cerizet, the once opulent friend and protector of Theodose, was the muddy mire still clinging to the Provencal, and the former manager of the joint-stock company saw very plainly that his tool wanted to brush himself on entering a sphere where decent clothing was a necessity.

"Well, my dear Theodose," began Thuillier, "we have hoped to see you every day this week, and every evening we find our hopes deceived. As this is our Sunday for a dinner, my sister and my wife have sent me here to beg you to come to us."

"I have been so busy," said Theodose, "that I have not had two minutes to give to any one, not even to you, whom I count among my friends, and with whom I have wished to talk about—"

"What? have you really been thinking seriously over what you said to me?" cried Thuillier, interrupting him.

"If you had not come here now for a full understanding, I shouldn't respect you as I do," replied la Peyrade, smiling. "You have been a sub-director, and therefore you must have the remains of ambition—which is deucedly legitimate in your case! Come, now, between ourselves, when one sees a Minard, that gilded pot, displaying himself at the Tuileries, and complimenting the king, and a Popinot about to become a minister of State, and then look at you! a man trained to administrative work, a man with thirty years' experience, who has seen six governments, left to plant balsams in a little garden! Heavens and earth!—I am frank, my dear Thuillier, and I'll say, honestly, that I want to advance you, because you'll draw me after you. Well, here's my plan. We are soon to elect a member of the council-general from this arrondissement; and that member must be you. And," he added, dwelling on the word, "it *will* be you! After that, you will certainly be deputy from the arrondissement when the Chamber is re-elected, which must surely be before long. The votes that elect you to the municipal council will stand by you in the election for deputy, trust me for that."

"But how will you manage all this?" cried Thuillier, fascinated.

"You shall know in good time; but you must let me conduct this long and difficult affair; if you commit the slightest indiscretion as to what is said, or planned, or agreed between us, I shall have to drop the whole matter, and good-bye to you!"

"Oh! you can rely on the absolute dumbness of a former sub-director; I've had secrets to keep."

"That's all very well; but these are secrets to keep from your wife and sister, and from Monsieur and Madame Colleville."

"Not a muscle of my face shall reveal them," said Thuillier, assuming a stolid air.

"Very good," continued Theodose. "I shall test you. In order to make yourself eligible, you must pay taxes on a certain amount of property, and you are not paying them."

"I beg your pardon; I'm all right for the municipal council at any rate; I pay two francs ninety-six centimes."

"Yes, but the tax on property necessary for election to the chamber is five hundred francs, and there is no time to lose in acquiring that property, because you must prove possession for one year."

"The devil!" cried Thuillier; "between now and a year hence to be taxed five hundred francs on property which—"

"Between now and the end of July, at the latest, you must pay that tax. Well, I feel enough interest in you to tell you the secret of an affair by which you might make from thirty to forty thousand francs a year, by employing a capital of one hundred and fifty thousand at most. I know that in your family it is your sister who does your business; I am far from thinking that a mistake; she has, they tell me, excellent judgment; and you must let me begin by obtaining her good-will and friendship, and proposing this investment to her. And this is why: If Mademoiselle Thuillier is not induced to put faith in my plan, we shall certainly have difficulty with her. Besides, it won't do for YOU to propose to her that she should put the investment of her money in your name. The idea had better come from me. As to my means of getting you elected to the municipal council, they are these: Phellion controls one quarter of the arrondissement; he and Laudigeois have lived in it these thirty years, and they are listened to like oracles. I have a friend who controls another quarter; and the rector of Saint-Jacques, who is not without influence, thanks to his virtues, disposes of certain votes. Dutocq, in his close relation to the people, and also the justice of peace, will help me, above all, as I'm not acting for myself; and Colleville, as secretary of the mayor's office, can certainly manage to obtain another fourth of the votes."

"You are right!" cried Thuillier. "I'm elected!"

"Do you think so?" said la Peyrade, in a voice of the deepest sarcasm. "Very good! then go and ask your friend Colleville to help you, and see what he'll say. No triumph in election cases is ever brought about by the candidate himself, but by his friends. He should never ask anything himself for himself; he must be invited to accept, and appear to be without ambition."

"La Peyrade!" cried Thuillier, rising, and taking the hand of the young lawyer, "you are a very capable man."

"Not as capable as you, but I have my merits," said the Provencal, smiling.

"If we succeed how shall I ever repay you?" asked Thuillier, naively.

"Ah! that, indeed! I am afraid you will think me impertinent, but remember, there is a true feeling in my heart which offers some excuse for me; in fact, it has given me the spirit to undertake this affair. I love—and I take you for my confidant."

"But who is it?" said Thuillier.

"Your dear little Celeste," replied la Peyrade. "My love for her will be a pledge to you of my devotion. What would I not do for a *father-in-law*! This is pure selfishness; I shall be working for myself."

"Hush!" cried Thuillier.

"Eh, my friend!" said la Peyrade, catching Thuillier round the body; "if I hadn't Flavie on my side, and if I didn't know *all* should I venture to be talking to you thus? But please say nothing to Flavie about this; wait till she speaks to you. Listen to me; I'm of the metal that makes ministers; I do not seek to obtain Celeste until I deserve her. You shall not be asked to give her to me until the day when your election as a deputy of Paris is assured. In order to be deputy of Paris, we must get the better of Minard; and in order to crush Minard you must keep in your own hands all your means of influence; for that reason use Celeste as a hope; we'll play them off, these people, against each other and fool them all—Madame Colleville and you and I will be persons of importance one of these days. Don't think me mercenary. I want Celeste without a 'dot,' with nothing more than her future expectations. To live in your family with you, to keep my wife in your midst, that is my desire. You see now that I have no hidden thoughts. As for you, my dear friend, six months after your election to the municipal council, you will have the cross of the Legion of honor, and when you are deputy you will be made an officer of it. As for your speeches in the Chamber—well! we'll write them together. Perhaps it would be desirable for you to write a book,—a serious book on matters half moral and philanthropic, half political; such, for instance, as charitable institutions considered from the highest stand-point; or reforms in the pawning system, the abuses of which are really frightful. Let us fasten some slight distinction to your name; it will help you,—especially in the arrondissement. Now, I say again, trust me, believe in me; do not think of taking me into your family until you have the ribbon in your buttonhole on the morrow of the day when you take your seat in the Chamber. I'll do more than that, however; I'll put you in the way of making forty thousand francs a year."

"For any one of those three things you shall have our Celeste," said Thuillier.

"Ah! what a pearl she is!" exclaimed la Peyrade, raising his eyes to heaven.

"I have the weakness to pray to God for her every day. She is charming; she is exactly like you—oh! nonsense; surely you needn't caution me! Dutocq told me all. Well, I'll be with you to-night. I must go to the Phellions' now, and begin to work our plan. You don't need me to caution you not to let it be known that you are thinking of me for Celeste; if you do, you'll cut off my arms and legs. Therefore, silence! even to Flavie. Wait till she speaks to you herself. Phellion shall to-night broach the matter of proposing you as candidate for the council."

"To-night?" said Thuillier.

"Yes, to-night," replied la Peyrade, "unless I don't find him at home now."

Thuillier departed, saying to himself:—

"That's a very superior man; we shall always understand each other. Faith! it might be hard to do better for Celeste. They will live with us, as in our own family, and that's a good deal! Yes, he's a fine fellow, a sound man."

To minds of Thuillier's calibre, a secondary consideration often assumes the importance of a principal reason. Theodose had behaved to him with charming bonhomie.

CHAPTER VII. THE WORTHY PHELLIONS

The house to which Theodose de la Peyrade now bent his steps had been the "hoc erat in votis" of Monsieur Phellion for twenty years; it was the house of the Phellions, just as much as Cerizet's frogged coat was the necessary complement of his personality.

This dwelling was stuck against the side of a large house, but only to the depth of one room (about twenty feet or so), and terminated at each end in a sort of pavilion with one window. Its chief charm was a garden, one hundred and eighty feet square, longer than the facade of the house by the width of a courtyard which opened on the street, and a little clump of lindens. Beyond the second pavilion, the courtyard had, between itself and the street, an iron railing, in the centre of which was a little gate opening in the middle.

This building, of rouge stone covered with stucco, and two storeys in height, had received a coat of yellow-wash; the blinds were painted green, and so were the shutters on the lower storey. The kitchen occupied the ground-floor of the pavilion on the courtyard, and the cook, a stout, strong girl, protected by two enormous dogs, performed the functions of portress. The facade, composed of five windows, and the two pavilions, which projected nine feet, were in the style Phellion. Above the door the master of the house had inserted a tablet of white marble, on which, in letters of gold, were read the words, "Aurea mediocritas." Above the sun-dial, affixed to one panel of the facade, he had also caused to be inscribed this sapient maxim: "Umbra mea vita, sic!"

The former window-sills had recently been superceded by sills of red Languedoc marble, found in a marble shop. At the bottom of the garden could be seen a colored statue, intended to lead casual observers to imagine that a nurse was carrying a child. The ground-floor of the house contained only the salon and the dining-room, separated from each other by the well of the staircase and the landing, which formed a sort of antechamber. At the end of the salon, in the other pavilion, was a little study occupied by Phellion.

On the first upper floor were the rooms of the father and mother and that of the young professor. Above were the chambers of the children and the servants; for Phellion, on consideration of his own age and that of his wife, had set up a male domestic, aged fifteen, his son having by that time entered upon his duties of tuition. To right, on entering the courtyard, were little offices where wood was stored, and where the former proprietor had lodged a porter. The Phellions were no doubt awaiting the marriage of their son to allow themselves that additional luxury.

This property, on which the Phellions had long had their eye, cost them eighteen thousand francs in 1831. The house was separated from the courtyard by a balustrade with a base of freestone and a coping of tiles; this little wall, which was breast-high, was lined with a hedge of Bengal roses, in the middle of which opened a wooden gate opposite and leading to the large gates on the street. Those who know the cul-de-sac of the Feuillantines, will understand that the Phellion house, standing at right angles to the street, had a southern exposure, and was protected on the north by the immense wall of the adjoining house, against which the smaller structure was built. The cupola of the Pantheon and that of the Val-de-Grace looked from there like two giants, and so diminished the sky space that, walking in the garden, one felt cramped and oppressed. No place could be more silent than this blind street.

Such was the retreat of the great unknown citizen who was now tasting the sweets of repose, after discharging his duty to the nation in the ministry of finance, from which he had retired as registration clerk after a service of thirty-six years. In 1832 he had led his battalion of the National Guard to the attack on Saint-Merri, but his neighbors had previously seen tears in his eyes at the thought of being obliged to fire on misguided Frenchmen. The affair was already decided by the time his legion crossed the pont Notre-Dame at a quick step, after debouching by the flower-market. This noble hesitation won him the respect of his whole quarter, but he lost the decoration of the Legion of honor; his colonel told him in a loud voice that, under arms, there was no such thing as deliberation,—a saying of Louis-Philippe to the National Guard of Metz. Nevertheless, the bourgeois virtues of Phellion, and the great respect in which he was held in his own quarter had kept him major of the battalion for eight years. He was now nearly sixty, and seeing the moment coming when he must lay off the sword and stock, he hoped that the king would deign to reward his services by granting him at last the Legion of honor.

Truth compels us to say, in spite of the stain this pettiness will put upon so fine a character, that Commander Phellion rose upon the tips of his toes at the receptions in the Tuileries, and did all that he could to put himself forward, even eyeing the citizen-king perpetually when he dined at his table. In short, he intrigued in a dumb sort of way; but had never yet obtained a look in return from the king of his choice. The worthy man had more than once thought, but was not yet decided, to beg Monsieur Minard to assist him in obtaining his secret desire.

Phellion, a man of passive obedience, was stoical in the matter of duty, and iron in all that touched his conscience. To complete this picture by a sketch of his person, we must add that at fifty-nine years of age Phellion had "thickened," to use a term of the bourgeois vocabulary. His face, of one monotonous tone and pitted with the small-pox, had grown to resemble a full moon; so that his lips, formerly large, now seemed of ordinary size. His eyes, much weakened, and protected by glasses, no longer showed the innocence of their light-blue orbs, which in former days had often excited a smile; his white hair now gave gravity to much that twelve years earlier had looked like silliness, and lent itself to ridicule. Time, which does such damage to faces with refined and delicate features, only improves those which, in their youth, have been course and massive. This was the case with Phellion. He occupied the leisure of his old age in making an abridgment of the History of France; for Phellion was the author of several works adopted by the University.

When la Peyrade presented himself, the family were all together. Madame Barniol was just telling her mother about one of her babies, which was slightly indisposed. They were dressed in their Sunday clothes, and were sitting before the fireplace of the wainscoted salon on chairs bought at a bargain; and they all felt an emotion when Genevieve, the cook and portress, announced the personage of whom they were just then speaking in connection with Celeste, whom, we must here state, Felix Phellion loved, to the extent of going to mass to behold her. The learned mathematician had made that effort in the morning, and the family were joking him about it in a pleasant way, hoping in their hearts that Celeste and her parents might understand the treasure that was thus offered to them.

"Alas! the Thuilliers seem to me infatuated with a very dangerous man," said Madame Phellion. "He took Madame Colleville by the arm this morning after church, and they went together to the Luxembourg."

"There is something about that lawyer," remarked Felix Phellion, "that strikes me as sinister. He might be found to have committed some crime and I shouldn't be surprised."

"That's going too far," said old Phellion. "He is cousin-germain to Tartuffe, that immortal figure cast in bronze by our honest Moliere; for Moliere, my children, had honesty and patriotism for the basis of his genius."

It was at that instant that Genevieve came in to say, "There's a Monsieur de la Peyrade out there, who wants to see monsieur."

"To see me!" exclaimed Phellion. "Ask him to come in," he added, with that solemnity in little things which gave him even now a touch of absurdity, though it always impressed his family, which accepted him as king.

Phellion, his two sons, and his wife and daughter, rose and received the circular bow made by the lawyer.

71

"To what do we owe the honor of your visit, monsieur?" asked Phellion, stiffly.

"To your importance in this arrondissement, my dear Monsieur Phellion, and to public interests," replied Theodose.

"Then let us go into my study," said Phellion.

"No, no, my friend," said the rigid Madame Phellion, a small woman, flat as a flounder, who retained upon her features the grim severity with which she taught music in boarding-schools for young ladies; "we will leave you."

An upright Erard piano, placed between the two windows and opposite to the fireplace, showed the constant occupation of a proficient.

"Am I so unfortunate as to put you to flight?" said Theodose, smiling in a kindly way at the mother and daughter. "You have a delightful retreat here," he continued. "You only lack a pretty daughter-in-law to pass the rest of your days in this 'aurea mediocritas,' the wish of the Latin poet, surrounded by family joys. Your antecedents, my dear Monsieur Phellion, ought surely to win you such rewards, for I am told that you are not only a patriot but a good citizen."

"Monsieur," said Phellion, embarrassed, "monsieur, I have only done my duty." At the word "daughter-in-law," uttered by Theodose, Madame Barniol, who resembled her mother as much as one drop of water is like another, looked at Madame Phellion and at Felix as if she would say, "Were we mistaken?"

The desire to talk this incident over carried all four personages into the garden, for, in March, 1840, the weather was spring-like, at least in Paris.

"Commander," said Theodose, as soon as he was alone with Phellion, who was always flattered by that title, "I have come to speak to you about the election—"

"Yes, true; we are about to nominate a municipal councillor," said Phellion, interrupting him.

"And it is apropos of that candidacy that I have come to disturb your Sunday joys; but perhaps in so doing we shall not go beyond the limits of the family circle."

It would be impossible for Phellion to be more Phellion than Theodose was Phellion at that moment.

"I shall not let you say another word," replied the commander, profiting by the pause made by Theodose, who watched for the effect of his speech. "My choice is made."

"We have had the same idea!" exclaimed Theodose; "men of the same character agree as well as men of the same mind."

"In this case I do not believe in that phenomenon," replied Phellion. "This arrondissement had for its representative in the municipal council the most virtuous of men, as he was the noblest of magistrates. I allude to the late Monsieur Popinot, the deceased judge of the Royal courts. When the question of replacing him came up, his nephew, the heir to his benevolence, did not reside in this quarter. He has since, however, purchased, and now occupies, the house where his uncle lived in the rue de la Montagne-Sainte-Genevieve; he is the physician of the Ecole Polytechnique and that of our hospitals; he does honor to this quarter; for these reasons, and to pay homage in the person of the nephew to the memory of the uncle, we have decided to nominate Doctor Horace Bianchon, member of the Academy of Sciences, as you are aware, and one of the most distinguished young men in the illustrious faculty of Paris. A man is not great in our eyes solely because he is celebrated; to my mind the late Councillor Popinot was almost another Saint Vincent de Paul."

"But a doctor is not an administrator," replied Theodose; "and, besides, I have come to ask your vote for a man to whom your dearest interests require that you should sacrifice a predilection, which, after all, is quite unimportant to the public welfare."

"Monsieur!" cried Phellion, rising and striking an attitude like that of Lafon in "Le Glorieux," "Do you despise me sufficiently to suppose that my personal interests could ever influence my political conscience? When a matter concerns the public welfare, I am a citizen—nothing more, and nothing less."

Theodose smiled to himself at the thought of the battle which was now to take place between the father and the citizen.

"Do not bind yourself to your present ideas, I entreat you," he said, "for this matter concerns the happiness of your dear Felix."

"What do you mean by those words?" asked Phellion, stopping short in the middle of the salon and posing, with his hand thrust through the bosom of his waistcoat from right to left, in the well-known attitude of Odilon Barrot.

"I have come in behalf of our mutual friend, the worthy and excellent Monsieur Thuillier, whose influence on the destiny of that beautiful Celeste Colleville must be well known to you. If, as I think, your son, whose merits are incontestable, and of whom both families may well be proud, if, I say, he is courting Celeste with a view to a marriage in which all expediencies may be combined, you cannot do more to promote that end than to obtain

73

Thuillier's eternal gratitude by proposing your worthy friend to the suffrages of your fellow-citizens. As for me, though I have lately come into the quarter, I can, thanks to the influence I enjoy through certain legal benefits done to the poor, materially advance his interests. I might, perhaps, have put myself forward for this position; but serving the poor brings in but little money; and, besides, the modesty of my life is out of keeping with such distinctions. I have devoted myself, monsieur, to the service of the weak, like the late Councillor Popinot,—a sublime man, as you justly remarked. If I had not already chosen a career which is in some sort monastic, and precludes all idea of marriage and public office, my taste, my second vocation, would lead me to the service of God, to the Church. I do not trumpet what I do, like the philanthropists; I do not write about it; I simply act; I am pledged to Christian charity. The ambition of our friend Thuillier becoming known to me, I have wished to contribute to the happiness of two young people who seem to me made for each other, by suggesting to you the means of winning the rather cold heart of Monsieur Thuillier."

Phellion was bewildered by this tirade, admirably delivered; he was dazzled, attracted; but he remained Phellion; he walked up to the lawyer and held out his hand, which la Peyrade took.

"Monsieur," said the commander, with emotion, "I have misjudged you. What you have done me the honor to confide to me will die *there*," laying his hand on his heart. "You are one of the men of whom we have too few,—men who console us for many evils inherent in our social state. Righteousness is seen so seldom that our too feeble natures distrust appearances. You have in me a friend, if you will allow me the honor of assuming that title. But you must learn to know me, monsieur. I should lose my own esteem if I nominated Thuillier. No, my son shall never own his happiness to an evil action on his father's part. I shall not change my candidate because my son's interests demand it. That is civic virtue, monsieur."

La Peyrade pulled out his handkerchief and rubbed it in his eye so that it drew a tear, as he said, holding out his hand to Phellion, and turning aside his head:—

"Ah! monsieur, how sublime a struggle between public and private duty! Had I come here only to see this sight, my visit would not have been wasted. You cannot do otherwise! In your place, I should do the same. You are that noblest thing that God has made—a righteous man! a citizen of the Jean-Jacques type! With many such citizens, oh France! my country! what mightest thou become! It is I, monsieur, who solicit, humbly, the honor to be your friend."

"What can be happening?" said Madame Phellion, watching the scene through the window. "Do see your father and that horrid man embracing each other."

Phellion and la Peyrade now came out and joined the family in the garden.

"My dear Felix," said the old man, pointing to la Peyrade, who was bowing to Madame Phellion, "be very grateful to that admirable young man; he will prove most useful to you."

The lawyer walked for about five minutes with Madame Barniol and Madame Phellion beneath the leafless lindens, and gave them (in consequence of the embarrassing circumstances created by Phellion's political obstinacy) a piece of advice, the effects of which were to bear fruit that evening, while its first result was to make both ladies admire his talents, his frankness, and his inappreciable good qualities. When the lawyer departed the whole family conducted him to the street gate, and all eyes followed him until he had turned the corner of the rue du Faubourg-Saint-Jacques. Madame Phellion then took the arm of her husband to return to the salon, saying:—

"Hey! my friend! what does this mean? You, such a good father, how can you, from excessive delicacy, stand in the way of such a fine marriage for our Felix?"

"My dear," replied Phellion, "the great men of antiquity, Brutus and others, were never fathers when called upon to be citizens. The bourgeoisie has, even more than the aristocracy whose place it has been called upon to take, the obligations of the highest virtues. Monsieur de Saint-Hilaire did not think of his lost arm in presence of the dead Turenne. We must give proof of our worthiness; let us give it at every state of the social hierarchy. Shall I instruct my family in the highest civic principles only to ignore them myself at the moment for applying them? No, my dear; weep, if you must, to-day, but to-morrow you will respect me," he added, seeing tears in the eyes of his starched better half.

These noble words were said on the sill of the door, above which was written, "Aurea mediocritas."

"I ought to have put, 'et digna,'" added Phellion, pointing to the tablet, "but those two words would imply self-praise."

"Father," said Marie-Theodore Phellion, the future engineer of "ponts et chaussees," when the family were once more seated in the salon, "it seems to me that there is nothing dishonorable in changing one's determination about a choice which is of no real consequence to public welfare."

"No consequence, my son!" cried Phellion. "Between ourselves I will say, and Felix shares my opinion, Monsieur Thuillier is absolutely without capacity; he knows nothing. Monsieur Horace Bianchon is an able man; he will obtain a thousand things for our arrondissement, and Thuillier will obtain none! Remember this, my son; to change a good determination for a bad one from motives of self-interest is one of those infamous actions which escape the control of men but are punished by God. I am, or I think I am, void of all blame before my conscience, and I owe it to you, my children, to leave my memory unstained among you. Nothing, therefore, can make me change my determination."

"Oh, my good father!" cried the little Barniol woman, flinging herself on a cushion at Phellion's knees, "don't ride your high horse! There are many fools and idiots in the municipal council, and France gets along all the same. That old Thuillier will adopt the opinions of those about him. Do reflect that Celeste will probably have five hundred thousand francs."

"She might have millions," said Phellion, "and I might see them there at my feet before I would propose Thuillier, when I owe to the memory of the best of men to nominate, if possible, Horace Bianchon, his nephew. From the heaven above us Popinot is contemplating and applauding me!" cried Phellion, with exaltation. "It is by such considerations as you suggest that France is being lowered, and the bourgeoisie are bringing themselves into contempt."

"My father is right," said Felix, coming out of a deep reverie. "He deserves our respect and love; as he has throughout the whole course of his modest and honored life. I would not owe my happiness either to remorse in his noble soul, or to a low political bargain. I love Celeste as I love my own family; but, above all that, I place my father's honor, and since this question is a matter of conscience with him it must not be spoken of again."

Phellion, with his eyes full of tears, went up to his eldest son and took him in his arms, saying, "My son! my son!" in a choking voice.

"All that is nonsense," whispered Madame Phellion in Madame Barniol's ear. "Come and dress me; I shall make an end of this; I know your father; he has put his foot down now. To carry out the plan that pious young man, Theodose, suggested, I want your help; hold yourself ready to give it, my daughter."

At this moment, Genevieve came in and gave a letter to Monsieur Phellion.

"An invitation for dinner to-day, for Madame Phellion and Felix and myself, at the Thuilliers'," he said.

The magnificent and surprising idea of Thuillier's municipal advancement, put forth by the "advocate of the poor" was not less upsetting in the Thuillier household than it was in the Phellion salon. Jerome Thuillier, without actually confiding anything to his sister, for he made it a point of honor to obey his Mephistopheles, had rushed to her in great excitement to say:—

"My dearest girl" (he always touched her heart with those caressing words), "we shall have some big-wigs at dinner to-day. I'm going to ask the Minards; therefore take pains about your dinner. I have written to Monsieur and Madame Phellion; it is rather late; but there's no need of ceremony with them. As for the Minards, I must throw a little dust in their eyes; I have a particular need of them."

"Four Minards, three Phellions, four Collevilles, and ourselves; that makes thirteen—"

"La Peyrade, fourteen; and it is worth while to invite Dutocq; he may be useful to us. I'll go up and see him."

"What are you scheming?" cried his sister. "Fifteen to dinner! There's forty francs, at the very least, waltzing off."

"You won't regret them, my dearest. I want you to be particularly agreeable to our young friend, la Peyrade. There's a friend, indeed! you'll soon have proofs of that! If you love me, cosset him well."

So saying, he departed, leaving Brigitte bewildered.

"Proofs, indeed! yes, I'll look out for proofs," she said. "I'm not to be caught with fine words, not I! He is an amiable fellow; but before I take him into my heart I shall study him a little closer."

After inviting Dutocq, Thuillier, having bedizened himself, went to the hotel Minard, rue des Macons-Sorbonne, to capture the stout Zelie, and gloss over the shortness of the invitation.

Minard had purchased one of those large and sumptuous habitations which the old religious orders built about the Sorbonne, and as Thuillier mounted the broad stone steps with an iron balustrade, that proved how arts of the second class flourished under Louis XIII., he envied both the mansion and its occupant,—the mayor.

This vast building, standing between a courtyard and garden, is noticeable as a specimen of the style, both noble and elegant, of the reign of Louis XIII., coming singularly, as it did, between the bad taste of the expiring renaissance and the heavy grandeur of Louis XIV., at its dawn. This transition period is shown in many public buildings. The massive scroll-work of several facades —that of the Sorbonne, for instance,—and columns rectified according to the rules of Grecian art, were beginning to appear in this architecture.

A grocer, a lucky adulterator, now took the place of the former ecclesiastical governor of an institution called in former times L'Economat; an establishment connected with the general agency of the old French clergy, and founded by the long-sighted genius of Richelieu. Thuillier's name opened for him the doors of the salon, where sat enthroned in velvet and gold, amid the most magnificent "Chineseries," the poor woman who weighed with all her avoirdupois on the hearts and minds of princes and princesses at the "popular balls" of the palace.

"Isn't she a good subject for 'La Caricature'?" said a so-called lady of the bedchamber to a duchess, who could hardly help laughing at the aspect of Zelie, glittering with diamonds, red as a poppy, squeezed into a gold brocade, and rolling along like the casts of her former shop.

"Will you pardon me, fair lady," began Thuillier, twisting his body, and pausing in pose number two of his imperial repertory, "for having allowed this invitation to remain in my desk, thinking, all the while, that it was sent? It is for to-day, but perhaps I am too late?"

Zelie examined her husband's face as he approached them to receive Thuillier; then she said:—

"We intended to drive into the country and dine at some chance restaurant; but we'll give up that idea and all the more readily because, in my opinion, it is getting devilishly vulgar to drive out of Paris on Sundays."

"We will have a little dance to the piano for the young people, if enough come, as I hope they will. I have sent a line to Phellion, whose wife is intimate with Madame Pron, the successor—"

"Successor*ess*," interrupted Madame Minard.

"No," said Thuillier, "it ought to be success'ress; just as we say may'ress, dropping the O, you know."

"Is it full dress?" asked Madame Minard.

"Heavens! no," replied Thuillier; "you would get me finely scolded by my sister. No, it is only a family party. Under the Empire, madame, we all devoted ourselves to dancing. At that great epoch of our national life they thought as much of a fine dancer as they did of a good soldier. Nowadays the country is so matter-of-fact."

"Well, we won't talk politics," said the mayor, smiling. "The King is grand; he is very able. I have a deep admiration for my own time, and for the institutions which we have given to ourselves. The King, you may be sure, knows very well what he is doing by the development of industries. He is struggling hand to hand against England; and we are doing him more harm during this fruitful peace than all the wars of the Empire would have done."

"What a deputy Minard would make!" cried Zelie, naively. "He practises speechifying at home. You'll help us to get him elected, won't you, Thuillier?"

"We won't talk politics now," replied Thuillier. "Come at five."

"Will that little Vinet be there?" asked Minard; "he comes, no doubt, for Celeste."

"Then he may go into mourning," replied Thuillier. "Brigitte won't hear of him."

Zelie and Minard exchanged a smile of satisfaction.

"To think that we must hob-nob with such common people, all for the sake of our son!" cried Zelie, when Thuillier was safely down the staircase, to which the mayor had accompanied him.

"Ha! he thinks to be deputy!" thought Thuillier, as he walked away. "These grocers! nothing satisfies them. Heavens! what would Napoleon say if he could see the government in the hands of such people! I'm a trained administrator, at any rate. What a competitor, to be sure! I wonder what la Peyrade will say?"

The ambitious ex-beau now went to invite the whole Laudigeois family for the evening, after which he went to the Collevilles', to make sure that Celeste should wear a becoming gown. He found Flavie rather pensive. She hesitated about coming, but Thuillier overcame her indecision.

"My old and ever young friend," he said, taking her round the waist, for she was alone in her little salon, "I won't have any secret from you. A great affair is in the wind for me. I can't tell you more than that, but I can ask you to be particularly charming to a certain young man—"

"Who is it?"

"La Peyrade."

"Why, Charles?"

"He holds my future in his hands. Besides, he's a man of genius. I know what that is. He's got this sort of thing,"—and Thuillier made the gesture of a dentist pulling out a back tooth. "We must bind him to us, Flavie. But, above all, don't let him see his power. As for me, I shall just give and take with him."

"Do you want me to be coquettish?"

"Not too much so, my angel," replied Thuillier, with a foppish air.

And he departed, not observing the stupor which overcame Flavie.

"That young man is a power," she said to herself. "Well, we shall see!"

For these reasons she dressed her hair with marabouts, put on her prettiest gown of gray and pink, which allowed her fine shoulders to be seen beneath a pelerine of black lace, and took care to keep Celeste in a little silk frock made with a yoke and a large plaited collarette, telling her to dress her hair plainly, a la Berthe.

CHAPTER VIII. AD MAJOREM THEODOSIS GLORIAM

At half-past four o'clock Theodose was at his post. He had put on his vacant, half-servile manner and soft voice, and he drew Thuillier at once into the garden.

"My friend," he said, "I don't doubt your triumph, but I feel the necessity of again warning you to be absolutely silent. If you are questioned about anything, especially about Celeste, make evasive answers which will keep your questioners in suspense. You must have learned how to do that in a government office."

"I understand!" said Thuillier. "But what certainty have you?"

"You'll see what a fine dessert I have prepared for you. But please be modest. There come the Minards; let me pipe to them. Bring them out here, and then disappear yourself."

After the first salutations, la Peyrade was careful to keep close to the mayor, and presently at an opportune moment he drew him aside to say:—

"Monsieur le maire, a man of your political importance doesn't come to bore himself in a house of this kind without an object. I don't want to fathom your motives—which, indeed, I have no right to do—and my part in this world is certainly not to mingle with earthly powers; but please pardon my apparent presumption, and deign to listen to a piece of advice which I shall venture to give you. If I do you a service to-day you are in a position to return it to me to-morrow; therefore, in case I should be so fortunate as to do you a good turn, I am really only obeying the law of self-interest. Our friend Thuillier is in despair at being a nobody; he has taken it into his head that he wants to become a personage in this arrondissement—"

"Ah! ah!" exclaimed Minard.

"Oh! nothing very exalted; he wants to be elected to the municipal council. Now, I know that Phellion, seeing the influence such a service would have on his family interests, intends to propose your poor friend as candidate. Well, perhaps you might think it wise, in your own interests, to be beforehand with him. Thuillier's nomination could only be favorable for you—I mean agreeable; and he'll fill his place in the council very well; there are some there who are not as strong as he. Besides, owing to his place to your support, he will see with your eyes; he already looks to you as one of the lights of the town."

"My dear fellow, I thank you very much," replied Minard. "You are doing me a service I cannot sufficiently acknowledge, and which proves to me—"

"That I don't like those Phellions," said la Peyrade, taking advantage of a slight hesitation on the part of the mayor, who feared to express an idea in which the lawyer might see contempt. "I hate people who make capital out of their honesty and coin money from fine sentiments."

"You know them well," said Minard; "they are sycophants. That man's whole life for the last ten years is explained by this bit of red ribbon," added the mayor, pointing to his own buttonhole.

"Take care!" said the lawyer, "his son is in love with Celeste, and he's fairly in the heart of the family."

"Yes, but my son has twelve thousand a year in his own right."

"Oh!" said Theodose, with a start, "Mademoiselle Brigitte was saying the other day that she wanted at least as much as that in Celeste's suitor. Moreover, six months hence you'll probably hear that Thuillier has a property worth forty thousand francs a year."

"The devil! well, I thought as much. Yes, certainly, he shall be made a member of the municipal council."

"In any case, don't say anything about me to him," said the advocate of the poor, who now hastened away to speak to Madame Phellion. "Well, my fair lady," he said, when he reached her, "have you succeeded?"

"I waited till four o'clock, and then that worthy and excellent man would not let me finish what I had to say. He is much to busy to accept such an office, and he sent a letter which Monsieur Phellion has read, saying that he, Doctor Bianchon, thanked him for his good intentions, and assured him that his own candidate was Monsieur Thuillier. He said that he should use all his influence in his favor, and begged my husband to do the same."

"And what did your excellent husband say?"

"'I have done my duty,' he said. 'I have not been false to my conscience, and now I am all for Thuillier.'"

"Well, then, the thing is settled," said la Peyrade. "Ignore my visit, and take all the credit of the idea to yourselves."

Then he went to Madame Colleville, composing himself in the attitude and manner of the deepest respect.

"Madame," he said, "have the goodness to send out to me here that kindly papa Colleville. A surprise is to be given to Monsieur Thuillier, and I want

Monsieur Colleville to be in the secret."

While la Peyrade played the part of man of the world with Colleville, and allowed himself various witty sarcasms when explaining to him Thuillier's candidacy, telling him he ought to support it, if only to exhibit his incapacity, Flavie was listening in the salon to the following conversation, which bewildered her for the moment and made her ears ring.

"I should like to know what Monsieur Colleville and Monsieur de la Peyrade can be saying to each other to make them laugh like that," said Madame Thuillier, foolishly, looking out of the window.

"A lot of improper things, as men always do when they talk together," replied Mademoiselle Thuillier, who often attacked men with the sort of instinct natural to old maids.

"No, they are incapable of that," said Phellion, gravely. "Monsieur de la Peyrade is one of the most virtuous young men I have ever met. People know what I think of Felix; well, I put the two on the same line; indeed, I wish my son had a little more of Monsieur de la Peyrade's beautiful piety."

"You are right; he is a man of great merit, who is sure to succeed," said Minard. "As for me, my suffrages—for I really ought not to say protection—are his."

"He pays more for oil than for bread," said Dutocq. "I know that."

"His mother, if he has the happiness to still possess her, must be proud of him," remarked Madame Thuillier, sententiously.

"He is a real treasure for us," said Thuillier. "If you only knew how modest he is! He doesn't do himself justice."

"I can answer for one thing," added Dutocq; "no young man ever maintained a nobler attitude in poverty; he triumphed over it; but he suffered —it is easy to see that."

"Poor young man!" cried Zelie. "Such things make my heart ache!"

"Any one could safely trust both secrets and fortune to him," said Thuillier; "and in these days that is the finest thing that can be said of a man."

"It is Colleville who is making him laugh," cried Dutocq.

Just then Colleville and la Peyrade returned from the garden the very best friends in the world.

"Messieurs," said Brigitte, "the soup and the King must never be kept waiting; give your hand to the ladies."

Five minutes after this little pleasantry (issuing from the lodge of her father the porter) Brigitte had the satisfaction of seeing her table surrounded by the principal personages of this drama; the rest, with the one exception of the odious Cerizet, arrived later.

The portrait of the former maker of canvas money-bags would be incomplete if we omitted to give a description of one of her best dinners. The physiognomy of the bourgeois cook of 1840 is, moreover, one of those details essentially necessary to a history of manners and customs, and clever housewives may find some lessons in it. A woman doesn't make empty bags for twenty years without looking out for the means to fill a few of them. Now Brigitte had one peculiar characteristic. She united the economy to which she owed her fortune with a full understanding of necessary expenses. Her relative prodigality, when it concerned her brother or Celeste, was the antipodes of avarice. In fact, she often bemoaned herself that she couldn't be miserly. At her last dinner she had related how, after struggling ten minute and enduring martyrdom, she had ended by giving ten francs to a poor workwoman whom she knew, positively, had been without food for two days.

"Nature," she said naively, "is stronger than reason."

The soup was a rather pale bouillon; for, even on an occasion like this, the cook had been enjoined to make a great deal of bouillon out of the beef supplied. Then, as the said beef was to feed the family on the next day and the day after that, the less juice it expended in the bouillon, the more substantial were the subsequent dinners. The beef, little cooked, was always taken away at the following speech from Brigitte, uttered as soon as Thuillier put his knife into it:—

"I think it is rather tough; send it away, Thuillier, nobody will eat it; we have other things."

The soup was, in fact, flanked by four viands mounted on old hot-water chafing-dishes, with the plating worn off. At this particular dinner (afterwards called that of the candidacy) the first course consisted of a pair of ducks with olives, opposite to which was a large pie with forcemeat balls, while a dish of eels "a la tartare" corresponded in like manner with a fricandeau on chicory. The second course had for its central dish a most dignified goose stuffed with chestnuts, a salad of vegetables garnished with rounds of beetroot opposite to custards in cups, while lower down a dish of turnips "au sucre" faced a timbale of macaroni. This gala dinner of the concierge type cost, at the utmost, twenty francs, and the remains of the feast provided the household for a couple of days; nevertheless, Brigitte would say:—

"Pest! when one has to have company how the money goes! It is fearful!"

The table was lighted by two hideous candlesticks of plated silver with four branches each, in which shone eight of those thrifty wax-candles that go by the name of Aurora. The linen was dazzling in whiteness, and the silver, with beaded edges, was the fruit, evidently, of some purchase made during the Revolution by Thuillier's father. Thus the fare and the service were in keeping with the house, the dining-room, and the Thuilliers themselves, who could never, under any circumstances, get themselves above this style of living. The Minards, Collevilles, and la Peyrade exchanged now and then a smile which betrayed their mutually satirical but repressed thoughts. La Peyrade, seated beside Flavie, whispered in her ear:—

"You must admit that they ought to be taught how to live. But those Minards are no better in their way. What cupidity! they've come here solely after Celeste. Your daughter will be lost to you if you let them have her. These parvenus have all the vices of the great lords of other days without their elegance. Minard's son, who has twelve thousand francs a year of his own, could very well find a wife elsewhere, instead of pushing his speculating rake in here. What fun it would be to play upon those people as one would on a bass-viol or a clarionet!"

While the dishes of the second course were being removed, Minard, afraid that Phellion would precede him, said to Thuillier with a grave air:—

"My dear Thuillier, in accepting your dinner, I did so for the purpose of making an important communication, which does you so much honor that all here present ought to be made participants in it."

Thuillier turned pale.

"Have you obtained the cross for me?" he cried, on receiving a glance from Theodose, and wishing to prove that he was not without craft.

"You will doubtless receive it ere long," replied the mayor. "But the matter now relates to something better than that. The cross is a favor due to the good opinion of a minister, whereas the present question concerns an election due to the consent of your fellow citizens. In a word, a sufficiently large number of electors in your arrondissement have cast their eyes upon you, and wish to honor you with their confidence by making you the representative of this arrondissement in the municipal council of Paris; which, as everybody knows, is the Council-general of the Seine."

"Bravo!" cried Dutocq.

Phellion rose.

"Monsieur le maire has forestalled me," he said in an agitated voice, "but it is so flattering for our friend to be the object of eagerness on the part of all good citizens, and to obtain the public vote of high and low, that I cannot complain of being obliged to come second only; therefore, all honor to the initiatory authority!" (Here he bowed respectfully to Minard.) "Yes, Monsieur Thuillier, many electors think of giving you their votes in that portion of the arrondissement where I keep my humble penates; and you have the special advantage of being suggested to their minds by a distinguished man." (Sensation.) "By a man in whose person we desired to honor one of the most virtuous inhabitants of the arrondissement, who for twenty years, I may say, was the father of it. I allude to the late Monsieur Popinot, counsellor, during his lifetime, to the Royal court, and our delegate in the municipal council of Paris. But his nephew, of whom I speak, Doctor Bianchon, one of our glories, has, in view of his absorbing duties, declined the responsibility with which we sought to invest him. While thanking us for our compliment he has—take note of this—indicated for our suffrages the candidate of Monsieur le maire as being, in his opinion, capable, owing to the position he formerly occupied, of exercising the magisterial functions of the aedileship."

And Phellion sat down amid approving murmurs.

"Thuillier, you can count on me, your old friend," said Colleville.

At this moment the guests were sincerely touched by the sight presented of old Mademoiselle Brigitte and Madame Thuillier. Brigitte, pale as though she were fainting, was letting the slow tears run, unheeded, down her cheeks, tears of deepest joy; while Madame Thuillier sat, as if struck by lightning, with her eyes fixed. Suddenly the old maid darted into the kitchen, crying out to Josephine the cook:—

"Come into the cellar my girl, we must get out the wine behind the wood!"

"My friends," said Thuillier, in a shaking voice, "this is the finest moment of my life, finer than even the day of my election, should I consent to allow myself to be presented to the suffrages of my fellow-citizens" ("You must! you must!"); "for I feel myself much worn down by thirty years of public service, and, as you may well believe, a man of honor has need to consult his strength and his capacities before he takes upon himself the functions of the aedileship."

"I expected nothing less of you, Monsieur Thuillier," cried Phellion. "Pardon me; this is the first time in my life that I have ever interrupted a superior; but there are circumstances—"

"Accept! accept!" cried Zelie. "Bless my soul! what we want are men like you to govern us."

"Resign yourself, my chief!" cried Dutocq, and, "Long live the future municipal councillor! but we haven't anything to drink——"

"Well, the thing is settled," said Minard; "you are to be our candidate."

"You think too much of me," replied Thuillier.

"Come, come!" cried Colleville. "A man who has done thirty years in the galleys of the ministry of finance is a treasure to the town."

"You are much too modest," said the younger Minard; "your capacity is well known to us; it remains a tradition at the ministry of finance."

"As you all insist——" began Thuillier.

"The King will be pleased with our choice; I can assure you of that," said Minard, pompously.

"Gentlemen," said la Peyrade, "will you permit a recent dweller in the faubourg Saint-Jacques to make one little remark, which is not without importance?"

The consciousness that everybody had of the sterling merits of the advocate of the poor produced the deepest silence.

"The influence of Monsieur le maire of an adjoining arrondissement, which is immense in ours where he has left such excellent memories; that of Monsieur Phellion, the oracle—yes, let the truth be spoken," he exclaimed, noticing a gesture made by Phellion—"the *oracle* of his battalion; the influence, no less powerful, which Monsieur Colleville owes to the frank heartiness of his manner, and to his urbanity; that of Monsieur Dutocq, the clerk of the justice court, which will not be less efficacious, I am sure; and the poor efforts which I can offer in my humble sphere of activity,—are pledges of success, but they are not success itself. To obtain a rapid triumph we should pledge ourselves, now and here, to keep the deepest secrecy on the manifestation of sentiments which has just taken place. Otherwise, we should excite, without knowing or willing it, envy and all the other secondary passions, which would create for us later various obstacles to overcome. The political meaning of the new social organization, its very basis, its token, and the guarantee for its continuance, are in a certain sharing of the governing power with the middle classes, classes who are the true strength of modern societies, the centre of morality, of all good sentiments and intelligent work. But we cannot conceal from ourselves that the principle of election, extended now to almost every function, has brought the interests of ambition, and the passion for being *something*, excuse the word, into social depths where they ought never to have penetrated. Some see good in this; others see evil; it is not my place to judge between them in presence of minds before whose eminence I bow. I content myself by simply suggesting this question in order to show the dangers which the banner of our friend must meet. See for yourselves! the decease of our late honorable representative in the municipal council dates back scarcely one week, and already the arrondissement is being canvassed by inferior ambitions. Such men put themselves forward to be seen at any price. The writ of convocation will, probably, not take effect for a month to come. Between now and then, imagine the intrigues! I entreat you not to expose our friend Thuillier to the blows of his competitors; let us not deliver him over to public discussion, that modern harpy which is but the trumpet of envy and calumny, the pretext seized by malevolence to belittle all that is great, soil all that is immaculate and dishonor whatever is sacred. Let us, rather, do as the Third Party is now doing in the Chamber,—keep silence and vote!"

"He speaks well," said Phellion to his neighbor Dutocq.

"And how strong the statement is!"

Envy had turned Minard and his son green and yellow.

"That is well said and very true," remarked Minard.

"Unanimously adopted!" cried Colleville. "Messieurs, we are men of honor; it suffices to understand each other on this point."

"Whoso desires the end accepts the means," said Phellion, emphatically.

At this moment, Mademoiselle Thuillier reappeared, followed by her two servants; the key of the cellar was hanging from her belt, and three bottles of champagne, three of hermitage, and one bottle of malaga were placed upon the table. She herself was carrying, with almost respectful care, a smaller bottle, like a fairy Carabosse, which she placed before her. In the midst of the hilarity caused by this abundance of excellent things—a fruit of gratitude, which the poor spinster in the delirium of her joy poured out with a profusion which put to shame the sparing hospitality of her usual fortnightly dinners—numerous dessert dishes made their appearance: mounds of almonds, raisins, figs, and nuts (popularly known as the "four beggars"), pyramids of oranges, confections, crystallized fruits, brought from the hidden depths of her cupboards, which would never have figured on the table-cloth had it not been for the "candidacy."

"Celeste, they will bring you a bottle of brandy which my father obtained in 1802; make an orange-salad!" cried Brigitte to her sister-in-law. "Monsieur Phellion, open the champagne; that bottle is for you three. Monsieur Dutocq, take this one. Monsieur Colleville, you know how to pop corks!"

The two maids distributed champagne glasses, also claret glasses, and wine glasses. Josephine also brought three more bottles of Bordeaux.

"The year of the comet!" cried Thuillier, laughing, "Messieurs, you have turned my sister's head."

"And this evening you shall have punch and cakes," she said. "I have sent to the chemists for some tea. Heavens! if I had only known the affair concerned an election," she cried, looking at her sister-in-law, "I'd have served the turkey."

A general laugh welcomed this speech.

"We have a goose!" said Minard junior.

"The carts are unloading!" cried Madame Thuillier, as "marrons glaces" and "meringues" were placed upon the table.

Mademoiselle Thuillier's face was blazing. She was really superb to behold. Never did sisterly love assume such a frenzied expression.

"To those who know her, it is really touching," remarked Madame Colleville.

The glasses were filled. The guests all looked at one another, evidently expecting a toast, whereupon la Peyrade said:—

"Messieurs, let us drink to something sublime."

Everybody looked curious.

"To Mademoiselle Brigitte!"

They all rose, clinked glasses, and cried with one voice, "Mademoiselle Brigitte!" so much enthusiasm did the exhibition of a true feeling excite.

"Messieurs," said Phellion, reading from a paper written in pencil, "To work and its splendors, in the person of our former comrade, now become one of the mayors of Paris,—to Monsieur Minard and his wife!"

After five minutes' general conversation Thuillier rose and said:—

"Messieurs, To the King and the royal family! I add nothing; the toast says all."

"To the election of my brother!" said Mademoiselle Thuillier a moment later.

"Now I'll make you laugh," whispered la Peyrade in Flavie's ear.

And he rose.

"To Woman!" he said; "that enchanting sex to whom we owe our happiness,—not to speak of our mothers, our sisters, and our wives!"

This toast excited general hilarity, and Colleville, already somewhat gay, exclaimed:—

"Rascal! you have stolen my speech!"

The mayor then rose; profound silence reigned.

"Messieurs, our institutions! from which come the strength and grandeur of dynastic France!"

The bottles disappeared amid a chorus of admiration as to the marvellous goodness and delicacy of their contents.

Celeste Colleville here said timidly:—

"Mamma, will you permit me to give a toast?"

The good girl had noticed the dull, bewildered look of her godmother, neglected and forgotten,—she, the mistress of that house, wearing almost the expression of a dog that is doubtful which master to obey, looking from the face of her terrible sister-in-law to that of Thuillier, consulting each countenance, and oblivious of herself; but joy on the face of that poor helot, accustomed to be nothing, to repress her ideas, her feelings, had the effect of a pale wintry sun behind a mist; it barely lighted her faded, flabby flesh. The gauze cap trimmed with dingy flowers, the hair ill-dressed, the gloomy brown gown, with no ornament but a thick gold chain—all, combined with the expression of her countenance, stimulated the affection of the young Celeste, who—alone in the world—knew the value of that woman condemned to silence but aware of all about her, suffering from all yet consoling herself in God and in the girl who now was watching her.

"Yes, let the dear child give us her little toast," said la Peyrade to Madame Colleville.

"Go on, my daughter," cried Colleville; "here's the hermitage still to be drunk—and it's hoary with age," he added.

"To my kind godmother!" said the girl, lowering her glass respectfully before Madame Thuillier, and holding it towards her.

The poor woman, startled, looked through a veil of tears first at her husband, and then at Brigitte; but her position in the family was so well known, and the homage paid by innocence to weakness had something so beautiful about it, that the emotion was general; the men all rose and bowed to Madame Thuillier.

"Ah! Celeste, I would I had a kingdom to lay at your feet," murmured Felix Phellion.

The worthy Phellion wiped away a tear. Dutocq himself was moved.

"Oh! the charming child!" cried Mademoiselle Thuillier, rising, and going round to kiss her sister-in-law.

"My turn now!" said Colleville, posing like an athlete. "Now listen: To friendship! Empty your glasses; refill your glasses. Good! To the fine arts,— the flower of social life! Empty your glasses; refill your glasses. To another such festival on the day after election!"

"What is that little bottle you have there?" said Dutocq to Mademoiselle Thuillier.

"That," she said, "is one of my three bottles of Madame Amphoux' liqueur; the second is for the day of Celeste's marriage; the third for the day on which her first child is baptized."

"My sister is losing her head," remarked Thuillier to Colleville.

The dinner ended with a toast, offered by Thuillier, but suggested to him by Theodose at the moment when the malaga sparkled in the little glasses like so many rubies.

"Colleville, messieurs, has drunk to *friendship*. I now drink, in this most generous wine, To my friends!"

An hurrah, full of heartiness, greeted that fine sentiment, but Dutocq remarked aside to Theodose:—

"It is a shame to pour such wine down the throats of such people."

"Ah! if we could only make such wine as that!" cried Zelie, making her glass ring by the way in which she sucked down the Spanish liquid. "What fortunes we could get!"

Zelie had now reached her highest point of incandescence, and was really alarming.

"Yes," replied Minard, "but ours is made."

"Don't you think, sister," said Brigitte to Madame Thuillier, "that we had better take coffee in the salon?"

Madame Thuillier obediently assumed the air of mistress of the house, and rose.

"Ah! you are a great wizard," said Flavie Colleville, accepting la Peyrade's arm to return to the salon.

"And yet I care only to bewitch you," he answered. "I think you more enchanting than ever this evening."

"Thuillier," she said, to evade the subject, "Thuillier made to think himself a political character! oh! oh!"

"But, my dear Flavie, half the absurdities of life are the result of such conspiracies; and men are not alone in these deceptions. In how many families one sees the husband, children, and friends persuading a silly mother that she is a woman of sense, or an old woman of fifty that she is young and beautiful. Hence, inconceivable contrarieties for those who go about the world with their eyes shut. One man owes his ill-savored conceit to the flattery of a mistress; another owes his versifying vanity to those who are paid to call him a great poet. Every family has its great man; and the result is, as we see it in the Chamber, general obscurity of the lights of France. Well, men of real mind are laughing to themselves about it, that's all. You are the mind and the beauty of this little circle of the petty bourgeoisie; it is this superiority which led me in the first instance to worship you. I have since longed to drag you out of it; for I love you sincerely—more in friendship than in love; though a great deal of love is gliding into it," he added, pressing her to his heart under cover of the recess of a window to which he had taken her.

"Madame Phellion will play the piano," cried Colleville. "We must all dance to-night—bottles and Brigitte's francs and all the little girls! I'll go and fetch my clarionet."

He gave his empty coffee-cup to his wife, smiling to see her so friendly with la Peyrade.

"What have you said and done to my husband?" asked Flavie, when Colleville had left them.

"Must I tell you all our secrets?"

"Ah! you don't love me," she replied, looking at him with the coquettish slyness of a woman who is not quite decided in her mind.

"Well, since you tell me yours," he said, letting himself go to the lively impulse of Provencal gaiety, always so charming and apparently so natural, "I will not conceal from you an anxiety in my heart."

He took her back to the same window and said, smiling:—

"Colleville, poor man, has seen in me the artist repressed by all these bourgeois; silent before them because I feel misjudged, misunderstood, and repelled by them. He has felt the heat of the sacred fire that consumes me. Yes I am," he continued, in a tone of conviction, "an artist in words after the manner of Berryer; I could make juries weep, by weeping myself, for I'm as nervous as a woman. Your husband, who detests the bourgeoisie, began to tease me about them. At first we laughed; then, in becoming serious, he found out that I was as strong as he. I told him of the plan concocted to make *something* of Thuillier, and I showed him all the good he could get himself out of a political puppet. 'If it were only,' I said to him, 'to make yourself Monsieur *de* Colleville, and to put your charming wife where I should like to see her, as the wife of a receiver-general, or deputy. To make yourself all that you and she ought to be, you have only to go and live a few years in the Upper or Lower Alps, in some hole of a town where everybody will like you, and your wife will seduce everybody; and this,' I added, 'you cannot fail to obtain, especially if you give your dear Celeste to some man who can influence the Chamber.' Good reasons, stated in jest, have the merit of penetrating deeper into some minds than if they were given soberly. So Colleville and I became the best friends in the world. Didn't you hear him say to me at table, 'Rascal! you have stolen my speech'? To-night we shall be theeing and thouing each other. I intend to have a choice little supper-party soon, where artists, tied to the proprieties at home, always compromise themselves. I'll invite him, and that will make us as solidly good friends as he is with Thuillier. There, my dear adorned one, is what a profound sentiment gives a man the courage to produce. Colleville must adopt me; so that I may visit your house by his invitation. But what couldn't you make me do? lick lepers, swallow live toads, seduce Brigitte—yes, if you say so, I'll impale my own heart on that great picket-rail to please you."

"You frightened me this morning," she said.

"But this evening you are reassured. Yes," he added, "no harm will ever happen to you through me."

"You are, I must acknowledge, a most extraordinary man."

"Why, no! the smallest as well as the greatest of my efforts are merely the reflections of the flame which you have kindled. I intend to be your son-in-law that we may never part. My wife, heavens! what could she be to me but a machine for child-bearing? whereas the divinity, the sublime being will be— you," he whispered in her ear.

"You are Satan!" she said, in a sort of terror.

"No, I am something of a poet, like all the men of my region. Come, be my Josephine! I'll go and see you to-morrow. I have the most ardent desire to see where you live and how you live, the furniture you use, the color of your stuffs, the arrangement of all things about you. I long to see the pearl in its shell."

He slipped away cleverly after these words, without waiting for an answer.

Flavie, to whom in all her life love had never taken the language of romance, sat still, but happy, her heart palpitating, and saying to herself that it was very difficult to escape such influence. For the first time Theodose had appeared in a pair of new trousers, with gray silk stockings and pumps, a waistcoat of black silk, and a cravat of black satin on the knot of which shone a plain gold pin selected with taste. He wore also a new coat in the last fashion, and yellow gloves, relieved by white shirt-cuffs; he was the only man who had manners, or deportment in that salon, which was now filling up for the evening.

Madame Pron, nee Barniol, arrived with two school-girls, aged seventeen, confided to her maternal care by families residing in Martinique. Monsieur Pron, professor of rhetoric in a college presided over by priests, belonged to the Phellion class; but, instead of expanding on the surface in phrases and demonstrations, and posing as an example, he was dry and sententious. Monsieur and Madame Pron, the flowers of the Phellion salon, received every Monday. Though a professor, the little man danced. He enjoyed great influence in the quarter enclosed by the boulevard du Mont-Parnasse, the Luxembourg, and the rue de Sevres. Therefore, as soon as Phellion saw his friend, he took him by the arm into a corner to inform him of the Thuillier candidacy. After ten minutes' consultation they both went to find Thuillier, and the recess of a window, opposite to that where Flavie still sat absorbed in her reflections, no doubt, heard a "trio" worthy, in its way, of that of the Swiss in "Guillaume Tell."

"Do you see," said Theodose, returning to Flavie, "the pure and honest Phellion intriguing over there? Give a personal reason to a virtuous man and he'll paddle in the slimiest puddle; he is hooking that little Pron, and Pron is taking it all in, solely to get your little Celeste for Felix Phellion. Separate them, and in ten minutes they'll get together again, and that young Minard will be growling round them like an angry bulldog."

Felix, still under the strong emotion imparted to him by Celeste's generous action and the cry that came from the girl's heart, though no one but Madame Thuillier still thought of it, became inspired by one of those ingenuous artfulnesses which are the honest charlatanism of true love; but he was not to the manner born of it, and mathematics, moreover, made him somewhat absent-minded. He stationed himself near Madame Thuillier, imagining that Madame Thuillier would attract Celeste to her side. This astute calculation succeeded all the better because young Minard, who saw in Celeste nothing more than a "dot," had no such sudden inspiration, and was drinking his coffee and talking politics with Laudigeois, Monsieur Barniol, and Dutocq by order of his father, who was thinking and planning for the general election of the legislature in 1842.

"Who wouldn't love Celeste?" said Felix to Madame Thuillier.

"Little darling, no one in the world loves me as she does," replied the poor slave, with difficulty restraining her tears.

"Ah! madame, we both love you," said the candid professor, sincerely.

"What are you saying to each other?" asked Celeste, coming up.

"My child," said the pious woman, drawing her god-daughter down to her and kissing her on the forehead. "He said that you both loved me."

"Do not be angry with my presumption, mademoiselle. Let me do all I can to prove it," murmured Felix. "Ah! I cannot help it, I was made this way; injustice revolts me to the soul! Yes, the Saviour of men was right to promise the future to the meek heart, to the slain lamb! A man who did not love you, Celeste, must have adored you after that sublime impulse of yours at table. Ah, yes! innocence alone can console the martyr. You are a kind young girl; you will be one of those wives who make the glory and the happiness of a family. Happy be he whom you will choose!"

"Godmamma, with what eyes do you think Monsieur Felix sees me?"

"He appreciates you, my little angel; I shall pray to God for both of you."

"If you knew how happy I am that my father can do a service to Monsieur Thuillier, and how I wish I could be useful to your brother—"

"In short," said Celeste, laughing, "you love us all."

"Well, yes," replied Felix.

True love wraps itself in the mysteries of reserve, even in its expression; it proves itself by itself; it does not feel the necessity, as a false love does, of lighting a conflagration. By an observer (if such a being could have glided into the Thuillier salon) a book might have been made in comparing the two scenes of love-making, and in watching the enormous preparations of Theodose and the simplicity of Felix: one was nature, the other was society,— the true and the false embodied. Noticing her daughter glowing with happiness, exhaling her soul through the pores of her face, and beautiful with the beauty of a young girl gathering the first roses of an indirect declaration, Flavie had an impulse of jealousy in her heart. She came across to Celeste and said in her ear:—

"You are not behaving well, my daughter; everybody is observing you; you are compromising yourself by talking so long to Monsieur Felix without knowing whether we approve of it."

"But, mamma, my godmother is here."

"Ah! pardon me, dear friend," said Madame Colleville; "I did not notice you."

"You do as others do," said the poor nonentity.

That reply stung Madame Colleville, who regarded it as a barbed arrow. She cast a haughty glance at Felix and said to Celeste, "Sit there, my daughter," seating herself at the same time beside Madame Thuillier and pointing to a chair on the other side of her.

"I will work myself to death," said Felix to Madame Thuillier. "I'll be a member of the Academy of Sciences; I'll make some great discovery, and win her hand by force of fame."

"Ah!" thought the poor woman to herself, "I ought to have had a gentle, peaceful, learned man like that. I might have slowly developed in a life of quietness. It was not thy will, O God! but, I pray thee, unite and bless these children; they are made for one another."

And she sat there, pensive, listening to the racket made by her sister-in-law —a ten-horse power at work—who now, lending a hand to her two servants, cleared the table, taking everything out of the dining-room to accommodate the dancers, vociferating, like the captain of a frigate on his quarter-deck when taking his ship into action: "Have you plenty of raspberry syrup?" "Run out and buy some more orgeat!" "There's not enough glasses. Where's the 'eau rougie'? Take those six bottles of 'vin ordinaire' and make more. Mind that Coffinet, the porter, doesn't get any." "Caroline, my girl, you are to wait at the sideboard; you'll have tongue and ham to slice in case they dance till morning. But mind, no waste! Keep an eye on everything. Pass me the broom; put more oil in those lamps; don't make blunders. Arrange the remains of the dessert so as to make a show on the sideboard; ask my sister to come and help us. I'm sure I don't know what she's thinking about, that dawdle! Heavens, how slow she is! Here, take away these chairs, they'll want all the room they can get."

The salon was full of Barniols, Collevilles, Phellions, Laudigeois, and many others whom the announcement of a dance at the Thuilliers', spread about in the Luxembourg between two and four in the afternoon, the hour at which the bourgeoisie takes its walk, had drawn thither.

"Are you ready, Brigitte?" said Colleville, bolting into the dining-room; "it is nine o'clock, and they are packed as close as herrings in the salon. Cardot, his wife and son and daughter and future son-in-law have just come, accompanied by that young Vinet; the whole faubourg Saint Antoine is debouching. Can't we move the piano in here?"

Then he gave the signal, by tuning his clarionet, the joyous sounds of which were greeted with huzzas from the salon.

It is useless to describe a ball of this kind. The toilets, faces, and conversations were all in keeping with one fact which will surely suffice even the dullest imagination; they passed round, on tarnished and discolored trays, common tumblers filled with wine, "eau rougie," and "eau sucree." The trays on which were glasses of orgeat and glasses of syrup and water appeared only at long intervals. There were five card-tables and twenty-five players, and eighteen dancers of both sexes. At one o'clock in the morning, all present— Madame Thuillier, Mademoiselle Brigitte, Madame Phellion, even Phellion himself—were dragged into the vivacities of a country-dance, vulgarly called "La Boulangere," in which Dutocq figured with a veil over his head, after the manner of the Kabyl. The servants who were waiting to escort their masters home, and those of the household, were audience to this performance; and after the interminable dance had lasted one whole hour it was proposed to carry Brigitte in triumph when she gave the announcement that supper was served. This circumstance made her see the necessity of hiding a dozen bottles of old burgundy. In short, the company had amused themselves so well, the matrons as well as the young girls, that Thuillier found occasion to say:—

"Well, well, this morning we little thought we should have such a fete to-night."

"There's never more pleasure," said the notary Cardot, "than in just such improvised balls. Don't talk to me of parties where everybody stands on ceremony."

This opinion, we may remark, is a standing axiom among the bourgeoisie.

"Well, for my part," said Madame Minard, "I prefer the dignified old ways."

"We didn't mean that for you, madame; your salon is the chosen haunt of pleasure," said Dutocq.

When "La Boulangere" came to an end, Theodose pulled Dutocq from the sideboard where he was preparing to eat a slice of tongue, and said to him:—

"Let us go; we must be at Cerizet's very early in the morning; we ought both of us to think over that affair; it is not so easy to manage as Cerizet seems to imagine."

"Why not?" asked Dutocq, bringing his slice of tongue to eat in the salon.

"Don't you know the law?"

"I know enough of it to be aware of the dangers of the affair. If that notary wants the house and we filch it from him, there are means by which he can recover it; he can put himself into the skin of a registered creditor. By the present legal system relating to mortgages, when a house is sold at the request

99

of creditors, if the price obtained for it at auction is not enough to pay all debts, the owners have the right to bid it in and hold it for a higher sum; now the notary, seeing himself caught, may back out of the sale in that way."

"Well," said la Peyrade, "it needs attention."

"Very good," replied Dutocq, "we'll go and see Cerizet."

These words, "go and see Cerizet," were overheard by Minard, who was following the two associates; but they offered no meaning to his mind. The two men were so outside of his own course and projects that he heard them without listening to them.

"This has been one of the finest days in our lives," said Brigitte to her brother, when she found herself alone with him in the deserted salon, at half-past two in the morning. "What a distinction! to be thus selected by your fellow-citizens!"

"Don't be mistaken about it, Brigitte; we owe it all, my child, to one man."

"What man?"

"To our friend, la Peyrade."

CHAPTER IX. THE BANKER OF THE POOR

It was not on the next day, Monday, but on the following day, Tuesday, that Dutocq and Theodose went to see Cerizet, the former having called la Peyrade's attention to the fact that Cerizet always absented himself on Sundays and Mondays, taking advantage of the total absence of clients on those days, which are devoted by the populace to debauch. The house toward which they directed their steps is one of the striking features in the faubourg Saint-Jacques, and it is quite as important to study it here as it was to study those of Phellion and Thuillier. It is not known (true, no commission has yet been appointed to examine this phenomenon), no one knows why certain quarters become degraded and vulgarized, morally as well as materially; why, for instance, the ancient residence of the court and the church, the Luxembourg and the Latin quarter, have become what they are to-day, in spite of the presence of the finest palaces in the world, in spite of the bold cupola of Sainte-Genevieve, that of Mansard on the Val-de-Grace, and the charms of the Jardin des Plantes. One asks one's self why the elegance of life has left that region; why the Vauquer houses, the Phellion and the Thuillier houses now swarm with tenants and boarders, on the site of so many noble and religious buildings, and why such mud and dirty trades and poverty should have fastened on a hilly piece of ground, instead of spreading out upon the flat land beyond the confines of the ancient city.

The angel whose beneficence once hovered above this quarter being dead, usury, on the lowest scale, rushed in and took his place. To the old judge, Popinot, succeeded Cerizet; and strange to say,—a fact which it is well to study,—the effect produced, socially speaking, was much the same. Popinot loaned money without interest, and was willing to lose; Cerizet lost nothing, and compelled the poor to work hard and stay virtuous. The poor adored Popinot, but they did not hate Cerizet. Here, in this region, revolves the lowest wheel of Parisian financiering. At the top, Nucingen & Co., the Kellers, du Tillet, and the Mongenods; a little lower down, the Palmas, Gigonnets, and Gobsecks; lower still, the Samonons, Chaboisseaus, and Barbets; and lastly (after the pawn-shops) comes this king of usury, who spreads his nets at the corners of the streets to entangle all miseries and miss none,—Cerizet, "money lender by the little week."

The frogged frock-coat will have prepared you for the den in which this convicted stock-broker carried on his present business.

The house was humid with saltpetre; the walls, sweating moisture, were enamelled all over with large slabs of mould. Standing at the corner of the rue des Postes and rue des Poules, it presented first a ground-floor, occupied partly by a shop for the sale of the commonest kind of wine, painted a coarse bright red, decorated with curtains of red calico, furnished with a leaden counter, and guarded by formidable iron bars. Above the gate of an odious alley hung a frightful lantern, on which were the words "Night lodgings here." The outer walls were covered with iron crossbars, showing, apparently, the insecurity of the building, which was owned by the wine-merchant, who also inhabited the entresol. The widow Poiret (nee Michonneau) kept furnished lodgings on the first, second, and third floors, consisting of single rooms for workmen and for the poorest class of students.

Cerizet occupied one room on the ground-floor and another in the entresol, to which he mounted by an interior staircase; this entresol looked out upon a horrible paved court, from which arose mephitic odors. Cerizet paid forty francs a month to the widow Poiret for his breakfast and dinner; he thus conciliated her by becoming her boarder; he also made himself acceptable to the wine-merchant by procuring him an immense sale of wine and liquors among his clients—profits realized before sunrise; the wine-shop beginning operations about three in the morning in summer, and five in winter.

The hour of the great Market, which so many of his clients, male and female, attended, was the determining cause of Cerizet's early hours. The Sieur Cadenet, the wine-merchant, in view of the custom which he owed to the usurer, had let him the two rooms for the low price of eighty francs a year, and had given him a lease for twelve years, which Cerizet alone had a right to break, without paying indemnity, at three months' notice. Cadenet always carried in a bottle of excellent wine for the dinner of this useful tenant; and when Cerizet was short of money he had only to say to his friend, "Cadenet, lend me a few hundred francs,"—loans which he faithfully repaid.

Cadenet, it was said, had proof of the widow Poiret having deposited in Cerizet's hands some two thousand francs for investment, which may explain the progress of the latter's affairs since the day when he first took up his abode in the quarter, supplied with a last note of a thousand francs and Dutocq's protection. Cadenet, prompted by a cupidity which success increased, had proposed, early in the year, to put twenty thousand francs into the hands of his friend Cerizet. But Cerizet had positively declined them, on the ground that he ran risks of a nature to become a possible cause of dispute with associates.

"I could only," he said to Cadenet, "take them at six per cent interest, and you can do better than that in your own business. We will go into partnership later, if you like, in some serious enterprise, some good opportunity which may require, say, fifty thousand francs. When you have got that sum to invest, let me know, and we'll talk about it."

Cerizet had only suggested the affair of the house to Theodose after making sure that among the three, Madame Poiret, Cadenet, and himself, it was impossible to raise the full sum of one hundred thousand francs.

The "lender by the little week" was thus in perfect safety in his den, where he could even, if necessity came, appeal to the law. On certain mornings there might be seen as many as sixty or eighty persons, men as often as women, either in the wine-shop, or the alley, or sitting on the staircase, for the distrustful Cerizet would only admit six persons at a time into his office. The first comers were first served, and each had to go by his number, which the wine-merchant, or his shop-boy, affixed to the hats of the man and the backs of the women. Sometimes the clients would sell to each other (as hackney-coachmen do on the cabstands), head numbers for tail numbers. On certain days, when the market business was pressing, a head number was often sold for a glass of brandy and a sou. The numbers, as they issued from Cerizet's office, called up the succeeding numbers; and if any disputes arose Cadenet put a stop to the fray at once my remarking:—

"If you get the police here you won't gain anything; *he*'ll shut up shop."

HE was Cerizet's name. When, in the course of the day, some hapless woman, without an atom of food in her room, and seeing her children pale with hunger, would come to borrow ten or twenty sous, she would say to the wine-merchant anxiously:—

"Is *he* there?"

Cadenet, a short, stout man, dressed in blue, with outer sleeves of black stuff and a wine-merchant's apron, and always wearing a cap, seemed an angel to these mothers when he replied to them:—

"*He* told me that you were an honest woman and I might give you forty sous. You know what you must do about it—"

And, strange to say, *he* was blessed by these poor people, even as they had lately blessed Popinot.

But Cerizet was cursed on Sunday mornings when accounts were settled; and they cursed him even more on Saturdays, when it was necessary to work in order to repay the sum borrowed with interest. But, after all, he was Providence, he was God from Tuesday to Friday of every week.

The room which he made his office, formerly the kitchen of the next floor, was bare; the beams of the ceiling had been whitewashed, but still bore marks of smoke. The walls, along which he had put benches, and the stone floor, retained and gave out dampness. The fireplace, where the crane remained, was partly filled by an iron stove in which Cerizet burned sea-coal when the weather was severe. A platform about half a foot high and eight feet square extended from the edge of the fireplace; on it was fastened a common table and an armchair with a round cushion covered with green leather. Behind him, Cerizet had sheathed the walls with planks; also protecting himself with a little wooden screen, painted white, from the draught between the window and door; but this screen, made of two leaves, was so placed that the warmth from the stove reached him. The window had enormous inside shutters of cast-iron, held, when closed, by a bar. The door commanded respect by an armor of the same character.

At the farther end of this room, in a corner, was a spiral-staircase, coming, evidently, from some pulled-down shop, and bought in the rue Chapon by Cadenet, who had fitted it through the ceiling into the room in the entresol occupied by Cerizet. In order to prevent all communication with the upper floors, Cerizet had exacted that the door of that room which opened on the common landing should be walled up. The place had thus become a fortress. The bedroom above had a cheap carpet bought for twenty francs, an iron bedstead, a bureau, three chairs, and an iron safe, made by a good workman, which Cerizet had bought at a bargain. He shaved before a glass on the chimney-piece; he owned two pairs of cotton sheets and six cotton shirts; the rest of his visible wardrobe was of the same character. Cadenet had once seen Cerizet dressed like a dandy of the period; he must, therefore, have kept hidden, in some drawer of his bureau, a complete disguise with which he could go to the opera, see the world, and not be recognized, for, had it not been that Cadenet heard his voice, he would certainly have asked him who he was.

What pleased the clients of this man most was his joviality and his repartees; he talked their language. Cadenet, his two shop-men, and Cerizet, living in the midst of dreadful misery, behaved with the calmness of undertakers in presence of afflicted heirs, of old sergeants of the Guard among heaps of dead. They no more shuddered on hearing cries of hunger and despair than surgeons shudder at the cries of their patients in hospital; they said, as the soldiers and the dressers said, the perfunctory words, "Have patience! a little courage! What's the good of grieving? Suppose you kill yourself, what then? One gets accustomed to everything; be reasonable!"

Though Cerizet took the precaution to hide the money necessary for his morning operations in the hollow seat of the chair in which he sat, taking out no more than a hundred francs at a time, which he put in the pockets of his trousers, never dipping into the funds of the chair except between the entrance of two batches of clients (keeping his door locked and not opening it till all was safely stowed in his pockets), he had really nothing to fear from the various despairs which found their way from all sides to this rendezvous of misery. Certainly, there are many different ways of being honest and virtuous; and the "Monograph of Virtue" has no other basis than this social axiom.[*] A man is false to his conscience; he fails, apparently, in delicacy; he forfeits that bloom of honor which, though lost, does not, as yet, mean general disrepute; at last, however, he fails decidedly in honor; if he falls into the hands of the correctional police, he is not, as yet, guilty of crime before the court of assizes; but after he is branded with infamy by the verdict of a jury he may still be honored at the galleys for the species of honor and integrity practised by criminals among themselves, which consists in not betraying each other, in sharing booty loyally, and in running all dangers. Well, this last form of honor —which is perhaps a calculation, a necessity, the practice of which offers certain opportunities for grandeur to the guilty man and the possibility of a return to good—reigned absolutely between Cerizet and his clients. Never did Cerizet make an error, nor his poor people either; neither side ever denied what was due, either capital or interests. Many a time Cerizet, who was born among the people, corrected from one week to another some accidental error, to the benefit of a poor man who had never discovered it. He was called a Jew, but an honest one, and his word in that city of sorrows was sacred. A woman died, causing a loss to him of thirty francs:

[*] A book on which the author has been at work since 1833, the year in which it was first announced.—Author's note.

"See my profits! there they go!" he said to his assemblage, "and you howl upon me! You know I'll never trouble the brats; in fact, Cadenet has already taken them bread and heel-taps."

After that it was said of him in both faubourgs:—

"He is not a bad fellow!"

The "loan by the little week," as interpreted by Cerizet, is not, considering all things, so cruel a thing as the pawn-shop. Cerizet loaned ten francs Tuesday on condition of receiving twelve francs Sunday morning. In five weeks he doubled his capital; but he had to make many compromises. His kindness consisted in accepting, from time to time, eleven francs and fifty centimes; sometimes the whole interest was still owing. When he gave fifty francs for sixty to a fruit-stall man, or a hundred francs for one hundred and twenty to a seller of peat-fuel, he ran great risks.

On reaching the rue des Poules through the rue des Postes, Theodose and Dutocq saw a great assemblage of men and women, and by the light which the wine-merchant's little oil-lamps cast upon these groups, they were horrified at beholding that mass of red, seamed, haggard faces; solemn with suffering, withered, distorted, swollen with wine, pallid from liquor; some threatening, others resigned, some sarcastic or jeering, others besotted; all rising from the midst of those terrible rags, which no designer can surpass in his most extravagant caricatures.

"I shall be recognized," said Theodose, pulling Dutocq away; "we have done a foolish thing to come here at this hour and take him in the midst of his business."

"All the more that Claparon may be sleeping in his lair, the interior of which we know nothing about. Yes, there are dangers for you, but none for me; I shall be thought to have business with my copying-clerk, and I'll go and tell him to come and dine with us; this is court day, so we can't have him to breakfast. I'll tell him to meet us at the 'Chaumiere' in one of the garden dining-rooms."

"Bad; anybody could listen to us there without being seen," said la Peyrade. "I prefer the 'Petit Rocher de Cancale'; we can go into a private room and speak low."

"But suppose you are seen with Cerizet?"

"Well, then, let's go to the 'Cheval Rouge,' quai de la Tournelle."

"That's best; seven o'clock; nobody will be there then."

Dutocq advanced alone into the midst of that congress of beggars, and he heard his own name repeated from mouth to mouth, for he could hardly fail to encounter among them some jail-bird familiar with the judge's office, just as Theodose was certain to have met a client.

In these quarters the justice-of-peace is the supreme authority; all legal contests stop short at his office, especially since the law was passed giving to those judges sovereign power in all cases of litigation involving not over one hundred and forty francs. A way was made for the judge's clerk, who was not less feared than the judge himself. He saw women seated on the staircase; a horrible display of pallor and suffering of many kinds. Dutocq was almost asphyxiated when he opened the door of the room in which already sixty persons had left their odors.

"Your number? your number?" cried several voices.

"Hold your jaw!" cried a gruff voice from the street, "that's the pen of the judge."

Profound silence followed. Dutocq found his copying clerk clothed in a jacket of yellow leather like that of the gloves of the gendarmerie, beneath which he wore an ignoble waistcoat of knitted wool. The reader must imagine the man's diseased head issuing from this species of scabbard and covered with a miserable Madras handkerchief, which, leaving to view the forehead and neck, gave to that head, by the gleam of a tallow candle of twelve to the pound, its naturally hideous and threatening character.

"It can't be done that way, papa Lantimeche," Cerizet was saying to a tall old man, seeming to be about seventy years of age, who was standing before him with a red woollen cap in his hand, exhibiting a bald head, and a breast covered with white hairs visible through his miserable linen jacket. "Tell me exactly what you want to undertake. One hundred francs, even on condition of getting back one hundred and twenty, can't be let loose that way, like a dog in a church—"

The five other applicants, among whom were two women, both with infants, one knitting, the other suckling her child, burst out laughing.

When Cerizet saw Dutocq, he rose respectfully and went rather hastily to meet him, adding to his client:—

"Take time to reflect; for, don't you see? it makes me doubtful to have such a sum as that, one hundred francs! asked for by an old journeyman locksmith!"

"But I tell you it concerns an invention," cried the old workman.

"An invention and one hundred francs!" said Dutocq. "You don't know the laws; you must take out a patent, and that costs two thousand francs, and you want influence."

"All that is true," said Cerizet, who, however, reckoned a good deal on such chances. "Come to-morrow morning, papa Lantimeche, at six o'clock, and we'll talk it over; you can't talk inventions in public."

Cerizet then turned to Dutocq whose first words were:—

"If the thing turns out well, half profits!"

"Why did you get up at this time in the morning to come here and say that to me?" demanded the distrustful Cerizet, already displeased with the mention of "half profits." "You could have seen me as usual at the office."

And he looked askance at Dutocq; the latter, while telling him his errand and speaking of Claparon and the necessity of pushing forward in the Theodose affair, seemed confused.

"All the same you could have seen me this morning at the office," repeated Cerizet, conducting his visitor to the door.

"There's a man," thought he, as he returned to his seat, "who seems to me to have breathed on his lantern so that I may not see clear. Well, well, I'll give up that place of copying clerk. Ha! your turn, little mother!" he cried; "you invent children! That's amusing enough, though the trick is well known."

It is all the more useless to relate the conversation which took place between the three confederates at the "Cheval Rouge," because the arrangements there concluded were the basis of certain confidences made, as we shall see, by Theodose to Mademoiselle Thuillier; but it is necessary to remark that the cleverness displayed by la Peyrade seemed almost alarming to Cerizet and Dutocq. After this conference, the banker of the poor, finding himself in company with such powerful players, had it in mind to make sure of his own stake at the first chance. To win the game at any price over the heads of the ablest gamblers, by cheating if necessary, is the inspiration of a special sort of vanity peculiar to friends of the green cloth. Hence came the terrible blow which la Peyrade was about to receive.

He knew his two associates well; and therefore, in spite of the perpetual activity of his intellectual forces, in spite of the perpetual watchfulness his personality of ten faces required, nothing fatigued him as much as the part he had to play with his two accomplices. Dutocq was a great knave, and Cerizet had once been a comic actor; they were both experts in humbug. A motionless face like Talleyrand's would have made then break at once with the Provencal, who was now in their clutches; it was necessary, therefore, that he should make a show of ease and confidence and of playing above board—the very height of art in such affairs. To delude the pit is an every-day triumph, but to deceive Mademoiselle Mars, Frederic Lemaitre, Potier, Talma, Monrose, is the acme of art.

This conference at the "Cheval Rouge" had therefore the result of giving to la Peyrade, who was fully as sagacious as Cerizet, a secret fear, which, during the latter period of this daring game, so fired his blood and heated his brain that there came moments when he fell into the morbid condition of the gambler, who follows with his eye the roll of the ball on which he has staked his last penny. The senses then have a lucidity in their action and the mind takes a range, which human knowledge has no means of measuring.

CHAPTER X. HOW BRIGITTE WAS WON

The day after this conference at the "Cheval Rouge," la Peyrade went to dine with the Thuilliers, and on the commonplace pretext of a visit to pay, Thuillier carried off his wife, leaving Theodose alone with Brigitte. Neither Thuillier, nor his sister, nor Theodose, were the dupes of this comedy; but the old beau of the Empire considered the manoeuvre a piece of diplomacy.

"Young man, do not take advantage of my sister's innocence; respect it," said Thuillier solemnly, as he departed.

"Mademoiselle," said Theodose, drawing his chair closer to the sofa where Brigitte sat knitting, "have you thought of inducing the business men of the arrondissement to support Thuillier's interests?"

"How can I?" she asked.

"Why! you are in close relations with Barbet and Metivier."

"Ah! you are right! Faith! you are no blunderer!" she said after a pause.

"When we love our friends, we serve them," he replied, sententiously.

To capture Brigitte would be like carrying the redoubt of the Moskowa, the culminating strategic point. But it was necessary to possess that old maid as the devil was supposed in the middle ages to possess men, and in a way to make any awakening impossible for her. For the last three days la Peyrade had been measuring himself for the task; he had carefully reconnoitred the ground to see all difficulty. Flattery, that almost infallible means in able hands, would certainly miscarry with a woman who for years had known she had no beauty. But a man of strong will finds nothing impregnable; the Lamarques could never have failed to take Capri. Therefore, nothing must be omitted from the memorable scene which was now to take place; all things about it had their own importance,—inflections of the voice, pauses, glances, lowered eyes.

"But," rejoined Brigitte, "you have already proved to us your affection."

"Your brother has told you—?"

"No, he merely told me that you had something to tell me."

"Yes, mademoiselle, I have; for you are the man of the family. In reflecting on this matter, I find many dangers for myself, such as a man only risks for his nearest and dearest. It involves a fortune; thirty to forty thousand francs a year, and not the slightest speculation—a piece of landed property. The hope of helping Thuillier to win such a fortune enticed me from the first. 'It fascinates me,' I said to him—for, unless a man is an absolute fool, he can't help asking himself: 'Why should he care to do us all this good?' So I told him frankly that in working for his interests, I flattered myself I was working for my own, as I'll explain to you later. If he wishes to be deputy, two things are absolutely necessary: to comply with the law as to property, and to win for his name some sort of public celebrity. If I myself push my devotion to the point of helping him to write a book on public financiering—or anything else, no matter what—which would give him that celebrity, I ought also to think of the other matter, his property—it would be absurd to expect you to give him this house—"

"For my brother? Why, I'd put it in his name to-morrow," cried Brigitte. "You don't know me."

"I don't know you thoroughly," said la Peyrade, "but I do know things about you which now make me regret that I did not tell you the whole affair from its origin; I mean from the moment when I conceived the plan to which Thuillier will owe his nomination. He will be hunted down by envy and jealousy, and the task of upholding him will be a hard one; we must, however, get the better of his rivals and take the wind out of their sails."

"But this affair," said Brigitte, "what are the difficulties?"

"Mademoiselle, the difficulties lie within my own conscience. Assuredly, I could not serve you in this matter without first consulting my confessor. From a worldly point of view—oh! the affair is perfectly legal, and I am—you'll understand me?—a barrister inscribed on the panel, that is, member of a bar controlled by the strictest rules. I am therefore incapable of proposing an enterprise which might give occasion for blame. In the first place, I myself don't make a penny by it."

Brigitte was on thorns; her face was flaming; she broke her wool, mended it, broke it again, and did not know which way to look.

"One can't get," she said, "in these days, forty thousand francs a year from landed property unless it is worth one million eight hundred thousand."

"Well, I will undertake that you shall see a piece of property and estimate yourself its probable revenue, which I can make Thuillier the owner of for fifty thousand francs down."

"Oh! if you can make us obtain that!" cried Brigitte, worked up to the highest excitement by the spur of her natural cupidity. "Go on, my dear Monsieur Theodose, and—"

She stopped short.

"Well, mademoiselle?"

"You will, perhaps, have done yourself a service."

"Ah! if Thuillier has told you my secret, I must leave this house."

Brigitte looked up.

"Did he tell you that I love Celeste?"

"No, on my word of honor!" cried Brigitte, "but I myself was just about to speak of her."

"And offer her to me? Oh! may God forgive us! I can only win her of herself, her parents, by a free choice—No, no, all I ask of you is your good-will, your protection. Promise me, as Thuillier has, in return for my services your influence, your friendship; tell me that you will treat me as a son. If you will do that, I will abide by your decision in this matter; I can trust it; I need not speak to my confessor. For the last two years, ever since I have seen much of this family, to whom I would fain give my powers and devote my utmost energy—for, I shall succeed! surely I shall!—I have observed that your integrity, your honor is that of the olden time, your judgment righteous and inflexible. Also, you have a knowledge of business; and these qualities combined are precious helps to a man. With a mother-in-law, as I may say, of your powers, I should find my home life relieved of a crowd of cares and details as to property, which hinder a man's advance in a political career if he is forced to attend to them. I admired you deeply on Sunday evening. Ah! you were fine! How you did manage matters! In ten minutes that dining-room was cleared! And, without going outside of your own apartment, you had everything at hand for the refreshments, for the supper! 'There,' I said to myself, as I watched you, 'is a true "maitresse-femme"—a masterly woman!'"

Brigitte's nostrils dilated; she breathed in the words of the young lawyer. He gave her a side-long glance to enjoy his triumph; he had touched the right chord in her breast.

At this moment he was standing, but he now resumed his seat beside her, and said:—

"Now here is our affair, dear aunt—for you will be a sort of aunt—"

"Hush! you naughty fellow!" said Brigitte, "and go on."

"I'll tell you the matter roughly—and remark, if you please, that I compromise myself in telling it to you; for these secrets are entrusted to me as a lawyer. Therefore understand that you and I are both committing a crime, so to speak, of leze-confidence! A notary of Paris was in partnership with an

113

architect; they bought land and built upon it; at the present moment, property has come down with a rush; they find themselves embarrassed—but all that doesn't concern us. Among the houses built by this illegal partnership—for notaries, you know, are sworn to have nothing to do with enterprises—is a very good one which, not being finished, must be sold at a great sacrifice; so great that they now ask only one hundred thousand francs for it, although the cost of the land and the building was at least four hundred thousand. As the whole interior is still unfinished, the value of what is still to do is easily appraised; it will probably not be more than fifty thousand francs. Now, owing to its excellent position, this house, when finished, will certainly bring in a rental, over and above the taxes, of forty thousand francs a year. It is built of freestone, the corners and copings of cut granite; the facade is covered with handsome carvings, on which they spent more than twenty thousand francs; the windows are plate glass with a new style of fastening called 'cremona.'"

"Well, where is the difficulty?"

"Just here: the notary wants to reserve to himself this bit of the cake he is forced to surrender; he is, under the name of a friend, the creditor who requests the sale of the property by the assignee of the bankruptcy. The case has not been brought into court; for legal proceedings cost so much money. The sale is to be made by voluntary agreement. Now, this notary has applied to one of my clients to lend him his name for this purchase. My client, a poor devil, says to me: 'There's a fortune to made out of that house by fooling the notary.'"

"And they do that sort of thing in business!" said Brigitte, quickly.

"If that were the only difficulty," continued Theodose, "it would be, as a friend of mine said to his pupil, who was complaining of the length of time it took to produce masterpieces in painting: 'My dear young fellow, if it were not so, our valets would be painting pictures.' But, mademoiselle, if we now get the better of this notary, who certainly deserves it, for he has compromised a number of private fortunes, yet, as he is a very shrewd man (though a notary), it might perhaps be very difficult to do it a second time, and here's the rub: When a piece of landed property is bought at a forced sale, if those who have lent money on that property see that is likely to be sold so low as not to cover the sum loaned upon it, they have the right, until the expiration of a certain time, to bid it in; that is, to offer more and keep the property in their own hands. If this trickster can't be hoodwinked as to the sale being a bona fide one until the time when his right to buy it expires, some other scheme must be resorted to. Now, is this business strictly legal? Am I justified in doing it for the benefit of a family I seek to enter? That is the question I have been revolving in my mind for the last three days."

Brigitte, we must acknowledge, hesitated, and Theodose then brought forward his last card:—

"Take the night to think of it," he said, "to-morrow we will talk it over."

"My young friend," said Brigitte, looking at the lawyer with an almost loving air, "the first thing to be done is to see the house. Where is it?"

"Near the Madeleine. That will be the heart of Paris in ten years. All that property has been desirable since 1819; the banker Du Tillet's fortune was derived from property about there. The famous failure of Maitre Roquin, which carried terror to all Paris, and did such harm to the confidence given to the notariat, was also caused by it; they went into heavy speculations on that land too soon; they should have waited until now."

"I remember about that," said Brigitte.

"The house might be finished by the end of the year," continued Theodose, "and the rentals could begin next spring."

"Could we go there to-morrow?"

"Dear aunt, I am at your orders."

"Ah ca!" she cried, "don't call me that before people. As to this affair," she continued, "I can't have any opinion until I have seen the house."

"It has six storeys; nine windows on the front; a fine courtyard, four shops, and it stands on a corner. Ah! that notary knows what he is about in wishing to hold on to such pieces of property! But let political events interfere, and down go the Funds! If I were you, I should sell out all that you and Madame Thuillier have on the Grand Livre and buy this fine piece of real estate for Thuillier, and I'd recover the fortune of that poor, pious creature by savings from its proceeds. Can the Funds go higher than they are to-day? One hundred and twenty-two! it is fabulous; I should make haste to sell."

Brigitte licked her lips; she perceived the means of keeping her own property intact, and of enriching her brother by this use of Madame Thuillier's fortune.

"My brother is right," she said to Theodose; "you certainly are a rare man; you'll get on in the world."

"And he'll walk before me," responded Theodose with a naivete that touched the old maid.

"You will live in the family," she said.

"There may be obstacles to that," he remarked. "Madame Thuillier is very queer at times; she doesn't like me."

"Ha! I'll settle that," cried Brigitte. "Do you attend to that affair and carry it through if it is feasible, and leave your interests in my hands."

"Thuillier, member of the municipal council, owner of an estate with a rental of forty thousand francs a year, with the cross of the Legion of honor and the author of a political work, grave, serious, important, will be deputy at the forthcoming general election. But, between ourselves, little aunt, one couldn't devote one's self so utterly except for a father-in-law."

"You are right."

"Though I have no fortune I shall have doubled yours; and if this affair goes through discreetly, others will turn up."

"Until I have seen the house," said Mademoiselle Thuillier again, "I can decide on nothing."

"Well then, send for a carriage to-morrow and let us go there. I will get a ticket early in the morning to view the premises."

"To-morrow, then, about mid-day," responded Brigitte, holding out her hand to Theodose that he might shake it, but instead of that he laid upon it the most respectful and the most tender kiss that Brigitte had ever in her life received.

"Adieu, my child," she said, as he reached the door.

She rang the bell hurriedly and when the servant came:—

"Josephine," she cried, "go at once to Madame Colleville, and ask her to come over and speak to me."

Fifteen minutes later Flavie entered the salon, where Brigitte was walking up and down, in a state of extreme agitation.

"My dear," she cried on seeing Flavie, "you can do me a great service, which concerns our dear Celeste. You know Tullia, don't you?—a danseuse at the opera; my brother was always dinning her into my ears at one time."

"Yes, I know her; but she is no longer a danseuse; she is Madame la Comtesse du Bruel. Her husband is peer of France!"

"Does she still like you?"

"We never see each other now."

"Well, I know that Chaffaroux, the rich contractor, is her uncle," said Brigitte. "He is old and wealthy. Go and see your former friend, and get her to give you a line of introduction to him, saying he would do her an eminent favor if he would give a piece of friendly advice to the bearer of the note, and then you and I will take it to him to-morrow about one o'clock. But tell Tullia she must request her uncle to keep secret about it. Go, my dear. Celeste, our dear child, will be a millionaire! I can't say more; but she'll have, from me, a husband who will put her on a pinnacle."

"Do you want me to tell you the first letters of his name?"

"Yes."

"T. P.,—Theodose de la Peyrade. You are right. That's a man who may, if supported by a woman like you, become a minister."

"It is God himself who has placed him in our house!" cried the old maid.

At this moment Monsieur and Madame Thuillier returned home.

Five days later, in the month of April, the ordinance which convoked the electors to appoint a member of the municipal council on the 20th of the same month was inserted in the "Moniteur," and placarded about Paris. For several weeks the ministry, called that of March 1st, had been in power. Brigitte was in a charming humor. She had been convinced of the truth of all la Peyrade's assertions. The house, visited from garret to cellar by old Chaffaroux, was admitted by him to be an admirable construction; poor Grindot, the architect, who was interested with the notary and Claparon in the affair, thought the old man was employed in the interests of the contractor; the old fellow himself thought he was acting in the interests of his niece, and he gave it as his opinion that thirty thousand francs would finish the house. Thus, in the course of one week la Peyrade became Brigitte's god; and she proved to him by the most naively nefarious arguments that fortune should be seized when it offered itself.

"Well, if there *is* any sin in the business," she said to him in the middle of the garden, "you can confess it."

"The devil!" cried Thuillier, "a man owes himself to his relatives, and you are one of us now."

"Then I decide to do it," replied la Peyrade, in a voice of emotion; "but on conditions that I must now distinctly state. I will not, in marrying Celeste, be accused of greed and mercenary motives. If you lay remorse upon me, at least you must consent that I shall remain as I am for the present. Do not settle upon Celeste, my old Thuillier, the future possession of the property I am about to obtain for you—"

"You are right."

"Don't rob yourself; and let my dear little aunt here act in the same way in relation to the marriage contract. Put the remainder of the capital in Madame

Thuillier's name, on the Grand Livre, and she can do what she likes with it. We shall all live together as one family, and I'll undertake to make my own fortune, now that I am free from anxiety about the future."

"That suits me," said Thuillier; "that's the talk of an honest man."

"Let me kiss you on the forehead, my son," said the old maid; "but, inasmuch as Celeste cannot be allowed to go without a 'dot,' we shall give her sixty thousand francs."

"For her dress," said la Peyrade.

"We are all three persons of honor," cried Thuillier. "It is now settled, isn't it? You are to manage the purchase of the house; we are to write together, you and I, my political work; and you'll bestir yourself to get me the decoration?"

"You will have that as soon as you are made a municipal councillor on the 1st of May. Only, my good friend, I must beg you, and you, too, dear aunt, to keep the most profound secrecy about me in this affair; and do not listen to the calumnies which all the men I am about to trick will spread about me. I shall become, you'll see, a vagabond, a swindler, a dangerous man, a Jesuit, an ambitious fortune-hunter. Can you hear those accusations against me with composure?"

"Fear nothing," replied Brigitte.

CHAPTER XI. THE REIGN OF THEODOSE

From that day forth Thuillier became a dear, good friend. "My dear, good friend," was the name given to him by Theodose, with voice inflections of varieties of tenderness which astonished Flavie. But "little aunt," a name that flattered Brigitte deeply, was only given in family secrecy, and occasionally before Flavie. The activity of Theodose and Dutocq, Cerizet, Barbet, Metivier, Minard, Phellion, Colleville, and others of the Thuillier circle was extreme. Great and small, they all put their hands to the work. Cadenet procured thirty votes in his section. On the 30th of April Thuillier was proclaimed member of the Council-general of the department of the Seine by an imposing majority; in fact, he only needed sixty more votes to make his election unanimous. May 1st Thuillier joined the municipal body and went to the Tuileries to congratulate the King on his fete-day, and returned home radiant. He had gone where Minard went!

Ten days later a yellow poster announced the sale of the house, after due publication; the price named being seventy-five thousand francs; the final purchase to take place about the last of July. On this point Cerizet and Claparon had an agreement by which Cerizet pledged the sum of fifteen thousand francs (in words only, be it understood) to Claparon in case the latter could deceive the notary and keep him quiet until the time expired during which he might withdraw the property by bidding it in. Mademoiselle Thuillier, notified by Theodose, agreed entirely to this secret clause, understanding perfectly the necessity of paying the culprits guilty of the treachery. The money was to pass through la Peyrade's hands. Claparon met his accomplice, the notary, on the Place de l'Observatoire by midnight. This young man, the successor of Leopold Hannequin, was one of those who run after fortune instead of following it leisurely. He now saw another future before him, and he managed his present affairs in order to be free to take hold of it. In this midnight interview, he offered Claparon ten thousand francs to secure himself in this dirty business,—a sum which was only to be paid on receipt, through Claparon, of a counter-deed from the nominal purchaser of the property. The notary was aware that that sum was all-important to Claparon to extricate him from present difficulties, and he felt secure of him.

"Who but you, in all Paris, would give me such a fee for such an affair?" Claparon said to him, with a false show of naivete. "You can sleep in peace; my ostensible purchaser is one of those men of honor who are too stupid to have ideas of your kind; he is a retired government employee; give him the money to make the purchase and he'll sign the counter-deed at once."

When the notary had made Claparon clearly understand that he could not get more than the ten thousand francs from him, Cerizet offered the latter twelve thousand down, and asked Theodose for fifteen thousand, intending to keep the balance for himself. All these scenes between the four men were seasoned with the finest speeches about feelings, integrity, and the honor that men owed to one another in doing business. While these submarine performances were going on, apparently in the interests of Thuillier, to whom Theodose related them with the deepest manifestations of disgust at being implicated therein, the pair were meditating the great political work which "my dear good friend" was to publish. Thus the new municipal councillor naturally acquired a conviction that he could never do or be anything without the help of this man of genius; whose mind so amazed him, and whose ability was now so important to him, that every day he became more and more convinced of the necessity of marrying him to Celeste, and of taking the young couple to live with him. In fact, after May the 1st, Theodose had already dined four times a week with "my dear, good friend."

This was the period when Theodose reigned without a dissenting voice in the bosom of that household, and all the friends of the family approved of him —for the following reason: The Phellions, hearing his praises sung by Brigitte and Thuillier, feared to displease the two powers and chorussed their words, even when such perpetual laudation seemed to them exaggerated. The same may be said of the Minards. Moreover la Peyrade's behavior, as "friend of the family" was perfect. He disarmed distrust by the manner in which he effaced himself; he was there like a new piece of furniture; and he contrived to make both the Phellions and Minards believe that Brigitte and Thuillier had weighed him, and found him too light in the scales to be anything more in the family than a young man whose services were useful to them.

"He may think," said Thuillier one day to Minard, "that my sister will put him in her will; he doesn't know her."

This speech, inspired by Theodose himself, calmed the uneasiness of Minard "pere."

"He is devoted to us," said Brigitte to Madame Phellion; "but he certainly owes us a great deal of gratitude. We have given him his lodging rent-free, and he dines with us almost every day."

This speech of the old maid, also instigated by Theodose, went from ear to ear among the families who frequented the Thuillier salon, and dissipated all fears. The young man called attention to the remarks of Thuillier and his sister with the servility of a parasite; when he played whist he justified the blunders of his dear, good friend, and he kept upon his countenance a smile, fixed and benign, like that of Madame Thuillier, ready to bestow upon all the bourgeois sillinesses of the brother and sister.

He obtained, what he wanted above all, the contempt of his true antagonists; and he used it as a cloak to hide his real power. For four consecutive months his face wore a torpid expression, like that of a snake as it gulps and digests its prey. But at times he would rush into the garden with Colleville or Flavie, to laugh and lay off his mask, and rest himself; or get fresh strength by giving way before his future mother-in-law to fits of nervous passion which either terrified or deeply touched her.

"Don't you pity me?" he cried to her the evening before the preparatory sale of the house, when Thuillier was to make the purchase at seventy-five thousand francs. "Think of a man like me, forced to creep like a cat, to choke down every pointed word, to swallow my own gall, and submit to your rebuffs!"

"My friend! my child!" Flavie replied, undecided in mind how to take him.

These words are a thermometer which will show the temperature at which this clever manipulator maintained his intrigue with Flavie. He kept her floating between her heart and her moral sense, between religious sentiments and this mysterious passion.

During this time Felix Phellion was giving, with a devotion and constancy worthy of all praise, regular lessons to young Colleville. He spent much of his time upon these lessons, feeling that he was thus working for his future family. To acknowledge this service, he was invited, by advice of Theodose to Flavie, to dine at the Collevilles' every Thursday, where la Peyrade always met him. Flavie was usually making either a purse or slippers or a cigar-case for the happy young man, who would say, deprecatingly:—

"I am only too well rewarded, madame, by the happiness I feel in being useful to you."

"We are not rich, monsieur," replied Colleville, "but, God bless me! we are not ungrateful."

Old Phellion would rub his hands as he listened to his son's account of these evenings, beholding his dear and noble Felix already wedded to Celeste.

But Celeste, the more she loved Felix, the more grave and serious she became with him; partly because her mother sharply lectured her, saying to her one evening:—

"Don't give any hope whatever to that young Phellion. Neither your father nor I can arrange your marriage. You have expectations to be consulted. It is much less important to please a professor without a penny than to make sure of the affection and good-will of Mademoiselle Brigitte and your godfather. If you don't want to kill your mother—yes, my dear, kill her—you must obey me in this affair blindly; and remember that what we want to secure, above all, is your good."

As the date of the final sale was set for the last of July, Theodose advised Brigitte by the end of June to arrange her affairs in time to be ready for the payment. Accordingly, she now sold out her own and her sister-in-law's property in the Funds. The catastrophe of the treaty of the four powers, an insult to France, is now an established historical fact; but it is necessary to remind the reader that from July to the last of August the French funds, alarmed by the prospect of war, a fear which Monsieur Thiers did much to promote, fell twenty francs, and the Three-per-cents went down to sixty. That was not all: this financial fiasco had a most unfortunate influence on the value of real estate in Paris; and all those who had such property then for sale suffered loss. These events made Theodose a prophet in the eyes of Brigitte and Thuillier, to whom the house was now about to be definitely sold for seventy-five thousand francs. The notary, involved in the political disaster, and whose practice was already sold, concealed himself for a time in the country; but he took with him the ten thousand francs for Claparon. Advised by Theodose, Thuillier made a contract with Grindot, who supposed he was really working for the notary in finishing the house; and as, during this period of financial depression, suspended work left many workmen with their arms folded, the architect was able to finish off the building in a splendid manner at a low cost. Theodose insisted that the agreement should be in writing.

This purchase increased Thuillier's importance ten-fold. As for the notary, he had temporarily lost his head in presence of political events which came upon him like a waterspout out of cloudless skies. Theodose, certain now of his supremacy, holding Thuillier fast by his past services and by the literary work in which they were both engaged, admired by Brigitte for his modesty and discretion,—for never had he made the slightest allusion to his own poverty or uttered one word about money,—Theodose began to assume an air that was rather less servile than it had been. Brigitte and Thuillier said to him one day:—

"Nothing can deprive you of our esteem; you are here in this house as if in your own home; the opinion of Minard and Phellion, which you seem to fear, has no more value for us than a stanza of Victor Hugo. Therefore, let them talk! Carry your head high!"

"But we shall still need them for Thuillier's election to the Chamber," said Theodose. "Follow my advice; you have found it good so far, haven't you? When the house is actually yours, you will have got it for almost nothing; for you can now buy into the Three-per-cents at sixty in Madame Thuillier's name, and thus replace nearly the whole of her fortune. Wait only for the expiration of the time allowed to the nominal creditor to buy it in, and have the fifteen thousand francs ready for our scoundrels."

Brigitte did not wait; she took her whole capital with the exception of a sum of one hundred and twenty thousand francs, and bought into the Three-per-cents in Madame Thuillier's name to the amount of twelve thousand francs a year, and in her own for ten thousand a year, resolving in her own mind to choose no other kind of investment in future. She saw her brother secure of forty thousand francs a year besides his pension, twelve thousand a year for Madame Thuillier and eighteen thousand a year for herself, besides the house they lived in, the rental of which she valued at eight thousand.

"We are worth quite as much as the Minards," she remarked.

"Don't chant victory before you win it," said Theodose. "The right of redemption doesn't expire for another week. I have attended to your affairs, but mine have gone terribly to pieces."

"My dear child, you have friends," cried Brigitte; "if you should happen to want five hundred francs or so, you will always find them here."

Theodose exchanged a smile with Thuillier, who hastened to carry him off, saying:—

"Excuse my poor sister; she sees the world through a small hole. But if you should want twenty-five thousand francs I'll lend them to you—out of my first rents," he added.

"Thuillier," exclaimed Theodose, "the rope is round my neck. Ever since I have been a barrister I have had notes of hand running. But say nothing about it," added Theodose, frightened himself at having let out the secret of his situation. "I'm in the claws of scoundrels, but I hope to crush them yet."

In telling this secret Theodose, though alarmed as he did so, had a two-fold purpose: first, to test Thuillier; and next, to avert the consequences of a fatal blow which might be dealt to him any day in a secret and sinister struggle he had long foreseen. Two words will explain his horrible position.

CHAPTER XII. DEVILS AGAINST DEVILS

During the extreme poverty of la Peyrade's first years in Paris, none but Cerizet had ever gone to see him in the wretched garret where, in severely cold weather, he stayed in bed for want of clothes. Only one shirt remained to him. For three days he lived on one loaf of bread, cutting it into measured morsels, and asking himself, "What am I to do?" At this moment it was that his former partner came to him, having just left prison, pardoned. The projects which the two men then formed before a fire of laths, one wrapped in his landlady's counterpane, the other in his infamy, it is useless to relate. The next day Cerizet, who had talked with Dutocq in the course of the morning, returned, bringing trousers, waistcoat, coat, hat, and boots, bought in the Temple, and he carried off Theodose to dine with himself and Dutocq. The hungry Provencal ate at Pinson's, rue de l'Ancienne Comedie, half of a dinner costing forty-seven francs. At dessert, after Theodose had drunk freely, Cerizet said to him:—

"Will you sign me bills of exchange for fifty thousand francs in your capacity as a barrister?"

"You couldn't get five thousand on them."

"That's not your affair, but ours; I mean monsieur's here, who is giving us this dinner, and mine, in a matter where you risk nothing, but in which you'll get your title as barrister, a fine practice, and the hand in marriage of a girl about the age of an old dog, and rich by twenty or thirty thousand francs a year. Neither Dutocq nor I can marry her; but we'll equip you, give you the look of a decent man, feed and lodge you, and set you up generally. Consequently, we want security. I don't say that on my own account, for I know you, but for monsieur here, whose proxy I am. We'll equip you as a pirate, hey! to do the white-slave trade! If we can't capture that 'dot,' we'll try other plans. Between ourselves, none of us need be particular what we touch —that's plain enough. We'll give you careful instructions; for the matter is certain to take time, and there'll probably be some bother about it. Here, see, I have brought stamped paper."

"Waiter, pens and ink!" cried Theodose.

"Ha! I like fellows of that kind!" exclaimed Dutocq.

"Sign: 'Theodose de la Peyrade,' and after your name put 'Barrister, rue Saint-Dominique d'Enfer,' under the words 'Accepted for ten thousand.' We'll date the notes and sue you,—all secretly, of course, but in order to have a hold upon you; the owners of a privateer ought to have security when the brig and the captain are at sea."

The day after this interview the bailiff of the justice-of-peace did Cerizet the service of suing la Peyrade secretly. He went to see the barrister that evening, and the whole affair was done without any publicity. The Court of commerce has a hundred such cases in the course of one term. The strict regulations of the council of barristers of the bar of Paris are well known. This body, and also the council of attorneys, exercise severe discipline over their members. A barrister liable to go to Clichy would be disbarred. Consequently, Cerizet, under Dutocq's advice, had taken against their puppet measures which were certain to secure to each of them twenty-five thousand francs out of Celeste's "dot." In signing the notes, Theodose saw but one thing,—his means of living secured; but as time had gone on, and the horizon grew clearer, and he mounted, step by step, to a better position on the social ladder, he began to dream of getting rid of his associates. And now, on obtaining twenty-five thousand francs from Thuillier, he hoped to treat on the basis of fifty per cent for the return of his fatal notes by Cerizet.

Unfortunately, this sort of infamous speculation is not an exceptional fact; it takes place in Paris under various forms too little disguised for the historian of manners and morals to pass them over unnoticed in a complete and accurate picture of society in the nineteenth century. Dutocq, an arrant scoundrel, still owed fifteen thousand francs on his practice, and lived in hopes of something turning up to keep his head, as the saying is, above water until the close of 1840. Up to the present time none of the three confederates had flinched or groaned. Each felt his strength and knew his danger. Equals they were in distrust, in watchfulness; equals, too, in apparent confidence; and equally stolid in silence and look when mutual suspicions rose to the surface of face or speech. For the last two months the position of Theodose was acquiring the strength of a detached fort. But Cerizet and Dutocq held it undermined by a mass of powder, with the match ever lighted; but the wind might extinguish the match or the devil might flood the mine.

The moment when wild beasts seize their food is always the most critical, and that moment had now arrived for these three hungry tigers. Cerizet would sometimes say to Theodose, with that revolutionary glance which twice in this century sovereigns have had to meet:—

"I have made you king, and here am I still nothing! for it is nothing not to be all."

A reaction of envy was rushing its avalanche through Cerizet. Dutocq was at the mercy of his copying clerk. Theodose would gladly have burned his copartners could he have burned their papers in the same conflagration. All three studied each other too carefully, in order to conceal their own thoughts, not to be in turn divined. Theodose lived a life of three hells as he thought of what lay below the cards, then of his own game, and then of his future. His speech to Thuillier was a cry of despair; he threw his lead into the waters of the old bourgeois and found there nothing more than twenty-five thousand francs.

"And," he said to himself as he went to his own room, "possibly nothing at all a month hence."

He new felt the deepest hatred to the Thuilliers. But Thuillier himself he held by a harpoon stuck into the depths of the man's vanity; namely, by the projected work, entitled "Taxation and the Sinking Fund," for which he intended to rearrange the ideas of the Saint-Simonian "Globe," giving them a systematic form, and coloring them with his fervid Southern diction. Thuillier's bureaucratic knowledge of the subject would be of use to him here. Theodose therefore clung to this rope, resolving to do battle, on so poor a base of operations, with the vanity of a fool, which, according to individual character, is either granite or sand. On reflection, Theodose was inclined to be content with the prospect.

On the evening before the right of redemption expired, Claparon and Cerizet proceeded to manipulate the notary in the following manner. Cerizet, to whom Claparon had revealed the password and the notary's retreat, went out to this hiding-place to say to the latter:—

"One of my friends, Claparon, whom you know, has asked me to come and see you; he will expect you to-morrow, in the evening, you know where. He has the paper you expect from him, which he will exchange with you for the ten thousand agreed upon; but I must be present, for five thousand of that sum belong to me; and I warn you, my dear monsieur, that the name in the counter-deed is in blank."

"I shall be there," replied the ex-notary.

The poor devil waited the whole night in agonies of mind that can well be imagined, for safety or inevitable ruin were in the balance. At sunrise he saw approaching him, instead of Claparon, a bailiff of the Court of commerce, who produced a judgment against him in regular form, and informed him that he must go with him to Clichy.

Cerizet had made an arrangement with one of the creditors of the luckless notary, pledging himself to deliver up the debtor on payment to himself of half the debt. Out of the ten thousand francs promised to Claparon, the victim of this trap was obliged, in order to obtain his liberty, to pay six thousand down, the amount of his debt.

On receiving his share of this extortion Cerizet said to himself: "There's three thousand to make Cerizet clear out."

Cerizet then returned to the notary and said: "Claparon is a scoundrel, monsieur; he has received fifteen thousand francs from the proposed purchaser of your house, who will now, of course, become the owner. Threaten to reveal his hiding-place to his creditors, and to have him sued for fraudulent bankruptcy, and he'll give you half."

In his wrath the notary wrote a fulminating letter to Claparon. Claparon, alarmed, feared an arrest, and Cerizet offered to get him a passport.

"You have played me many a trick, Claparon," he said, "but listen to me now, and you can judge of my kindness. I possess, as my whole means, three thousand francs; I'll give them to you; start for America, and make your fortune there, as I'm trying to make mine here."

That evening Claparon, carefully disguised by Cerizet, left for Havre by the diligence. Cerizet remained master of the fifteen thousand francs to be paid to Claparon, and he awaited Theodose with the payment thereof tranquilly.

"The limit for bidding-in is passed," thought Theodose, as he went to find Dutocq and ask him to bring Cerizet to his office. "Suppose I were now to make an effort to get rid of my leech?"

"You can't settle this affair anywhere but at Cerizet's, because Claparon must be present, and he is hiding there," said Dutocq.

Accordingly, Theodose went, between seven and eight o'clock, to the den of the "banker of the poor," whom Dutocq had notified of his coming. Cerizet received him in the horrible kitchen where miseries and sorrows were chopped and cooked, as we have seen already. The pair then walked up and down, precisely like two animals in a cage, while mutually playing the following scene:—

"Have you brought the fifteen thousand francs?"

"No, but I have them at home."

"Why not have them in your pocket?" asked Cerizet, sharply.

"I'll tell you," replied Theodose, who, as he walked from the rue Saint-Dominique to the Estrapade, had decided on his course of action.

The Provencal, writhing upon the gridiron on which his partners held him, became suddenly possessed with a good idea, which flashed from the body of the live coal under him. Peril has gleams of light. He resolved to rely on the power of frankness, which affects all men, even swindlers. Every one is grateful to an adversary who bares himself to the waist in a duel.

"Well!" said Cerizet, "now the humbug begins."

The words seemed to come wholly through the hole in his nose with horrible intonations.

"You have put me in a magnificent position, and I shall never forget the service you have done me, my friend," began Theodose, with emotion.

"Oh, that's how you take it, is it?" said Cerizet.

"Listen to me; you don't understand my intentions."

"Yes, I do!" replied the lender by "the little week."

"No, you don't."

"You intend not to give up those fifteen thousand francs."

Theodose shrugged his shoulders and looked fixedly at Cerizet, who, struck by the two motions, kept silence.

"Would you live in my position, knowing yourself within range of a cannon loaded with grape-shot, without feeling a strong desire to get out of it? Now listen to me carefully. You are doing a dangerous business, and you would be glad enough to have some solid protection in the very heart of the magistracy of Paris. If I can continue my present course, I shall be substitute attorney-general, possibly attorney-general, in three years. I offer you to-day the offices of a devoted friendship, which will serve you hereafter most assuredly, if only to replace you in a honorable position. Here are my conditions—"

"Conditions!" exclaimed Cerizet.

"In ten minutes I will bring you twenty-five thousand francs if you return to me all the notes which you have against me."

"But Dutocq? and Claparon?" said Cerizet.

"Leave them in the lurch!" replied Theodose, with his lips at Cerizet's ear.

"That's a pretty thing to say!" cried Cerizet. "And so you have invented this little game of hocus-pocus because you hold in your fingers fifteen thousand francs that don't belong to you!"

"But I've added ten thousand francs to them. Besides, you and I know each other."

"If you are able to get ten thousand francs out of your bourgeois you can surely get fifteen," said Cerizet. "For thirty thousand I'm your man. Frankness for frankness, you know."

"You ask the impossible," replied Theodose. "At this very moment, if you had to do with Claparon instead of with me, your fifteen thousand would be lost, for Thuillier is to-day the owner of that house."

"I'll speak to Claparon," said Cerizet, pretending to go and consult him, and mounting the stairs to the bedroom, from which Claparon had only just departed on his road to Havre.

The two adversaries had been speaking, we should here remark, in a manner not to be overheard; and every time that Theodose raised his voice Cerizet would make a gesture, intimating that Claparon, from above, might be listening. The five minutes during which Theodose heard what seemed to be the murmuring of two voices were torture to him, for he had staked his very life upon the issue. Cerizet at last came down, with a smile upon his lips, his eyes sparkling with infernal mischief, his whole frame quivering in his joy, a Lucifer of gaiety!

"I know nothing, so it seems!" he cried, shaking his shoulders, "but Claparon knows a great deal; he has worked with the big-wig bankers, and when I told what you wanted he began to laugh, and said, 'I thought as much!' You will have to bring me the twenty-five thousand you offer me to-morrow morning, my lad; and as much more before you can recover your notes."

"Why?" asked Theodose, feeling his spinal column liquidizing as if the discharge of some inward electric fluid had melted it.

"The house is ours."

"How?"

"Claparon has bit it in under the name of one of his creditors, a little toad named Sauvaignou. Desroches, the lawyer, has taken the case, and you'll get a notice to-morrow. This affair will oblige Claparon, Dutocq, and me to raise funds. What would become of me without Claparon! So I forgive him—yes, I forgave him, and though you may not believe it, my dear friend, I actually kissed him! Change your terms."

The last three words were horrible to hear, especially when illustrated by the face of the speaker, who amused himself by playing a scene from the "Legataire," all the while studying attentively the Provencal's character.

"Oh, Cerizet!" cried Theodose; "I, who wished to do you so much good!"

"Don't you see, my dear fellow," returned Cerizet, "that between you and me there ought to be *this*,—" and he struck his heart,—"of which you have none. As soon as you thought you had a lever on us, you have tried to knock us over. I saved you from the horrors of starvation and vermin! You'll die like the idiot you are. We put you on the high-road to fortune; we gave you a fine social skin and a position in which you could grasp the future—and look what you do! *Now* I know you! and from this time forth, we shall go armed."

"Then it is war between us!" exclaimed Theodose.

"You fired first," returned Cerizet.

"If you pull me down, farewell to your hopes and plans; if you don't pull me down, you have in me an enemy."

"That's just what I said yesterday to Dutocq; but, how can we help it? We are forced to choose between two alternatives—we must go according to circumstances. I'm a good-natured fellow myself," he added, after a pause; "bring me your twenty-five thousand francs to-morrow morning and Thuillier shall keep the house. We'll continue to help you at both ends, but you'll have to pay up, my boy. After what has just happened that's pretty kind, isn't it?"

And Cerizet patted Theodose on the shoulder, with a cynicism that seemed to brand him more than the iron of the galleys.

"Well, give me till to-morrow at mid-day," replied the Provencal, "for there'll be, as you said, some manipulation to do."

"I'll try to keep Claparon quiet; he's in such a hurry, that man!"

"To-morrow then," said Theodose, in the tone of a man who decides his course.

"Good-night, friend," said Cerizet, in his nasal tone, which degraded the finest word in the language. "There's one who has got a mouthful to suck!" thought Cerizet, as he watched Theodose going down the street with the step of a dazed man.

When la Peyrade reached the rue des Postes he went with rapid strides to Madame Colleville's house, exciting himself as he walked along, and talking aloud. The fire of his roused passions and the sort of inward conflagration of which many Parisians are conscious (for such situations abound in Paris) brought him finally to a pitch of frenzy and eloquence which found expression, as he turned into the rue des Deux-Eglises, in the words:—

"I will kill him!"

"There's a fellow who is not content!" said a passing workman, and the jesting words calmed the incandescent madness to which Theodose was a prey.

As he left Cerizet's the idea came to him to go to Flavie and tell her all. Southern natures are born thus—strong until certain passions arise, and then collapsed. He entered Flavie's room; she was alone, and when she saw Theodose she fancied her last hour had come.

"What is the matter?" she cried.

"I—I—" he said. "Do you love me, Flavie?"

"Oh! how can you doubt it?"

"Do you love me absolutely?—if I were criminal, even?"

"Has he murdered some one?" she thought, replying to his question by a nod.

Theodose, thankful to seize even this branch of willow, drew a chair beside Flavie's sofa, and there gave way to sobs that might have touched the oldest judge, while torrents of tears began to flow from his eyes.

Flavie rose and left the room to say to her maid: "I am not at home to any one." Then she closed all doors and returned to Theodose, moved to the utmost pitch of maternal solicitude. She found him stretched out, his head thrown back, and weeping. He had taken out his handkerchief, and when Flavie tried to move it from his face it was heavy with tears.

"But what is the matter?" she asked; "what ails you?"

Nature, more impressive than art, served Theodose well; no longer was he playing a part; he was himself; this nervous crisis and these tears were the winding up of his preceding scenes of acted comedy.

"You are a child," she said, in a gentle voice, stroking his hair softly.

"I have but you, you only, in all the world!" he replied, kissing her hands with a sort of passion; "and if you are true to me, if you are mine, as the body belongs to the soul and the soul to the body, then—" he added, recovering himself with infinite grace, "*Then* I can have courage."

He rose, and walked about the room.

"Yes, I will struggle; I will recover my strength, like Antaeus, from a fall; I will strangle with my own hands the serpents that entwine me, that kiss with serpent kisses, that slaver my cheeks, that suck my blood, my honor! Oh, misery! oh, poverty! Oh, how great are they who can stand erect and carry high their heads! I had better have let myself die of hunger, there, on my wretched pallet, three and a half years ago! A coffin is a softer bed to lie in than the life I lead! It is eighteen months that I have *fed on bourgeois*! and now, at the moment of attaining an honest, fortunate life, a magnificent future, at the moment when I was about to sit down to the social banquet, the executioner strikes me on the shoulder! Yes, the monster! he struck me there, on my shoulder, and said to me: 'Pay thy dues to the devil, or die!' And shall I not crush them? Shall I not force my arm down their throats to their very entrails? Yes, yes, I will, I will! See, Flavie, my eyes are dry now. Ha, ha! now I laugh; I feel my strength come back to me; power is mine! Oh! say that you love me; say it again! At this moment it sounds like the word 'Pardon' to the man condemned to death!"

"You are terrible, my friend!" cried Flavie. "Oh! you are killing me."

She understood nothing of all this, but she fell upon the sofa, exhausted by the spectacle. Theodose flung himself at her feet.

"Forgive me! forgive me!" he said.

"But what is the matter? what is it?" she asked again.

"They are trying to destroy me. Oh! promise to give me Celeste, and you shall see what a glorious life I will make you share. If you hesitate—very good; that is saying you will be wholly mine, and I will have you!"

He made so rapid a movement that Flavie, terrified, rose and moved away.

"Oh! my saint!" he cried, "at thy feet I fall—a miracle! God is for me, surely! A flash of light has come to me—an idea—suddenly! Oh, thanks, my good angel, my grand Saint-Theodose! thou hast saved me!"

Flavie could not help admiring that chameleon being; one knee on the floor, his hands crossed on his breast, and his eyes raised to heaven in religious ecstasy, he recited a prayer; he was a fervent Catholic; he reverently crossed himself. It was fine; like the vision of Saint-Jerome.

"Adieu!" he said, with a melancholy look and a moving tone of voice.

"Oh!" cried Flavie, "leave me this handkerchief."

Theodose rushed away like one possessed, sprang into the street, and darted towards the Thuilliers', but turned, saw Flavie at her window, and made her a little sign of triumph.

"What a man!" she thought to herself.

"Dear, good friend," he said to Thuillier, in a calm and gentle, almost caressing voice, "we have fallen into the hands of atrocious scoundrels. But I mean to read them a lesson."

"What has happened?" asked Brigitte.

"They want twenty-five thousand francs, and, in order to get the better of us, the notary, or his accomplices, have determined to bid in the property. Thuillier, put five thousand francs in your pocket and come with me; I will secure that house to you. I am making myself implacable enemies!" he cried; "they are seeking to destroy me morally. But all I ask is that you will disregard their infamous calumnies and feel no change of heart to me. After all, what is it? If I succeed, you will only have paid one hundred and twenty-five thousand francs for the house instead of one hundred and twenty."

"Provided the same thing doesn't happen again," said Brigitte, uneasily, her eyes dilating under the effect of a violent suspicion.

"Preferred creditors have alone the right to bid in property, and as, in this case, there is but one, and he has used that right, we are safe. The amount of his claim is really only two thousand francs, but there are lawyers, attorneys, and so forth, to pay in such matters, and we shall have to drop a note of a thousand francs to make the creditor happy."

"Go, Thuillier," said Brigitte, "get your hat and gloves, and take the money —from you know where."

"As I paid those fifteen thousand francs without success, I don't wish to have any more money pass through my hands. Thuillier must pay it himself," said Theodose, when he found himself alone with Brigitte. "You have, however, gained twenty thousand on the contract I enabled you to make with Grindot, who thought he was serving the notary, and you own a piece of property which in five years will be worth nearly a million. It is what is called a 'boulevard corner.'"

Brigitte listened uneasily, precisely like a cat which hears a mouse within the wall. She looked Theodose straight in the eye, and, in spite of the truth of his remarks, doubts possessed her.

"What troubles you, little aunt?"

"Oh! I shall be in mortal terror until that property is securely ours."

"You would be willing to give twenty thousand francs, wouldn't you," said Theodose, "to make sure that Thuillier was what we call, in law, 'owner not dispossessable' of that property? Well, then, remember that I have saved you twice that amount."

"Where are we going?" asked Thuillier, returning.

"To Maitre Godeschal! We must employ him as our attorney."

"But we refused him for Celeste."

"Well, that's one reason for going to him," replied Theodose. "I have taken his measure; he's a man of honor, and he'll think it a fine thing to do you a service."

Godeschal, now Derville's successor, had formerly been, for more than two years, head-clerk with Desroches. Theodose, to whom that circumstance was known, seemed to hear the name flung into his ear in the midst of his despair by an inward voice, and he foresaw a possibility of wrenching from the hands of Claparon the weapon with which Cerizet had threatened him. He must, however, in the first instance, gain an entrance to Desroches, and get some light on the actual situation of his enemies. Godeschal, by reason of the intimacy still existing between the former clerk and his old master, could be his go-between. When the attorneys of Paris have ties like those which bound Godeschal and Desroches together, they live in true fraternity, and the result is a facility in arranging any matters which are, as one may say, arrangeable. They obtain from one another, on the ground of reciprocity, all possible concessions by the application of the proverb, "Pass me the rhubarb, and I'll pass you the senna," which is put in practice in all professions, between ministers, soldiers, judges, business men; wherever, in short, enmity has not raised barriers too strong and high between the parties.

"I gain a pretty good fee out of this compromise," is a reason that needs no expression in words: it is visible in the gesture, the tone, the glance; and as attorneys and solicitors meet constantly on this ground, the matter, whatever it is, is arranged. The counterpoise of this fraternal system is found in what we may call professional conscience. The public must believe the physician who says, giving medical testimony, "This body contains arsenic"; nothing is supposed to exceed the integrity of the legislator, the independence of the cabinet minister. In like manner, the attorney of Paris says to his brother lawyer, good-humoredly, "You can't obtain that; my client is furious," and the other answers, "Very good; I must do without it."

Now, la Peyrade, a shrewd man, had worn his legal gown about the Palais long enough to know how these judicial morals might be made to serve his purpose.

"Sit in the carriage," he said to Thuillier, when they reached the rue Vivienne, where Godeschal was now master of the practice he had formerly served as clerk. "You needn't show yourself until he undertakes the affair."

It was eleven o'clock at night; la Peyrade was not mistaken in supposing that he should find a newly fledged master of a practice in his office at that hour.

"To what do I owe this visit, monsieur?" said Godeschal, coming forward to meet the barrister.

Foreigners, provincials, and persons in high society may not be aware that barristers are to attorneys what generals are to marshals. There exists a line of demarcation, strictly maintained, between the order of barristers and the guild of attorneys and solicitors in Paris. However venerable an attorney may be, however capable and strong in his profession, he must go to the barrister. The attorney is the administrator, who maps out the plan of the campaign, collects the munitions of war, and puts the force in motion; the barrister gives battle. It is not known why the law gives a man two men to defend him any more than it is known why an author is forced to have both printer and publisher. The rules of the bar forbid its members to do any act belonging to the guild of attorneys. It is very rare that a barrister puts his foot in an attorney's office; the two classes meet in the law-courts. In society, there is no barrier between them, and some barristers, those in la Peyrade's situation particularly, demean themselves by calling occasionally on attorneys, though even these cases are rare, and are usually excused by some special urgency.

"I have come on important business," replied la Peyrade; "it concerns, especially, a question of delicacy which you and I ought to solve together. Thuillier is below, in a carriage, and I have come up to see you, not as a barrister, but as his friend. You are in a position to do him an immense service; and I have told him that you have too noble a soul (as a worthy successor of our great Derville must have) not to put your utmost capacity at his orders. Here's the affair."

After explaining, wholly to his own advantage, the swindling trick which must, he said, be met with caution and ability, the barrister developed his plan of campaign.

"You ought, my dear maitre, to go this very evening to Desroches, explain the whole plot and persuade him to send to-morrow for his client, this Sauvaignou. We'll confess the fellow between us, and if he wants a note for a thousand francs over and above the amount of his claim, we'll let him have it; not counting the five hundred for you and as much more for Desroches, provided Thuillier receives the relinquishment of his claim by ten o'clock to-morrow morning. What does this Sauvaignou want? Nothing but money. Well, a haggler like that won't resist the attraction of an extra thousand francs, especially if he is only the instrument of a cupidity behind him. It is no matter to us how he fights it out with those who prompt him. Now, then, do you think you can get the Thuillier family out of this?"

"I'll go and see Desroches at once," said Godeschal.

"Not before Thuillier gives you a power of attorney and five hundred francs. The money should be on the table in a case like this."

After the interview with Thuillier was over, la Peyrade took Godeschal in the carriage to the rue du Bethizy, where Desroches lived, explaining that it was on their way back to the rue Saint-Dominique d'Enfer. When they stopped at Desroches's door la Peyrade made an appointment with Godeschal to meet him there the next morning at seven o'clock.

La Peyrade's whole future and fortune lay in the outcome of this conference. It is therefore not astonishing that he disregarded the customs of the bar and went to Desroches's office, to study Sauvaignou and take part in the struggle, in spite of the danger he ran in thus placing himself visibly before the eyes of one of the most dreaded attorneys in Paris.

As he entered the office and made his salutations, he took note of Sauvaignou. The man was, as the name had already told him, from Marseilles,—the foreman of a master-carpenter, entrusted with the giving out of sub-contracts. The profits of this work consisted of what he could make between the price he paid for the work and that paid to him by the master-carpenter; this agreement being exclusive of material, his contract being only for labor. The master-carpenter had failed. Sauvaignou had thereupon appealed to the court of commerce for recognition as creditor with a lien on the property. He was a stocky little man, dressed in a gray linen blouse, with a cap on his head, and was seated in an armchair. Three banknotes, of a thousand francs each, lying visibly before him on Desroches's desk, informed la Peyrade that the negotiation had already taken place, and that the lawyers were worsted. Godeschal's eyes told the rest, and the glance which Desroches cast at the "poor man's advocate" was like the blow of a pick-axe into the earth of a grave. Stimulated by his danger, the Provencal became magnificent. He coolly took up the bank-notes and folded them, as if to put them in his pocket, saying to Desroches:—

"Thuillier has changed his mind."

"Very good; then we are all agreed," said the terrible attorney.

"Yes; your client must now hand over to us the fifty thousand francs we have spent on finishing the house, according to the contract between Thuillier and Grindot. I did not tell you that yesterday," he added, turning to Godeschal.

"Do you hear that?" said Desroches to Sauvaignou. "That's a case I shall not touch without proper guarantees."

"But, messieurs," said Sauvaignou, "I can't negotiate this matter until I have seen the worthy man who paid me five hundred francs on account for having signed him that bit of a proxy."

"Are you from Marseilles?" said la Peyrade, in patois.

"Oh! if he tackles him with patois the fellow is beaten," said Godeschal to

138

Desroches in a low tone.

"Yes, monsieur," replied the Marseillais.

"Well, you poor devil," continued Theodose, "don't you see that they want to ruin you? Shall I tell you what you ought to do? Pocket these three thousand francs, and when your worthy man comes after you, take your rule and hit him a rap over the knuckles; tell him he's a rascal who wants you to do his dirty work, and instead of that you revoke your proxy and will pay him his five hundred francs in the week with three Thursdays. Then be off with you to Marseilles with these three thousand francs and your savings in your pocket. If anything happens to you there, let me know through these gentlemen, and I'll get you out of the scrape; for, don't you see? I'm not only a Provencal, but I'm also one of the leading lawyers in Paris, and the friend of the poor."

When the workman found a compatriot sanctioning in a tone of authority the reasons by which he could betray Cerizet, he capitulated, asking, however, for three thousand five hundred francs. That demand having been granted he remarked:—

"It is none too much for a rap over the knuckles; he might put me in prison for assault."

"Well, you needn't strike unless he insults you," replied la Peyrade, "and that's self-defence."

When Desroches had assured him that la Peyrade was really a barrister in good standing, Sauvaignou signed the relinquishment, which contained a receipt for the amount, principal and interest, of his claim, made in duplicate between himself and Thuillier, and witnessed by the two attorneys; so that the paper was a final settlement of the whole matter.

"We'll leave the remaining fifteen hundred between you," whispered la Peyrade to Desroches and Godeschal, "on condition that you give me the relinquishment, which I will have Thuillier accept and sign before his notary, Cardot. Poor man! he never closed his eyes all night!"

"Very well," replied Desroches. "You may congratulate yourself," he added, making Sauvaignou sign the paper, "that you've earned that money pretty easily."

"It is really mine, isn't it, monsieur?" said the Marseillais, already uneasy.

"Yes, and legally, too," replied Desroches, "only you must let your man know this morning that you have revoked your proxy under date of yesterday. Go out through my clerk's office, here, this way."

Desroches told his head-clerk what the man was to do, and he sent a pupil-clerk with him to see that a sheriff's officer carried the notice to Cerizet before ten o'clock.

"I thank you, Desroches," said la Peyrade, pressing the attorney's hand; "you think of everything; I shall never forget this service."

"Don't deposit the deed with Cardot till after twelve o'clock," returned Desroches.

"Hay! comrade," cried the barrister, in Provencal, following Sauvaignou into the next room, "take your Margot to walk about Belleville, and be sure you don't go home."

"I hear," said Sauvaignou. "I'm off to-morrow; adieu!"

"Adieu," returned la Peyrade, with a Provencal cry.

"There is something behind all this," said Desroches in an undertone to Godeschal, as la Peyrade followed Sauvaignou into the clerk's office.

"The Thuilliers get a splendid piece of property for next to nothing," replied Godeschal; "that's all."

"La Peyrade and Cerizet look to me like two divers who are fighting under water," replied Desroches. "What am I to say to Cerizet, who put the matter into my hands?" he added, as the barrister returned to them.

"Tell him that Sauvaignou forced your hand," replied la Peyrade.

"And you fear nothing?" said Desroches, in a sudden manner.

"I? oh no! I want to give Cerizet a lesson."

"To-morrow, I shall know the truth," said Desroches, in a low tone, to Godeschal; "no one chatters like a beaten man."

La Peyrade departed, carrying with him the deed of relinquishment. At eleven o'clock he was in the courtroom of the justice-of-peace, perfectly calm, and firm. When he saw Cerizet come in, pale with rage, his eyes full of venom, he said in his ear:—

"My dear friend, I'm a pretty good fellow myself, and I hold that twenty-five thousand francs in good bank-bills at your disposal, whenever you will return to me those notes of mine which you hold."

Cerizet looked at the advocate of the poor, without being able to say one word in reply; he was green; the bile had struck in.

CHAPTER XIII. THE PERVERSITY OF DOVES

"I am a non-dispossessable property-owner!" cried Thuillier, coming home after visiting his notary. "No human power can get that house away from me. Cardot says so."

The bourgeoisie think much more of what their notary tells them than of what their attorney says. The notary is nearer to them than any other ministerial officer. The Parisian bourgeois never pays a visit to his attorney without a sense of fear; whereas he mounts the stairs with ever-renewed pleasure to see his notary; he admires that official's virtue and his sound good sense.

"Cardot, who is looking for an apartment for one of his clients, wants to know about our second floor," continued Thuillier. "If I choose he'll introduce to me on Sunday a tenant who is ready to sign a lease for eighteen years at forty thousand francs and taxes! What do you say to that, Brigitte?"

"Better wait," she replied. "Ah! that dear Theodose, what a fright he gave me!"

"Hey! my dearest girl, I must tell you that when Cardot asked who put me in the way of this affair he said I owed him a present of at least ten thousand francs. The fact is, I owe it all to him."

"But he is the son of the house," responded Brigitte.

"Poor lad! I'll do him the justice to say that he asks for nothing."

"Well, dear, good friend," said la Peyrade, coming in about three o'clock, "here you are, richissime!"

"And through you, Theodose."

"And you, little aunt, have you come to life again? Ah! you were not half as frightened as I was. I put your interests before my own; I haven't breathed freely till this morning at eleven o'clock; and yet I am sure now of having two mortal enemies at my heels in the two men I have tricked for your sake. As I walked home, just now, I asked myself what could be your influence over me to make me commit such a crime, and whether the happiness of belonging to your family and becoming your son could ever efface the stain I have put upon my conscience."

"Bah! you can confess it," said Thuillier, the free-thinker.

"And now," said Theodose to Brigitte, "you can pay, in all security, the cost of the house,—eighty thousand francs, and thirty thousand to Grindot; in all, with what you have paid in costs, one hundred and twenty thousand; and this last twenty thousand added make one hundred and forty thousand. If you let the house outright to a single tenant ask him for the last year's rent in advance, and reserve for my wife and me the whole of the first floor above the entresol. Make those conditions and you'll still get your forty thousand francs a year. If you should want to leave this quarter so as to be nearer the Chamber, you can always take up your abode with us on that vast first floor, which has stables and coach-house belonging to it; in fact, everything that is needful for a splendid life. And now, Thuillier, I am going to get the cross of the Legion of honor for you."

Hearing this last promise, Brigitte cried out in her enthusiasm:—

"Faith! my dear boy, you've done our business so well that I'll leave you to manage that of letting the house."

"Don't abdicate, dear aunt," replied Theodose. "God keep me from ever taking a step without you! You are the good genius of this family; I think only of the day when Thuillier will take his seat in the Chamber. If you let the house you will come into possession of your forty thousand francs for the last year of the lease in two months from now; and that will not prevent Thuillier from drawing his quarterly ten thousand of the rental."

After casting this hope into the mind of the old maid, who was jubilant, Theodose drew Thuillier into the garden and said to him, without beating round the bush:—

"Dear, good friend, find means to get ten thousand francs from your sister, and be sure not to let her suspect that you pay them to me; tell her that sum is required in the government office to facilitate your appointment as chevalier of the Legion of honor; tell her, too, that you know the persons among whom that sum should be distributed."

"That's a good idea," said Thuillier; "besides, I'll pay it back to her when I get my rents."

"Have the money ready this evening, dear friend. Now I am going out on business about your cross; to-morrow we shall know something definitely about it."

"What a man you are!" cried Thuillier.

"The ministry of the 1st of March is going to fall, and we must get it out of them beforehand," said Theodose, shrewdly.

He now hurried to Madame Colleville, crying out as he entered her room:

"I've conquered! We shall have a piece of landed property for Celeste worth a million, a life-interest in which will be given to her by her marriage-contract; but keep the secret, or your daughter will be hunted down by peers of France. Besides, this settlement will only be made in my favor. Now dress yourself, and let us go and call on Madame du Bruel; she can get the cross for Thuillier. While you are getting under arms I'll do a little courting to Celeste; you and I can talk as we drive along."

La Peyrade had seen, as he passed the door of the salon, Celeste and Felix Phellion in close conversation. Flavie had such confidence in her daughter that she did not fear to leave them together. Now that the great success of the morning was secured, Theodose felt the necessity of beginning his courtship of Celeste. It was high time, he thought, to bring about a quarrel between the lovers. He did not, therefore, hesitate to apply his ear to the door of the salon before entering it, in order to discover what letters of the alphabet of love they were spelling; he was even invited to commit this domestic treachery by sounds from within, which seemed to say that they were disputing. Love, according to one of our poets, is a privilege which two persons mutually take advantage of to cause each other, reciprocally, a great deal of sorrow about nothing at all.

When Celeste knew that Felix was elected by her heart to be the companion of her life, she felt a desire, not so much to study him as to unite herself closely with him by that communion of souls which is the basis of all affections, and leads, in youthful minds, to involuntary examination. The dispute to which Theodose was now to listen took its rise in a disagreement which had sprung up within the last few days between the mathematician and Celeste. The young girl's piety was real; she belonged to the flock of the truly faithful, and to her, Catholicism, tempered by that mysticism which attracts young souls, was an inward poem, a life within her life. From this point young girls are apt to develop into either extremely high-minded women or saints. But, during this beautiful period of their youth they have in their heart, in their ideas, a sort of absolutism: before their eyes is the image of perfection, and all must be celestial, angelic, or divine to satisfy them. Outside of their ideal, nothing of good can exist; all is stained and soiled. This idea causes the rejection of many a diamond with a flaw by girls who, as women, fall in love with paste.

Now, Celeste had seen in Felix, not irreligion, but indifference to matters of religion. Like most geometricians, chemists, mathematicians, and great naturalists, he had subjected religion to reason; he recognized a problem in it as insoluble as the squaring of the circle. Deist "in petto," he lived in the religion of most Frenchmen, not attaching more importance to it than he did to the new laws promulgated in July. It was necessary to have a God in heaven, just as they set up a bust of the king at the mayor's office. Felix Phellion, a worthy son of his father, had never drawn the slightest veil over his opinions or his conscience; he allowed Celeste to read into them with the candor and the inattention of a student of problems. The young girl, on her side, professed a horror for atheism, and her conscience assured her that a deist was cousin-germain to an atheist.

"Have you thought, Felix, of doing what you promised me?" asked Celeste, as soon as Madame Colleville had left them alone.

"No, my dear Celeste," replied Felix.

"Oh! to have broken his word!" she cried, softly.

"But to have kept it would have been a profanation," said Felix. "I love you so deeply, with a tenderness so little proof against your wishes, that I promised a thing contrary to my conscience. Conscience, Celeste, is our treasure, our strength, our mainstay. How can you ask me to go into a church and kneel at the feet of a priest, in whom I can see only a man? You would despise me if I obeyed you."

"And so, my dear Felix, you refuse to go to church," said Celeste, casting a tearful glance at the man she loved. "If I were your wife you would let me go alone? You do not love me as I love you! for, alas! I have a feeling in my heart for an atheist contrary to that which God commands."

"An atheist!" cried Felix. "Oh, no! Listen to me, Celeste. There is certainly a God; I believe in that; but I have higher ideas of Him than those of your priests; I do not wish to bring Him down to my level; I want to rise to Him. I listen to the voice He has put within me,—a voice which honest men call conscience, and I strive not to darken that divine ray as it comes to me. For instance, I will never harm others; I will do nothing against the commandments of universal morality, which was that of Confucius, Moses, Pythagoras, Socrates, as well as of Jesus Christ. I will stand in the presence of God; my actions shall be my prayers; I will never be false in word or deed; never will I do a base or shameful thing. Those are the precepts I have learned from my virtuous father, and which I desire to bequeath to my children. All the good that I can do I shall try to accomplish, even if I have to suffer for it. What can you ask more of a man than that?"

This profession of the Phellion faith caused Celeste to sadly shake her head.

"Read attentively," she replied, "'The Imitation of Jesus Christ.' Strive to convert yourself to the holy Catholic, apostolic, and Roman Church, and you will see how empty your words are. Hear me, Felix; marriage is not, the Church says, the affair of a day, the mere satisfaction of our own desires; it is made for eternity. What! shall we be united day and night, shall we form one flesh, one word, and yet have two languages, two faiths in our heart, and a cause of perpetual dissension? Would you condemn me to weep tears over the state of your soul,—tears that I must ever conceal from you? Could I address myself in peace to God when I see his arm stretched out in wrath against you? Must my children inherit the blood of a deist and his convictions? Oh! God, what misery for a wife! No, no, these ideas are intolerable. Felix! be of my faith, for I cannot share yours. Do not put a gulf between us. If you loved me, you would already have read 'The Imitation of Jesus Christ.'"

The Phellion class, sons of the "Constitutionnel," dislike the priestly mind. Felix had the imprudence to reply to this sort of prayer from the depths of an ardent heart:—

"You are repeating, Celeste, the lessons your confessor teaches you; nothing, believe me, is more fatal to happiness than the interference of priests in a home."

"Oh!" cried Celeste, wounded to the quick, for love alone inspired her, "you do not love! The voice of my heart is not in unison with yours! You have not understood me, because you have not listened to me; but I forgive you, for you know not what you say."

She wrapped herself in solemn silence, and Felix went to the window and drummed upon the panes,—music familiar to those who have indulged in poignant reflections. Felix was, in fact, presenting the following delicate and curious questions to the Phellion conscience.

"Celeste is a rich heiress, and, in yielding against the voice of natural religion, to her ideas, I should have in view the making of what is certainly an advantageous marriage,—an infamous act. I ought not, as father of a family, to allow the priesthood to have an influence in my home. If I yield to-day, I do a weak act, which will be followed by many others equally pernicious to the authority of a husband and father. All this is unworthy of a philosopher."

Then he returned to his beloved.

"Celeste, I entreat you on my knees," he said, "not to mingle that which the law, in its wisdom, has separated. We live in two worlds,—society and heaven. Each has its own way of salvation; but as to society, is it not obeying God to obey the laws? Christ said: 'Render unto Caesar that which is Caesar's.' Caesar is the body politic. Dear, let us forget our little quarrel."

"Little quarrel!" cried the young enthusiast; "I want you to have my whole heart as I want to have the whole of yours; and you make it into two parts! Is not that an evil? You forget that marriage is a sacrament."

"Your priesthood have turned your head," exclaimed the mathematician, impatiently.

"Monsieur Phellion," said Celeste, interrupting him hastily, "enough of this!"

It was at this point of the quarrel that Theodose considered it judicious to enter the room. He found Celeste pale, and the young professor as anxious as a lover should be who has just irritated his mistress.

"I heard the word 'enough'; then something is too much?" he said, inquiringly, looking in turn from Celeste to Felix.

"We were talking religion," replied Felix, "and I was saying to mademoiselle how dangerous ecclesiastical influence is in the bosom of families."

"That was not the point, monsieur," said Celeste, sharply; "it was to know if husband and wife could be of one heart when the one is an atheist and the other Catholic."

"Can there be such a thing as atheists?" cried Theodose, with all the signs of extreme wonderment. "Could a true Catholic marry a Protestant? There is no safety possible for a married pair unless they have perfect conformity in the matter of religious opinions. I, who come from the Comtat, of a family which counts a pope among its ancestors—for our arms are: gules, a key argent, with supporters, a monk holding a church, and a pilgrim with a staff, or, and the motto, 'I open, I shut'—I am, of course, intensely dogmatic on such points. But in these days, thanks to our modern system of education, it does not seem to me strange that religion should be called into question. I myself would never marry a Protestant, had she millions, even if I loved her distractedly. Faith is a thing that cannot be tampered with. 'Una fides, unus Dominus,' that is my device in life."

"You hear that!" cried Celeste, triumphantly, looking at FelixPhellion.

"I am not openly devout," continued la Peyrade. "I go to mass at six every morning, that I may not be observed; I fast on Fridays; I am, in short, a son of the Church, and I would not undertake any serious enterprise without prayer, after the ancient fashion of our ancestors; but no one is able to notice my religion. A singular thing happened to our family during the Revolution of 1789, which attached us more closely than ever to our holy mother the Church. A poor young lady of the elder branch of the Peyrades, who owned

147

the little estate of la Peyrade,—for we ourselves are Peyrades of Canquoelle, but the two branches inherit from one another,—well, this young lady married, six years before the Revolution, a barrister who, after the fashion of the times, was Voltairean, that is to say, an unbeliever, or, if you choose, a deist. He took up all the revolutionary ideas, and practised the charming rites that you know of in the worship of the goddess Reason. He came into our part of the country imbued with the ideas of the Convention, and fanatical about them. His wife was very handsome; he compelled her to play the part of Liberty; and the poor unfortunate creature went mad. She died insane! Well, as things are going now it looks as if we might have another 1793."

This history, invented on the spot, made such an impression on Celeste's fresh and youthful imagination that she rose, bowed to the young men and hastened to her chamber.

"Ah! monsieur, why did you tell her that?" cried Felix, struck to the heart by the cold look the young girl, affecting profound indifference, cast upon him. She fancied herself transformed into a goddess of Reason.

"Why not? What were you talking about?" asked Theodose.

"About my indifference to religion."

"The great sore of this century," replied Theodose, gravely.

"I am ready," said Madame Colleville, appearing in a toilet of much taste. "But what is the matter with my poor daughter? She is crying!"

"Crying? madame," exclaimed Felix; "please tell her that I will study 'The Imitation of Christ' at once."

Felix left the house with Theodose and Flavie, whose arm the barrister pressed to let her know he would explain in the carriage the apparent dementia of the young professor.

An hour later, Madame Colleville and Celeste, Colleville and Theodose were entering the Thuilliers' apartment to dine there. Theodose and Flavie took Thuillier into the garden, where the former said to him:—

"Dear, good friend! you will have the cross within a week. Our charming friend here will tell you about our visit to the Comtesse du Bruel."

And Theodose left Thuillier, having caught sight of Desroches in the act of being brought by Mademoiselle Thuillier into the garden; he went, driven by a terrible and glacial presentiment, to meet him.

"My good friend," said Desroches in his ear, "I have come to see if you can procure at once twenty-five thousand francs plus two thousand six hundred and eighty for costs."

"Are you acting for Cerizet?" asked the barrister.

"Cerizet has put all the papers into the hands of Louchard, and you know what you have to expect if arrested. Is Cerizet wrong in thinking you have twenty-five thousand francs in your desk? He says you offered them to him and he thinks it only natural not to leave them in your hands."

"Thank you for taking the step, my good friend," replied Theodose. "I have been expecting this attack."

"Between ourselves," replied Desroches, "you have made an utter fool of him, and he is furious. The scamp will stop at nothing to get his revenge upon you—for he'll lose everything if he forces you to fling your barrister's gown, as they say, to the nettles and go to prison."

"I?" said Theodose. "I'm going to pay him. But even so, there will still be five notes of mine in his hands, for five thousand francs each; what does he mean to do with them?"

"Oh! after the affair of this morning, I can't tell you; my client is a crafty, mangy cur, and he is sure to have his little plans."

"Look here, Desroches," said Theodose, taking the hard, unyielding attorney round the waist, "those papers are in your hands, are not they?"

"Will you pay them?"

"Yes, in three hours."

"Very good, then. Be at my office at nine o'clock; I'll receive the money and give you your notes; *but*, at half-past nine o'clock, they will be in the sheriff's hands."

"To-night, then, at nine o'clock," said Theodose.

"Nine o'clock," repeated Desroches, whose glance had taken in the whole family, then assembled in the garden.

Celeste, with red eyes, was talking to her godmother; Colleville and Brigitte, Flavie and Thuillier were on the steps of the broad portico leading to the entrance-hall. Desroches remarked to Theodose, who followed him to the door:—

"You can pay off those notes."

At a single glance the shrewd attorney had comprehended the whole scheme of the barrister.

149

CHAPTER XIV. ONE OF CERIZET'S FEMALE CLIENTS

The next morning, at daybreak, Theodose went to the office of the banker of the poor, to see the effect produced upon his enemy by the punctual payment of the night before, and to make another effort to get rid of his hornet.

He found Cerizet standing up, in conference with a woman, and he received an imperative sign to keep at a distance and not to interrupt the interview. The barrister was therefore reduced to conjectures as to the importance of this woman, an importance revealed by the eager look on the face of the lender "by the little week." Theodose had a presentiment, though a very vague one, that the upshot of this conference would have some influence on Cerizet's own arrangements, for he suddenly beheld on that crafty countenance the change produced by a dawning hope.

"But, my dear mamma Cardinal—"

"Yes, my good monsieur—"

"What is it you want—?"

"It must be decided—"

These beginnings, or these ends of sentences were the only gleams of light that the animated conversation, carried on in the lowest tones with lip to ear and ear to lip, conveyed to the motionless witness, whose attention was fixed on Madame Cardinal.

Madame Cardinal was one of Cerizet's earliest clients; she peddled fish. If Parisians know these creations peculiar to their soil, foreigners have no suspicion of their existence; and Mere Cardinal—technologically speaking, of course, deserved all the interest she excited in Theodose. So many women of her species may be met with in the streets that the passers-by give them no more attention than they give to the three thousand pictures of the Salon. But as she stood in Cerizet's office the Cardinal had all the value of an isolated masterpiece; she was a complete and perfect type of her species.

The woman was mounted on muddy sabots; but her feet, carefully wrapped in gaiters, were still further protected by stout and thick-ribbed stockings. Her cotton gown, adorned with a glounce of mud, bore the imprint of the strap which supported the fish-basket. Her principal garment was a shawl of what was called "rabbit's-hair cashmere," the two ends of which were knotted

152

behind, above her bustle—for we must needs employ a fashionable word to express the effect produced by the transversal pressure of the basket upon her petticoats, which projected below it, in shape like a cabbage. A printed cotton neckerchief, of the coarsest description, gave to view a red neck, ribbed and lined like the surface of a pond where people have skated. Her head was covered in a yellow silk foulard, twined in a manner that was rather picturesque. Short and stout, and ruddy of skin, Mere Cardinal probably drank her little drop of brandy in the morning. She had once been handsome. The Halle had formerly reproached her, in the boldness of its figurative speech, for doing "a double day's-work in the twenty-four." Her voice, in order to reduce itself to the diapason of ordinary conversation, was obliged to stifle its sound as other voices do in a sick-room; but at such times it came thick and muffled, from a throat accustomed to send to the farthest recesses of the highest garret the names of the fish in their season. Her nose, a la Roxelane, her well-cut lips, her blue eyes, and all that formerly made up her beauty, was now buried in folds of vigorous flesh which told of the habits and occupations of an outdoor life. The stomach and bosom were distinguished for an amplitude worthy of Rubens.

"Do you want to make me lie in the straw?" she said to Cerizet. "What do I care for the Toupilliers? Ain't I a Toupillier myself? What do you want to do with them, those Toupilliers?"

This savage outburst was hastily repressed by Cerizet, who uttered a prolonged "Hush-sh!" such as all conspirators obey.

"Well, go and find out all you can about it, and come back to me," said Cerizet, pushing the woman toward the door, and whispering, as he did so, a few words in her ear.

"Well, my dear friend," said Theodose to Cerizet, "you have got your money?"

"Yes," returned Cerizet "we have measured our claws, they are the same length, the same strength, and the same sharpness. What next?"

"Am I to tell Dutocq that you received, last night, twenty-five thousand francs?"

"Oh! my dear friend, not a word, if you love me!" cried Cerizet.

"Listen," said Theodose. "I must know, once for all, what you want. I am positively determined not to remain twenty-four hours longer on the gridiron where you have got me. Cheat Dutocq if you will; I am utterly indifferent to that; but I intend that you and I shall come to an understanding. It is a fortune that I have paid you, twenty-five thousand francs, and you must have earned ten thousand more in your business; it is enough to make you an honest man. Cerizet, if you will leave me in peace, if you won't prevent my marriage with Mademoiselle Colleville, I shall certainly be king's attorney-general, or something of that kind in Paris. You can't do better than make sure of an influence in that sphere."

"Here are my conditions; and they won't allow of discussion; you can take them or leave them. You will obtain for me the lease of Thuillier's new house for eighteen years, and I'll hand you back one of your five notes cancelled, and you shall not find me any longer in your way. But you will have to settle with Dutocq for the remaining four notes. You got the better of *me*, and I know Dutocq hasn't the force to stand against you."

"I'll agree to that, provided you'll pay a rent of forty-eight thousand francs for the house, the last year in advance, and begin the lease in October."

"Yes; but I shall not give for the last year's rent more than forty-three thousand francs; your note will pay the remainder. I have seen the house, and examined it. It suits me very well."

"One last condition," said Theodose; "you'll help me against Dutocq?"

"No," said Cerizet, "you'll cook him brown yourself; he doesn't need any basting from me; he'll give out his gravy fast enough. But you ought to be reasonable. The poor fellow can't pay off the last fifteen thousand francs due on his practice, and you should reflect that fifteen thousand francs would certainly buy back your notes."

"Well; give me two weeks to get your lease——"

"No, not a day later than Monday next! Tuesday your notes will be in Louchard's hands; unless you pay them Monday, or Thuillier signs the lease."

"Well, Monday, so be it!" said Theodose; "are we friends?"

"We shall be Monday," responded Cerizet.

"Well, then, Monday you'll pay for my dinner," said Theodose, laughing.

"Yes, at the Rocher de Cancale, if I have the lease. Dutocq shall be there—we'll all be there—ah! it is long since I've had a good laugh."

Theodose and Cerizet shook hands, saying, reciprocally:—

"We'll meet soon."

Cerizet had not calmed down so suddenly without reasons. In the first place, as Desroches once said, "Bile does not facilitate business," and the usurer had too well seen the justice of that remark not to coolly resolve to get something out of his position, and to squeeze the jugular vein of the crafty

Provencal until he strangled him.

"It is a fair revenge," Desroches said to him; "mind you extract its quintessence. You hold that fellow."

For ten years past Cerizet had seen men growing rich by practising the trade of principal tenant. The principal tenant is, in Paris, to the owners of houses what farmers are to country landlords. All Paris has seen one of its great tailors, building at his own cost, on the famous site of Frascati, one of the most sumptuous of houses, and paying, as principal tenant, fifty thousand francs a year for the ground rent of the house, which, at the end of nineteen years' lease, was to become the property of the owner of the land. In spite of the costs of construction, which were something like seven hundred thousand francs, the profits of those nineteen years proved, in the end, very large.

Cerizet, always on the watch for business, had examined the chances for gain offered by the situation of the house which Thuillier had *stolen*,—as he said to Desroches,—and he had seen the possibility of letting it for sixty thousand at the end of six years. There were four shops, two on each side, for it stood on a boulevard corner. Cerizet expected, therefore, to get clear ten thousand a year for a dozen years, allowing for eventualities and sundries attendant on renewal of leases. He therefore proposed to himself to sell his money-lending business to the widow Poiret and Cadenet for ten thousand francs; he already possessed thirty thousand; and the two together would enable him to pay the last year's rent in advance, which house-owners in Paris usually demand as a guarantee from a principal tenant on a long lease. Cerizet had spent a happy night; he fell asleep in a glorious dream; he saw himself in a fair way to do an honest business, and to become a bourgeois like Thuillier, like Minard, and so many others.

But he had a waking of which he did not dream. He found Fortune standing before him, and emptying her gilded horns of plenty at his feet in the person of Madame Cardinal. He had always had a liking for the woman, and had promised her for a year past the necessary sum to buy a donkey and a little cart, so that she could carry on her business on a large scale, and go from Paris to the suburbs. Madame Cardinal, widow of a porter in the corn-market, had an only daughter, whose beauty Cerizet had heard of from some of the mother's cronies. Olympe Cardinal was about thirteen years of age at the time, 1837, when Cerizet began his system of loans in the quarter; and with a view to an infamous libertinism, he had paid great attention to the mother, whom he rescued from utter misery, hoping to make Olympe his mistress. But suddenly, in 1838, the girl left her mother, and "made her life," to use an expression by which the lower classes in Paris describe the abuse of the most precious gifts of nature and youth.

To look for a girl in Paris is to look for a smelt in the Seine; nothing but chance can throw her into the net. The chance came. Mere Cardinal, who to entertain a neighbor had taken her to the Bobino theatre, recognized in the leading lady her own daughter, whom the first comedian had held under his control for three years. The mother, gratified at first at beholding her daughter in a fine gown of gold brocade, her hair dressed like that of a duchess, and wearing open-worked stockings, satin shoes, and receiving the plaudits of the audience, ended by screaming out from her seat in the gallery:—

"You shall soon hear of me, murderer of your own mother! I'll know whether miserable strolling-players have the right to come and debauch young girls of sixteen!"

She waited at the stage-door to capture her daughter, but the first comedian and the leading lady had no doubt jumped across the footlights and left the theatre with the audience, instead of issuing by the stage-door, where Madame Cardinal and her crony, Mere Mahoudeau, made an infernal rumpus, which two municipal guards were called upon to pacify. Those august personages, before whom the two women lowered the diapason of their voices, called the mother's attention to the fact that the girl was of legitimate theatrical age, and that instead of screaming at the door after the director, she could summon him before the justice-of-peace, or the police-court, whichever she pleased.

The next day Madame Cardinal intended to consult Cerizet, in view of the fact that he was a clerk in the office of the justice-of-peace; but, before reaching his lair in the rue des Poules, she was met by the porter of a house in which an uncle of hers, a certain Toupillier, was living, who told her that the old man hadn't probably two days to live, being then in the last extremity.

"Well, how do you expect me to help it?" replied the widow Cardinal.

"We count on you, my dear Madame Cardinal; we know you won't forget the good advice we'll give you. Here's the thing. Lately, your poor uncle, not being able to stir round, has trusted me to go and collect the rents of his house, rue Notre-Dame de Nazareth, and the arrears of his dividends at the Treasury, which come to eighteen hundred francs."

By this time the widow Cardinal's eyes were becoming fixed instead of wandering.

"Yes, my dear," continued Perrache, a hump-backed little concierge; "and, seeing that you are the only person who ever thinks about him, and that you come and see him sometimes, and bring him fish, perhaps he may make a bequest in your favor. My wife, who has been nursing him for the last few days since he has been so ill, spoke to him of you, but he wouldn't have you told about his illness. But now, don't you see, it is high time you should show yourself there. It is pretty nigh two months since he has been able to attend to business."

"You may well think, you old thief," replied Madame Cardinal, hurrying at top speed toward the rue Honore-Chevalier, where her uncle lived in a wretched garret, "that the hair would grow on my hand before I could ever imagine that. What! my uncle Toupillier rich! the old pauper of the church of Saint-Sulpice!"

"Ah!" returned the porter, "but he fed well. He went to bed every night with his best friend, a big bottle of Roussillon. My wife has tasted it, though he told us it was common stuff. The wine-merchant in the rue des Canettes supplies it to him."

"Don't say a word about all this," said the widow, when she parted from the man who had given her the information. "I'll take care and remember you—if anything comes of it."

Toupillier, former drum-major in the French Guards, had been for the two years preceding 1789 in the service of the Church as beadle of Saint-Sulpice. The Revolution deprived him of that post, and he then dropped down into a state of abject misery. He was even obliged to take to the profession of model, for he *enjoyed*, as they say, a fine physique. When public worship was restored, he took up his beadle's staff once more; but in 1816 he was dismissed, as much on account of his immorality as for his political opinions. Nevertheless, he was allowed to stay about the door of the church and distribute the holy water. Later, an unfortunate affair, which we shall presently mention, made him lose even that position; but, still finding means to keep to the sanctuary, he obtained permission to be allowed as a pauper in the porch. At this period of life, being then seventy-two years of age, he made himself ninety-six, and began the profession of centenarian.

In all Paris it was impossible to find another such beard and head of hair as Toupillier's. As he walked he appeared bent double; he held a stick in his shaking hand,—a hand that was covered with lichen, like a granite rock, and with the other he held out the classic hat with a broad brim, filthy and battered, into which, however, there fell abundant alms. His legs were swathed in rags and bandages, and his feet shuffled along in miserable overshoes of woven mat-weed, inside of which he had fastened excellent cork soles. He washed his face with certain compounds, which gave it an appearance of forms of illness, and he played the senility of a centenarian to the life. He reckoned himself a hundred years old in 1830, at which time his actual age was eighty; he was the head of the paupers of Saint-Sulpice, the master of the place, and all those who came to beg under the arcades of the church, safe from the persecutions of the police and beneath the protection of the beadle and the giver of holy water, were forced to pay him a sort of tithe.

When a new heir, a bridegroom, or some godfather left the church, saying, "Here, this is for all of you; don't torment any of my party," Toupillier, appointed by the beadle to receive these alms, pocketed three-fourths, and distributed only the remaining quarter among his henchmen, whose tribute amounted to a sou a day. Money and wine were his last two passions; but he regulated the latter and gave himself up to the former, with neglecting his personal comfort. He drank at night only, after his dinner, and for twenty years he slept in the arms of drunkenness, his last mistress.

In the early morning he was at his post with all his faculties. From then until his dinner, which he took at Pere Lathuile's (made famous by Charlet), he gnawed crusts of bread by way of nourishment; and he gnawed them artistically, with an air of resignation which earned him abundant alms. The beadle and the giver of holy water, with whom he may have had some private understanding, would say of him:—

"He is one of the worthy poor of the church; he used to know the rector Languet, who built Saint-Sulpice; he was for twenty years beadle of the church before the Revolution, and he is now over a hundred years old."

This little biography, well known to all the pious attendants of the church, was, of course, the best of his advertisements, and no hat was so well lined as his. He bought his house in 1826, and began to invest his money in the Funds in 1830. From the value of the two investments he must have made something like six thousand francs a year, and probably turned them over by usury, after Cerizet's own fashion; for the sum he paid for the house was forty thousand francs, while his investment in 1830 was forty-eight thousand more. His niece, deceived by the old man as much as he deceived the functionaries and the pious souls of the church, believed him the most miserable of paupers, and when she had any fish that were spoiling she sometimes took them to the aged beggar.

Consequently, she now felt it her right to get what she could in return for her pity and her liberality to an uncle who was likely to have a crowd of collateral heirs; she herself being the third and last Toupillier daughter. She had four brothers, and her father, a porter with a hand-cart, had told her, in her childhood, of three aunts and four uncles, who all led an existence of the baser sort.

After inspecting the sick man, she went, at full speed, to consult Cerizet, telling him, in the first place, how she had found her daughter, and then the reasons and indications which made her think that her uncle Toupillier was hoarding a pile of gold in his mattress. Mere Cardinal did not feel herself strong enough to seize upon the property, legally or illegally, and she therefore came to confide in Cerizet and get his advice.

So, then, the banker of the poor, like other scavengers, had, at last, found diamonds in the slime in which he had paddled for the last four years, being always on the watch for some such chance,—a chance, they say, occasionally met with in the purlieus, which give birth to heiresses in sabots. This was the secret of his unexpected gentleness to la Peyrade, the man whose ruin he had vowed. It is easy to imagine the anxiety with which he awaited the return of Madame Cardinal, to whom this wily schemer of nefarious plots had given means to verify her suspicions as to the existence of the hoarded treasure, promising her complete success if she would trust him to obtain for her so rich a harvest. He was not the man to shrink from a crime, above all, when he saw that others could commit it, while he obtained the benefits.

"Well, monsieur," cried the fishwife, entering Cerizet's den with a face as much inflamed by cupidity as by the haste of her movements, "my uncle sleeps on more than a hundred thousand francs in gold, and I am certain that those Perraches, by dint of nursing him, have smelt the rat."

"Shared among forty heirs that won't be much to each," said Cerizet. "Listen to me, Mere Cardinal: I'll marry your daughter; give her your uncle's gold, and I'll guarantee to you a life-interest in the house and the dividends from the money in the Funds."

"We sha'n't run any risk?"

"None, whatever."

"Agreed, then," said the widow Cardinal, holding out her hand to her future son-in-law. "Six thousand francs a year; hey! what a fine life I'll have."

"With a son-in-law like me!" added Cerizet.

"I shall be a bourgeoisie of Paris!"

"Now," resumed Cerizet, after a pause, "I must study the ground. Don't leave your uncle alone a minute; tell the Perraches that you expect a doctor. I'll be the doctor, and when I get there you must seem not to know me."

"Aren't you sly, you old rogue," said Madame Cardinal, with a punch on Cerizet's stomach by way of farewell.

An hour later, Cerizet, dressed in black, disguised by a rusty wig and an artificially painted physiognomy, arrived at the house in the rue Honore-Chevalier in the regulation cabriolet. He asked the porter to tell him how to find the lodging of an old beggar named Toupillier.

"Is monsieur the doctor whom Madame Cardinal expects?" asked Perrache.

Cerizet had no doubt reflected on the gravity of the affair he was undertaking, for he avoided giving an answer to that question.

"Is this the way?" he said, turning at random to one side of the courtyard.

"No, monsieur," replied Perrache, who then took him to the back stairs of the house, which led up to the wretched attic occupied by the pauper.

Nothing remained for the inquisitive porter to do but to question the driver of the cabriolet; to which employment we will leave him, while we pursue our own inquiries elsewhere.

CHAPTER XV

The house in which Toupillier lived is one of those which have lost half their depth, owing to the straightening of the line of the street, the rue Honore-Chevalier being one of the narrowest in the Saint-Sulpice quarter. The owner, forbidden by the law to repair it, or to add new storeys, was compelled to let the wretched building in the condition in which he bought it. It consisted of a first storey above the ground-floor, surmounted by garrets, with two small wings running back on either side. The courtyard thus formed ended in a garden planted with trees, which was always rented to the occupant of the first floor. This garden, separated by an iron railing from the courtyard, would have allowed a rich owner to sell the front buildings to the city, and to build a new house upon the courtyard; but the whole of the first floor was let on an eighteen years' lease to a mysterious personage, about whom neither the official policing of the concierge nor the curiosity of the other tenants could find anything to censure.

This tenant, now seventy years of age, had built, in 1829, an outer stairway, leading from the right wing of the first floor to the garden, so that he could get there without going through the courtyard. Half the ground-floor was occupied by a book-stitcher, who for the last ten years had used the stable and coach-house for workshops. A book-binder occupied the other half. The binder and the stitcher lived, each of them, in half the garret rooms over the front building on the street. The garrets above the rear wings were occupied, the one on the right by the mysterious tenant, the one on the left by Toupillier, who paid a hundred francs a year for it, and reached it by a dark staircase, lighted by small round windows. The porte-cochere was made in the circular form indispensable in a street so narrow that two carriages cannot pass in it.

Cerizet laid hold of the rope which served as a baluster, to climb the species of ladder leading to the room where the so-called beggar was dying,— a room in which the odious spectacle of pretended pauperism was being played. In Paris, everything that is done for a purpose is thoroughly done. Would-be paupers are as clever at mounting their disguise as shopkeepers in preparing their show-windows, or sham rich men in obtaining credit.

The floor had never been swept; the bricks had disappeared beneath layers of dirt, dust, dried mud, and any and every thing thrown down by Toupillier. A miserable stove of cast-iron, the pipe of which entered a crumbling chimney, was the most apparent piece of furniture in this hovel. In an alcove stood a bed, with tester and valence of green serge, which the moths had transformed into lace. The window, almost useless, had a heavy coating of grease upon its panes, which dispensed with the necessity of curtains. The whitewashed walls presented to the eye fuliginous tones, due to the wood and peat burned by the pauper in his stove. On the fireplace were a broken water-pitcher, two bottles, and a cracked plate. A worm-eaten chest of drawers contained his linen and decent clothes. The rest of the furniture consisted of a night-table of the commonest description, another table, worth about forty sous, and two kitchen chairs with the straw seats almost gone. The extremely picturesque costume of the centenarian pauper was hanging from a nail, and below it, on the floor, were the shapeless mat-weed coverings that served him for shoes, the whole forming, with his amorphous old hat and knotty stick, a sort of panoply of misery.

As he entered, Cerizet gave a rapid glance at the old man, whose head lay on a pillow brown with grease and without a pillow-case; his angular profile, like those which engravers of the last century were fond of making out of rocks in the landscapes they engraved, was strongly defined in black against the green serge hangings of the tester. Toupillier, a man nearly six feet tall, was looking fixedly at some object at the foot of his bed; he did not move on hearing the groaning of the heavy door, which, being armed with iron bolts and a strong lock, closed his domicile securely.

"Is he conscious?" said Cerizet, before whom Madame Cardinal started back, not having recognized him till he spoke.

"Pretty nearly," she replied.

"Come out on the staircase, so that he doesn't hear us," whispered Cerizet. "This is how we'll manage it," he continued, in the ear of his future mother-in-law. "He is weak, but he isn't so very low; we have fully a week before us. I'll send you a doctor who'll suit us,—you understand? and later in the evening I'll bring you six poppy-heads. In the state he's in, you see, a decoction of poppy-heads will send him into a sound sleep. I'll send you a cot-bed on pretence of your sleeping in the room with him. We'll move him from one bed to the other, and when we've found the money there won't be any difficulty in carrying it off. But we ought to know who the people are who live in this old barrack. If Perrache suspects, as you think, about the money, he might give an alarm, and so many tenants, so many spies, you know—"

"Oh! as for that," said Madame Cardinal, "I've found out already that Monsieur du Portail, the old man who occupies the first floor, has charge of an insane woman; I heard their Dutch servant-woman, Katte, calling her Lydie this morning. The only other servant is an old valet named Bruneau; he does everything, except cook."

"But the binder and the stitcher down below," returned Cerizet, "they begin work very early in the morning—Well, anyhow, we must study the matter," he added, in the tone of a man whose plans are not yet decided. "I'll go to the mayor's office of your arrondissement, and get Olympe's register of birth, and put up the banns. The marriage must take place a week from Saturday."

"How he goes it, the rascal!" cried the admiring Madame Cardinal, pushing her formidable son-in-law by the shoulder.

As he went downstairs Cerizet was surprised to see, through one of the small round windows, an old man, evidently du Portail, walking in the garden with a very important member of the government, Comte Martial de la Roche-Hugon. He stopped in the courtyard when he reached it, as if to examine the old house, built in the reign of Louis XIV., the yellow walls of which, though of freestone, were bent like the elderly beggar they contained. Then he looked at the workshops, and counted the workmen. The house was otherwise as silent as a cloister. Being observed himself, Cerizet departed, thinking over in his mind the various difficulties that might arise in extracting the sum hidden beneath the dying man.

"Carry off all that gold at night?" he said to himself; "why, those porters will be on the watch, and twenty persons might see us! It is hard work to carry even twenty-five thousand francs of gold on one's person."

Societies have two goals of perfection; the first is a state of civilization in which morality equally infused and pervasive does not admit even the idea of crime; the Jesuits reached that point, formerly presented by the primitive Church. The second is the state of another civilization in which the supervision of citizens over one another makes crime impossible. The end which modern society has placed before itself is the latter; namely, that in which a crime presents such difficulties that a man must abandon all reasoning in order to commit it. In fact, iniquities which the law cannot reach are not left actually unpunished, for social judgment is even more severe than that of courts. If a man like Minoret, the post-master at Nemours [see "Ursule Mirouet"] suppresses a will and no one witnesses the act, the crime is traced home to him by the watchfulness of virtue as surely as a robbery is followed up by the detective police. No wrong-doing passes actually unperceived; and wherever a lesion in rectitude takes place the scar remains. Things can be no more made to disappear than men; so carefully, in Paris especially, are articles and objects ticketed and numbered, houses watched, streets observed, places spied upon. To live at ease, crime must have a sanction like that of the Bourse; like that conceded by Cerizet's clients; who never complained of his usury, and, indeed, would have been troubled in mind if their flayer were not in his den of a Tuesday.

"Well, my dear monsieur," said Madame Perrache, the porter's wife, as he passed her lodge, "how do you find him, that friend of God, that poor man?"

"I am not the doctor," replied Cerizet, who now decidedly declined that role. "I am Madame Cardinal's business man. I have just advised her to have a cot-bed put up, so as to nurse her uncle night and day; though, perhaps, she will have to get a regular nurse."

"I can help her," said Madame Perrache. "I nurse women in childbed."

"Well, we'll see about it," said Cerizet; "I'll arrange all that. Who is the tenant on your first floor?"

"Monsieur du Portail. He has lodged here these thirty years. He is a man with a good income, monsieur; highly respectable, and elderly. You know people who invest in the Funds live on their incomes. He used to be in business. But it is more than eleven years now since he has been trying to restore the reason of a daughter of one of his friends, Mademoiselle Lydie de la Peyrade. She has the best advice, I can tell you; the very first doctors in Paris; only this morning they had a consultation. But so far nothing has cured her; and they have to watch her pretty close; for sometimes she gets up and walks at night—"

"Mademoiselle Lydie de la Peyrade!" exclaimed Cerizet; "are you sure of the name?"

"I've heard Madame Katte, her nurse, who also does the cooking, call her so a thousand times, monsieur; though, generally, neither Monsieur Bruneau, the valet, nor Madame Katte say much. It's like talking to the wall to try and get any information out of them. We have been porters here these twenty years and we've never found out anything about Monsieur du Portail yet. More than that, monsieur, he owns the little house alongside; you see the double door from here. Well, he can go out that way and receive his company too, and we know nothing about it. Our owner doesn't know anything more than we do; when people ring at that door, Monsieur Bruneau goes and opens it."

"Then you didn't see the gentleman who is talking with him in the garden go by this way?"

"Bless me! no, that I didn't!"

"Ah!" thought Cerizet as he got into the cabriolet, "she must be the daughter of that uncle of Theodose. I wonder if du Portail can be the secret benefactor who sent money from time to time to that rascal? Suppose I send an anonymous letter to the old fellow, warning him of the danger the barrister runs from those notes for twenty-five thousand francs?"

An hour later the cot-bed had arrived for Madame Cardinal, to whom the inquisitive portress offered her services to bring her something to eat.

"Do you want to see the rector?" Madame Cardinal inquired of her uncle.

She had noticed that the arrival of the bed seemed to draw him from his somnolence.

"I want wine!" replied the pauper.

"How do you feel now, Pere Toupillier?" asked Madame Perrache, in a coaxing voice.

"I tell you I want wine," repeated the old man, with an energetic insistence scarcely to be expected of his feebleness.

"We must first find out if it is good for you, uncle," said Madame Cardinal, soothingly. "Wait till the doctor comes."

"Doctor! I won't have a doctor!" cried Toupillier; "and you, what are you doing here? I don't want anybody."

"My good uncle, I came to know if you'd like something tasty. I've got some nice fresh soles—hey! a bit of fried sole, with a squeeze of lemon on it?"

"Your fish, indeed!" cried Toupillier; "all rotten! That last you brought me, more than six weeks ago, it is there in the cupboard; you can take it away with you."

"Heavens! how ungrateful sick men are!" whispered the widow Cardinal to Perrache.

Nevertheless, to exhibit solicitude, she arranged the pillow under the patient's head, saying:—

"There! uncle, don't you feel better like that?"

"Let me alone!" shouted Toupillier, angrily; "I want no one here; I want wine; leave me in peace."

"Don't get angry, little uncle; we'll fetch you some wine."

"Number six wine, rue des Canettes," cried the pauper.

"Yes, I know," replied Madame Cardinal; "but let me count out my coppers. I want to get something better for you than that kind of wine; for, don't you see, an uncle, he's a kind of father, and one shouldn't mind what one does for him."

So saying, she sat down, with her legs apart, on one of the dilapidated chairs, and poured into her apron the contents of her pockets, namely: a knife, her snuff-box, two pawn-tickets, some crusts of bread, and a handful of copper, from which she extracted a few silver bits.

This exhibition, intended to prove her generous and eager devotion, had no result. Toupillier seemed not to notice it. Exhausted by the feverish energy with which he had demanded his favorite remedy, he made an effort to change his position, and, with his back turned to his two nurses, he again muttered: "Wine! wine!" after which nothing more was heard of him but a stentorous breathing, that plainly showed the state of his lungs, which were beginning to congest.

"I suppose I must go and fetch his wine!" said the Cardinal, restoring to her pockets, with some ill-humor, the cargo she had just pulled out of them.

"If you don't want to go—" began Madame Perrache, always ready to offer her services.

The fishwife hesitated for a moment; then, reflecting that something might be got out of a conversation with the wine-merchant, and sure, moreover, that as long as Toupillier lay on his gold she could safely leave him alone with the portress, she said:—

"Thank you, Madame Perrache, but I'd better make acquaintance with his trades-folk."

Then, having spied behind the night-table a dirty bottle which might hold about two quarts,—

"Did he say the rue des Canelles?" she inquired of the portress.

"Corner of the rue Guisarde," replied Madame Perrache. "Monsieur Legrelu, a tall, fine man with big whiskers and no hair." Then, lowering her voice, she added: "His number-six wine, you know, is Roussillon, and the best, too. However, the wine-merchant knows; it is enough if you tell him you have come from his customer, the pauper of Saint-Sulpice."

"No need to tell me anything twice," said the Cardinal, opening the door and making, as they say, a false exit. "Ah ca!" she said, coming back; "what does he burn in his stove, supposing I want to heat some remedy for him?"

"Goodness!" said the portress, "he doesn't make much provision for winter, and here we are in the middle of summer!"

"And not a saucepan! not a pot, even! Gracious! what a way to live. I'll have to fetch him some provisions; I hope nobody will see the things I bring back; I'd be ashamed they should—"

"I'll lend you a hand-bag," said the portress, always ready and officious.

"No, I'll buy a basket," replied the fishwife, more anxious about what she expected to carry away than what she was about to bring home to the pauper. "There must be some Auvergnat in the neighborhood who sells wood," she added.

"Corner of the rue Ferou; you'll find one there. A fine establishment, with logs of wood painted in a kind of an arcade all round the shop—so like, you'd think they were going to speak to you."

Before going finally off, Madame Cardinal went through a piece of very deep hypocrisy. We have seen how she hesitated about leaving the portress alone with the sick man:—

"Madame Perrache," she said to her, "you won't leave him, the poor darling, will you, till I get back?"

It may have been noticed that Cerizet had not decided on any definite course of action in the new affair he was now undertaking. The part of doctor, which for a moment he thought of assuming, frightened him, and he gave himself out, as we have seen, to Madame Perrache as the business agent of his accomplice. Once alone, he began to see that his original idea complicated with a doctor, a nurse, and a notary, presented the most serious difficulties. A regular will drawn in favor of Madame Cardinal was not a thing to be improvised in a moment. It would take some time to acclimatize the idea in the surly and suspicious mind of the old pauper, and death, which was close at hand, might play them a trick at any moment, and balk the most careful preparations.

It was true that unless a will were made the income of eight thousand francs on the Grand Livre and the house in the rue Notre-Dame de Nazareth would go to the heirs-at-law, and Madame Cardinal would get only her share of the property; but the abandonment of this visible portion of the inheritance was the surest means of laying hands on the invisible part of it. Besides, if the latter were secured, what hindered their returning to the idea of a will?

Resolving, therefore, to confine the *operation* to the simplest terms at first, Cerizet summed them up in the manoeuvre of the poppy-heads, already mentioned, and he was making his way back to Toupillier's abode, armed with that single weapon of war, intending to give Madame Cardinal further instructions, when he met her, bearing on her arm the basket she had just bought; and in that basket was the sick man's panacea.

"Upon my word!" cried the usurer, "is this the way you keep your watch?"

"I had to go out and buy him wine," replied the Cardinal; "he is howling like a soul in hell that he wants to be at peace, and to be let alone, and get his wine! It is his one idea that Roussillon is good for his disease. Well, when he has drunk it, I dare say he will be quieter."

"You are right," said Cerizet, sententiously; "never contradict a sick man. But this wine, you know, ought to be improved; by infusing these" (and lifting one of the covers of the basket he slipped in the poppies) "you'll procure the poor man a good, long sleep,—five or six hours at least. This evening I'll come and see you, and nothing, I think, need prevent us from examining a little closer those matters of inheritance."

"I see," said Madame Cardinal, winking.

"To-night, then," said Cerizet, not wishing to prolong the conversation.

He had a strong sense of the difficulty and danger of the affair, and was very reluctant to be seen in the street conversing with his accomplice.

Returning to her uncle's garret, Madame Cardinal found him still in a state of semi-torpor; she relieved Madame Perrache, and bade her good-bye, going to the door to receive a supply of wood, all sawed, which she had ordered from the Auvergnat in the rue Ferou.

Into an earthen pot, which she had bought of the right size to fit upon the hole in the stoves of the poor where they put their soup-kettles, she now threw the poppies, pouring over them two-thirds of the wine she had brought back with her. Then she lighted a fire beneath the pot, intending to obtain the decoction agreed upon as quickly as possible. The crackling of the wood and the heat, which soon spread about the room, brought Toupillier out of his stupor. Seeing the stove lighted he called out:—

"Who is making a fire here? Do you want to burn the house down?"

"Why, uncle," said the Cardinal, "it is wood I bought with my own money, to warm your wine. The doctor doesn't want you to drink it cold."

"Where is it, that wine?" demanded Toupillier, calming down a little at the thought that the fire was not burning at his expense.

"It must come to a boil," said his nurse; "the doctor insisted upon that. Still, if you'll be good I'll give you half a glass of it cold, just to wet your whistle. I'll take that upon myself, but don't you tell the doctor."

"Doctor! I won't have a doctor; they are all scoundrels, invented to kill people," cried Toupillier, whom the idea of drink had revived. "Come, give me the wine!" he said, in the tone of a man whose patience had come to an end.

Convinced that though this compliance would do no harm it could do no good, Madame Cardinal poured out half a glass, and while she gave it with one hand to the sick man, with the other she raised him to a sitting posture that he might drink it.

With his fleshless, eager fingers Toupillier clutched the glass, emptied it at a gulp, and exclaimed:—

"Ah! that's a fine drop, that is! though you've watered it."

"You mustn't say that, uncle; I went and bought it myself of Pere Legrelu, and I've given it you quite pure. But you let me simmer the rest; the doctor said I might then give you all you wanted."

Toupillier resigned himself with a shrug of the shoulders. At the end of fifteen minutes, the infusion being in condition to serve, Madame Cardinal brought him, without further appeal, a full cup of it.

The avidity with which the old pauper drank it down prevented him from noticing at first that the wine was drugged; but as he swallowed the last drops he tasted the sickly and nauseating flavor, and flinging the cup on the bed he cried out that some one was trying to poison him.

"Poison! nonsense!" said the fishwife, pouring into her own mouth a few drops of that which remained in the bottle, declaring to the old man that if the wine did not seem to him the same as usual, it was because his mouth had a "bad taste to it."

Before the end of the dispute, which lasted some time, the narcotic began to take effect, and at the end of an hour the sick man was sound asleep.

While idly waiting for Cerizet, an idea took possession of the Cardinal's mind. She thought that in view of their comings and goings with the treasure, it would be well if the vigilance of the Perrache husband and wife could be dulled in some manner. Consequently, after carefully flinging the refuse poppy-heads into the privy, she called to the portress:—

"Madame Perrache, come up and taste his wine. Wouldn't you have thought to hear him talk he was ready to drink a cask of it? Well, a cupful satisfied him."

"Your health!" said the portress, touching glasses with the Cardinal, who was careful to have hers filled with the unboiled wine. Less accomplished as a gourmet than the old beggar, Madame Perrache perceived nothing in the insidious liquid (cold by the time she drank it) to make her suspect its narcotic character; on the contrary, she declared it was "velvet," and wished that her husband were there to have a share in the treat. After a rather long gossip, the two women separated. Then, with the cooked meat she had provided for herself, and the remains of the Roussillon, Madame Cardinal made a repast which she finished off with a siesta. Without mentioning the emotions of the day, the influence of one of the most heady wines of the country would have sufficed to explain the soundness of her sleep; when she woke darkness was coming on.

Her first care was to give a glance at her patient; his sleep was restless, and he was dreaming aloud.

"Diamonds," he said; "those diamonds? At my death, but not before."

"Gracious!" thought Madame Cardinal, "that was the one thing lacking,— diamonds! that he should have diamonds!"

Then, as Toupillier seemed to be in the grasp of a violent nightmare, she leaned over him so as not to lose a word of his speech, hoping to gather from it some important revelation. At this moment a slight rap given to the door, from which the careful nurse had removed the key, announced the arrival of Cerizet.

"Well?" he said, on entering.

"He has taken the drug. He's been sound asleep these two hours; just now, in dreaming, he was talking of diamonds."

"Well," said Cerizet, "it wouldn't be surprising if we found some. These paupers when they set out to be rich, like to pile up everything."

"Ah ca!" cried the Cardinal, suddenly, "what made you go and tell Mere Perrache that you were my man of business, and that you weren't a doctor? I thought we agreed this morning that you were coming as a doctor?"

Cerizet did not choose to admit that the usurpation of that title had seemed to him dangerous; he feared to discourage his accomplice.

"I saw that the woman was going to propose a consultation," he replied, "and I got out of it that way."

"Goodness!" exclaimed Madame Cardinal, "they say fine minds come together; that was my dodge, too. Calling you my man of business seemed to give that old pilferer a few ideas. Did they see you come in, those porters?"

"I thought, as I went by," replied Cerizet, "that the woman was asleep in her chair."

"And well she might be," said the Cardinal, significantly.

"What, really?" said Cerizet.

"Parbleu!" replied the fishwife; "what's enough for one is enough for two; the rest of the stuff went that way."

"As for the husband, he was there," said Cerizet; "for he gave me a gracious sign of recognition, which I could have done without."

"Wait till it is quite dark, and we'll play him a comedy that shall fool him finely."

Accordingly, ten minutes later, the fishwife, with a vim that delighted the usurer, organized for the innocent porter the comedy of a *monsieur* who would not, out of politeness, let her accompany him to the door; she herself with equal politeness insisting. Appearing to conduct the sham physician into the street gate she pretended that the wind had blown out of her lamp, and under pretext of relighting it she put out that of Perrache. All this racket, accompanied by exclamations and a bewildering loquacity, was so briskly carried out that the porter, if summoned before the police-court, would not have hesitated to swear that the doctor, whose arrival he had witnessed, left the house between nine and ten o'clock.

When the two accomplices were thus in tranquil possession of the field of operations Madame Cardinal hung up her rabbit's-hair shawl before the window to exclude all possible indiscretion on the part of a neighbor. In the Luxembourg quarter life quiets down early. By ten o'clock all the sounds in the house as well as those out of doors were stilled, and Cerizet declared that the moment had come to go to work; by beginning at once they were certain that the sleeper would remain under the influence of the drug; besides, if the booty were found at once, Madame Cardinal could, under pretence of a sudden attack on her patient, which required her to fetch a remedy from the apothecary, get the porter to open the street gate for her without suspicion. As all porters pull the gate-cord from their beds, Cerizet would be able to get away at the same time without notice.

Powerful in advice, Cerizet was a very incapable hand in action; and, without the robust assistance of Mere Cardinal he could never have lifted what might almost be called the corpse of the former drum-major. Completely insensible, Toupillier was now an inert mass, a dead-weight, which could, fortunately, be handled without much precaution, and the athletic Madame Cardinal, gathering strength from her cupidity, contrived, notwithstanding Cerizet's insufficient assistance, to effect the transfer of her uncle from one bed to the other.

On rummaging the bed from which the body was moved, nothing was found, and Madame Cardinal, pressed by Cerizet to explain why she had confidently asserted that her uncle "was lying on one hundred thousand francs in gold," was forced to admit that a talk with Madame Perrache, and her own fervid imagination were the sole grounds of her certainty. Cerizet was furious; having for one whole day dallied with the idea and hope of fortune, having, moreover, entered upon a dangerous and compromising course of action, only to find himself, at the supreme moment, face to face with—nothing! The disappointment was so bitter that if he had not been afraid of the muscular strength of his future mother-in-law, he would have rushed upon her with some frantic intention.

His anger, however, spent itself in words. Harshly abused, Madame Cardinal contented herself by remarking that all hope was not lost, and then, with a faith that ought to have moved mountains, she set to work to empty the straw from the mattress she had already vainly explored in all directions. But Cerizet would not allow that extreme measure; he remarked that after the autopsy of a straw mattress such detritus would remain upon the floor as must infallibly give rise to suspicion. But the Cardinal, who thought this caution ridiculous, was determined to, at least, take apart the flock bedstead. The passion of the search gave extraordinary vigilance to her senses, and as she raised the wooden side-frame she heard the fall of some tiny object on the floor. Seizing the light she began to search in the mound of filth of all kinds that was under the bed, and finally laid her hand on a bit of polished steel about half an inch long, the use of which was to her inexplicable.

"That's a key!" cried Cerizet, who was standing beside her with some indifference, but whose imagination now set off at a gallop.

"Ha! ha! you see I was right," cried the Cardinal. "But what can it open?" she added, on reflection; "nothing bigger than a doll's house."

"No," said Cerizet, "it is a modern invention, and very strong locks can be opened with that little instrument."

With a rapid glance he took in all the pieces of furniture in the room; went to the bureau and pulled out the drawers; looked in the stove, in the table; but nowhere did he find a lock to which the little key could be adapted.

Suddenly the Cardinal had a flash of illumination.

"See here!" she said. "I remarked that the old thief, as he lay on his bed, never took his eyes off the wall just opposite to him."

"A cupboard hidden in the wall!" cried Cerizet, seizing the light eagerly; "it is not impossible!"

Examining attentively the door of the alcove, which was opposite the bed's head, he could see nothing there but a vast accumulation of dust and spiders' webs. He next employed the sense of touch, and began to rap and sound the wall in all directions. At the spot to which Toupillier's constant gaze was directed he thought he perceived in a very narrow space a slight sonority, and he presently perceived that he was rapping on wood. He then rubbed the spot vigorously with his handkerchief, and beneath the thick layer of dust and dirt which he thus removed he found a piece of oak plank carefully inserted in the wall. On one side of this plank was a small round hole; it was that of the lock which the key fitted!

While Cerizet was turning the key, which worked with great difficulty, Madame Cardinal, holding the light, was pale and breathless; but, oh! cruel deception! the cupboard, at last unlocked and open, showed only an empty space, into which the light in her hand fell uselessly.

Allowing this bacchante to give vent to her despair by saluting her much-beloved uncle with the harshest epithets, Cerizet quietly inserted his arm into the cupboard, and after feeling it over at the back, he cried out, "An iron safe!" adding, impatiently, "Give me more light, Madame Cardinal."

Then, as the light did not penetrate to the depths of the cupboard, he snatched the candle from the bottle, where, in default of a candlestick, the Cardinal had stuck it, and, taking it in his hand, moved it carefully over all parts of the iron safe, the existence of which was now a certainty.

"There is no visible lock," he said. "There must be a secret opening."

"Isn't he sly, that old villain!" exclaimed Madame Cardinal, while Cerizet's bony fingers felt the side of the safe over minutely.

"Ha!" he exclaimed, after groping for ten minutes, "I have it!"

During this time Madame Cardinal's life seemed actually suspended.

Under the pressure which Cerizet now applied, the iron side rose quickly into the thickness of the wall above, and in the midst of a mass of gold thrown pell-mell into a large excavation that was now exposed to view, lay a case of red morocco, which, from its size and appearance, gave promise of magnificent booty.

"I take the diamonds for myself," said Cerizet, when he had opened the case and seen the splendid jewels it contained; "you won't know how to get rid of them. I'll leave you the gold for your share. As for the house and the money in the Funds, they are not worth the trouble it would be to get the old fellow to make a will."

"Not so fast, my little man!" replied the Cardinal, who thought this decision rather summary; "we will first count the money—"

"Hush!" exclaimed Cerizet, apparently listening to a sound.

"What is it?" asked the Cardinal.

"Don't you hear some one moving below?"

"No, I hear nothing."

Cerizet, making her a sign to be silent, listened attentively.

"I hear a step on the stairs," he said, a moment later.

Then he hastily replaced the morocco case, and made desperate but unavailing efforts to lower the panel.

"Yes!" cried Madame Cardinal, terrified; "some one is really coming." Then, fastening to a hope of safety, she added, "I dare say it is that insane girl; they say she walks at night."

At any rate, the insane girl (if it were she) had a key to the room, for a moment later, this key was inserted in the lock. With a rapid glance Madame Cardinal measured the distance to the door; should she have time to push the bolt? No; certain that it was then too late, so she blew out the candle to give herself at least some chances in the darkness.

Useless effort! the intruder who now appeared had brought a candle with him.

When Madame Cerizet saw that she had to do with a small, old man of puny appearance, she flung herself before him with flaming eyes, like a lioness from whom the hunter is seeking to take her cubs.

"Be calm, my good woman," said the little man, in a jeering tone; "the police are sent for; they will be here in a moment."

At the word "police" the Cardinal's legs gave way.

"But, monsieur," she said, "why the police? we are not robbers."

"No matter for that; if I were in your place I shouldn't wait for them," said the little old man; "they make unfortunate mistakes sometimes."

"Can I clear out?" asked the woman, incredulously.

"Yes, if you empty your pockets of anything which has, *by accident*, got into them."

"Oh! my good monsieur, I haven't a thing in my hands or my pockets; I wasn't here to harm any one,—only to nurse my poor dear uncle; you can search me."

"Come, be off with you! that will do," said the old man.

Madame Cardinal did not oblige him to repeat the order, and she rapidly disappeared down the staircase.

Cerizet made as though he would take the same road.

"You, monsieur, are quite another thing," said the little old man. "You and I must talk together; but if you are tractable, the affair between us can be settled amicably."

Whether it was that the narcotic had ceased to operate, or that the noise going on about Toupillier put an end to his sleep, he now opened his eyes and cast around him the glance of a man who endeavors to remember where he is; then, seeing his precious cupboard open, he found in the emotion that sight produced the strength to cry out two or three times, "Help! help! robbers!" in a voice that was loud enough to rouse the house.

"No, Toupillier," said the little old man; "you have not been robbed; I came here in time to prevent it; nothing has been taken."

"Why don't you arrest that villain?" shouted the old pauper, pointing to Cerizet.

"Monsieur is not a thief," replied the old man. "On the contrary, he came up with me to lend assistance." Then, turning to Cerizet, he added, in a low voice: "I think, my good friend, that we had better postpone the interview I desire to have with you until to-morrow. Come at ten o'clock to the adjoining house, and ask for Monsieur du Portail. After what has passed this evening, there will, I ought to warn you, be some danger to you in not accepting this conference. I shall find you elsewhere, infallibly; for I have the honor to know who you are; you are the man whom the Opposition journals were accustomed to call 'the courageous Cerizet.'"

In spite of the profound sarcasm of this remark, Cerizet, perceiving that he was not to be treated more rigorously than Madame Cardinal, felt so pleased with this conclusion that he promised, very readily, to keep the appointment, and then slipped away with all the haste he could.

CHAPTER XVI. DU PORTAIL

The next day Cerizet did not fail to appear at the rendezvous given to him. Examined, at first, through the wicket of the door, he was admitted, after giving his name, into the house, and was ushered immediately to the study of Monsieur du Portail, whom he found at his desk.

Without rising, and merely making a sign to his guest to take a chair, the little old man continued the letter he was then writing. After sealing it with wax, with a care and precision that denoted a nature extremely fastidious and particular, or else a man accustomed to discharge diplomatic functions, du Portail rang for Bruneau, his valet, and said, as he gave him the letter:—

"For the justice-of-peace of the arrondissement."

Then he carefully wiped the steel pen he had just used, restored to their places, symmetrically, all the displaced articles on his desk, and it was only when these little arrangements were completed that he turned to Cerizet, and said:—

"You know, of course, that we lost that poor Monsieur Toupillier last night?"

"No, really?" said Cerizet, putting on the most sympathetic air he could manage. "This is my first knowledge of it."

"But you probably expected it. When one gives a dying man an immense bowl of hot wine, which has also been narcotized,—for the Perrache woman slept all night in a sort of lethargy after drinking a small glass of it,—it is evident that the catastrophe has been hastened."

"I am ignorant, monsieur," said Cerizet, with dignity, "of what Madame Cardinal may have given to her uncle. I have no doubt committed a great piece of thoughtlessness in assisting this woman to obtain an inheritance to which she assured me she had legal rights; but as to attempting the life of that old pauper, I am quite incapable of such a thing; nothing of the kind ever entered my mind."

"You wrote me this letter, I think," said du Portail, abruptly, taking from beneath a bohemian glass bowl a paper which he offered to Cerizet.

"A letter?" replied Cerizet, with the hesitation of a man who doesn't know whether to lie or speak the truth.

"I am quite sure of what I say," continued du Portail. "I have a mania for autographs, and I possess one of yours, obtained at the period when the

178

Opposition exalted you to the glorious rank of martyr. I have compared the two writings, and I find that you certainly wrote me, yesterday, the letter which you hold in your hand, informing me of the money embarrassments of young la Peyrade at the present moment."

"Well," said Cerizet, "knowing that you had given a home to Mademoiselle de la Peyrade, who is probably cousin of Theodose, I thought I recognized in you the mysterious protector from whom, on more than one occasion, my friend has received the most generous assistance. Now, as I have a sincere affection for that poor fellow, it was in his interests that I permitted myself—"

"You did quite right," interrupted du Portail. "I am delighted to have fallen in with a friend of la Peyrade. I ought not to conceal from you that it was this particular fact which protected you last night. But tell me, what is this about notes for twenty-five thousand francs? Is our friend so badly off in his affairs? Is he leading a dissipated life?"

"On the contrary," replied Cerizet, "he's a puritan. Given to the deepest piety, he did not choose to take, as a barrister, any other cases but those of the poor. He is now on the point of making a rich marriage."

"Ah! is he going to be married? and to whom?"

"To a Demoiselle Colleville, daughter of the secretary of the mayor of the 12th arrondissement. In herself, the girl has no fortune, but a certain Monsieur Thuillier, her godfather, member of the Council-general of the Seine, has promised her a suitable 'dot.'"

"Who has handled this affair?"

"La Peyrade has been devoted to the Thuillier family, into which he was introduced by Monsieur Dutocq, clerk of the justice-of-peace of their arrondissement."

"But you wrote me that these notes were signed in favor of Monsieur Dutocq. The affair is a bit of matrimonial brokerage, in short?"

"Well, something of that kind," replied Cerizet. "You know, monsieur, that in Paris such transactions are very common. Even the clergy won't disdain to have a finger in them."

"Is the marriage a settled thing?"

"Yes, and within the last few days especially."

"Well, my good sir, I rely on you to put an end to it. I have other views for Theodose,—another marriage to propose to him."

"Excuse me!" said Cerizet, "to break up this marriage would make it

179

impossible for him to pay his notes; and I have the honor to call your attention to the fact that these particular bills of exchange are serious matters. Monsieur Dutocq is in the office of the justice-of-peace; in other words, he couldn't be easily defeated in such a matter."

"The debt to Monsieur Dutocq you shall buy off yourself," replied du Portail. "Make arrangements with him to that effect. Should Theodose prove reluctant to carry out my plans, those notes may become a useful weapon in our hands. You will take upon yourself to sue him for them, and you shall have no money responsibility in the matter. I will pay you the amount of the notes for Dutocq, and your costs in suing Theodose."

"You are square in business, monsieur," said Cerizet. "There's some pleasure in being your agent. Now, if you think the right moment has come, I should be glad if you would give me some better light on the mission you are doing me the honor to place in my hands."

"You spoke just now," replied du Portail, "of the cousin of Theodose, Mademoiselle Lydie de la Peyrade. This young woman, who is not in her first youth, for she is nearly thirty, is the natural daughter of the celebrated Mademoiselle Beaumesnil of the Theatre Francais and Peyrade, the commissary-general of police under the Empire, and the uncle of our friend. Until his death, which occurred suddenly, leaving his daughter, whom he loved tenderly, without means of support, I was bound to that excellent man with the warmest friendship."

Glad to show that he had some knowledge of du Portail's interior life, Cerizet hastened to remark:—

"And you have secretly fulfilled the duties of that friendship, monsieur; for, in taking into your home that interesting orphan you assumed a difficult guardianship. Mademoiselle de la Peyrade's state of health requires, I am told, a care not only affectionate, but persevering."

"Yes," replied du Portail, "the poor girl, after the death of her father, was so cruelly tried that her mind has been somewhat affected; but a fortunate change has lately occurred in her condition, and only yesterday I called in consultation Doctor Bianchon and the two physicians-in-charge of Bicetre and the Salpetriere. These gentlemen unanimously declare that marriage and the birth of a first child would undoubtedly restore her to perfect health. You can readily understand that the remedy is too easy and agreeable not to be attempted."

"Then," said Cerizet, "it is to Mademoiselle Lydie de la Peyrade, his cousin, that you wish to marry Theodose."

"You have said it," returned du Portail, "and you must not think that our young friend, if he accepts the marriage, will be called upon to show a gratuitous devotion. Lydie is very agreeable in person; she has talents, a charming disposition, and she can bring to bear, in her husband's interest, a strong influence in public life. She has, moreover, a pretty fortune, consisting of what her mother left her, and of my entire property, which, having no heirs myself, I intend to secure to her in the marriage contract. Besides all this, she has this very night acquired a not inconsiderable legacy."

"What!" exclaimed Cerizet, "do you mean that old Toupillier—"

"By a will in his own handwriting, which I have here, that old pauper constitutes her his sole legatee. You see, therefore, that I showed some kindness in not proceeding against you and Madame Cardinal for your little attempt last night; it was simply our property that you were trying to pillage."

"Heavens!" cried Cerizet, "I won't pretend to excuse Madame Cardinal's misconduct; and yet, as one of the legal heirs, dispossessed by a stranger, she had, it seems to me, some right to the indulgence which you certainly showed to her."

"In that you are mistaken," said du Portail; "the apparent liberality of the old beggar to Mademoiselle de la Peyrade happens to be only a restitution."

"A restitution!" exclaimed Cerizet, in a tone of curiosity.

"A restitution," repeated du Portail, "and nothing is easier than to prove it. Do you remember the robbery of some diamonds from one of our dramatic celebrities about ten years ago?"

"Yes," replied Cerizet. "I was manager of one of my newspapers at the time, and I used to write the 'Paris items.' But stay, I remember, the actress who lost them was Mademoiselle Beaumesnil."

"Precisely; the mother of Mademoiselle de la Peyrade."

"Consequently, this miserable old Toupillier—no, I remember that the thief was convicted; his name was Charles Crochard. It was said, under the rose, that he was the natural son of a great personage, the Comte de Granville, attorney-general under the Restoration." [See "A Double Life."]

"Well," said du Portail, "this is how it happened. The robbery was committed in a house in the rue de Tournon, occupied by Mademoiselle Beaumesnil. Charles Crochard, who was a handsome fellow, was said to have the run of it—"

"Yes, yes," cried Cerizet, "I remember Mademoiselle Beaumesnil's embarrassment when she gave her testimony—and also the total extinction of voice that attacked her when the judge asked her age."

"The robbery," continued du Portail, "was audaciously committed in the daytime; and no sooner did Charles Crochard get possession of the casket than he went to the church of Saint-Sulpice, where he had an appointment with an accomplice, who, being supplied with a passport, was to start immediately with the diamonds for foreign parts. It so chanced that on entering the church, instead of meeting the man he expected, who was a trifle late, Charles Crochard came face to face with a celebrated agent of the detective force, who was well known to him, inasmuch as the young rascal was not at his first scrimmage with the police. The absence of his accomplice, this encounter with the detective, and, lastly, a rapid movement made by the latter, by the merest chance, toward the door, induced the robber to fancy he was being watched. Losing his head under this idea, he wanted, at any cost, to put the casket out of his possession, knowing that if arrested, as he expected, at the door of the church, it would be a damning proof against him. Catching sight at that moment of Toupillier, who was then the giver of holy water, 'My man,' said he, making sure that no one overheard their colloquy, 'will you take care of this little package for me? It is a box of lace. I am going near by to a countess who is slow to pay her bill; and if I have the lace with me she'll want to see it, for it is a new style, and she'll ask me to leave it with her on credit, instead of paying the bill; therefore I don't want to take it. But,' he added, 'be sure not to touch the paper that wraps the box, for there's nothing harder than to do up a package in the same folds—'"

"The booby!" cried Cerizet, naively; "why, that very caution would make the man want to open it."

"You are an able casuist," said du Portail. "Well, an hour later, Charles Crochard, finding that nothing happened to him, returned to the church to obtain his deposit, but Toupillier was no longer there. You can imagine the anxiety with which Charles Crochard attended early mass the next day, and approached the giver of holy water, who was there, sure enough, attending to his functions. But night, they say, brings counsel; the worthy beggar audaciously declared that he had received no package, and did not know what his interlocutor meant."

"And there was no possibility of arguing with him, for that would be exposure," remarked Cerizet, who was not far from sympathizing in a trick so boldly played.

"No doubt," resumed du Portail; "the robbery was already noised about, and Toupillier, who was a very able fellow, had calculated that Charles Crochard would not dare to publicly accuse him, for that would reveal the theft. In fact, on his trial Charles Crochard never said a word of his mishap, and during the six years he spent at the galleys (he was condemned to ten, but four were remitted) he did not open his lips to a single soul about the treachery of which he had been a victim."

"That was pretty plucky," said Cerizet; the tale excited him, and he showed openly that he saw the matter as an artist and a connoisseur.

"In that interval," continued du Portail, "Madame Beaumesnil died, leaving her daughter a few fragments of a once great fortune, and the diamonds which the will expressly stated Lydie was to receive 'in case they were recovered.'"

"Ha! ha!" exclaimed Cerizet, "bad for Toupillier, because, having to do with a man of your calibre—"

"Charles Crochard's first object on being liberated was vengeance on Toupillier, and his first step was to denounce him to the police as receiver of the stolen property. Taken in hand by the law, Toupillier defended himself with such singular good-humor, being able to show that no proof whatever existed against him, that the examining judge let him off. He lost his place, however, as giver of holy water, obtaining, with great difficulty, permission to beg at the door of the church. For my part, I was certain of his guilt; and I managed to have the closest watch kept upon him; though I relied far more upon myself. Being a man of means and leisure, I stuck, as you may say, to the skin of my thief, and did, in order to unmask him, one of the cleverest things of my career. He was living at that time in the rue du Coeur-Volant. I succeeded in becoming the tenant of the room adjoining his; and one night, through a gimlet hole I had drilled in the partition, I saw my man take the case of diamonds from a very cleverly contrived hiding-place. He sat for an hour gazing at them and fondling them; he made them sparkle in the light, he pressed them passionately to his lips. The man actually loved those diamonds for themselves, and had never thought of turning them to money."

"I understand," said Cerizet,—"a mania like that of Cardillac, the jeweller, which has now been dramatized."

"That is just it," returned du Portail; "the poor wretch was in love with that casket; so that when, shortly after, I entered his room and told him I knew all, he proposed to me to leave him the life use of what he called the consolation of his old age, pledging himself to make Mademoiselle de la Peyrade his sole heir, revealing to me at the same time the existence of a hoard of gold (to which he was adding every day), and also the possession of a house and an investment in the Funds."

"If he made that proposal in good faith," said Cerizet, "it was a desirable one. The interest of the capital sunk in the diamonds was more than returned by that from the other property."

"You now see, my dear sir," said du Portail, "that I was not mistaken in trusting him. All my precautions were well taken; I exacted that he should occupy a room in the house I lived in, where I could keep a close eye upon him. I assisted him in making that hiding-place, the secret of which you discovered so cleverly; but what you did not find out was that in touching the spring that opened the iron safe you rang a bell in my apartment, which warned me of any attempt that was made to remove our treasure."

"Poor Madame Cardinal!" cried Cerizet, good-humoredly, "how far she was from suspecting it!"

"Now here's the situation," resumed du Portail. "On account of the interest I feel in the nephew of my old friend, and also, on account of the relationship, this marriage seems to me extremely desirable; in short, I unite Theodose to his cousin and her 'dot.' As it is possible that, considering the mental state of his future wife, Theodose may object to sharing my views, I have not thought it wise to make this proposal directly to himself. You have suddenly turned up upon my path; I know already that you are clever and wily, and that knowledge induces me to put this little matrimonial negotiation into your hands. Now, I think, you understand the matter thoroughly; speak to him of a fine girl, with one little drawback, but, on the other hand, a comfortable fortune. Do not name her to him; and come here and let me know how the proposal has been taken."

"Your confidence delights me as much as it honors me," replied Cerizet, "and I will justify it the best I can."

"We must not expect too much," said du Portail. "Refusal will be the first impulse of a man who has an affair on hand elsewhere; but we need not consider ourselves beaten. I shall not easily give up a plan which I know to be just, even if I push my zeal so far as to put la Peyrade under lock and key in Clichy. I am resolved not to take no for his answer to a proposal of which, in the end, he cannot fail to see the propriety. Therefore, in any case, buy up those notes from Monsieur Dutocq."

"At par?" asked Cerizet.

"Yes, at par, if you cannot do better; we are not going to haggle over a few thousand francs; only, when this transaction is arranged, Monsieur Dutocq must pledge us either his assistance, or, at the very least, his neutrality. After what you have said of the other marriage, it is unnecessary for me to warn you that there is not a moment to lose in putting our irons into the fire."

"Two days hence I have an appointment with la Peyrade," said Cerizet. "We have a little matter of business of our own to settle. Don't you think it would be best to wait till then, when I can introduce the proposal incidentally? In case of resistance, I think that arrangement would best conduce to OUR dignity."

"So be it," said du Portail; "it isn't much of a delay. Remember, monsieur, that if you succeed you have, in place of a man able to bring you to a stern account for your *imprudent assistance* to Madame Cardinal, a greatly obliged person, who will be ready at all times to serve you, and whose influence is greater than is generally supposed."

After these friendly words, the pair separated with a thoroughly good understanding, and well satisfied with each other.

CHAPTER XVII. IN WHICH THE LAMB DEVOURS THE WOLF

The evening before the day already agreed upon, Theodose received from Cerizet the following note:—

"To-morrow, lease or no lease, Rocher de Cancale, half-past six o'clock."

As for Dutocq, Cerizet saw him every day, for he was still his copying clerk; he therefore gave him his invitation by word of mouth; but the attentive reader must remark a difference in the hour named: "Quarter-past-six, Rocher de Cancale," said Cerizet. It was evident, therefore, that he wanted that fifteen minutes with Dutocq before the arrival of la Peyrade.

These minutes the usurer proposed to employ in jockeying Dutocq in the purchase of the notes; he fancied that if the proposition to buy them were suddenly put before him without the slightest preparation it might be more readily received. By not leaving the seller time to bethink himself, perhaps he might lead him to loosen his grasp, and the notes once bought below par, he could consider at his leisure whether to pocket the difference or curry favor with du Portail for the discount he had obtained. Let us say, moreover, that apart from self-interest, Cerizet would still have endeavored to scrape a little profit out of his friend; 'twas an instinct and a need of his nature. He had as great a horror for straight courses as the lovers of English gardens show in the lines of their paths.

Dutocq, having still a portion of the cost of his practice to pay off, was forced to live very sparingly, so that a dinner at the Rocher de Cancale was something of an event in the economy of his straitened existence. He arrived, therefore, with that punctuality which testifies to an interest in the occasion, and precisely at a quarter past six he entered the private room of the restaurant where Cerizet awaited him.

"It is queer," he said; "here we are returned to precisely the situation in which we began our business relationship with la Peyrade,—except, to be sure, that this present place of meeting of the three emperors is more comfortable; I prefer the Tilsit of the rue Montgorgeuil to the Tilsit of the Cheval Rouge."

"Faith!" said Cerizet, "I don't know that the results justify the change, for, to be frank, where are the profits to *us* in the scheme of our triumvirate?"

"But," said Dutocq, "it was a bargain with a long time limit. It can't be said that la Peyrade has lost much time in getting installed—forgive the pun—at the Thuilleries. The scamp has made his way pretty fast, you must own that."

"Not so fast but what his marriage," said Cerizet, "is at the present moment a very doubtful thing."

"Doubtful!" cried Dutocq; "why doubtful?"

"Well, I am commissioned to propose to him another wife, and I'm not sure that any choice is left to him."

"What the devil are you about, my dear fellow, lending your hand in this way to another marriage when you know we have a mortgage on the first?"

"One isn't always master of circumstances, my friend; I saw at once when the new affair was laid before me that the one we had settled on must infallibly go by the board. Consequently, I've tried to work it round in our interests, yours and mine."

"Ah ca! do you mean they are pulling caps for this Theodose? Who is the new match? Has she money?"

"The 'dot' is pretty good; quite as much as Mademoiselle Colleville's."

"Then I wouldn't give a fig for it. La Peyrade has signed those notes and he will pay them."

"Will he pay them? that's the question. You are not a business man, neither is Theodose; it may come into his head to dispute the validity of those notes. What security have we that if the facts about their origin should come out, and the Thuillier marriage shouldn't come off, the court of commerce mightn't annul them as 'obligations without cause.' For my part, I should laugh at such a decision; I can stand it; and, moreover, my precautions are taken; but you, as clerk to a justice-of-peace, don't you see that such an affair would give the chancellor a bone to pick with you?"

"But, my good fellow," said Dutocq, with the ill-humor of a man who sees himself face to face with an argument he can't refute, "you seem to have a mania for stirring up matters and meddling with—"

"I tell you again," said Cerizet, "this came to me; I didn't seek it; but I saw at once that there was no use struggling against the influence that is opposing us; so I chose the course of saving ourselves by a sacrifice."

"A sacrifice! what sort of sacrifice?"

"Parbleu! I've sold my share of those notes, leaving those who bought them to fight it out with Master barrister."

"Who is the purchaser?"

"Who do you suppose would step into my shoes unless it were the persons who have an interest in this other marriage, and who want to hold a power over Theodose, and control him by force if necessary."

"Then my share of the notes is equally important to them?"

"No doubt; but I couldn't speak for you until I had consulted you."

"What do they offer?"

"Hang it! my dear fellow, the same that I accepted. Knowing better than you the danger of their competition I sold out to them on very bad terms."

"Well, but what are they, those terms?"

"I gave up my shares for fifteen thousand francs."

"Come, come!" said Dutocq, shrugging his shoulders, "what you are after is to recover a loss (if you made it) by a commission on my share—and perhaps, after all, the whole thing is only a plot between you and la Peyrade —"

"At any rate, my good friend, you don't mince your words; an infamous thought comes into your head and you state it with charming frankness. Luckily you shall presently hear me make the proposal to Theodose, and you are clever enough to know by his manner if there has been any connivance between us."

"So be it!" said Dutocq. "I withdraw the insinuation; but I must say your employers are pirates; I call their proposal throttling people. I have not, like you, something to fall back upon."

"Well, you poor fellow, this is how I reasoned: I said to myself, That good Dutocq is terribly pressed for the last payment on his practice; this will give him enough to pay it off at one stroke; events have proved that there are great uncertainties about our Theodose-and-Thuillier scheme; here's money down, live money, and therefore it won't be so bad a bargain after all."

"It is a loss of two-fifths!"

"Come," said Cerizet, "you were talking just now of commissions. I see a means of getting one for you if you'll engage to batter down this Colleville marriage. If you will cry it down as you have lately cried it up I shouldn't despair of getting you a round twenty thousand out of the affair."

"Then you think that this new proposal will not be agreeable to la Peyrade, —that he'll reject it? Is it some heiress on whom he has already taken a mortgage?"

"All that I can tell you is that these people expect some difficulty in bringing the matter to a conclusion."

"Well, I don't desire better than to follow your lead and do what is disagreeable to la Peyrade; but five thousand francs—think of it!—it is too much to lose."

At this moment the door opened, and a waiter ushered in the expected guest.

"You can serve dinner," said Cerizet to the waiter; "we are all here."

It was plain that Theodose was beginning to take wing toward higher social spheres; elegance was becoming a constant thought in his mind. He appeared in a dress suit and varnished shoes, whereas his two associates received him in frock-coats and muddy boots.

"Gentlemen," he said, "I think I am a little late, but that devil of a Thuillier is the most intolerable of human beings about a pamphlet I am concocting for him. I was unlucky enough to agree to correct the proofs with him, and over every paragraph there's a fight. 'What I can't understand,' he says, 'the public can't, either. I'm not a man of letters, but I'm a practical man'; and that's the way we battle it, page after page. I thought the sitting this afternoon would never end."

"How unreasonable you are, my dear fellow," said Dutocq; "when a man wants to succeed he must have the courage to make sacrifices. Once married, you can lift your head."

"Ah, yes!" said la Peyrade with a sigh, "I'll lift it; for since the day you made me eat this bread of anguish I've become terribly sick of it."

"Cerizet," said Dutocq, "has a plan that will feed you more succulently."

Nothing more was said at the moment, for justice had to be done to the excellent fare ordered by Cerizet in honor of his coming lease. As usually happens at dinners where affairs are likely to be discussed, each man, with his mind full of them, took pains not to approach those topics, fearing to compromise his advantages by seeming eager; the conversation, therefore, continued for a long time on general subjects, and it was not until the dessert was served that Cerizet brought himself to ask la Peyrade what had been settled about the terms of his lease.

"Nothing, my friend," replied Theodose.

"What! nothing? I certainly allowed you time enough to decide the matter."

"Well, as to that, something is decided. There will not be any principal tenant at all; Mademoiselle Brigitte is going to let the house herself."

"That's a singular thing," said Cerizet, stiffly. "After your agreement with me, I certainly did not expect such a result as this."

"How can I help it, my dear fellow? I agreed with you, barring amendments on the other side; I wasn't able to give another turn to the affair. In her natural character as a managing woman and a sample of perpetual motion, Brigitte has reflected that she might as well manage that house herself and put into her own pocket the profits you proposed to make. I said all I could about the cares and annoyances which she would certainly saddle upon herself. 'Oh! nonsense!' she said; 'they'll stir my blood and do my health good!'"

"It is pitiable!" said Cerizet. "That poor old maid will never know which end to take hold of; she doesn't imagine what it is to have an empty house, and which must be filled with tenants from garret to cellar."

"I plied her with all those arguments," replied la Peyrade; "but I couldn't move her resolution. Don't you see, my dear democrats, you stirred up the revolution of '89; you thought to make a fine speculation in dethroning the noble by the bourgeois, and the end of it is you are shoved out yourselves. This looks like paradox; but you've found out now that the peasant and clodhopper isn't malleable; he can't be forced down and kept under like the noble. The aristocracy, on behalf of its dignity, would not condescend to common cares, and was therefore dependent on a crowd of plebeian servitors to whom it had to trust for three-fourths of the actions of its own life. That was the reign of stewards and bailiffs, wily fellows, into whose hands the interests of the great families passed, and who fed and grew fat on the parings of the great fortunes they managed. But now-a-days, utilitarian theories, as they call them, have come to the fore,—'We are never so well served as by ourselves,' 'There's no shame in attending to one's own business,' and many other bourgeois maxims which have suppressed the role of intermediaries. Why shouldn't Mademoiselle Brigitte Thuillier manage her own house when dukes and peers go in person to the Bourse, where such men sign their own leases and read the deeds before they sign them, and go themselves to the notary, whom, in former days, they considered a servant.'"

During this time Cerizet had time to recover from the blow he had just received squarely in the face, and to think of the transition he had to make from one set of interests to the other, of which he was now the agent.

"What you are declaiming there is all very clever," he said, carelessly, "but the thing that proves to me our defeat is the fact that you are not on the terms with Mademoiselle Thuillier you would have us believe you are. She is slipping through your fingers; and I don't think that marriage is anything like as certain as Dutocq and I have been fancying it was."

"Well, no doubt," said la Peyrade, "there are still some touches to be given to our sketch, but I believe it is well under way."

"And I think, on the contrary, that you have lost ground; and the reason is simple: you have done those people an immense service; and that's a thing never forgiven."

"Well, we shall see," said la Peyrade. "I have more than one hold upon them."

"No, you are mistaken. You thought you did a brilliant thing in putting them on a pinnacle, but the fact is you emancipated them; they'll keep you now at heel. The human heart, particularly the bourgeois heart, is made that way. If I were in your place I shouldn't feel so sure of being on solid ground, and if something else turned up that offered me a good chance—"

"What! just because I couldn't get you the lease of that house do you want to knock everything to pieces?"

"No," said Cerizet, "I am not looking at the matter in the light of my own interests; I don't doubt that as a trustworthy friend you have done every imaginable thing to promote them; but I think the manner in which you have been shoved aside a very disturbing symptom. It even decides me to tell you something I did not intend to speak of; because, in my opinion, when persons start a course they ought to keep on steadily, looking neither forward nor back, and not allowing themselves to be diverted to other aspirations."

"Ah ca!" cried la Peyrade, "what does all this verbiage mean? Have you anything to propose to me? What's the price of it?"

"My dear Theodose," said Cerizet, paying no attention to the impertinence, "you yourself can judge of the value of discovering a young girl, well brought-up, adorned with beauty and talents and a 'dot' equal to that of Celeste, which she has in her own right, *plus* fifty thousand francs' worth of diamonds (as Mademoiselle Georges says on her posters in the provinces), and, moreover,—a fact which ought to strike the mind of an ambitious man, —a strong political influence, which she can use for a husband."

"And this treasure you hold in your hand?" said la Peyrade, in a tone of incredulity.

"Better still, I am authorized to offer it to you; in fact, I might say that I am charged to do so."

"My friend, you are poking fun at me; unless, indeed, this phoenix has some hideous or prohibitory defect."

"Well, I'll admit," said Cerizet, "that there is a slight objection, not on the score of family, for, to tell the truth, the young woman has none—"

"Ah!" said la Peyrade, "a natural child—Well, what next?"

"Next, she is not so very young,—something like twenty-nine or so; but there's nothing easier than to turn an elderly girl into a young widow if you have imagination."

"Is that all the venom in it?"

"Yes, all that is irreparable."

"What do you mean by that? Is it a case of rhinoplasty?"

Addressed to Cerizet the word had an aggressive air, which, in fact, was noticeable since the beginning of the dinner in the whole manner and conversation of the barrister. But it did not suit the purpose of the negotiator to resent it.

"No," he replied, "our nose is as well made as our foot and our waist; but we may, perhaps, have a slight touch of hysteria."

"Oh! very good," said la Peyrade; "and as from hysteria to insanity there is but a step—"

"Well, yes," interrupted Cerizet, hastily, "sorrows have affected our brain slightly; but the doctors are unanimous in their diagnosis; they all say that after the birth of the first child not a trace will remain of this little trouble."

"I am willing to admit that doctors are infallible," replied la Peyrade; "but, in spite of your discouragement, you must allow me, my friend, to persist in my suit to Mademoiselle Colleville. Perhaps it is ridiculous to confess it, but the truth is I am gradually falling in love with that little girl. It isn't that her beauty is resplendent, or that the glitter of her 'dot' has dazzled me, but I find in that child a great fund of sound sense joined to simplicity; and, what to mind is of greater consequence, her sincere and solid piety attracts me; I think a husband ought to be very happy with her."

"Yes," said Cerizet, who, having been on the stage, may very well have known his Moliere, "this marriage will crown your wishes with all good; it will be filled with sweetness and with pleasures."

The allusion to Tartuffe was keenly felt by la Peyrade, who took it up and said, hotly:—

"The contact with innocence will disinfect me of the vile atmosphere in which I have lived too long."

"And you will pay your notes of hand," added Cerizet, "which I advise you to do with the least possible delay; for Dutocq here was saying to me just now that he would like to see the color of your money."

"I? not at all," interposed Dutocq. "I think, on the contrary, that our friend has a right to the delay."

"Well," said la Peyrade, "I agree with Cerizet. I hold that the less a debt is due, and therefore the more insecure and open to contention it is, the sooner one ought to free one's self by paying it."

"But, my dear la Peyrade," said Dutocq, "why take this bitter tone?"

Pulling from his pocket a portfolio, la Peyrade said:—

"Have you those notes with you, Dutocq?"

"Faith! no, my dear fellow," replied Dutocq, "I don't carry them about with me; besides, they are in Cerizet's hands."

"Well," said the barrister, rising, "whenever you come to my house I'll pay you on the nail, as Cerizet can tell you."

"What! are you going to leave us without your coffee?" said Cerizet, amazed to the last degree.

"Yes; I have an arbitration case at eight o'clock. Besides, we have said all we had to say. You haven't your lease, but you've got your twenty five thousand francs in full, and those of Dutocq are ready for him whenever he chooses to come to my office. I see nothing now to prevent me from going where my private business calls me, and I therefore very cordially bid you good-bye."

"Ah ca! Dutocq," cried Cerizet, as la Peyrade disappeared, "this means a rupture."

"Prepared with the utmost care," added Dutocq. "Did you notice the air with which he pulled out that pocket-book?"

"But where the devil," said the usurer, "could he have got the money?"

"Probably," replied Dutocq, sarcastically, "where he got that with which he paid you in full for those notes you sold at a sacrifice."

"My dear Dutocq," said Cerizet, "I'll explain to you the circumstances under which that insolent fellow freed himself, and you'll see if he didn't rob me of fifteen thousand francs."

"Possibly, but you, my worthy clerk, were trying to get ten thousand away from me."

"No, no; I was positively ordered to buy up your claim; and you ought to remember that my offer had risen to twenty thousand when Theodose came in."

"Well," said Dutocq, "when we leave here we'll go to your house, where you will give me those notes; for, you'll understand that to-morrow morning, at the earliest decent hour, I shall go to la Peyrade's office; I don't mean to let his paying humor cool."

"And right you are; for I can tell you now that before long there'll be a fine upset in his life."

"Then the thing is really serious—this tale of a crazy woman you want him to marry? I must say that in his place, with these money-matters evidently on the rise, I should have backed out of your proposals just as he did. Ninas and Ophelias are all very well on the stage, but in a home—"

"In a home, when they bring a 'dot,' we can be their guardian," replied Cerizet, sententiously. "In point of fact, we get a fortune and not a wife."

"Well," said Dutocq, "that's one way to look at it."

"If you are willing," said Cerizet, "let us go and take our coffee somewhere else. This dinner has turned out so foolishly that I want to get out of this room, where there's no air." He rang for the waiter. "Garcon!" he said, "the bill."

"Monsieur, it is paid."

"Paid! by whom?"

"By the gentleman who just went out."

"But this is outrageous," cried Cerizet. "I ordered the dinner, and you allow some one else to pay for it!"

"It wasn't I, monsieur," said the waiter; "the gentleman went and paid the 'dame du comptoir'; she must have thought it was arranged between you. Besides, it is not so uncommon for gentlemen to have friendly disputes about paying."

"That's enough," said Cerizet, dismissing the waiter.

"Won't these gentlemen take their coffee?—it is paid for," said the man before he left the room.

"A good reason for not taking it," replied Cerizet, angrily. "It is really inconceivable that in a house of this kind such an egregious blunder should be committed. What do you think of such insolence?" he added, when the waiter had left the room.

"Bah!" exclaimed Dutocq, taking his hat, "it is a schoolboy proceeding; he

195

wanted to show he had money; it is easy to see he never had any before."

"No, no! that's not it," said Cerizet; "he meant to mark the rupture. 'I will not owe you even a dinner,' is what he says to me."

"But, after all," said Dutocq, "this banquet was given to celebrate your enthronement as principal tenant of the grand house. Well, he has failed to get you the lease, and I can understand that his conscience was uneasy at letting you pay for a dinner which, like those notes of mine, were an 'obligation without cause.'"

Cerizet made no reply to this malicious observation. They had reached the counter where reigned the dame who had permitted the improper payment, and, for the sake of his dignity, the usurer thought it proper to make a fuss. After which the two men departed, and the copying-clerk took his employer to a low coffee-house in the Passage du Saumon. There Cerizet recovered his good-humor; he was like a fish out of water suddenly returned to his native element; for he had reached that state of degradation when he felt ill at ease in places frequented by good society; and it was with a sort of sensuous pleasure that he felt himself back in the vulgar place where they were noisily playing pool for the benefit of a "former conqueror of the Bastille."

In this establishment Cerizet enjoyed the fame of being a skilful billiard-player, and he was now entreated to take part in a game already begun. In technical language, he "bought his ball"; that is, one of the players sold him his turn and his chances. Dutocq profited by this arrangement to slip away, on pretence of inquiring for a sick friend.

Presently, in his shirt-sleeves, with a pipe between his lips, Cerizet made one of those masterly strokes which bring down the house with frantic applause. As he waited a moment, looking about him triumphantly, his eye lighted on a terrible kill-joy. Standing among the spectators with his chin on his cane, du Portail was steadily watching him.

A tinge of red showed itself in Cerizet's cheeks. He hesitated to bow or to recognize the old gentleman, a most unlikely person to meet in such a place. Not knowing how to take the unpleasant encounter, he went on playing; but his hand betrayed his uneasiness, and presently an unlucky stroke threw him out of the game. While he was putting on his coat in a tolerably ill-humor, du Portail passed, almost brushing him, on his way to the door.

"Rue Montmartre, at the farther end of the Passage," said the old man, in a low tone.

When they met, Cerizet had the bad taste to try to explain the disreputable position in which he had just been detected.

"But," said du Portail, "in order to see you there, I had to be there myself."

"True," returned Cerizet. "I was rather surprised to see a quiet inhabitant of the Saint-Sulpice quarter in such a place."

"It merely proves to you," said the little old man, in a tone which cut short all explanation, and all curiosity, "that I am in the habit of going pretty nearly everywhere, and that my star leads me into the path of those persons whom I wish to meet. I was thinking of you at the very moment you came in. Well, what have you done?"

"Nothing good," replied Cerizet. "After playing me a devilish trick which deprived me of a magnificent bit of business, our man rejected your overture with scorn. There is no hope whatever in that claim of Dutocq's; for la Peyrade is chock-full of money; he wanted to pay the notes just now, and to-morrow morning he will certainly do so."

"Does he regard his marriage to this Demoiselle Colleville as a settled thing?"

"He not only considers it settled, but he is trying now to make people believe it is a love-match. He rattled off a perfect tirade to convince me that he is really in love."

"Very well," said du Portail, wishing, perhaps, to show that he could, on occasion, use the slang of a low billiard-room, "'stop the charge'" (meaning: Do nothing more); "I will undertake to bring monsieur to reason. But come and see me to-morrow, and tell me all about the family he intends to enter. You have failed in this affair; but don't mind that; I shall have others for you."

So saying, he signed to the driver of an empty citadine, which was passing, got into it, and, with a nod to Cerizet, told the man to drive to the rue Honore-Chevalier.

As Cerizet walked down the rue Montmartre to regain the Estrapade quarter, he puzzled his brains to divine who that little old man with the curt speech, the imperious manner, and a tone that seemed to cast upon all those with whom he spoke a boarding-grapnel, could be; a man, too, who came from such a distance to spend his evening in a place where, judging by his clothes alone, he had no business to be.

Cerizet had reached the Market without finding any solution to that problem, when he was roughly shaken out of it by a heavy blow in the back. Turning hastily, he found himself in presence of Madame Cardinal, an encounter with whom, at a spot where she came every morning to get fish to peddle, was certainly not surprising.

Since that evening in Toupillier's garret, the worthy woman, in spite of the clemency so promptly shown to her, had judged it imprudent to make other than very short apparitions in her own domicile, and for the last two days she had been drowning among the liquor-dealers (called "retailers of comfort") the pangs of her defeat. With flaming face and thickened voice she now addressed her late accomplice:—

"Well, papa," she said, "what happened after I left you with that little old fellow?"

"I made him understand in a very few words," replied the banker of the poor, "that it was all a mistake as to me. In this affair, my dear Madame Cardinal, you behaved with a really unpardonable heedlessness. How came you to ask my assistance in obtaining your inheritance from your uncle, when with proper inquiry you might have known there was a natural daughter, in whose favor he had long declared he should make a will? That little old man, who interrupted you in your foolish attempt to anticipate your legacy, was no other than the guardian of the daughter to whom everything is left."

"Ha! guardian, indeed! a fine thing, guardian!" cried the Cardinal. "To talk of a woman of my age, just because I wanted to see if my uncle owned anything at all, to talk to *me* of the police! It's hateful! it's *disgusting!*"

"Come, come!" said Cerizet, "you needn't complain; you got off cheaply."

"Well, and you, who broke the locks and said you were going to take the diamonds, under color of marrying my daughter! Just as if she would have you,—a legitimate daughter like her! 'Never, mother,' said she; 'never will I give my heart to a man with such a nose.'"

"So you've found her, have you?" said Cerizet.

"Not until last night. She has left her blackguard of a player, and she is now, I flatter myself, in a fine position, eating money; has her citadine by the month, and is much respected by a barrister who would marry her at once, but he has got to wait till his parents die, for the father happens to be mayor, and the government wouldn't like it."

"What mayor?"

"11th arrondissement,—Minard, powerfully rich, used to do a business in cocoa."

"Ah! very good! very good! I know all about him. You say Olympe is living with his son?"

"Well, not to say living together, for that would make talk, though he only sees her with good motives. He lives at home with his father, but he has bought their furniture, and has put it, and my daughter, too, into a lodging in the Chausee d'Antin; stylish quarter, isn't it?"

"It seems to me pretty well arranged," said Cerizet; "and as Heaven, it appears, didn't destine us for each other—"

"No, yes, well, that's how it was; and I think that girl is going to give me great satisfaction; and there's something I want to consult you about."

"What?" demanded Cerizet.

"Well, my daughter being in luck, I don't think I ought to continue to cry fish in the streets; and now that my uncle has disinherited me, I have, it seems to me, a right to an 'elementary allowance.'"

"You are dreaming, my poor woman; your daughter is a minor; it is you who ought to be feeding her; the law doesn't require her to give you aliment."

"Then do you mean," said Madame Cardinal, "that those who have nothing are to give to those who have much? A fine thing such a law as that! It's as bad as guardians who, for nothing at all, talk about calling the police. Yes! I'd like to see 'em calling the police to me! Let 'em guillotine me! It won't prevent my saying that the rich are swindlers; yes, swindlers! and the people ought to make another revolution to get their rights; and *then*, my lad, you, and my daughter, and barrister Minard, and that little old guardian, you'll all come down under it—"

Perceiving that his ex-mother-in-law was reaching stage of exaltation that was not unalarming, Cerizet hastened to get away, her epithets pursuing him for more than a hundred feet; but he comforted himself by thinking that he would make her pay for them the next time she came to his back to ask for a "convenience."

CHAPTER XVIII. SET A SAINT TO CATCH A SAINT

As he approached his own abode, Cerizet, who was nothing so little as courageous, felt an emotion of fear. He perceived a form ambushed near the door, which, as he came nearer, detached itself as if to meet him. Happily, it was only Dutocq. He came for his notes. Cerizet returned them in some ill-humor, complaining of the distrust implied in a visit at such an hour. Dutocq paid no attention to this sensitiveness, and the next morning, very early, he presented himself at la Peyrade's.

La Peyrade paid, as he had promised, on the nail, and to a few sentinel remarks uttered by Dutocq as soon as the money was in his pocket, he answered with marked coldness. His whole external appearance and behavior was that of a slave who has burst his chain and has promised himself not to make a gospel use of his liberty.

As he conducted his visitor to the door, the latter came face to face with a woman in servant's dress, who was just about to ring the bell. This woman was, apparently, known to Dutocq, for he said to her:—

"Ha ha! little woman; so we feel the necessity of consulting a barrister? You are right; at the family council very serious matters were brought up against you."

"Thank God, I fear no one. I can walk with my head up," said the person thus addressed.

"So much the better for you," replied the clerk of the justice-of-peace; "but you will probably be summoned before the judge who examines the affair. At any rate, you are in good hands here; and my friend la Peyrade will advise you for the best."

"Monsieur is mistaken," said the woman; "it is not for what he thinks that I have come to consult a lawyer."

"Well, be careful what you say and do, my dear woman, for I warn you you are going to be finely picked to pieces. The relations are furious against you, and you can't get the idea out of their heads that you have got a great deal of money."

While speaking thus, Dutocq kept his eye on Theodose, who bore the look uneasily, and requested his client to enter.

Here follows a scene which had taken place the previous afternoon between this woman and la Peyrade.

La Peyrade, we may remember, was in the habit of going to early mass at his parish church. For some little time he had felt himself the object of a singular attention which he could not explain on the part of the woman whom we have just seen entering his office, who daily attended the church at, as Dorine says, his "special hour." Could it be for love? That explanation was scarcely compatible with the maturity and the saintly, beatific air of this person, who, beneath a plain cap, called "a la Janseniste," by which fervent female souls of that sect were recognized, affected, like a nun, to hide her hair. On the other hand, the rest of her clothing was of a neatness that was almost dainty, and the gold cross at her throat, suspended by a black velvet ribbon, excluded the idea of humble and hesitating mendicity.

The morning of the day on which the dinner at the Rocher de Cancale was to take place, la Peyrade, weary of a performance which had ended by preoccupying his mind, went up to the woman and asked her pointblank if she had any request to make of him.

"Monsieur," she answered, in a tone of solemnity, "is, I think, the celebrated Monsieur de la Peyrade, the advocate of the poor?"

"I am la Peyrade; and I have had, it is true, an opportunity to render services to the indigent persons of this quarter."

"Would it, then, be asking too much of monsieur's goodness that he should suffer me to consult him?"

"This place," replied la Peyrade, "is not well chosen for such consultation. What you have to say to me seems important, to judge by the length of time you have been hesitating to speak to me. I live near here, rue Saint-Dominique d'Enfer, and if you will take the trouble to come to my office—"

"It will not annoy monsieur?"

"Not in the least; my business is to hear clients."

"At what hour—lest I disturb monsieur—?"

"When you choose; I shall be at home all the morning."

"Then I will hear another mass, at which I can take the communion. I did not dare to do so at this mass, for the thought of speaking to monsieur so distracted my mind. I will be at monsieur's house by eight o'clock, when I have ended my meditation, if that hour does not inconvenience him."

"No; but there is no necessity for all this ceremony," replied la Peyrade, with some impatience.

Perhaps a little professional jealousy inspired his ill-humor, for it was evident that he had to do with an antagonist who was capable of giving him points.

At the hour appointed, not a minute before nor a minute after, the pious woman rang the bell, and the barrister having, not without some difficulty, induced her to sit down, he requested her to state her case. She was then seized with that delaying little cough with which we obtain a respite when brought face to face with a difficult subject. At last, however, she compelled herself to approach the object of her visit.

"It is to ask monsieur," she said, "if he would be so very good as to inform me whether it is true that a charitable gentleman, now deceased, has bequeathed a fund to reward domestic servants who are faithful to their masters."

"Yes," replied la Peyrade; "that is to say, Monsieur de Montyon founded 'prizes for virtue,' which are frequently given to zealous and exemplary domestic servants. But ordinary good conduct is not sufficient; there must be some act or acts of great devotion, and truly Christian self-abnegation."

"Religion enjoins humility upon us," replied the pious woman, "and therefore I dare not praise myself; but inasmuch as for the last twenty years I have lived in the service of an old man of the dullest description, a savant, who has wasted his substance on inventions, so that I myself have had to feed and clothe him, persons have thought that I am not altogether undeserving of that prize."

"It is certainly under such conditions that the Academy selects its candidates," said la Peyrade. "What is your master's name?"

"Pere Picot; he is never called otherwise in our quarter; sometimes he goes out into the streets as if dressed for the carnival, and all the little children crowd about him, calling out: 'How d'ye do, Pere Picot! Good-morning, Pere Picot!' But that's how it is; he takes no care of his dignity; he goes about full of his own ideas; and though I kill myself trying to give him appetizing food, if you ask him what he has had for his dinner he can't tell you. Yet he's a man full of ability, and he has taught good pupils. Perhaps monsieur knows young Phellion, a professor in the College of Saint-Louis; he was one of his scholars, and he comes to see him very often."

"Then," said la Peyrade, "your master is a mathematician?"

"Yes, monsieur; mathematics have been his bane; they have flung him into a set of ideas which don't seem to have any common-sense in them ever since he has been employed at the Observatory, near here."

"Well," said la Peyrade, "you must bring testimony proving your long devotion to this old man, and I will then draw up a memorial to the Academy and take the necessary steps to present it."

"How good monsieur is!" said the pious woman, clasping her hands; "and if he would also let me tell him of a little difficulty—"

"What is it?"

"They tell me, monsieur, that to get this prize persons must be really very poor."

"Not exactly; still, the Academy does endeavor to choose whose who are in straitened circumstances, and who have made sacrifices too heavy for their means."

"Sacrifices! I think I may indeed say I have made sacrifices, for the little property I inherited from my parents has all been spent in keeping the old man, and for fifteen years I have had no wages, which, at three hundred francs a year and compound interest, amount now to a pretty little sum; as monsieur, I am sure, will agree."

At the words "compound interest," which evidenced a certain amount of financial culture, la Peyrade looked at this Antigone with increased attention.

"In short," he said, "your difficulty is—"

"Monsieur will not think it strange," replied the saintly person, "that a very rich uncle dying in England, who had never done anything for his family in his lifetime, should have left me twenty-five thousand francs."

"Certainly," said the barrister, "there's nothing in that but what is perfectly natural and proper."

"But, monsieur, I have been told that the possession of this money will prevent the judges from considering my claims to the prize."

"Possibly; because seeing you in possession of a little competence, the sacrifices which you apparently intend to continue in favor of your master will be less meritorious."

"I shall never abandon him, poor, dear man, in spite of his faults, though I know that this poor little legacy which Heaven has given me is in the greatest danger from him."

"How so?" asked la Peyrade, with some curiosity.

"Eh! monsieur, let him only get wind of that money, and he'd snap it up at a mouthful; it would all go into his inventions of perpetual motion and other machines of various kinds which have already ruined him, and me, too."

"Then," said la Peyrade, "your desire is that this legacy should remain completely unknown, not only to your master but to the judges of the Academy?"

"How clever monsieur is, and how well he understands things!" she replied, smiling.

"And also," continued the barrister, "you don't want to keep that money openly in your possession?"

"For fear my master should find it out and get it away from me? Exactly. Besides, as monsieur will understand, I shouldn't be sorry, in order to supply the poor dear man with extra comforts, that the sum should bear interest."

"And the highest possible interest," said the barrister.

"Oh! as for that, monsieur, five or six per cent."

"Very good; then it is not only about the memorial to the Academy for the prize of virtue, but also about an investment of your legacy that you have so long been desirous of consulting me?"

"Monsieur is so kind, so charitable, so encouraging!"

"The memorial, after I have made a few inquiries, will be easy enough; but an investment, offering good security, the secret of which you desire to keep, is much less readily obtained."

"Ah! if I dared to—" said the pious woman, humbly.

"What?" asked la Peyrade.

"Monsieur understands me?"

"I? not the least in the world."

"And yet I prayed earnestly just now that monsieur might be willing to keep this money for me. I should feel such confidence if it were in his hands; I know he would return it to me, and never speak of it."

La Peyrade gathered, at this instant, the fruit of his comedy of legal devotion to the necessitous classes. The choir of porters chanting his praises to the skies could alone have inspired this servant-woman with the boundless confidence of which he found himself the object. His thoughts reverted instantly to Dutocq and his notes, and he was not far from thinking that this woman had been sent to him by Providence. But the more he was inclined to profit by this chance to win his independence, the more he felt the necessity of seeming to yield only to her importunity; consequently his objections were many.

205

Moreover, he had no great belief in the character of his client, and did not care, as the common saying is, to uncover Saint Peter to cover Saint Paul; in other words, to substitute for a creditor who, after all, was his accomplice, a woman who might at any time become exacting and insist in repayment in some public manner that would injure his reputation. He decided, therefore, to play the game with a high hand.

"My good woman," he said, "I am not in want of money, and I am not rich enough to pay interest on twenty-five thousand francs for which I have no use. All that I can do for you is to place that sum, in my name, with the notary Dupuis. He is a religious man; you can see him every Sunday in the warden's pew in our church. Notaries, you know, never give receipts, therefore I could not give you one myself; I can only promise to leave among my papers, in case of death, a memorandum which will secure the restitution of the money into your hands. The affair, you see, is one of blind confidence, and I am very unwilling to make it. If I do so, it is only to oblige a person whose piety and the charitable use she intends to make of the proceeds of her little fortune entitle her to my good-will."

"If monsieur thinks that the matter cannot be otherwise arranged—"

"This appears to me the only possible way," said la Peyrade. "I shall hope to get you six per cent interest, and you may rely that it will be paid with the utmost regularity. But remember, six months, or even a year, may elapse before the notary will be in a position to repay this money, because notaries invest such trust funds chiefly in mortgages which require a certain time to mature. Now, when you have obtained the prize for virtue, which, according to all appearance, I can readily do for you, there will be no reason to hide your little property any longer,—a reason which I fully understand; but you will not be able to withdraw it from the notary's hands immediately; and in case of any difficulty arising, I should be forced to explain the situation, the manner in which you have concealed your prosperity from your master, to whom you have been supposed to be wholly devoted. This, as you will see, would put you in the position of falsely professing virtue, and would do great harm to your reputation for piety."

"Oh! monsieur," said the saintly woman, "can it be that any one would think me a person who did not speak the truth?"

"Bless you! my good creature, in business it is necessary to foresee everything. Money embroils the best friends, and leads to actions they never foresaw. Therefore reflect; you can come and see me again in a few days. It is possible that between now and then you will find some better investment; and I myself, who am doing at this moment a thing I don't altogether like, may have found other difficulties which I do not now expect."

This threat, adroitly thrown out as an afterthought, was intended to immediately clinch the matter.

"I have reflected carefully," said the pious woman, "and I feel sure that in the hands of so religious a man as monsieur I run no risks."

Taking from her bosom a little pocket-book, she pulled out twenty-five bank notes. The rapid manner in which she counted them was a revelation to la Peyrade. The woman was evidently accustomed to handle money, and a singular idea darted through his mind.

"Can it be that she is making me a receiver of stolen property? No," he said aloud, "in order to draw up the memorial for the Academy, I must, as I told you, make a few inquiries; and that will give me occasion to call upon you. At what hour can I see you alone?"

"At four o'clock, when monsieur goes to take his walk in the Luxembourg."

"And where do you live?"

"Rue du Val-de-Grace, No. 9."

"Very good; at four o'clock; and if, as I doubt not, the result of my inquiry is favorable, I will take your money then. Otherwise, if there are not good grounds for your application for the prize of virtue there will be no reason why you should make a mystery of your legacy. You could then invest it in some more normal manner than that I have suggested to you."

"Oh! how cautious monsieur is!" she said, with evident disappointment, having thought the affair settled. "This money, God be thanked! I have not stolen, and monsieur can make what inquiries he likes about me in the quarter."

"It is quite indispensable that I should do so," said la Peyrade, dryly, for he did not at all like, under this mask of simplicity, the quick intelligence that penetrated his thoughts. "Without being a thief, a woman may very well not be a Sister of Charity; there's a wide margin between the two extremes."

"As monsieur chooses," she replied; "he is doing me so great a service that I ought to let him take all precautions."

Then, with a piously humble bow, she went away, taking her money with her.

"The devil!" thought la Peyrade; "that woman is stronger than I; she swallows insults with gratitude and without the sign of a grimace! I have never yet been able to master myself like that."

He began now to fear that he had been too timid, and to think that his would-be creditor might change her mind before he could pay her the visit he had promised. But the harm was done, and, although consumed with anxiety lest he had lost a rare chance, he would have cut off a leg sooner than yield to his impulse to go to her one minute before the hour he had fixed. The information he obtained about her in the quarter was rather contradictory. Some said his client was a saint; otherwise declared her to be a sly creature; but, on the whole, nothing was said against her morality that deterred la Peyrade from taking the piece of luck she had offered him.

When he met her at four o'clock he found her in the same mind.

With the money in his pocket he went to dine with Cerizet and Dutocq at the Rocher de Cancale; and it is to the various emotions he had passed through during the day that we must attribute the sharp and ill-considered manner in which he conducted his rupture with his two associates. This behavior was neither that of his natural disposition nor of his acquired temperament; but the money that was burning in his pockets had slightly intoxicated him; its very touch had conveyed to him an excitement and an impatience for emancipation of which he was not wholly master. He flung Cerizet over in the matter of the lease without so much as consulting Brigitte; and yet, he had not had the full courage of his duplicity; for he had laid to the charge of the old woman a refusal which was merely the act of his own will, prompted by bitter recollections of his fruitless struggles with the man who had so long oppressed him.

In short, during the whole day, la Peyrade had not shown himself the able and infallible man that we have hitherto seen him. Once before, when he carried the fifteen thousand francs entrusted to him by Thuillier, he had been led by Cerizet into an insurrectionary proceeding which necessitated the affair of Sauvaignou. Perhaps, on the whole, it is more difficult to be strong under good than under evil fortune. The Farnese Hercules, calm and in still repose, expresses more energetically the plenitude of muscular power than a violent and agitated Hercules represented in the over-excited energy of his labors.

PART II. THE PARVENUS

CHAPTER I. PHELLION, UNDER A NEW ASPECT

Between the first and second parts of this history an immense event had taken place in the life of Phellion.

There is no one who has not heard of the misfortunes of the Odeon, that fatal theatre which, for years, ruined all its directors. Right or wrong, the quarter in which this dramatic impossibility stands is convinced that its prosperity depends upon it; so that more than once the mayor and other authorities of the arrondissement have, with a courage that honors them, taken part in the most desperate efforts to galvanize the corpse.

Now to meddle with theatrical matters is one of the eternally perennial ambitions of the lesser bourgeoisie. Always, therefore, the successive saviours of the Odeon feel themselves magnificently rewarded if they are given ever so small a share in the administration of that enterprise. It was at some crisis in its affairs that Minard, in his capacity as mayor of the 11th arrondissement, had been called to the chairmanship of the committee for reading plays, with the power to join unto himself as assistants a certain number of the notables of the Latin quarter,—the selection being left to him.

We shall soon know exactly how near was the realization of la Peyrade's projects for the possession of Celeste's "dot"; let us merely say now that these projects in approaching maturity had inevitably become noised abroad; and as this condition of things pointed, of course, to the exclusion of Minard junior and also of Felix the professor, the prejudice hitherto manifested by Minard pere against old Phellion was transformed into an unequivocal disposition towards friendly cordiality; there is nothing that binds and soothes like the feeling of a checkmate shared in common. Judged without the evil eye of paternal rivalry, Phellion became to Minard a Roman of incorruptible integrity and a man whose little treatises had been adopted by the University, —in other words, a man of sound and tested intellect.

So that when it became the duty of the mayor to select the members of the dramatic custom-house, of which he was now the head, he immediately thought of Phellion. As for the great citizen, he felt, on the day when a post was offered to him in that august tribunal, that a crown of gold had been placed upon his brow.

It will be well understood that it was not lightly, nor without having deeply meditated, that a man of Phellion's solemnity had accepted the high and

212

sacred mission which was offered to him. He said within himself that he was called upon to exercise the functions of a magistracy, a priestly office.

"To judge of men," he replied to Minard, who was much surprised at his hesitation, "is an alarming task, but to judge of minds!—who can believe himself equal to such a mission?"

Once more the family—that rock on which the firmest resolutions split—had threatened to infringe on the domain of his conscience. The thought of boxes and tickets of which the future member of the committee could dispose in favor of his own kin had excited in the household so eager a ferment that his freedom of decision seemed for a moment in danger. But, happily, Brutus was able to decide himself in the same direction along which a positive uprising of the whole Phellionian tribe intended to push him. From the observations of Barniol, his son-in-law, and also by his own personal inspiration, he became persuaded that by his vote, always given to works of irreproachable morality, and by his firm determination to bar the way to all plays that mothers of families could not take their daughters to witness, he was called upon to render the most signal services to morals and public order. Phellion, to use his own expression, had therefore become a member of the areopagus presided over by Minard, and—still speaking as he spoke—he was issuing from the exercise of his functions, which were both delicate and interesting, when the conversation we are about to report took place. A knowledge of this conversation is necessary to an understanding of the ulterior events of this history, and it will also serve to put into relief the envious insight which is one of the most marked traits of the bourgeois character.

The session of the committee had been extremely stormy. On the subject of a tragedy entitled, "The Death of Hercules," the classic party and the romantic party, whom the mayor had carefully balanced in the composition of his committee, had nearly approached the point of tearing each other's hair out. Twice Phellion had risen to speak, and his hearers were astonished at the quantity of metaphors the speech of a major of the National Guard could contain when his literary convictions were imperilled. As the result of a vote, victory remained with the opinions of which Phellion was the eloquent organ. It was while descending the stairway of the theatre with Minard that he remarked:—

"We have done a good work this day. 'The Death of Hercules' reminded me of 'The Death of Hector,' by the late Luce de Lancival; the work we have just accepted sparkles with sublime verses."

"Yes," said Minard, "the versification has taste; there are some really fine lines in it, and I admit to you that I think this sort of literature rather above the anagrams of Master Colleville."

"Oh!" replied Minard, "Colleville's anagrams are mere witticisms, which have nothing in common with the sterner accents of Melpomene."

"And yet," said Minard, "I can assure you he attaches the greatest importance to that rubbish, and apropos to his anagrams, as, indeed, about many other things, he is not a little puffed up. Since their emigration to the Madeleine quarter it seems to me that not only the Sieur Colleville, but his wife and daughter, and the Thuilliers and the whole coterie have assumed an air of importance which is rather difficult to justify."

"No wonder!" said Phellion; "one must have a pretty strong head to stand the fumes of opulence. Our friends have become so very rich by the purchase of that property where they have gone to live that we ought to forgive them for a little intoxication; and I must say the dinner they gave us yesterday for a house-warming was really as well arranged as it was succulent."

"I myself," said Minard, "have given a few remarkable dinners to which men in high government positions have not disdained to come, yet I am not puffed up with pride on that account; such as my friends have always known me, that I have remained."

"You, Monsieur le maire, have long been habituated to the splendid existence you have made for yourself by your high commercial talents; our friends, on the contrary, so lately embarked on the smiling ship of Fortune, have not yet found, as the vulgar saying is, their sea-legs."

And then to cut short a conversation in which Phellion began to think the mayor rather "caustic," he made as if he intended to take leave of him. In order to reach their respective homes they did not always take the same way.

"Are you going through the Luxembourg?" asked Minard, not allowing Phellion to give him the slip.

"I shall cross it, but I have an appointment to meet Madame Phellion and the little Barniols at the end of the grand alley."

"Then," said Minard, "I'll go with you and have the pleasure of making my bow to Madame Phellion; and I shall get the fresh air at the same time, for, in spite of hearing fine things, one's head gets tired at the business we have just been about."

Minard had felt that Phellion gave rather reluctant assent to his sharp remarks about the new establishment of the Thuilliers, and he did not attempt to renew the subject; but when he had Madame Phellion for a listener, he was very sure that his spite would find an echo.

"Well, fair lady," he began, "what did you think of yesterday's dinner?"

"It was very fine," replied Madame Phellion; "as I tasted that soup 'a la bisque' I knew that some caterer, like Chevet, had supplanted the cook. But the whole affair was dull; it hadn't the gaiety of our old meetings in the Latin quarter. And then, didn't it strike you, as it did me, that Madame and Mademoiselle Thuillier no longer seemed mistresses of their own house? I really felt as if I were the guest of Madame—what *is* her name? I never can remember it."

"Torna, Comtesse de Godollo," said Phellion, intervening. "The name is euphonious enough to remember."

"Euphonious if you like, my dear; but to me it never seems a name at all."

"It is a Magyar, or to speak more commonly, a Hungarian name. Our own name, if we wanted to discuss it, might be said to be a loan from the Greek language."

"Very likely; at any rate we have the advantage of being known, not only in our own quarter, but throughout the tuition world, where we have earned an honorable position; while this Hungarian countess, who makes, as they say, the good and the bad weather in the Thuilliers' home, where does she come from, I'd like to know? How did such a fine lady,—for she has good manners and a very distinguished air, no one denies her that,—how came she to fall in love with Brigitte; who, between ourselves, keeps a sickening odor of the porter's lodge about her. For my part, I think this devoted friend is an intriguing creature, who scents money, and is scheming for some future gain."

"Ah ca!" said Minard, "then you don't know the original cause of the intimacy between Madame la Comtesse de Godollo and the Thuilliers?"

"She is a tenant in their house; she occupies the entresol beneath their apartment."

"True, but there's something more than that in it. Zelie, my wife, heard it from Josephine, who wanted, lately, to enter our service; the matter came to nothing, for Francoise, our woman, who thought of marrying, changed her mind. You must know, fair lady, that it was solely Madame de Godollo who brought about the emigration of the Thuilliers, whose upholsterer, as one might say, she is."

"What! their upholsterer?" cried Phellion,—"that distinguished woman, of whom one may truly say, 'Incessu patuit dea'; which in French we very inadequately render by the expression, 'bearing of a queen'?"

"Excuse me," said Minard. "I did not mean that Madame de Godollo is actually in the furniture business; but, at the time when Mademoiselle Thuillier decided, by la Peyrade's advice, to manage the new house herself, that little fellow, who hasn't all the ascendancy over her mind he thinks he has, couldn't persuade her to move the family into the splendid apartment where they received us yesterday. Mademoiselle Brigitte objected that she should have to change her habits, and that her friends and relations wouldn't follow her to such a distant quarter—"

"It is quite certain," interrupted Madame Phellion, "that to make up one's mind to hire a carriage every Sunday, one wants a prospect of greater pleasure than can be found in that salon. When one thinks that, except on the day of the famous dance of the candidacy, they never once opened the piano in the rue Saint-Dominique!"

"It would have been, I am sure, most agreeable to the company to have a talent like yours put in requisition," remarked Minard; "but those are not ideas that could ever come into the mind of that good Brigitte. She'd have seen two more candles to light. Five-franc pieces are her music. So, when la Peyrade and Thuillier insisted that she should move into the apartment in the Place de la Madeleine, she thought of nothing but the extra costs entailed by the removal. She judged, rightly enough, that beneath those gilded ceilings her old 'penates' might have a singular effect."

"See how all things link together," remarked Phellion, "and how, from the summits of society, luxury infiltrates itself, sooner or later, through the lower classes, leading to the ruin of empires."

"You are broaching there, my dear commander," said Minard, "one of the most knotty questions of political economy. Many good minds think, on the contrary, that luxury is absolutely demanded in the interests of commerce, which is certainly the life of States. In any case, this view, which isn't yours, appears to have been that of Madame de Godollo, for, they tell me, her apartment is very coquettishly furnished; and to coax Mademoiselle Brigitte into the same path of elegance she made a proposal to her as follows: 'A friend of mine,' she said, 'a Russian princess for whom one of the first upholsterers has just made splendid furniture, is suddenly recalled to Russia by the czar, a gentleman with whom no one dares to trifle. The poor woman is therefore obliged to turn everything she owns here into money as fast as possible; and I feel sure she would sell this furniture for ready money at a quarter of the price it cost her. All of it is nearly new, and some things have never been used at all.'"

"So," cried Madame Phellion, "all that magnificence displayed before our eyes last night was a magnificent economical bargain?"

"Just so," replied Minard; "and the thing that decided Mademoiselle Brigitte to take that splendid chance was not so much the desire to renew her shabby furniture as the idea of doing an excellent stroke of business. In that old maid there's always something of Madame la Ressource in Moliere's 'Miser.'"

"I think, Monsieur le maire, that you are mistaken," said Phellion. "Madame la Ressource is a character in 'Turcaret,' a very immoral play by the late Le Sage."

"Do you think so?" said Minard. "Well, very likely. But what is certain is that, though the barrister ingratiated himself with Brigitte in helping her to buy the house, it was by this clever jockeying about the furniture that the foreign countess got upon the footing with Brigitte that you now see. You may have remarked, perhaps, that a struggle is going on between those two influences; which we may designate as the house, and its furniture."

"Yes, certainly," said Madame Phellion, with a beaming expression that bore witness to the interest she took in the conversation, "it did seem to me that the great lady allowed herself to contradict the barrister, and did it, too, with a certain sharpness."

"Very marked sharpness," resumed Minard, "and that intriguing fellow perceives it. It strikes me that the lady's hostility makes him uneasy. The Thuilliers he got cheaply; for, between ourselves you know, there's not much in Thuillier himself; but he feels now that he has met a tough adversary, and he is looking anxiously for a weak spot on which to attack her."

"Well, that's justice," said Madame Phellion. "For some time past that man, who used to make himself so small and humble, has been taking airs of authority in the house which are quite intolerable; he behaves openly as the son-in-law; and you know very well, in that affair of Thuillier's election he jockeyed us all, and made us the stepping-stone for his matrimonial ambition."

"Yes; but I can assure you," said Minard, "that at the present time his influence is waning. In the first place, he won't find every day for his dear, good friend, as he calls him, a fine property worth a million to be bought for a bit of bread."

"Then they did get that house very cheap?" said Madame Phellion, interrogatively.

"They got it for nothing, as the result of a dirty intrigue which the lawyer Desroches related to me the other day. If it ever became known to the council of the bar, that little barrister would be badly compromised. The next thing is the coming election to the Chamber. Eating gives appetite, as they say, and our good Thuillier is hungry; but he begins to perceive that Monsieur de la Peyrade, when it becomes a question of getting him that mouthful, hasn't his former opportunity to make dupes of us. That is why the family is turning more and more to Madame de Godollo, who seems to have some very high acquaintances in the political world. Besides all this, in fact, without dwelling on the election business, which is still a distant matter, this Hungarian countess is becoming, every day, more and more a necessity to Brigitte; for it must be owned that without the help of the great lady, the poor soul would look in the midst of her gilded salon like a ragged gown in a bride's trousseau."

"Oh, Monsieur le maire, you are cruel," said Madame Phellion, affecting compunction.

"No, but say," returned Minard, "with your hand on your conscience, whether Brigitte, whether Madame Thuillier could preside in such a salon? No, it is the Hungarian countess who does it all. She furnished the rooms; she selected the male domestic, whose excellent training and intelligence you must have observed; it was she who arranged the menu of that dinner; in short, she is the providence of the parvenu colony, which, without her intervention, would have made the whole quarter laugh at it. And—now this is a very noticeable thing—instead of being a parasite like la Peyrade, this Hungarian lady, who seems to have a fortune of her own, proves to be not only disinterested, but generous. The two gowns that you saw Brigitte and Madame Thuillier wear last night were a present from her, and it was because she came herself to superintend the toilet of our two 'amphitryonesses' that you were so surprised last night not to find them rigged in their usual dowdy fashion."

"But what can be the motive," asked Madame Phellion, "of this maternal and devoted guardianship?"

"My dear wife," said Phellion, solemnly, "the motives of human actions are not always, thank God! selfishness and the consideration of vile interests. There are hearts in this world that find pleasure in doing good for its own sake. This lady may have seen in our good friends a set of people about to enter blindly into a sphere they knew nothing about, and having encouraged their first steps by the purchase of this furniture, she may, like a nurse attached to her nursling, find pleasure in giving them the milk of her social knowledge and her counsels."

"He seems to keep aloof from our strictures, the dear husband!" cried Minard; "but just see how he goes beyond them!"

"I!" said Phellion; "it is neither my intention nor my habit to do so."

"All the same it would be difficult to say more neatly that the Thuilliers are geese, and that Madame de Godollo is bringing them up by hand."

"I do not accept for these friends of ours," said Phellion, "a characterization so derogatory to their repute. I meant to say that they were lacking, perhaps, in that form of experience, and that this noble lady has placed at their service her knowledge of the world and its usages. I protest against any interpretation of my language which goes beyond my thought thus limited."

"Well, anyhow, you will agree, my dear commander, that in the idea of giving Celeste to this la Peyrade, there is something more than want of experience; there is, it must be said, blundering folly and immorality; for really the goings on of that barrister with Madame Colleville—"

"Monsieur le maire," interrupted Phellion, with redoubled solemnity, "Solon, the law-giver, decreed no punishment for parricide, declaring it to be an impossible crime. I think the same thing may be said of the offence to which you seem to make allusion. Madame Colleville granting favors to Monsieur de la Peyrade, and all the while intending to give him her daughter? No, monsieur, no! that passes imagination. Questioned on this subject, like Marie Antoinette, by a human tribunal, Madame Colleville would answer with the queen, 'I appeal to all mothers.'"

"Nevertheless, my friend," said Madame Phellion, "allow me to remind you that Madame Colleville is excessively light-minded, and has given, as we al know, pretty good proofs of it."

"Enough, my dear," said Phellion. "The dinner hour summons us; I think that, little by little, we have allowed this conversation to drift toward the miry slough of backbiting."

"You are full of illusions, my dear commander," said Minard, taking Phellion by the hand and shaking it; "but they are honorable illusions, and I envy them. Madame, I have the honor—" added the mayor, with a respectful bow to Madame Phellion.

And each party took its way.

CHAPTER II. THE PROVENCAL'S PRESENT POSITION

The information acquired by the mayor of the 11th arrondissement was by no means incorrect. In the Thuillier salon, since the emigration to the Madeleine quarter, might be seen daily, between the tart Brigitte and the plaintive Madame Thuillier, the graceful and attractive figure of a woman who conveyed to this salon an appearance of the most unexpected elegance. It was quite true that through the good offices of this lady, who had become her tenant in the new house, Brigitte had made a speculation in furniture not less advantageous in its way, but more avowable, than the very shady purchase of the house itself. For six thousand francs in ready money she had obtained furniture lately from workshops representing a value of at least thirty thousand.

It was still further true that in consequence of a service which went deep into her heart, Brigitte was showing to the beautiful foreign countess the respectful deference which the bourgeoisie, in spite of its sulky jealousy, is much less indisposed to give to titles of nobility and high positions in the social hierarchy than people think. As this Hungarian countess was a woman of great tact and accomplished training, in taking the direction which she had thought it wise to assume over the affairs of her proteges, she had been careful to guard her influence from all appearance of meddlesome and imperious dictation. On the contrary, she flattered Brigitte's claim to be a model housekeeper; in her own household expenses she affected to ask the spinster's advice; so that by reserving to herself the department of luxurious expenses, she had more the air of giving information than of exercising supervision.

La Peyrade could not disguise from himself that a change was taking place. His influence was evidently waning before that of this stranger; but the antagonism of the countess was not confined to a simple struggle for influence. She made no secret of being opposed to his suit for Celeste; she gave her unequivocal approval to the love of Felix Phellion, the professor. Minard, by whom this fact was not unobserved, took very good care, in the midst of his other information, not to mention it to those whom it most concerned.

La Peyrade was all the more anxious at being thus undermined by a hostility the cause of which was inexplicable to him, because he knew he had himself to blame for bringing this disquieting adversary into the very heart of his citadel. His first mistake was in yielding to the barren pleasure of disappointing Cerizet in the lease of the house. If Brigitte by his advice and urging had not taken the administration of the property into her own hands there was every probability that she would never have made the acquaintance of Madame de Godollo. Another imprudence had been to urge the Thuilliers to leave their old home in the Latin quarter.

At this period, when his power and credit had reached their apogee, Theodose considered his marriage a settled thing; and he now felt an almost childish haste to spring into the sphere of elegance which seemed henceforth to be his future. He had therefore furthered the inducements of the countess, feeling that he thus sent the Thuilliers before him to make his bed in the splendid apartment he intended to share with them. By thus removing them from their old home he saw another advantage,—that of withdrawing Celeste from daily intercourse with a rival who seemed to him dangerous. Deprived of the advantage of propinquity, Felix would be forced to make his visits farther apart; and therefore there would be greater facilities to ruin him in the girl's heart, where he was installed on condition of giving religious satisfaction,—a requirement to which he showed himself refractory.

But in all these plans and schemes various drawbacks confronted him. To enlarge the horizon of the Thuilliers was for la Peyrade to run the chance of creating competition for the confidence and admiration of which he had been till then the exclusive object. In the sort of provincial life they had hitherto lived, Brigitte and his dear, good friend placed him, for want of comparison, at a height from which the juxtaposition of other superiorities and elegances must bring him down. So, then, apart from the blows covertly dealt him by Madame de Godollo, the idea of the transpontine emigration had proved to be, on the whole, a bad one.

The Collevilles had followed their friends the Thuilliers, to the new house near the Madeleine, where an entresol at the back had been conceded to them at a price conformable to their budget. But Colleville declared it lacked light and air, and being obliged to go daily from the boulevard of the Madeleine to the faubourg Saint-Jacques, where his office was, he fumed against the arrangement of which he was the victim, and felt at times that la Peyrade was a tyrant. Madame Colleville, on the other hand, had flung herself into an alarming orgy of bonnets, mantles, and new gowns, requiring the presentation of a mass of bills, which led not infrequently to scenes in the household which were more or less stormy. As for Celeste, she had undoubtedly fewer opportunities to see young Phellion, but she had also fewer chances to rush into religious controversy; and absence, which is dangerous to none but inferior attachments, made her think more tenderly and less theologically of the man of her dreams.

But all these false calculations of Theodose were as nothing in the balance with another cause for his diminishing influence which was now to weigh heavily on his situation.

He had assured Thuillier that, after a short delay and the payment of ten thousand francs, to which his dear, good friend submitted with tolerable grace, the cross of the Legion of honor would arrive to realize the secret desire of all his life. Two months had now passed without a sign of that glorious rattle; and the former sub-director, who would have felt such joy in parading his red ribbon on the boulevard of the Madeleine, of which he was now one of the most assiduous promenaders, had nothing to adorn his buttonhole but the flowers of the earth, the privilege of everybody,—of which he was far less proud than Beranger.

La Peyrade had, to be sure, mentioned an unforeseen and inexplicable difficulty by which all the efforts of the Comtesse du Bruel had been paralyzed; but Thuillier did not take comfort in the explanation; and on certain days, when the disappointment became acute, he was very near saying with Chicaneau in Les Plaideurs, "Return my money."

However, no outbreak happened, for la Peyrade held him in leash by the famous pamphlet on "Taxation and the Sliding-Scale"; the conclusion of which had been suspended during the excitement of the moving; for during that agitating period Thuillier had been unable to give proper care to the correction of proofs, about which, we may remember, he had reserved the right of punctilious examination. La Peyrade had now reached a point when he was forced to see that, in order to restore his influence, which was daily evaporating, he must strike some grand blow; and it was precisely this nagging and vexatious fancy about the proofs that the barrister decided to take as the starting-point of a scheme, both deep and adventurous, which came into his mind.

One day, when the pair were engaged on the sheets of the pamphlet, a discussion arose upon the word "nepotism," which Thuillier wished to eliminate from one of la Peyrade's sentences, declaring that never had he met with it anywhere; it was pure neologism—which, to the literary notions of the bourgeoisie, is equivalent to the idea of 1793 and the Terror.

Generally la Peyrade took the ridiculous remarks of his dear, good friend pretty patiently; but on this occasion he made himself exceedingly excited, and signified to Thuillier that he might terminate himself a work to which he applied such luminous and intelligent criticism; after which remark he departed and was not seen again for several days.

At first Thuillier supposed this outbreak to be a mere passing effect of ill-humor; but when la Peyrade's absence grew prolonged he felt the necessity of taking some conciliatory step, and accordingly he went to see the barrister, intending to make honorable amends and so put an end to his sulkiness. Wishing, however, to give this advance an air which allowed an honest issue to his own self-love, he entered la Peyrade's room with an easy manner, and said, cheerfully:—

"Well, my dear fellow, it turns out that we were both right: 'nepotism' means the authority that the nephews of popes take in public affairs. I have searched the dictionary and it gives no other explanation; but, from what Phellion tells me, I find that in the political vocabulary the meaning of the word has been extended to cover the influence which corrupt ministers permit certain persons to exercise illegally. I think, therefore, that we may retain the expression, though it is certainly not taken in that sense by Napoleon Landais."

La Peyrade, who, in receiving his visitor, had affected to be extremely busy in sorting his papers, contented himself by shrugging his shoulders and saying nothing.

"Well," said Thuillier, "have you got the last proofs? We ought to be getting on."

"If you have sent nothing to the printing-office," replied la Peyrade, "of course there are no proofs. I myself haven't touched the manuscript."

"But, my dear Theodose," said Thuillier, "it isn't possible that for such a trifle you are affronted. I don't pretend to be a writer, only as my name is on the book I have, I think, the right to my opinion about a word."

"But 'Mossie' Phellion," replied Theodose, "is a writer; and inasmuch as you have consulted him, I don't see why you can't engage him to finish the work in which, for my part, I have resolved not to co-operate any longer."

"Heavens! what temper!" cried Thuillier; "here you are furious just because I seemed to question a word and then consulted some one. You know very well that I have read passages to Phellion, Colleville, Minard, and Barniol as if the work were mine, in order to see the effect it would produce upon the public; but that's no reason why I should be willing to give my name to the things they are capable of writing. Do you wish me to give you a proof of the confidence I have in you? Madame la Comtesse de Godollo, to whom I read a few pages last night, told me that the pamphlet was likely to get me into trouble with the authorities; but I wouldn't allow what she said to have any influence upon me."

"Well," said la Peyrade, "I think that the oracle of the family sees the matter clearly; and I've no desire to bring your head to the scaffold."

"All that is nonsense," said Thuillier. "Have you, or have you not, an intention to leave me in the lurch?"

"Literary questions make more quarrels among friends than political questions," replied Theodose. "I wish to put an end to these discussions between us."

"But, my dear Theodose, never have I assumed to be a literary man. I think I have sound common-sense, and I say out my ideas; you can't be angry at that; and if you play me this trick, and refuse to collaborate any longer, it is because you have some other grudge against me that I know nothing about."

"I don't see why you call it a trick. There's nothing easier for you than not to write a pamphlet; you'll simply be Jerome Thuillier, as before."

"And yet it was you yourself who declared that this publication would help my election; besides, I repeat, I have read passages to all our friends, I have announced the matter in the municipal council, and if the work were not to appear I should be dishonored; people would be sure to say the government had bought me up."

"You have only to say that you are the friend of Phellion, the incorruptible; that will clear you. You might even give Celeste to his booby of a son; that alliance would certainly protect you from all suspicion."

"Theodose," said Thuillier, "there is something in your mind that you don't tell me. It is not natural that for a simple quarrel about a word you should wish to lose a friend like me."

"Well, yes, there is," replied la Peyrade, with the air of a man who makes up his mind to speak out. "I don't like ingratitude."

"Nor I either; I don't like it," said Thuillier, hotly; "and if you accuse me of so base an action, I summon you to explain yourself. We must get out of these hints and innuendoes. What do you complain of? What have you against a man whom only a few days ago you called your friend?"

"Nothing and everything," replied la Peyrade. "You and your sister are much too clever to break openly with a man who, at the risk of his reputation, has put a million in your hands. But I am not so simple that I don't know how to detect changes. There are people about you who have set themselves, in an underhand way, to destroy me; and Brigitte has only one thought, and that is, how to find a decent way of not keeping her promises. Men like me don't wait till their claims are openly protested, and I certainly do not intend to

225

impose myself on any family; still, I was far, I acknowledge, from expecting such treatment."

"Come, come," said Thuillier, kindly, seeing in the barrister's eye the glint of a tear of which he was completely the dupe, "I don't know what Brigitte may have been doing to you, but one thing is very certain: I have never ceased to be your most devoted friend."

"No," said la Peyrade, "since that mishap about the cross I am only good, as the saying is, to throw to the dogs. How could I have struggled against secret influences? Possibly it is that pamphlet, about which you have talked a great deal too much, that has hindered your appointment. The ministers are so stupid! They would rather wait and have their hand forced by the fame of the publication than do the thing with a good grace as the reward of your services. But these are political mysteries which would never enter your sister's mind."

"The devil!" cried Thuillier. "I think I've got a pretty observing eye, and yet I can't see the slightest change in Brigitte toward you."

"Oh, yes!" said la Peyrade, "your eyesight is so good that you have never seen perpetually beside her that Madame de Godollo, whom she now thinks she can't live without."

"Ha, ha!" said Thuillier, slyly, "so it is a little jealousy, is it, in our mind?"

"Jealousy!" retorted la Peyrade. "I don't know if that's the right word, but certainly your sister—whose mind is nothing above the ordinary, and to whom I am surprised that a man of your intellectual superiority allows a supremacy in your household which she uses and abuses—"

"How can I help it, my dear fellow," interrupted Thuillier, sucking in the compliment; "she is so absolutely devoted to me."

"I admit the weakness, but, I repeat, your sister doesn't fit into your groove. Well, I say that when a man of the value which you are good enough to recognize in me, does her the honor to consult her and devote himself to her as I have done, it can hardly be agreeable to him to find himself supplanted by a woman who comes from nobody knows where—and all because of a few trumpery chairs and tables she has helped her to buy!"

"With women, as you know very well," replied Thuillier, "household affairs have the first place."

"And Brigitte, who wants a finger in everything, also assumes to carry matters with a high hand in affairs of the heart. As you are so extraordinarily clear-sighted you ought to have seen that in Brigitte's mind nothing is less certain than my marriage with Mademoiselle Colleville; and yet my love has been solemnly authorized by you."

"Good gracious!" cried Thuillier, "I'd like to see any one attempt to meddle with my arrangements!"

"Well, without speaking of Brigitte, I can tell you of another person," said Theodose, "who is doing that very thing; and that person is Mademoiselle Celeste herself. In spite of their quarrels about religion, her mind is none the less full of that little Phellion."

"But why don't you tell Flavie to put a stop to it?"

"No one knows Flavie, my dear Thuillier, better than you. She is a woman rather than a mother. I have found it necessary to do a little bit of courting to her myself, and, you understand, while she is willing for this marriage she doesn't desire it very much."

"Well," said Thuillier, "I'll undertake to speak to Celeste myself. It shall never be said that a slip of a girl lays down the law to me."

"That's exactly what I don't want you to do," cried la Peyrade. "Don't meddle in all this. Outside of your relations to your sister you have an iron will, and I will never have it said that you exerted your authority to put Celeste in my arms; on the contrary, I desire that the child may have complete control over her own heart. The only thing I request is that she shall decide positively between Felix Phellion and myself; because I do not choose to remain any longer in this doubtful position. It is true we agreed that the marriage should only take place after you became a deputy; but I feel now that it is impossible to allow the greatest event of my life to remain at the mercy of doubtful circumstances. And, besides, such an arrangement, though at first agreed upon, seems to me now to have a flavor of a bargain which is unbecoming to both of us. I think I had better make you a confidence, to which I am led by the unpleasant state of things now between us. Dutocq may have told you, before you left the apartment in the rue Saint-Dominique, that an heiress had been offered to me whose immediate fortune is larger than that which Mademoiselle Colleville will eventually inherit. I refused, because I have had the folly to let my heart be won, and because an alliance with a family as honorable as yours seemed to me more desirable; but, after all, it is as well to let Brigitte know that if Celeste refuses me, I am not absolutely turned out into the cold."

"I can easily believe that," said Thuillier; "but as for putting the whole decision into the hands of that little girl, especially if she has, as you tell me, a fancy for Felix—"

"I can't help it," said the barrister. "I must, at any price, get out of this

227

position; it is no longer tenable. You talk about your pamphlet; I am not in a fit condition to finish it. You, who have been a man of gallantry, you must know the dominion that women, fatal creatures! exercise over our whole being."

"Bah!" said Thuillier, conceitedly, "they cared for me, but I did not often care for them; I took them, and left them, you know."

"Yes, but I, with my Southern nature, love passionately; and Celeste has other attractions besides fortune. Brought up in your household, under your own eye, you have made her adorable. Only, I must say, you have shown great weakness in letting that young fellow, who does not suit her in any respect, get such hold upon her fancy."

"You are quite right; but the thing began in a childish friendship; she and Felix played together. You came much later; and it is a proof of the great esteem in which we hold you, that when you made your offer we renounced our earlier projects."

"*You* did, yes," said la Peyrade, "and with some literary manias—which, after all, are frequently full of sense and wit—you have a heart of gold; with you friendship is a sure thing, and you know what you mean. But Brigitte is another matter; you'll see, when you propose to her to hasten the marriage, what a resistance she will make."

"I don't agree with you. I think that Brigitte has always wanted you and still wants you for son-in-law—if I may so express myself. But whether she does or not, I beg you to believe that in all important matters I know how to have my will obeyed. Only, let us come now to a distinct understanding of what you wish; then we can start with the right foot foremost, and you'll see that all will go well."

"I wish," replied la Peyrade, "to put the last touches to your pamphlet; for, above all things, I think of you."

"Certainly," said Thuillier, "we ought not to sink in port."

"Well, in consequence of the feeling that I am oppressed, stultified by the prospect of a marriage still so doubtful, I am certain that not a page of manuscript could be got out of me in any form, until the question is settled."

"Very good," said Thuillier; "then how do you present that question?"

"Naturally, if Celeste's decision be against me, I should wish an immediate solution. If I am condemned to make a marriage of convenience I ought to lose no time in taking the opportunity I mentioned to you."

"So be it; but what time do you intend to allow us?"

"I should think that in fifteen days a girl might be able to make up her mind."

"Undoubtedly," replied Thuillier; "but it is very repugnant to me to let Celeste decide without appeal."

"For my part, I will take that risk; in any case, I shall be rid of uncertainty; and that is really my first object. Between ourselves, I am not risking as much as you think. It will take more than fifteen days for a son of Phellion, in other words, obstinacy incarnate in silliness, to have done with philosophical hesitations; and it is very certain that Celeste will not accept him for a husband unless he gives her some proofs of conversion."

"That's probable. But suppose Celeste tries to dawdle; suppose she refuses to accept the alternative?"

"That's your affair," said the Provencal. "I don't know how you regard the family in Paris; I only know that in my part of the country it is an unheard-of thing that a girl should have such liberty. If you, your sister (supposing she plays fair in the matter), and the father and mother can't succeed in making a girl whom you dower agree to so simple a thing as to make a perfectly free choice between two suitors, then good-bye to you! You'll have to write upon your gate-post that Celeste is queen and sovereign of the house."

"Well, we haven't got to that point yet," said Thuillier, with a capable air.

"As for you, my old fellow," resumed la Peyrade, "I must postpone our business until after Celeste's decision. Be that in my favor or not, I will then go to work, and in three days the pamphlet can be finished."

"Now," said Thuillier, "I know what you have had on your mind. I'll talk about it with Brigitte."

"That's a sad conclusion," said la Peyrade; "but, unhappily, so it is."

"What do you mean by that?"

"I would rather, as you can easily imagine, hear you say of yourself that the thing shall be done; but old habits can't be broken up."

"Ah ca! do you think I'm a man without any will, any initiative of my own?"

"No! but I'd like to be hidden in a corner and hear how you will open the subject with your sister."

"Parbleu! I shall open it frankly. I WILL, very firmly said, shall meet every one of her objections."

"Ah, my poor fellow!" said la Peyrade, clapping him on the shoulder, "from Chrysale down how often have we seen brave warriors lowering their penants before the wills of women accustomed to master them!"

"We'll see about *that*," replied Thuillier, making a theatrical exit.

The eager desire to publish his pamphlet, and the clever doubt thrown upon the strength of his will had made him furious,—an actual tiger; and he went away resolved, in case of opposition, to reduce his household, as the saying is, by fire and sword.

When he reached home Thuillier instantly laid the question before Brigitte. She, with her crude good sense and egotism, pointed out to him that by thus hastening the period formerly agreed upon for the marriage, they committed the blunder of disarming themselves; they could not be sure that when the election took place la Peyrade would put the same zeal into preparing for it. "It might be," said the old maid, "just as it has been about the cross."

"There's this difference," said Thuillier; "the cross doesn't depend directly upon la Peyrade, whereas the influence he exerts in the 12th arrondissement he can employ as he will."

"And suppose he willed, after we have feathered his nest," said Brigitte, "to work his influence for his own election? He is very ambitious, you know."

This danger did not fail to strike the mind of the future legislator, who thought, however, that he might feel some security in the honor and morality of la Peyrade.

"A man's honor can't be very delicate," returned Brigitte, "when he tries to get out of a bargain; and this fashion of dangling a bit of sugar before us about getting your pamphlet finished, doesn't please me at all. Can't you get Phellion to help you, and do without Theodose? Or, I dare say, Madame de Godollo, who knows everybody in politics, could find you a journalist—they say there are plenty of them out at elbows; a couple of hundred francs would do the thing."

"But the secret would get into the papers," said Thuillier. "No, I must absolutely have Theodose; he knows that, and he makes these conditions. After all, we did promise him Celeste, and it is only fulfilling the promise a year earlier—what am I saying?—a few months, a few weeks, possibly; for the king may dissolve the Chamber before any one expects it."

"But suppose Celeste won't have him?" objected Brigitte.

"Celeste! Celeste, indeed!" ejaculated Thuillier; "she *must* have whomsoever we choose. We ought to have thought of that when we made the engagement with la Peyrade; our word is passed now, you know. Besides, if the child is allowed to choose between la Peyrade and Phellion—"

"So you really think," said the sceptical old maid, "that if Celeste decides for Phellion you can still count on la Peyrade's devotion?"

"What else can I do? Those are his conditions. Besides, the fellow has calculated the whole thing; he knows very well that Felix will never bring himself in two weeks to please Celeste by going to confession, and unless he does, that little monkey will never accept him for a husband. La Peyrade's game is very clever."

"Too clever," said Brigitte. "Well, settle the matter as you choose; I shall not meddle; all this manoeuvring is not to my taste."

Thuillier went to see Madame Colleville, and intimated to her that she must inform Celeste of the designs upon her.

Celeste had never been officially authorized to indulge her sentiment for Felix Phellion. Flavie, on the contrary, had once expressly forbidden her to encourage the hopes of the young professor; but as, on the part of Madame Thuillier, her godmother and her confidant, she knew she was sustained in her inclination, she had let herself gently follow it without thinking very seriously of the obstacles her choice might encounter. When, therefore, she was ordered to choose at once between Felix and la Peyrade, the simple-hearted girl was at first only struck by the advantages of one half of the alternative, and she fancied she did herself a great service by agreeing to an arrangement which made her the mistress of her own choice and allowed her to bestow it as her heart desired.

But la Peyrade was not mistaken in his calculation when he reckoned that the religious intolerance of the young girl on one side, and the philosophical inflexibility of Phellion's son on the other, would create an invincible obstacle to their coming together.

CHAPTER III. GOOD BLOOD CANNOT LIE

The evening of the day on which Flavie had communicated to Celeste the sovereign orders of Thuillier, the Phellions called to spend the evening with Brigitte, and a very sharp engagement took place between the two young people. Mademoiselle Colleville did not need to be told by her mother that it would be extremely unbecoming if she allowed Felix to know of the conditional approval that was granted to their sentiments. Celeste had too much delicacy, and too much real religious feeling to wish to obtain the conversion of the man she loved on any other ground than that of his conviction. Their evening was therefore passed in theological debate; but love is so strange a Proteus, and takes so many and such various forms, that though it appeared on this occasion in a black gown and a mob cap, it was not at all as ungraceful and displeasing as might have been imagined. But Phellion junior was in this encounter, the solemnity of which he little knew, unlucky and blundering to the last degree. Not only did he concede nothing, but he took a tone of airy and ironical discussion, and ended by putting poor Celeste so beside herself that she finally declared an open rupture and forbade him to appear in her presence again.

It was just the case for a lover more experienced than the young savant to reappear the very next day, for young hearts are never so near to understanding each other as when they have just declared the necessity of eternal separation. But this law is not one of logarithms, and Felix Phellion, being incapable of guessing it, thought himself positively and finally banished; so much so, that during the fifteen days granted to the poor girl to deliberate (as says the Code in the matter of beneficiary bequests), although he was expected day by day, and from minute to minute by Celeste, who gave no more thought to la Peyrade than if he had nothing to do with the question, the deplorably stupid youth did not have the most distant idea of breaking his ban.

Luckily for this hopeless lover, a beneficent fairy was watching over him, and the evening before the day on which the young girl was to make her decision the following affair took place.

It was Sunday, the day on which the Thuilliers still kept up their weekly receptions.

Madame Phellion, convinced that the housekeeping leakage, vulgarly called "the basket dance," was the ruin of the best-regulated households, was in the habit of going in person to her tradespeople. From time immemorial in

234

the Phellion establishment, Sunday was the day of the "pot-au-feu," and the wife of the great citizen, in that intentionally dowdy costume in which good housekeepers bundle themselves when they go to market, was prosaically returning from a visit to the butcher, followed by her cook and the basket, in which lay a magnificent cut of the loin of beef. Twice had she rung her own doorbell, and terrible was the storm gathering on the head of the foot-boy, who by his slowness in opening the door was putting his mistress in a situation less tolerable than that of Louis XIV., who had only *almost* waited. In her feverish impatience Madame Phellion had just given the bell a third and ferocious reverberation, when, judge of her confusion, a little coupe drew up with much clatter at the door of her house, and a lady descended, whom she recognized, at this untimely hour, as the elegant Comtesse Torna de Godollo!

Turning a purplish scarlet, the unfortunate bourgeoise lost her head, and, floundering in excuses, she was about to complicate the position by some signal piece of awkwardness, when, happily for her, Phellion, attracted by the noise of the bell, and attired in a dressing-gown and Greek cap, came out of his study to inquire what was the matter. After a speech, the pompous charm of which did much to compensate for his dishabille, the great citizen, with the serenity that never abandoned him, offered his hand very gallantly to the lady, and having installed her in the salon, said:—

"May I, without indiscretion, ask Madame la comtesse what has procured for us the unhoped-for advantage of this visit?"

"I have come," said the lady, "to talk with Madame Phellion on a matter which must deeply interest her. I have no other way of meeting her without witnesses; and therefore, though I am hardly known to Madame Phellion, I have taken the liberty to call upon her here."

"Madame, your visit is a great honor to this poor dwelling. But where is Madame Phellion?" added the worthy man, impatiently, going towards the door.

"No, I beg of you, don't disturb her," said the countess; "I have heedlessly come at a moment when she is busy with household cares. Brigitte has been my educator in such matters, and I know the respect we ought to pay to good housekeepers. Besides, I have the pleasure of your presence, which I scarcely expected."

Before Phellion could reply to these obliging words, Madame Phellion appeared. A cap with ribbons had taken the place of the market bonnet, and a large shawl covered the other insufficiencies of the morning toilet. When his wife arrived, the great citizen made as though he would discreetly retire.

"Monsieur Phellion," said the countess, "you are not one too many in the conference I desire with madame; on the contrary, your excellent judgment will be most useful in throwing light upon a matter as interesting to you as to your wife. I allude to the marriage of your son."

"The marriage of my son!" cried Madame Phellion, with a look of astonishment; "but I am not aware that anything of the kind is at present in prospect."

"The marriage of Monsieur Felix with Mademoiselle Celeste is, I think, one of your strongest desires—"

"But we have never," said Phellion, "taken any overt steps for that object."

"I know that only too well," replied the countess; "on the contrary, every one in your family seems to study how to defeat my efforts in that direction. However, one thing is clear in spite of the reserve, and, you must allow me to say so, the clumsiness in which the affair has been managed, and that is that the young people love each other, and they will both be unhappy if they do not marry. Now, to prevent this catastrophe is the object with which I have come here this morning."

"We cannot, madame, be otherwise than deeply sensible of the interest you are so good as to show in the happiness of our son," said Phellion; "but, in truth, this interest—"

"Is something so inexplicable," interrupted the countess, "that you feel a distrust of it?"

"Oh! madame!" said Phellion, bowing with an air of respectful dissent.

"But," continued the lady, "the explanation of my proceeding is very simple. I have studied Celeste, and in that dear and artless child I find a moral weight and value which would make me grieve to see her sacrificed."

"You are right, madame," said Madame Phellion. "Celeste is, indeed, an angel of sweetness."

"As for monsieur Felix, I venture to interest myself because, in the first place, he is the son of so virtuous a father—"

"Oh, madame! I entreat—" said Phellion, bowing again.

"—and he also attracts me by the awkwardness of true love, which appears in all his actions and all his words. We mature women find an inexpressible charm in seeing the tender passion under a form which threatens us with no deceptions and no misunderstandings."

"My son is certainly not brilliant," said Madame Phellion, with a faint tone of sharpness; "he is not a fashionable young man."

"But he has the qualities that are most essential," replied the countess, "and a merit which ignores itself,—a thing of the utmost consequence in all intellectual superiority—"

"Really, madame," said Phellion, "you force us to hear things that—"

"That are not beyond the truth," interrupted the countess. "Another reason which leads me to take a deep interest in the happiness of these young people is that I am not so desirous for that of Monsieur Theodose de la Peyrade, who is false and grasping. On the ruin of their hopes that man is counting to carry out his swindling purposes."

"It is quite certain," said Phellion, "that there are dark depths in Monsieur de la Peyrade where light does not penetrate."

"And as I myself had the misfortune to marry a man of his description, the thought of the wretchedness to which Celeste would be condemned by so fatal a connection, impels me, in the hope of saving her, to the charitable effort which now, I trust, has ceased to surprise you."

"Madame," said Phellion, "we do not need the conclusive explanations by which you illumine your conduct; but as to the faults on our part, which have thwarted your generous efforts, I must declare that in order to avoid committing them in future, it seems to me not a little desirable that you should plainly indicate them."

"How long is it," asked the countess, "since any of your family have paid a visit to the Thuilliers'?"

"If my memory serves me," said Phellion, "I think we were all there the Sunday after the dinner for the house-warming."

"Fifteen whole days of absence!" exclaimed the countess; "and you think that nothing of importance could happen in fifteen days?"

"No, indeed! did not three glorious days in July, 1830, cast down a perjured dynasty and found the noble order of things under which we now live?"

"You see it yourself!" said the countess. "Now, tell me, during that evening, fifteen days ago, did nothing serious take place between your son and Celeste?"

"Something did occur," replied Phellion,—"a very disagreeable conversation on the subject of my son's religious opinions; it must be owned that our good Celeste, who in all other respects has a charming nature, is a trifle fanatic in the matter of piety."

237

"I agree to that," said the countess; "but she was brought up by the mother whom you know; she was never shown the face of true piety; she saw only the mimicry of it. Repentant Magdalens of the Madame Colleville species always assume an air of wishing to retire to a desert with their death's-head and crossed bones. They think they can't get salvation at a cheaper rate. But after all, what did Celeste ask of Monsieur Felix? Merely that he would read 'The Imitation of Christ.'"

"He has read it, madame," said Phellion, "and he thinks it a book extremely well written; but his convictions—and that is a misfortune—have not been affected by the perusal."

"And do you think he shows much cleverness in not assuring his mistress of some little change in his inflexible convictions?"

"My son, madame, has never received from me the slightest lesson in cleverness; loyalty, uprightness, those are the principles I have endeavored to inculcate in him."

"It seems to me, monsieur, that there is no want of loyalty when, in dealing with a troubled mind, we endeavor to avoid wounding it. But let us agree that Monsieur Felix owed it to himself to be that iron door against which poor Celeste's applications beat in vain; was that a reason for keeping away from her and sulking in his tent for fifteen whole days? Above all, ought he to have capped these sulks by a proceeding which I can't forgive, and which—only just made known to us—has struck the girl's heart with despair, and also with a feeling of extreme irritation?"

"My son capable of any such act! it is quite impossible, madame!" cried Phellion. "I know nothing of this proceeding; but I do not hesitate to affirm that you have been ill-informed."

"And yet, nothing is more certain. Young Colleville, who came home to-day for his half-holiday, has just told us that Monsieur Felix, who had previously gone with the utmost punctuality to hear him recite has ceased entirely to have anything to do with him. Unless your son is ill, I do not hesitate to say that this neglect is the greatest of blunders, in the situation in which he now stands with the sister he ought not to have chosen this moment to put an end to these lessons."

The Phellions looked at each other as if consulting how to reply.

"My son," said Madame Phellion, "is not exactly ill; but since you mention a fact which is, I acknowledge, very strange and quite out of keeping with his nature and habits, I think it right to tell you that from the day when Celeste seemed to signify that all was at an end between them, a very extraordinary

238

change has come over Felix, which is causing Monsieur Phellion and myself the deepest anxiety."

"Yes, madame," said Phellion, "the young man is certainly not in his normal condition."

"But what is the matter with him?" asked the countess, anxiously.

"The night of that scene with Celeste," replied Phellion, "after his return home, he wept a flood of hot tears on his mother's bosom, and gave us to understand that the happiness of his whole life was at an end."

"And yet," said Madame de Godollo, "nothing very serious happened; but lovers always make the worst of things."

"No doubt," said Madame Phellion; "but since that night Felix has not made the slightest allusion to his misfortune, and the next day he went back to his work with a sort of frenzy. Does that seem natural to you?"

"It is capable of explanation; work is said to be a great consoler."

"That is most true," said Phellion; "but in Felix's whole personality there is something excited, and yet repressed, which is difficult to describe. You speak to him, and he hardly seems to hear you; he sits down to table and forgets to eat, or takes his food with an absent-mindedness which the medical faculty consider most injurious to the process of digestion; his duties, his regular occupations, we have to remind him of—him, so extremely regular, so punctual! The other day, when he was at the Observatory, where he now spends all his evenings, only coming home in the small hours, I took it upon myself to enter his room and examine his papers. I was terrified, madame, at finding a paper covered with algebraic calculations which, by their vast extent appeared to me to go beyond the limits of the human intellect."

"Perhaps," said the countess, "he is on the road to some great discovery."

"Or to madness," said Madame Phellion, in a low voice, and with a heavy sigh.

"That is not probable," said Madame de Godollo; "with an organization so calm and a mind so well balanced, he runs but little danger of that misfortune. I know myself of another danger that threatens him to-morrow, and unless we can take some steps this evening to avert it, Celeste is positively lost to him."

"How so?" said the husband and wife together.

"Perhaps you are not aware," replied the countess, "that Thuillier and his sister have made certain promises to Monsieur de la Peyrade about Celeste?"

"We suspected as much," replied Madame Phellion.

239

"The fulfilment of these pledges was postponed to a rather distant period, and subordinated to certain conditions. Monsieur de la Peyrade, after enabling them to buy the house near the Madeleine, pledged himself not only to obtain the cross for Monsieur Thuillier, but to write in his name a political pamphlet, and assist him in his election to the Chamber of Deputies. It sounds like the romances of chivalry, in which the hero, before obtaining the hand of the princess, is compelled to exterminate a dragon."

"Madame is very witty," said Madame Phellion, looking at her husband, who made her a sign not to interrupt.

"I have no time now," said the countess; "in fact it would be useless to tell you the manoeuvres by which Monsieur de la Peyrade has contrived to hasten the period of this marriage; but it concerns you to know that, thanks to his duplicity, Celeste is being forced to choose between him and Monsieur Felix; fifteen days were given her in which to make her choice; the time expires to-morrow, and, thanks to the unfortunate state of feeling into which your son's attitude has thrown her, there is very serious danger of seeing her sacrifice to her wounded feelings the better sentiments of her love and her instincts."

"But what can be done to prevent it?" asked Phellion.

"Fight, monsieur; come this evening in force to the Thuilliers'; induce Monsieur Felix to accompany you; lecture him until he promises to be a little more flexible in his philosophical opinions. Paris, said Henri IV., is surely worth a mass. But let him avoid all such questions; he can certainly find in his heart the words and tones to move a woman who loves him; it requires so little to satisfy her! I shall be there myself, and I will help him to my utmost ability; perhaps, under the inspiration of the moment, I may think of some way to do effectually. One thing is very certain: we have to fight a great battle to-night, and if we do not ALL do our duty valorously, la Peyrade may win it."

"My son is not here, madame," said Phellion, "and I regret it, for perhaps your generous devotion and urgent words would succeed in shaking off his torpor; but, at any rate, I will lay before him the gravity of the situation, and, beyond all doubt, he will accompany us to-night to the Thuilliers'."

"It is needless to say," added the countess, rising, "that we must carefully avoid the very slightest appearance of collusion; we must not converse together; in fact, unless it can be done in some casual way, it would be better not to speak."

"I beg you to rely, madame, upon my prudence," replied Phellion, "and kindly accept the assurance—"

"Of your most distinguished sentiments," interrupted the countess, laughing.

"No, madame," replied Phellion, gravely, "I reserve that formula for the conclusion of my letters; I beg you to accept the assurance of my warmest and most unalterable gratitude."

"We will talk of that when we are out of danger," said Madame de Godollo, moving towards the door; "and if Madame Phellion, the tenderest and most virtuous of mothers, will grant me a little place in her esteem, I shall count myself more than repaid for my trouble."

Madame Phellion plunged headlong into a responsive compliment; and the countess, in her carriage, was at some distance from the house before Phellion had ceased to offer her his most respectful salutations.

As the Latin-quarter element in Brigitte's salon became more rare and less assiduous, a livelier Paris began to infiltrate it. Among his colleagues in the municipal council and among the upper employees of the prefecture of the Seine, the new councillor had made several very important recruits. The mayor, and the deputy mayors of the arrondissement, on whom, after his removal to the Madeleine quarter, Thuillier had called, hastened to return the civility; and the same thing happened with the superior officers of the first legion. The house itself had produced a contingent; and several of the new tenants contributed, by their presence, to change the aspect of the dominical meetings. Among the number we must mention Rabourdin [see "Bureaucracy"], the former head of Thuillier's office at the ministry of finance. Having had the misfortune to lose his wife, whose salon, at an earlier period, checkmated that of Madame Colleville, Rabourdin occupied as a bachelor the third floor, above the apartment let to Cardot, the notary. As the result of an odious slight to his just claims, Rabourdin had voluntarily resigned his public functions. At this time, when he again met Thuillier, he was director of one of those numerous projected railways, the construction of which is always delayed by either parliamentary rivalry or parliamentary indecision. Let us say, in passing, that the meeting with this able administrator, now become an important personage in the financial world, was an occasion to the worthy and honest Phellion to display once more his noble character. At the time of the resignation to which Rabourdin had felt himself driven, Phellion alone, of all the clerks in the office, had stood by him in his misfortunes. Being now in a position to bestow a great number of places, Rabourdin, on meeting once more his faithful subordinate, hastened to offer him a position both easy and lucrative.

"Mossieu," said Phellion, "your benevolence touches me and honors me, but my frankness owes you an avowal, which I beg you not to take in ill part:

I do not believe in 'railways,' as the English call them."

"That's an opinion to which you have every right," said Rabourdin, smiling; "but, meanwhile, until the contrary is proved, we pay the employees in our office well, and I should be glad to have you with me in that capacity. I know by experience that you are a man on whom I can count."

"Mossieu," returned the great citizen, "I did my duty at that time, and nothing more. As for the offer you have been so good as to make to me, I cannot accept it; satisfied with my humble fortunes, I feel neither the need nor the desire to re-enter an administrative career; and, in common with the Latin poet, I may say, 'Claudite jam rivos, pueri, sat prata biberunt.'"

Thus elevated in the character of its habitues, the salon Thuillier still needed a new element of life. Thanks to the help of Madame de Godollo, a born organizer, who successfully put to profit the former connection of Colleville with the musical world, a few artists came to make diversion from bouillotte and boston. Old-fashioned and venerable, those two games were forced to beat a retreat before whist, the only manner, said the Hungarian countess, in which respectable people can kill time.

Like Louis XVI., who began by putting his own hand to reforms which subsequently engulfed his throne, Brigitte had encouraged, at first, this domestic revolution; the need of sustaining her position suitably in the new quarter to which she had emigrated had made her docile to all suggestions of comfort and elegance. But the day on which occurred the scene we are about to witness, an apparently trivial detail had revealed to her the danger of the declivity on which she stood. The greater number of the new guests, recently imported by Thuillier, knew nothing of his sister's supremacy in his home. On arrival, therefore, they all asked Thuillier to present them to *Madame*, and, naturally, Thuillier could not say to them that his wife was a figure-head who groaned under the iron hand of a Richelieu, to whom the whole household bent the knee. It was therefore not until the first homage rendered to the sovereign "de jure" was paid, that the new-comers were led up to Brigitte, and by reason of the stiffness which displeasure at this misplacement of power gave to her greeting they were scarcely encouraged to pay her any further attentions. Quick to perceive this species of overthrow, Queen Elizabeth said to herself, with that profound instinct of domination which was her ruling passion:—

"If I don't take care I shall soon be nobody in this house."

Burrowing into that idea, she came to think that if the project of making a common household with la Peyrade, then Celeste's husband, were carried out, the situation which was beginning to alarm her would become even worse.

From that moment, and by sudden intuition, Felix Phellion, that good young man, with his head too full of mathematics ever to become a formidable rival to her sovereignty, seemed to her a far better match than the enterprising lawyer, and she was the first, on seeing the Phellion father and mother arrive without the son, to express regret at his absence. Brigitte, however, was not the only one to feel the injury that the luckless professor was doing to his prospects in thus keeping away from her reception. Madame Thuillier, with simple candor, and Celeste with feigned reserve, both made manifest their displeasure. As for Madame de Godollo, who, in spite of a very remarkable voice, usually required much pressing before she would sing (the piano having been opened since her reign began), she now went up to Madame Phellion and asked her to accompany her, and between two verses of a song she said in her ear:—

"Why isn't your son here?"

"He is coming," said Madame Phellion. "His father talked to him very decidedly; but to-night there happens to be a conjunction of I don't know what planets; it is a great night at the Observatory, and he did not feel willing to dispense with—"

"It is inconceivable that a man should be so foolish!" exclaimed Madame de Godollo; "wasn't theology bad enough, that he must needs bring in astronomy too?"

And her vexation gave to her voice so vibrating a tone that her song ended in the midst of what the English call a thunder of applause. La Peyrade, who feared her extremely, was not one of the last, when she returned to her place, to approach her, and express his admiration; but she received his compliments with a coldness so near to incivility that their mutual hostility was greatly increased. La Peyrade turned away to console himself with Madame Colleville, who had still too many pretensions to beauty not to be the enemy of a woman made to intercept all homage.

"So you also, you think that woman sings well?" she said, contemptuously, to Theodose.

"At any rate, I have been to tell her so," replied la Peyrade, "because without her, in regard to Brigitte, there's no security. But do just look at your Celeste; her eyes never leave that door, and every time a tray is brought in, though it is an hour at least since the last guest came, her face expresses disappointment."

We must remark, in passing, that since the reign of Madame de Godollo trays were passed round on the Sunday reception days, and that without scrimping; on the contrary, they were laden with ices, cakes, and syrups, from

Taurade's, then the best confectioner.

"Don't harass me!" cried Flavie. "I know very well what that foolish girl has in her mind; and your marriage will take place only too soon."

"But you know it is not for myself I make it," said la Peyrade; "it is a necessity for the future of all of us. Come, come, there are tears in your eyes! I shall leave you; you are not reasonable. The devil! as that Prudhomme of a Phellion says, 'Whoso wants the end wants the means.'"

And he went toward the group composed of Celeste, Madame Thuillier, Madame de Godollo, Colleville, and Phellion. Madame Colleville followed him; and, under the influence of the feeling of jealousy she had just shown, she became a savage mother.

"Celeste," she said, "why don't you sing? These gentlemen wish to hear you."

"Oh, mamma!" cried the girl, "how can I sing after Madame de Godollo, with my poor thread of a voice? Besides, you know I have a cold."

"That is to say that, as usual, you make yourself pretentious and disagreeable; people sing as they can sing; all voices have their own merits."

"My dear," said Colleville, who, having just lost twenty francs at the card-tables, found courage in his ill-humor to oppose his wife, "that saying, 'People sing as they can sing' is a bourgeois maxim. People sing with a voice, if they have one; but they don't sing after hearing such a magnificent opera voice as that of Madame la comtesse. For my part, I readily excuse Celeste for not warbling to us one of her sentimental little ditties."

"Then it is well worth while," said Flavie, leaving the group, "to spend so much money on expensive masters who are good for nothing."

"So," said Colleville, resuming the conversation which the invasion of Flavie had interrupted, "Felix no longer inhabits this earth; he lives among the stars?"

"My dear and former colleague," said Phellion, "I am, as you are, annoyed with my son for neglecting, as he does, the oldest friends of his family; and though the contemplation of those great luminous bodies suspended in space by the hand of the Creator presents, in my opinion, higher interest than it appears to have to your more eager brain, I think that Felix, by not coming here to-night, as he promised me he would, shows a want of propriety, about which, I can assure you I shall speak my mind."

"Science," said la Peyrade, "is a fine thing, but it has, unfortunately, the attribute of making bears and monomaniacs."

"Not to mention," said Celeste, "that it destroys all religious sentiments."

"You are mistaken there, my dear child," said Madame de Godollo. "Pascal, who was himself a great example of the falseness of your point of view, says, if I am not mistaken, that a little science draws us from religion, but a great deal draws us back to it."

"And yet, madame," said Celeste, "every one admits that Monsieur Felix is really very learned; when he helped my brother with his studies nothing could be, so Francois told me, clearer or more comprehensible than his explanations; and you see, yourself, he is not the more religious for that."

"I tell you, my dear child, that Monsieur Felix is not irreligious, and with a little gentleness and patience nothing would be easier than to bring him back."

"Bring back a savant to the duties of religion!" exclaimed la Peyrade. "Really, madame, that seems to me very difficult. These gentlemen put the object of their studies before everything else. Tell a geometrician or a geologist, for example, that the Church demands, imperatively, the sanctification of the Sabbath by the suspension of all species of work, and they will shrug their shoulders, though God Himself did not disdain to rest from His labors."

"So that in not coming here this evening," said Celeste, naively, "Monsieur Felix commits not only a fault against good manners, but a sin."

"But, my dearest," said Madame de Godollo, "do you think that our meeting here this evening to sing ballads and eat ices and say evil of our neighbor—which is the customary habit of salons—is more pleasing to God than to see a man of science in his observatory busied in studying the magnificent secrets of His creation?"

"There's a time for all things," said Celeste; "and, as Monsieur de la Peyrade says, God Himself did not disdain to rest."

"But, my love," said Madame de Godollo, "God has time to do so; He is eternal."

"That," said la Peyrade, "is one of the wittiest impieties ever uttered; those are the reasons that the world's people put forth. They interpret and explain away the commands of God, even those that are most explicit and imperative; they take them, leave them, or choose among them; the free-thinker subjects them to his lordly revision, and from free-thinking the distance is short to free actions."

During this harangue of the barrister Madame de Godollo had looked at the clock; it then said half-past eleven. The salon began to empty. Only one card-table was still going on, Minard, Thuillier, and two of the new acquaintances being the players. Phellion had just quitted the group with which he had so far been sitting, to join his wife, who was talking with Brigitte in a corner; by the vehemence of his pantomimic action it was easy to see that he was filled with some virtuous indignation. Everything seemed to show that all hope of seeing the arrival of the tardy lover was decidedly over.

"Monsieur," said the countess to la Peyrade, "do you consider the gentlemen attached to Saint-Jacques du Haut Pas in the rue des Postes good Catholics?"

"Undoubtedly," replied the barrister, "religion has no more loyal supporters."

"This morning," continued the countess, "I had the happiness to be received by Pere Anselme. He is thought the model of all Christian virtues, and yet the good father is a very learned mathematician."

"I have not said, madame, that the two qualities were absolutely incompatible."

"But you did say that a true Christian could not attend to any species of work on Sunday. If so, Pere Anselme must be an unbeliever; for when I was admitted to his room I found him standing before a blackboard with a bit of chalk in his hand, busy with a problem which was, no doubt, knotty, for the board was three-parts covered with algebraic signs; and I must add that he did not seem to care for the scandal this ought to cause, for he had with him an individual whom I am not allowed to name, a younger man of science, of great promise, who was sharing his profane occupation."

Celeste and Madame Thuillier looked at each other, and both saw a gleam of hope in the other's eyes.

"Why can't you tell us the name of that young man of science?" Madame Thuillier ventured to say, for she never put any diplomacy into the expression of her thoughts.

"Because he has not, like Pere Anselme, the saintliness which would absolve him in the eyes of monsieur here for this flagrant violation of the Sabbath. Besides," added Madame de Godollo, in a significant manner, "he asked me not to mention that I had met him there."

"Then you know a good many scientific young men?" said Celeste, interrogatively; "this one and Monsieur Felix—that makes two."

"My dear love," said the countess, "you are an inquisitive little girl, and you will not make me say what I do not choose to say, especially after a confidence that Pere Anselme made to me; for if I did, your imagination would at once set off at a gallop."

The gallop had already started, and every word the countess said only added to the anxious eagerness of the young girl.

"As for me," said la Peyrade, sarcastically, "I shouldn't be at all surprised if Pere Anselme's young collaborator was that very Felix Phellion. Voltaire always kept very close relations with the Jesuits who brought him up; but he never talked religion with them."

"Well, my young savant does talk of it to his venerable brother in science; he submits his doubts to him; in fact, that was the beginning of their scientific intimacy."

"And does Pere Anselme," asked Celeste, "hope to convert him?"

"He is sure of it," replied the countess. "His young collaborator, apart from a religious education which he certainly never had, has been brought up to the highest principles; he knows, moreover, that his conversion to religion would make the happiness of a charming girl whom he loves, and who loves him. Now, my dear, you will not get another word out of me, and you may think what you like."

"Oh! godmother!" whispered Celeste, yielding to the freshness of her feelings, "suppose it were he!"

And the tears filled her eyes as she pressed Madame Thuillier's hand.

At this moment the servant threw open the door of the salon, and, singular complication! announced Monsieur Felix Phellion.

The young professor entered the room, bathed in perspiration, his cravat in disorder, and himself out of breath.

"A pretty hour," said Phellion, sternly, "to present yourself."

"Father," said Felix, moving to the side of the room where Madame Thuillier and Celeste were seated, "I could not leave before the end of the phenomenon; and then I couldn't find a carriage, and I have run the whole way."

"Your ears ought to have burned as you came," said la Peyrade, "for you have been for the last half-hour in the minds of these ladies, and a great problem has been started about you."

Felix did not answer. He saw Brigitte entering the salon from the dining-room where she had gone to tell the man-servant not to bring in more trays, and he hurried to greet her.

After listening to a few reproaches for the rarity of his visits and receiving forgiveness in a very cordial "Better late than never," he turned towards his pole, and was much astonished to hear himself addressed by Madame de Godollo as follows:—

"Monsieur," she said, "I hope you will pardon the indiscretion I have, in the heat of conversation, committed about you. I have told these ladies where I met you this morning."

"Met me?" said Felix; "if I had the honor to meet you, madame, I did not see you."

An almost imperceptible smile flickered on la Peyrade's lips.

"You saw me well enough to ask me to keep silence as to where I had met you; but, at any rate, I did not go beyond a simple statement; I said you saw Pere Anselme sometimes, and had certain scientific relations with him; also that you defended your religious doubts to him as you do to Celeste."

"Pere Anselme!" said Felix, stupidly.

"Yes, Pere Anselme," said la Peyrade, "a great mathematician who does not despair of converting you. Mademoiselle Celeste wept for joy."

Felix looked around him with a bewildered air. Madame de Godollo fixed upon him a pair of eyes the language of which a poodle could have understood.

"I wish," he said finally, "I could have given that joy to Mademoiselle Celeste, but I think, madame, you are mistaken."

"Ah! monsieur, then I must be more precise," said the countess, "and if your modesty still induces you to hide a step that can only honor you, you can contradict me; I will bear the mortification of having divulged a secret which, I acknowledge, you trusted implicitly to my discretion."

Madame Thuillier and Celeste were truly a whole drama to behold; never were doubt and eager expectation more plainly depicted on the human face. Measuring her words deliberately, Madame de Godollo thus continued:—

"I said to these ladies, because I know how deep an interest they take in your salvation, and because you are accused of boldly defying the commandments of God by working on Sundays, that I had met you this morning at the house of Pere Anselme, a mathematician like yourself, with whom you were busy in solving a problem; I said that your scientific intercourse with that saintly and enlightened man had led to other explanations between you; that you had submitted to him your religious doubts, and he did not despair of removing them. In the confirmation you can

248

give of my words there is nothing, I am sure, to wound your self-esteem. The matter was simply a surprise you intended for Celeste, and I have had the stupidity to divulge it. But when she hears you admit the truth of my words you will have given her such happiness that I shall hope to be forgiven."

"Come, monsieur," said la Peyrade, "there's nothing absurd or mortifying in having sought for light; you, so honorable and so truly an enemy to falsehood, you cannot deny what madame affirms with such decision."

"Well," said Felix, after a moment's hesitation, "will you, Mademoiselle Celeste, allow me to say a few words to you in private, without witnesses?"

Celeste rose, after receiving an approving sign from Madame Thuillier. Felix took her hand and led her to the recess of the nearest window.

"Celeste," he said, "I entreat you: wait! See," he added, pointing to the constellation of Ursa Minor, "beyond those visible stars a future lies before us; I will place you there. As for Pere Anselme, I cannot admit what has been said, for it is not true. It is an invented tale. But be patient with me; you shall soon know all."

"He is mad!" said the young girl, in tones of despair, as she resumed her place beside Madame Thuillier.

Felix confirmed this judgment by rushing frantically from the salon, without perceiving the emotion in which his father and his mother started after him. After this sudden departure, which stupefied everybody, la Peyrade approached Madame de Godollo very respectfully, and said to her:—

"You must admit, madame, that it is difficult to drag a man from the water when he persists in being drowned."

"I had no idea until this moment of such utter simplicity," replied the countess; "it is too silly. I pass over to the enemy; and with that enemy I am ready and desirous to have, whenever he pleases, a frank and honest explanation."

CHAPTER IV. HUNGARY VERSUS PROVENCE

The next day Theodose felt himself possessed by two curiosities: How would Celeste behave as to the option she had accepted? and this Comtesse Torna de Godollo, what did she mean by what she had said; and what did she want with him?

The first of these questions seemed, undoubtedly, to have the right of way, and yet, by some secret instinct, la Peyrade felt more keenly drawn toward the conclusion of the second problem. He decided, therefore, to take his first step in that direction, fully understanding that he could not too carefully arm himself for the interview to which the countess had invited him.

The morning had been rainy, and this great calculator was, of course, not ignorant how much a spot of mud, tarnishing the brilliancy of varnished boots, could lower a man in the opinion of some. He therefore sent his porter for a cabriolet, and about three o'clock in the afternoon he drove from the rue Saint-Dominique d'Enfer toward the elegant latitudes of the Madeleine. It may well be believed that certain cares had been bestowed upon his toilet, which ought to present a happy medium between the negligent ease of a morning costume and the ceremonious character of an evening suit. Condemned by his profession to a white cravat, which he rarely laid aside, and not venturing to present himself in anything but a dress-coat, he felt himself being drawn, of necessity, to one of the extremes he desired to avoid. However by buttoning up his coat and wearing tan instead of straw-colored gloves, he managed to *unsolemnize* himself, and to avoid that provincial air which a man in full dress walking the streets of Paris while the sun is above the horizon never fails to convey.

The wary diplomatist was careful not to drive to the house where he was going. He was unwilling to be seen from the countess' entresol issuing from a hired cab, and from the first floor he feared to be discovered stopping short on his way up at the lower floor,—a proceeding which could not fail to give rise to countless conjectures.

He therefore ordered the driver to pull up at the corner of the rue Royale, whence, along a pavement that was now nearly dry, he picked his way on tiptoe to the house. It so chanced that he was not seen by either the porter or his wife; the former being beadle of the church of the Madeleine, was absent at a service, and the wife had just gone up to show a vacant apartment to a lodger. Theodose was therefore able to glide unobserved to the door of the sanctuary he desired to penetrate. A soft touch of his hand to the silken bell-rope caused a sound which echoed from the interior of the apartment. A few seconds elapsed, and then another and more imperious bell of less volume seemed to him a notification to the maid that her delay in opening the door was displeasing to her mistress. A moment later, a waiting-woman, of middle age, and too well trained to dress like a "soubrette" of comedy, opened the door to him.

The lawyer gave his name, and the woman ushered him into a dining-room, severely luxurious, where she asked him to wait. A moment later, however, she returned, and admitted him into the most coquettish and splendid salon it was possible to insert beneath the low ceilings of an entresol. The divinity of the place was seated before a writing-table covered with a Venetian cloth, in which gold glittered in little spots among the dazzling colors of the tapestry.

"Will you allow me, monsieur, to finish a letter of some importance?" she said.

The barrister bowed in sign of assent. The handsome Hungarian then concluded a note on blue English paper, which she placed in an envelope; after sealing it carefully, she rang the bell. The maid appeared immediately and lighted a little spirit lamp; above the lamp was suspended a sort of tiny crucible, in which was a drop of sealing-wax; as soon as this had melted, the maid poured it on the envelope, presenting to her mistress a seal with armorial bearings. This the countess imprinted on the wax with her own beautiful hands, and then said:—

"Take the letter at once to that address."

The woman made a movement to take the letter, but, either from haste or inadvertence, the paper fell from her hand close to la Peyrade's feet. He stooped hastily to pick it up, and read the direction involuntarily. It bore the words, "His Excellency the Minister of Foreign Affairs"; the significant words, "For him only," written higher up, seemed to give this missive a character of intimacy.

"Pardon, monsieur," said the countess, receiving the paper, which he had the good taste to return to her own hands in order to show his eagerness to serve her. "Be so good, mademoiselle, as to carry that in a way not to lose it," she added in a dry tone to the unlucky maid. The countess then left her writing-table and took her seat on a sofa covered with pearl-gray satin.

During these proceedings la Peyrade had the satisfaction of making an inventory of all the choice things by which he was surrounded. Paintings by good masters detached themselves from walls of even tone; on a pier-table stood a very tall Japanese vase; before the windows the jardinieres were filled with lilium rubrum, showing its handsome reversely curling petals surmounted by white and red camellias and a dwarf magnolia from China, with flowers of sulphur white with scarlet edges. In a corner was a stand of arms, of curious shapes and rich construction, explained, perhaps, by the lady's Hungarian nationality—always that of the hussar. A few bronzes and statuettes of exquisite selection, chairs rolling softly on Persian carpets, and a perfect anarchy of stuffs of all kinds completed the arrangement of this salon, which the lawyer had once before visited with Brigitte and Thuillier before the countess moved into it. It was so transformed that it seemed to him unrecognizable. With a little more knowledge of the world la Peyrade would have been less surprised at the marvellous care given by the countess to the decoration of the room. A woman's salon is her kingdom, and her absolute domain; there, in the fullest sense of the word, she reigns, she governs; there she offers battle, and nearly always comes off victorious.

Coquettishly lying back in a corner of the sofa, her head carelessly supported by an arm the form and whiteness of which could be seen nearly to the elbow through the wide, open sleeve of a black velvet dressing-gown, her Cinderella foot in its dainty slipper of Russia leather resting on a cushion of orange satin, the handsome Hungarian had the look of a portrait by Laurence or Winterhalter, plus the naivete of the pose.

"Monsieur," she said, with the slightly foreign accent which lent an added charm to her words, "I cannot help thinking it rather droll that a man of your mind and rare penetration should have thought you had an enemy in me."

"But, Madame la comtesse," replied la Peyrade, allowing her to read in his eyes an astonishment mingled with distrust, "all the appearances, you must admit, were of that nature. A suitor interposes to break off a marriage which has been offered to me with every inducement; this rival does me the service of showing himself so miraculously stupid and awkward that I could easily have set him aside, when suddenly a most unlooked-for and able auxiliary devotes herself to protecting him on the very ground where he shows himself most vulnerable."

"You must admit," said the countess, laughing, "that the protege showed himself a most intelligent man, and that he seconded my efforts valiantly."

"His clumsiness could not have been, I think, very unexpected to you," replied la Peyrade; "therefore the protection you have deigned to give him is the more cruel to me."

"What a misfortune it would be," said the countess, with charmingly affected satire, "if your marriage with Mademoiselle Celeste were prevented! Do you really care so much, monsieur, for that little school-girl?"

In that last word, especially the intonation with which it was uttered, there was more than contempt, there was hatred. This expression did not escape an observer of la Peyrade's strength, but not being a man to advance very far on a single remark he merely replied:—

"Madame, the vulgar expression, to 'settle down,' explains this situation, in which a man, after many struggles and being at an end of his efforts and his illusions, makes a compromise with the future. When this compromise takes the form of a young girl with, I admit, more virtue than beauty, but one who brings to a husband the fortune which is indispensable to the comfort of married life, what is there so astonishing in the fact that his heart yields to gratitude and that he welcomes the prospect of a placid happiness?"

"I have always thought," replied the countess, "that the power of a man's intellect ought to be the measure of his ambition; and I imagined that one so wise as to make himself, at first, the poor man's lawyer, would have in his heart less humble and less pastoral aspirations."

"Ah! madame," returned la Peyrade, "the iron hand of necessity compels us to strange resignations. The question of daily bread is one of those before which all things bend the knee. Apollo was forced to 'get a living,' as the shepherd of Admetus."

"The sheepfold of Admetus," said Madame de Godollo, "was at least a royal fold; I don't think Apollo would have resigned himself to be the shepherd of a—bourgeois."

The hesitation that preceded that last word seemed to convey in place of it a proper name; and la Peyrade understood that Madame de Godollo, out of pure clemency, had suppressed that of Thuillier, had turned her remark upon the species and not the individual.

"I agree, madame, that your distinction is a just one," he replied, "but in this case Apollo has no choice."

"I don't like persons who charge too much," said the countess, "but still less do I like those who sell their merchandise below the market price; I always suspect such persons of trying to dupe me by some clever and complicated trick. You know very well, monsieur, your own value, and your hypocritical humility displeases me immensely. It proves to me that my kindly overtures have not produced even a beginning of confidence between us."

"I assure you, madame, that up to the present time life has never justified the belief in any dazzling superiority in me."

"Well, really," said the Hungarian, "perhaps I ought to believe in the humility of a man who is willing to accept the pitiable finale of his life which

I threw myself into the breach to prevent."

"Just as I, perhaps," said la Peyrade, with a touch of sarcasm, "ought to believe in the reality of a kindness which, in order to save me, has handled me so roughly."

The countess cast a reproachful look upon her visitor; her fingers crumpled the ribbons of her gown; she lowered her eyes, and gave a sigh, so nearly imperceptible, so slight, that it might have passed for an accident in the most regular breathing.

"You are rancorous," she said, "and you judge people by one aspect only. After all," she added, as if on reflection, "you are perhaps right in reminding me that I have taken the longest way round by meddling, rather ridiculously, in interests that do not concern me. Go on, my dear monsieur, in the path of this glorious marriage which offers you so many combined inducements; only, let me hope that you may not repent a course with which I shall no longer interfere."

The Provencal had not been spoilt by an experience of "bonnes fortunes." The poverty against which he had struggled so long never leads to affairs of gallantry, and since he had thrown off its harsh restraint, his mind being wholly given up to the anxious work of creating his future, the things of the heart had entered but slightly into his life; unless we must except the comedy he had played on Flavie. We can therefore imagine the perplexity of this novice in the matter of adventures when he saw himself placed between the danger of losing what seemed to be a delightful opportunity, and the fear of finding a serpent amid the beautiful flowers that were offered to his grasp. Too marked a reserve, too lukewarm an eagerness, might wound the self-love of that beautiful foreigner, and quench the spring from which he seemed invited to draw. On the other hand, suppose that appearance of interest were only a snare? Suppose this kindness (ill-explained, as it seemed to him), of which he was so suddenly the object, had no other purpose than to entice him into a step which might be used to compromise him with the Thuilliers? What a blow to his reputation for shrewdness, and what a role to play!—that of the dog letting go the meat for the shadow!

We know that la Peyrade was trained in the school of Tartuffe, and the frankness with which that great master declares to Elmire that without receiving a few of the favors to which he aspired he could not trust in her tender advances, seemed to the barrister a suitable method to apply to the present case, adding, however, a trifle more softness to the form.

"Madame la comtesse," he said, "you have turned me into a man who is much to be pitied. I was cheerfully advancing to this marriage, and you take

255

all faith in it away from me. Suppose I break it off, what use can I—with that great capacity you see in me—make of the liberty I thus recover?"

"La Bruyere, if I am not mistaken, said that nothing freshens the blood so much as to avoid committing a folly."

"That may be; but it is, you must admit, a negative benefit; and I am of an age and in a position to desire more serious results. The interest that you deign to show to me cannot, I think, stop short at the idea of merely putting an end to my present prospects. I love Mademoiselle Colleville with a love, it is true, which has nothing imperative about it; but I certainly love her, her hand is promised to me, and before renouncing it—"

"So," said the countess, hastily, "in a given case you would not be averse to a rupture? And," she added, in a more decided tone, "there would be some chance of making you see that in taking your first opportunity you cut yourself off from a better future, in which a more suitable marriage may present itself?"

"But, at least, madame, I must be enabled to foresee it definitely."

This persistence in demanding pledges seemed to irritate the countess.

"Faith," she said, "is only a virtue when it believes without seeing. You doubt yourself, and that is another form of stupidity. I am not happy, it seems, in my selection of those I desire to benefit."

"But, madame, it cannot be indiscreet to ask to know in some remote way at least, what future your kind good-will has imagined for me."

"It is very indiscreet," replied the countess, coldly, "and it shows plainly that you offer me only a conditional confidence. Let us say no more. You are certainly far advanced with Mademoiselle Colleville; she suits you, you say, in many ways; therefore marry her. I say again, you will no longer find me in your way."

"But does Mademoiselle Colleville really suit me?" resumed la Peyrade; "that is the very point on which you have lately raised my doubts. Do you not think there is something cruel in casting me first in one direction and then in the other without affording me any ground to go upon?"

"Ah!" said the countess, in a tone of impatience, "you want my opinion on the premises! Well, monsieur, there is one very conclusive fact to which I can bring proof: Celeste does not love you."

"So I have thought," said la Peyrade, humbly. "I felt that I was making a marriage of mere convenience."

"And she cannot love you, because," continued Madame de Godollo, with animation, "she cannot comprehend you. Her proper husband is that blond little man, insipid as herself; from the union of those two natures without life or heat will result in that lukewarm existence which, in the opinion of the world where she was born and where she has lived, is the ne plus ultra of conjugal felicity. Try to make that little simpleton understand that when she had a chance to unite herself with true talent she ought to have felt highly honored! But, above all, try to make her miserable, odious family and surroundings understand it! Enriched bourgeois, parvenus! there's the roof beneath which you think to rest from your cruel labor and your many trials! And do you believe that you will not be made to feel, twenty times a day, that your share in the partnership is distressingly light in the scale against their money? On one side, the Iliad, the Cid, Der Freyschutz, and the frescos of the Vatican; on the other, three hundred thousand francs in good, ringing coin! Tell me which side they will trust and admire! The artist, the man of imagination who falls into the bourgeois atmosphere—shall I tell you to what I compare him? To Daniel cast into the lion's den, less the miracle of Holy Writ."

This invective against the bourgeoisie was uttered in a tone of heated conviction which could scarcely fail to be communicated.

"Ah! madame," cried la Peyrade, "how eloquently you say things which again and again have entered my troubled and anxious mind! But I have felt myself lashed to that most cruel fate, the necessity of gaining a position—"

"Necessity! position!" interrupted the countess, again raising the temperature of her speech,—"words void of meaning! which have not even sound to able men, though they drive back fools as though they were formidable barriers. Necessity! does that exist for noble natures, for those who know how to will? A Gascon minister uttered a saying which ought to be engraved on the doors of all careers: 'All things come to him who knows how to wait.' Are you ignorant that marriage, to men of a high stamp, is either a chain which binds them to the lowest vulgarities of existence, or a wing on which to rise to the highest summits of the social world? The wife you need, monsieur,—and she would not be long wanting to your career if you had not, with such incredible haste, accepted the first 'dot' that was offered you,—the wife you should have chosen is a woman capable of understanding you, able to divine your intellect; one who could be to you a fellow-worker, an intellectual confidant, and not a mere embodiment of the 'pot-au-feu'; a woman capable of being now your secretary, but soon the wife of a deputy, a minister, an ambassador; one, in short, who could offer you her heart as a mainspring, her salon for a stage, her connections for a ladder, and who, in return for all she would give you of ardor and strength, asks only to shine beside your throne in the rays of the glory she predicts for you!"

Intoxicated, as it were, with the flow of her own words, the countess was really magnificent; her eyes sparkled, her nostrils dilated; the prospect her vivid eloquence thus unrolled she seemed to see, and touch with her quivering fingers. For a moment, la Peyrade was dazzled by this sunrise which suddenly burst upon his life.

However, as he was a man most eminently prudent, who had made it his rule of life never to lend except on sound and solvent security, he was still impelled to weigh the situation.

"Madame la comtesse," he said, "you reproached me just now for speaking like a bourgeois, and I, in return, am afraid that you are talking like a goddess. I admire you, I listen to you, but I am not convinced. Such devotions, such sublime abnegations may be met with in heaven, but in this low world who can hope to be the object of them?"

"You are mistaken, monsieur," replied the countess, with solemnity; "such devotions are rare, but they are neither impossible nor incredible; only, it is necessary to have the heart to find them, and, above all, the hand to take them when they are offered to you."

So saying, the countess rose majestically.

La Peyrade saw that he had ended by displeasing her, and he felt that she dismissed him. He rose himself, bowed respectfully, and asked to be received again.

"Monsieur," said Madame de Godollo, "we Hungarians, primitive people and almost savages that we are, have a saying that when our door is open both sides of it are opened wide; when we close it it is double-locked and bolted."

That dignified and ambiguous speech was accompanied by a slight inclination of the head. Bewildered, confounded by this behavior, to him so new, which bore but little resemblance to that of Flavie, Brigitte, and Madame Minard, la Peyrade left the house, asking himself again and again whether he had played his game properly.

CHAPTER V. SHOWING HOW NEAR THE TARPEIAN ROCK IS TO THE CAPITOL

On leaving Madame de Godollo, la Peyrade felt the necessity of gathering himself together. Beneath the conversation he had just maintained with this strange woman, what could he see,—a trap, or a rich and distinguished marriage offered to him. Under such a doubt as this, to press Celeste for an immediate answer was neither clever nor prudent; it was simply to bind himself, and close the door to the changes, still very ill-defined, which seemed offered to him. The result of the consultation which Theodose held with himself as he walked along the boulevard was that he ought, for the moment, to think only of gaining time. Consequently, instead of going to the Thuilliers' to learn Celeste's decision, he went home, and wrote the following little note to Thuillier:—

> My dear Thuillier,—You will certainly not think it extraordinary that I should not present myself at your house to-day,—partly because I fear the sentence which will be pronounced upon me, and partly because I do not wish to seem an impatient and unmannerly creditor. A few days, more or less, will matter little under such circumstances, and yet Mademoiselle Colleville may find them desirable for the absolute freedom of her choice. I shall, therefore, not go to see you until you write for me.
>
> I am now more calm, and I have added a few more pages to our manuscript; it will take but little time to hand in the whole to the printer.

Ever yours,

Theodose de la Peyrade.

Two hours later a servant, dressed in what was evidently the first step towards a livery, which the Thuilliers did not as yet venture to risk, the "male domestic," whom Minard had mentioned to the Phellions, arrived at la Peyrade's lodgings with the following note:—

> Come to-night, without fail. We will talk over the whole affair with Brigitte.

Your most affectionately devoted Jerome Thuillier.

"Good!" said la Peyrade; "evidently there is some hindrance on the other side; I shall have time to turn myself round."

That evening, when the servant announced him in the Thuillier salon, the Comtesse de Godollo, who was sitting with Brigitte, hastened to rise and leave the room. As she passed la Peyrade she made him a very ceremonious bow. There was nothing conclusive to be deduced from this abrupt departure, which might signify anything, either much or nothing.

After talking of the weather and so forth for a time, as persons do who have met to discuss a delicate subject about which they are not sure of coming to an understanding, the matter was opened by Brigitte, who had sent her brother to take a walk on the boulevard, telling him to leave her to manage the affair.

"My dear boy," she said to Theodose, "it was very nice of you not to come here to-day like a *grasp-all*, to put your pistol at our throats, for we were not, as it happened, quite ready to answer you. I think," she added, "that our little Celeste needs a trifle more time."

"Then," said la Peyrade, quickly, "she has not decided in favor of Monsieur Felix Phellion?"

"Joker!" replied the old maid, "you know very well you settled that business last night; but you also know, of course, that her own inclinations incline her that way."

"Short of being blind, I must have seen that," replied la Peyrade.

"It is not an obstacle to my projects," continued Mademoiselle Thuillier; "but it serves to explain why I ask for Celeste a little more time; and also why I have wished all along to postpone the marriage to a later date. I wanted to give you time to insinuate yourself into the heart of my dear little girl—but you and Thuillier upset my plans."

"Nothing, I think, has been done without your sanction," said la Peyrade, "and if, during these fifteen days, I have not talked with you on the subject, it was out of pure delicacy. Thuillier told me that everything was agreed upon with you."

"On the contrary, Thuillier knows very well that I refused to mix myself up on your new arrangements. If you had not made yourself so scarce lately, I might have been the first to tell you that I did not approve of them. However, I can truly say I did nothing to hinder their success."

"But that was too little," said la Peyrade; "your active help was absolutely necessary."

"Possibly; but I, who know women better than you, being one of them,—I felt very sure that if Celeste was told to choose between two suitors she would consider that a permission to think at her ease of the one she liked best. I myself had always left her in the vague as to Felix, knowing as I did the proper moment to settle her mind about him."

"So," said la Peyrade, "you mean that she refuses me."

"It is much worse than that," returned Brigitte; "she accepts you, and is willing to pledge her word; but it is so easy to see she regards herself as a victim, that if I were in your place I should feel neither flattered nor secure in such a position."

In any other condition of mind la Peyrade would probably have answered that he accepted the sacrifice, and would make it his business to win the heart which at first was reluctantly given; but delay now suited him, and he replied to Brigitte with a question:—

"Then what do you advise? What course had I better take?"

"Finish Thuillier's pamphlet, in the first place, or he'll go crazy; and leave me to work the other affair in your interests," replied Brigitte.

"But am I in friendly hands? For, to tell you the truth, little aunt, I have not been able to conceal from myself that you have, for some time past, changed very much to me."

"Changed to you! What change do you see in me, addled-pate that you are?"

"Oh! nothing very tangible," said la Peyrade; "but ever since that Countess Torna has had a footing in your house—"

"My poor boy, the countess has done me many services, and I am very grateful to her; but is that any reason why I should be false to you, who have done us still greater services?"

"But you must admit," said la Peyrade, craftily, "that she has told you a great deal of harm of me."

"Naturally she has; these fine ladies are all that way; they expect the whole world to adore them, and she sees that you are thinking only of Celeste; but all she has said to me against you runs off my mind like water from varnished cloth."

"So, then, little aunt, I may continue to count on you?" persisted la Peyrade.

"Yes; provided you are not tormenting, and will let me manage this affair."

"Tell me how you are going to do it?" asked la Peyrade, with an air of great good-humor.

"In the first place, I shall signify to Felix that he is not to set foot in this house again."

"Is that possible?" said the barrister; "I mean can it be done civilly?"

"Very possible; I shall make Phellion himself tell him. He's a man who is always astride of principles, and he'll be the first to see that if his son will not do what is necessary to obtain Celeste's hand he ought to deprive us of his presence."

"What next?" asked la Peyrade.

"Next, I shall signify to Celeste that she was left at liberty to choose one husband or the other, and as she did not choose Felix she must make up her mind to take you, a pious fellow, such as she wants. You needn't be uneasy; I'll sing your praises, especially your generosity in not profiting by the arrangement she agreed to make to-day. But all that will take a week at least, and if Thuillier's pamphlet isn't out before then, I don't know but what we shall have to put him in a lunatic asylum."

"The pamphlet can be out in two days. But is it very certain, little aunt, that we are playing above-board? Mountains, as they say, never meet, but men do; and certainly, when the time comes to promote the election, I can do Thuillier either good or bad service. Do you know, the other day I was terribly frightened. I had a letter from him in my pocket, in which he spoke of the pamphlet as being written by me. I fancied for a moment that I had dropped it in the Luxembourg. If I had, what a scandal it would have caused in the quarter."

"Who would dare to play tricks with such a wily one as you?" said Brigitte, fully comprehending the comminatory nature of la Peyrade's last words, interpolated into the conversation without rhyme or reason. "But really," she added, "why should you complain of us? It is you who are behindhand in your promises. That cross which was to have been granted within a week, and that pamphlet, which ought to have appeared a long time ago—"

"The pamphlet and the cross will both appear in good time; the one will bring the other," said la Peyrade, rising. "Tell Thuillier to come and see me to-morrow evening, and I think we can then correct the last sheet. But, above all, don't listen to the spitefulness of Madame de Godollo; I have an idea that in order to make herself completely mistress of this house she wants to alienate all your old friends, and also that she is casting her net for Thuillier."

"Well, in point of fact," said the old maid, whom the parting shot of the infernal barrister had touched on the ever-sensitive point of her authority, "I must look into that matter you speak of there; she is rather coquettish, that little woman."

La Peyrade gained a second benefit out of that speech so adroitly flung out; he saw by Brigitte's answer to it that the countess had not mentioned to her the visit he had paid her during the day. This reticence might have a serious meaning.

Four days later, the printer, the stitcher, the paper glazier having fulfilled their offices, Thuillier had the inexpressible happiness of beginning on the boulevards a promenade, which he continued through the Passages, and even to the Palais-Royal, pausing before all the book-shops where he saw, shining in black letters on a yellow poster, the famous title:—

TAXATION AND THE SLIDING-SCALE by J. Thuillier, Member of the Council-General of the Seine.

Having reached the point of persuading himself that the care he had bestowed upon the correction of proofs made the merit of the work his own, his paternal heart, like that of Maitre Corbeau, could not contain itself for joy. We ought to add that he held in very low esteem those booksellers who did not announce the sale of the new work, destined to become, as he believed, a European event. Without actually deciding the manner in which he would punish their indifference, he nevertheless made a list of these rebellious persons, and wished them as much evil as if they had offered him a personal affront.

The next day he spent a delightful morning in writing a certain number of letters, sending the publication to friends, and putting into paper covers some fifty copies, to which the sacramental phrase, "From the author," imparted to his eyes an inestimable value.

But the third day of the sale brought a slight diminution of his happiness. He had chosen for his editor a young man, doing business at a breakneck pace, who had lately established himself in the Passage des Panoramas, where he was paying a ruinous rent. He was the nephew of Barbet the publisher, whom Brigitte had had as a tenant in the rue Saint-Dominique d'Enfer. This Barbet junior was a youth who flinched at nothing; and when he was presented to Thuillier by his uncle, he pledged himself, provided he was not shackled in his advertising, to sell off the first edition and print a second within a week.

Now, Thuillier had spent about fifteen hundred francs himself on costs of publication, such, for instance, as copies sent in great profusion to the newspapers; but at the close of the third day *seven* copies only had been sold, and three of those on credit. It might be believed that in revealing to the horror-stricken Thuillier this paltry result the young publisher would have lost at least something of his assurance. On the contrary, this Guzman of the book-trade hastened to say:—

"I am delighted at what has happened. If we had sold a hundred copies it would trouble me far more than the fifteen hundred now on our hands; that's what I call hanging fire; whereas this insignificant sale only proves that the edition will go off like a rocket."

"But when?" asked Thuillier, who thought this view paradoxical.

"Parbleu!" said Barbet, "when we get notices in the newspapers. Newspaper notices are only useful to arouse attention. 'Dear me!' says the public, 'there's a publication that must be interesting.' The title is good, —'Taxation and the Sliding-Scale,'—but I find that the more piquant a title is, the more buyers distrust it, they have been taken in so often; they wait for the notices. On the other hand, for books that are destined to have only a limited sale, a hundred ready-made purchasers will come in at once, but after that, good-bye to them; we don't place another copy."

"Then you don't think," said Thuillier, "that the sale is hopeless?"

"On the contrary, I think it is on the best track. When the 'Debats,' the 'Constitutionnel,' the 'Siecle,' and the 'Presse' have reviewed it, especially if the 'Debats' mauls it (they are ministerial, you know), it won't be a week before the whole edition is snapped up."

"You say that easily enough," replied Thuillier; "but how are we to get hold of those gentlemen of the press?"

"Ah! I'll take care of that," said Barbet. "I am on the best of terms with the managing editors; they say the devil is in me, and that I remind them of Ladvocat in his best days."

"But then, my dear fellow, you ought to have seen to this earlier."

"Ah! excuse me, papa Thuillier; there's only one way of seeing to the journalists; but as you grumbled about the fifteen hundred francs for the advertisements, I did not venture to propose to you another extra expense."

"What expense?" asked Thuillier, anxiously.

"When you were nominated to the municipal council, where was the plan mooted?" asked the publisher.

"Parbleu! in my own house," replied Thuillier.

"Yes, of course, in your own house, but at a dinner, followed by a ball, and the ball itself crowned by a supper. Well, my dear master, there are no two ways to do this business; Boileau says:—

"'All is done through the palate, and not through the mind;
And it is by our dinners we govern mankind.'"

"Then you think I ought to give a dinner to those journalists?"

"Yes; but not at your own house; for these journalists, you see, if women are present, get stupid; they have to behave themselves. And, besides, it isn't dinner they want, but a breakfast—that suits them best. In the evening these gentlemen have to go to first representations, and make up their papers, not to speak of their own little private doings; whereas in the mornings they have nothing to think about. As for me, it is always breakfasts that I give."

"But that costs money, breakfasts like that," said Thuillier; "journalists are gourmands."

"Bah! twenty francs a head, without wine. Say you have ten of them; three hundred francs will see you handsomely through the whole thing. In fact, as a matter of economy, breakfasts are preferable; for a dinner you wouldn't get off under five hundred francs."

"How you talk, young man!" said Thuillier.

"Oh, hang it! everybody knows it costs dear to get elected to the Chamber; and all this favors your nomination."

"But how can I invite those gentlemen? Must I go and see them myself?"

"Certainly not; send them your pamphlet and appoint them to meet you at Philippe's or Vefour's—they'll understand perfectly."

"Ten guests," said Thuillier, beginning to enter into the idea. "I did not know there were so many leading journals."

"There are not," said the publisher; "but we must have the little dogs as well, for they bark loudest. This breakfast is certain to make a noise, and if you don't ask them they'll think you pick and choose, and everyone excluded will be your enemy."

"Then you think it is enough merely to send the invitations?"

"Yes; I'll make the list, and you can write the notes and send them to me. I'll see that they are delivered; some of them I shall take in person."

"If I were sure," said Thuillier, undecidedly, "that this expense would have the desired effect—"

"*If I were sure*,—that's a queer thing to say," said Barbet. "My dear master, this is money placed on mortgage; for it, I will guarantee the sale of fifteen hundred copies,—say at forty sous apiece; allowing the discounts, that makes three thousand francs. You see that your costs and extra costs are covered, and more than covered."

"Well," said Thuillier, turning to go, "I'll talk to la Peyrade about it."

"As you please, my dear master; but decide soon, for nothing gets mouldy so fast as a book; write hot, serve hot, and buy hot,—that's the rule for authors, publishers, and public; all is bosh outside of it, and no good to touch."

When la Peyrade was consulted, he did not think in his heart that the remedy was heroic, but he had now come to feel the bitterest animosity against Thuillier, so that he was well pleased to see this new tax levied on his self-important inexperience and pompous silliness.

As for Thuillier, the mania for posing as a publicist and getting himself talked about so possessed him that although he moaned over this fresh bleeding of his purse, he had decided on the sacrifice before he even spoke to la Peyrade. The reserved and conditional approval of the latter was, therefore, more than enough to settle his determination, and the same evening he returned to Barbet junior and asked for the list of guests whom he ought to invite.

Barbet gaily produced his little catalogue. Instead of the ten guests originally mentioned, there proved to be fifteen, not counting himself or la Peyrade, whom Thuillier wanted to second him in this encounter with a set of men among whom he himself felt he should be a little out of place. Casting his eyes over the list, he exclaimed, vehemently:—

"Heavens! my dear fellow, here are names of papers nobody ever heard of. Where's the 'Moralisateur,' the 'Lanterne de Diogene,' the 'Pelican,' the 'Echo de la Bievre'?"

"You'd better be careful how you scorn the 'Echo de la Bievre,'" said Barbet; "why, that's the paper of the 12th arrondissement, from which you expect to be elected; its patrons are those big tanners of the Mouffetard quarter!"

"Well, let that go—but the 'Pelican'?"

"The 'Pelican'? that's a paper you'll find in every dentist's waiting-room; dentists are the first *puffists* in the world! How many teeth do you suppose are daily pulled in Paris?"

"Come, come, nonsense," said Thuillier, who proceeded to mark out certain names, reducing the whole number present to fourteen.

"If one falls off we shall be thirteen," remarked Barbet.

"Pooh!" said Thuillier, the free-thinker, "do you suppose I give in to that superstition?"

The list being finally closed and settled at fourteen, Thuillier seated himself at the publisher's desk and wrote the invitations, naming, in view of the urgency of the purpose, the next day but one for the meeting, Barbet having assured him that no journalist would object to the shortness of the invitation. The meeting was appointed at Vefour's, the restaurant par excellence of the bourgeoisie and all provincials.

Barbet arrived on the day named before Thuillier, who appeared in a cravat which alone was enough to create a stir in the satirical circle in which he was about to produce himself. The publisher, on his own authority, had changed various articles on the bill of fare as selected by his patron, more especially directing that the champagne, ordered in true bourgeois fashion to be served with the dessert, should be placed on the table at the beginning of breakfast, with several dishes of shrimps, a necessity which had not occurred to the amphitryon.

Thuillier, who gave a lip-approval to these amendments, was followed by la Peyrade; and then came a long delay in the arrival of the guests. Breakfast was ordered at eleven o'clock; at a quarter to twelve not a journalist had appeared. Barbet, who was never at a loss, made the consoling remark that breakfasts at restaurants were like funerals, where, as every one knew, eleven o'clock meant mid-day.

Sure enough, shortly before that hour, two gentlemen, with pointed beards, exhaling a strong odor of tobacco, made their appearance. Thuillier thanked them effusively for the "honor" they had done him; after which came another long period of waiting, of which we shall not relate the tortures. At one o'clock the assembled contingent comprised five of the invited guests, Barbet and la Peyrade not included. It is scarcely necessary to say that none of the self-respecting journalists of the better papers had taken any notice of the absurd invitation.

Breakfast now had to be served to this reduced number. A few polite phrases that reached Thuillier's ears about the "immense" interest of his publication, failed to blind him to the bitterness of his discomfiture; and without the gaiety of the publisher, who had taken in hand the reins his patron, gloomy as Hippolytus on the road to Mycenae, let fall, nothing could have surpassed the glum and glacial coldness of the meeting.

After the oysters were removed, the champagne and chablis which had washed them down had begun, nevertheless, to raise the thermometer, when, rushing into the room where the banquet was taking place, a young man in a cap conveyed to Thuillier a most unexpected and crushing blow.

"Master," said the new-comer to Barbet (he was a clerk in the bookseller's shop), "we are done for! The police have made a raid upon us; a commissary and two men have come to seize monsieur's pamphlet. Here's a paper they have given me for you."

"Look at that," said Barbet, handing the document to la Peyrade, his customary assurance beginning to forsake him.

"A summons to appear at once before the court of assizes," said la Peyrade, after reading a few lines of the sheriff's scrawl.

Thuillier had turned as pale as death.

"Didn't you fulfil all the necessary formalities?" he said to Barbet, in a choking voice.

"This is not a matter of formalities," said la Peyrade, "it is a seizure for what is called press misdemeanor, exciting contempt and hatred of the government; you probably have the same sort of compliment awaiting you at home, my poor Thuillier."

"Then it is treachery!" cried Thuillier, losing his head completely.

"Hang it, my dear fellow! you know very well what you put in your pamphlet; for my part, I don't see anything worth whipping a cat for."

"There's some misunderstanding," said Barbet, recovering courage; "it will all be explained, and the result will be a fine cause of complaint—won't it, messieurs?"

"Waiter, pens and ink!" cried one of the journalists thus appealed to.

"Nonsense! you'll have time to write your article later," said another of the brotherhood; "what has a bombshell to do with this 'filet saute'?"

That, of course, was a parody on the famous speech of Charles XII., King of Sweden, when a shot interrupted him while dictating to a secretary.

"Messieurs," said Thuillier, rising, "I am sure you will excuse me for leaving you. If, as Monsieur Barbet thinks, there is some misunderstanding, it ought to be explained at once; I must therefore, with your permission, go to the police court. La Peyrade," he added in a significant tone, "you will not refuse, I presume, to accompany me. And you, my dear publisher, you would do well to come too."

"No, faith!" said Barbet, "when I breakfast, I breakfast; if the police have committed a blunder, so much the worse for them."

"But suppose the matter is serious?" cried Thuillier, in great agitation.

"Well, I should say, what is perfectly true, that I had never read a line of your pamphlet. One thing is very annoying; those damned juries hate beards, and I must cut off mine if I'm compelled to appear in court."

"Come, my dear amphitryon, sit down again," said the editor of the "Echo de la Bievre," "we'll stand by you; I've already written an article in my head which will stir up all the tanners in Paris; and, let me tell you, that honorable corporation is a power."

"No, monsieur," replied Thuillier, "no; a man like me cannot rest an hour under such an accusation as this. Continue your breakfast without us; I hope soon to see you again. La Peyrade, are you coming?"

"He's charming, isn't he?" said Barbet, when Thuillier and his counsel had left the room. "To ask me to leave a breakfast after the oysters, and go and talk with the police! Come, messieurs, close up the ranks," he added, gaily.

"Tiens!" said one of the hungry journalists, who had cast his eyes into the garden of the Palais-Royal, on which the dining-room of the restaurant opened, "there's Barbanchu going by; suppose I call him in?"

"Yes, certainly," said Barbet junior, "have him up."

"Barbanchu! Barbanchu!" called out the journalist.

Barbanchu, his hat being over his eyes, was some time in discovering the cloud above him whence the voice proceeded.

"Here, up here!" called the voice, which seemed to Barbanchu celestial when he saw himself hailed by a man with a glass of champagne in his hand. Then, as he seemed to hesitate, the party above called out in chorus:—

"Come up! come up! *There's fat to be had*!"

When Thuillier left the office of the public prosecutor he could no longer have any illusions. The case against him was serious, and the stern manner in which he had been received made him see that when the trial came up he would be treated without mercy. Then, as always happens among accomplices after the non-success of an affair they have done in common, he turned upon la Peyrade in the sharpest manner: La Peyrade had paid no attention to what he wrote; he had given full swing to his stupid Saint-Simonian ideas; *he* didn't care for the consequences; it was not *he* who would have to pay the fine and go to prison! Then, when la Peyrade answered that the matter did not look to him serious, and he expected to get a verdict of acquittal without difficulty, Thuillier burst forth upon him, vehemently:—

"Parbleu! the thing is plain enough; monsieur sees nothing in it? Well, I shall not put my honor and my fortune into the hands of a little upstart like yourself; I shall take some great lawyer if the case comes to trial. I've had enough of your collaboration by this time."

Under the injustice of these remarks la Peyrade felt his anger rising. However, he saw himself disarmed, and not wishing to come to an open rupture, he parted from Thuillier, saying that he forgave a man excited by fear, and would go to see him later in the afternoon, when he would probably be calmer; they could then decide on what steps they had better take.

Accordingly, about four o'clock, the Provencal arrived at the house in the Place de la Madeleine. Thuillier's irritation was quieted, but frightful consternation had taken its place. If the executioner were coming in half an hour to lead him to the scaffold he could not have been more utterly unstrung and woe-begone. When la Peyrade entered Madame Thuillier was trying to make him take an infusion of linden-leaves. The poor woman had come out of her usual apathy, and proved herself, beside the present Sabinus, another Eponina.

As for Brigitte, who presently appeared, bearing a foot-bath, she had no mercy or restraint towards Theodose; her sharp and bitter reproaches, which were out of all proportion to the fault, even supposing him to have committed one would have driven a man of the most placid temperament beside himself. La Peyrade felt that all was lost to him in the Thuillier household, where they now seemed to seize with joy the occasion to break their word to him and to give free rein to revolting ingratitude. On an ironical allusion by Brigitte to the manner in which he decorated his friends, la Peyrade rose and took leave, without any effort being made to retain him.

After walking about the streets for awhile, la Peyrade, in the midst of his indignation, turned to thoughts of Madame de Godollo, whose image, to tell the truth, had been much in his mind since their former interview.

CHAPTER VI. 'TWAS THUS THEY BADE ADIEU

Not only once when the countess met the barrister at the Thuilliers had she left the room; but the same performance took place at each of their encounters; and la Peyrade had convinced himself, without knowing exactly why, that in each case, this affectation of avoiding him, signified something that was not indifference. To have paid her another visit immediately would certainly have been very unskilful; but now a sufficient time had elapsed to prove him to be a man who was master of himself. Accordingly, he returned upon his steps to the Boulevard de la Madeleine, and without asking the porter if the countess was at home, he passed the lodge as if returning to the Thuilliers', and rang the bell of the entresol.

The maid who opened the door asked him, as before, to wait until she notified her mistress; but, on this occasion, instead of showing him into the dining-room, she ushered him into a little room arranged as a library.

He waited long, and knew not what to think of the delay. Still, he reassured himself with the thought that if she meant to dismiss him he would not have been asked to wait at all. Finally the maid reappeared, but even then it was not to introduce him.

"Madame la comtesse," said the woman, "was engaged on a matter of business, but she begged monsieur be so kind as to wait, and to amuse himself with the books in the library, because she might be detained longer than she expected."

The excuse, both in form and substance, was certainly not discouraging, and la Peyrade looked about him to fulfil the behest to amuse himself. Without opening any of the carved rosewood bookcases, which enclosed a collection of the most elegantly bound volumes he had ever laid his eyes upon, he saw on an oblong table with claw feet a pell-mell of books sufficient for the amusement of a man whose attention was keenly alive elsewhere.

But, as he opened one after another of the various volumes, he began to fancy that a feast of Tantalus had been provided for him: one book was English, another German, a third Russian; there was even one in cabalistic letters that seemed Turkish. Was this a polyglottic joke the countess had arranged for him?

One volume, however, claimed particular attention. The binding, unlike those of the other books, was less rich than dainty. Lying by itself at a corner of the table, it was open, with the back turned up, the edges of the leaves resting on the green table-cloth in the shape of a tent. La Peyrade took it up, being careful not to lose the page which it seemed to have been some one's intention to mark. It proved to be a volume of the illustrated edition of Monsieur Scribe's works. The engraving which presented itself on the open page to la Peyrade's eyes, was entitled "The Hatred of a Woman"; the principal personage of which is a young widow, desperately pursuing a poor young man who cannot help himself. There is hatred all round. Through her devilries she almost makes him lose his reputation, and does make him miss a rich marriage; but the end is that she gives him more than she took away from him, and makes a husband of the man who was thought her victim.

If chance had put this volume apart from the rest, and had left it open at the precise page where la Peyrade found it marked, it must be owned that, after what had passed between himself and the countess, chance can sometimes seem clever and adroit. As he stood there, thinking over the significance which this more or less accidental combination might have, la Peyrade read through a number of scenes to see whether in the details as well as the general whole they applied to the present situation. While thus employed, the sound of an opening door was heard, and he recognized the silvery and slightly drawling voice of the countess, who was evidently accompanying some visitor to the door.

"Then I may promise the ambassadress," said a man's voice, "that you will honor her ball with your presence?"

"Yes, commander, if my headache, which is just beginning to get a little better, is kind enough to go away."

"Au revoir, then, fairest lady," said the gentleman. After which the doors were closed, and silence reigned once more.

The title of commander reassured la Peyrade somewhat, for it was not the rank of a young dandy. He was nevertheless curious to know who this personage was with whom the countess had been shut up so long. Hearing no one approach the room he was in, he went to the window and opened the curtain cautiously, prepared to let it drop back at the slightest noise, and to make a quick right-about-face to avoid being caught, "flagrante delicto," in curiosity. An elegant coupe, standing at a little distance, was now driven up to the house, a footman in showy livery hastened to open the door, and a little old man, with a light and jaunty movement, though it was evident he was one of those relics of the past who have not yet abandoned powder, stepped quickly into the carriage, which was then driven rapidly away. La Peyrade had time to observe on his breast a perfect string of decorations. This, combined with the powdered hair, was certain evidence of a diplomatic individual.

La Peyrade had picked up his book once more, when a bell from the inner room sounded, quickly followed by the appearance of the maid, who invited him to follow her. The Provencal took care *not* to replace the volume where he found it, and an instant later he entered the presence of the countess.

A pained expression was visible on the handsome face of the foreign countess, who, however, lost nothing of her charm in the languor that seemed to overcome her. On the sofa beside her was a manuscript written on gilt-edged paper, in that large and opulent handwriting which indicates an official communication from some ministerial office or chancery. She held in her hand a crystal bottle with a gold stopper, from which she frequently inhaled the contents, and a strong odor of English vinegar pervaded the salon.

"I fear you are ill, madame," said la Peyrade, with interest.

"Oh! it is nothing," replied the countess; "only a headache, to which I am very subject. But you, monsieur, what has become of you? I was beginning to lose all hope of ever seeing you again. Have you come to announce to me some great news? The period of your marriage with Mademoiselle Colleville is probably so near that I think you can speak of it."

This opening disconcerted la Peyrade.

"But, madame," he answered, in a tone that was almost tart, "you, it seems to me, must know too well everything that goes on in the Thuillier household not to be aware that the event you speak of is not approaching, and, I may add, not probable."

"No, I assure you, I know nothing; I have strictly forbidden myself from taking any further interest in an affair which I felt I had meddled with very foolishly. Mademoiselle Brigitte and I talk of everything except Celeste's marriage."

"And it is no doubt the desire to allow me perfect freedom in the matter that induces you to take flight whenever I have the honor to meet you in the Thuillier salon?"

"Yes," said the countess, "that ought to be the reason that makes me leave the room; else, why should I be so distant?"

"Ah! madame, there are other reasons that might make a woman avoid a man's presence. For instance, if he has displeased her; if the advice, given to him with rare wisdom and kindness, was not received with proper eagerness and gratitude."

"Oh, my dear monsieur," she replied, "I have no such ardor in proselytizing that I am angry with those who are not docile to my advice. I am, like others, very apt to make mistakes."

"On the contrary, madame, in the matter of my marriage your judgment was perfectly correct."

"How so?" said the countess, eagerly. "Has the seizure of the pamphlet, coming directly after the failure to obtain the cross, led to a rupture?"

"No," said la Peyrade, "my influence in the Thuillier household rests on a solid basis; the services I have rendered Mademoiselle Brigitte and her brother outweigh these checks, which, after all, are not irreparable."

"Do you really think so?" said the countess.

"Certainly," replied la Peyrade; "when the Comtesse du Bruel takes it into her head to seriously obtain that bit of red ribbon, she can do so, in spite of all obstacles that are put in her way."

The countess received this assertion with a smile, and shook her head.

"But, madame, only a day or two ago Madame du Bruel told Madame Colleville that the unexpected opposition she had met with piqued her, and that she meant to go in person to the minister."

"But you forget that since then this seizure has been made by the police; it is not usual to decorate a man who is summoned before the court of assizes. You seem not to notice that the seizure argues a strong ill-will against Monsieur Thuillier, and, I may add, against yourself, monsieur, for you are known to be the culprit. You have not, I think, taken all this into account. The authorities appear to have acted not wholly from legal causes."

La Peyrade looked at the countess.

"I must own," he said, after that rapid glance, "that I have tried in vain to find any passage in that pamphlet which could be made a legal pretext for the seizure."

"In my opinion," said the countess, "the king's servants must have a vivid imagination to persuade themselves they were dealing with a seditious publication. But that only proves the strength of the underground power which is thwarting all your good intentions in favor of Monsieur Thuillier."

"Madame," said la Peyrade, "do you know our secret enemies?"

"Perhaps I do," replied the countess, with another smile.

"May I dare to utter a suspicion, madame?" said la Peyrade, with some agitation.

"Yes, say what you think," replied Madame de Godollo. "I shall not blame you if you guess right."

"Well, madame, our enemies, Thuillier's and mine, are—a woman."

"Supposing that is so," said the countess; "do you know how many lines Richelieu required from a man's hand in order to hang him?"

"Four," replied la Peyrade.

"You can imagine, then, that a pamphlet of two hundred pages might afford a—slightly intriguing woman sufficient ground for persecution."

"I see it all, madame, I understand it!" cried la Peyrade, with animation. "I believe that woman to be one of the elite of her sex, with as much mind and malice as Richelieu! Adorable magician! it is she who has set in motion the police and the gendarmes; but, more than that, it is she who withholds that cross the ministers were about to give."

"If that be so," said the countess, "why struggle against her?"

"Ah! I struggle no longer," said la Peyrade. Then, with an assumed air of contrition, he added, "You must, indeed, *hate* me, madame."

"Not quite as much as you may think," replied the countess; "but, after all, suppose that I do hate you?"

"Ah! madame," cried la Peyrade, ardently, "I should then be the happiest of unhappy men; for that hatred would seem to me sweeter and more precious than your indifference. But you do not hate me; why should you feel to me that most blessed feminine sentiment which Scribe has depicted with such delicacy and wit?"

Madame de Godollo did not answer immediately. She lowered her eyelids, and the deeper breathing of her bosom gave to her voice when she did speak a tremulous tone:—

"The hatred of a woman!" she said. "Is a man of your stoicism able to perceive it?"

"Ah! yes, madame," replied la Peyrade, "I do indeed perceive it, but not to revolt against it; on the contrary, I bless the harshness that deigns to hurt me. Now that I know my beautiful and avowed enemy, I shall not despair of touching her heart; for never again will I follow any road but the one that she points out to me, never will I march under any banner but hers. I shall wait— for her inspiration, to think; for her will, to will; for her commands, to act. In all things I will be her auxiliary,—more than that, her slave; and if she still repulses me with that dainty foot, that snowy hand, I will bear it resignedly, asking, in return for such obedience one only favor,—that of kissing the foot that spurns me, of bathing with tears the hand that threatens me."

During this long cry of the excited heart, which the joy of triumph wrung from a nature so nervous and impressionable as that of the Provencal, he had slidden from his chair, and now knelt with one knee on the ground beside the countess, in the conventional attitude of the stage, which is, however, much more common in real life than people suppose.

"Rise, monsieur," said the countess, "and be so good as to answer me." Then, giving him a questioning look from beneath her beautiful frowning brows, she continued: "Have you well-weighed the outcome of the words you have just uttered? Have you measured the full extent of your pledge, and its depth? With your hand on your heart and on your conscience, are you a man to fulfil those words? Or are you one of the falsely humble and perfidious men who throw themselves at our feet only to make us lose the balance of our will and our reason?"

"I!" exclaimed la Peyrade; "never can I react against the fascination you have wielded over me from the moment of our first interview! Ah! madame, the more I have resisted, the more I have struggled, the more you ought to trust in my sincerity and its tardy expression. What I have said, I think; that which I think aloud to-day I have thought in my soul since the hour when I first had the honor of admittance to you; and the many days I have passed in struggling against this allurement have ended in giving me a firm and deliberate will, which understands itself, and is not cast down by your severity."

"Severity?" said the countess; "possibly. But you ought to think of the kindness too. Question yourself carefully. We foreign women do not understand the careless ease with which a Frenchwoman enters upon a solemn engagement. To us, our *yes* is sacred; our word is a bond. We do and we will nothing by halves. The arms of my family bear a motto which seems significant under the present circumstances,—'All or Nothing'; that is saying much, and yet, perhaps, not enough."

"That is how I understand my pledge," replied la Peyrade; "and on leaving this room my first step will be to break with that ignoble past which for an instant I seemed to hold in the balance against the intoxicating future you do not forbid me to expect."

"No," said the countess, "do it calmly and advisedly; I do not like rash conduct; you will not please me by taking open steps. These Thuilliers are not really bad at heart; they humiliated you without knowing that they did so; their world is not yours. Is that their fault? Loosen the tie between you, but do not violently break it. And, above all, reflect. Your conversion to my beliefs is

278

of recent date. What man is certain of what his heart will say to him to-morrow?"

"Madame," said la Peyrade, "I am that man. We men of Southern blood do not love as you say a Frenchwoman loves."

"But," said the countess, with a charming smile, "I thought it was hatred we were talking of."

"Ah, madame," cried the barrister, "explained and understood as it has been, that word is still a thing that hurts me. Tell me rather, not that you love me, but that the words you deigned to say to me at our first interview were indeed the expression of your thoughts."

"My friend," said the countess, dwelling on the word; "one of your moralists has said: 'There are persons who say, *that is* or *that is not*.' Do me the favor to count me among such persons."

So saying, she held out her hand to her suitor with a charming gesture of modesty and grace. La Peyrade, quite beside himself, darted upon that beautiful hand and devoured it with kisses.

"Enough, child!" said the countess, gently freeing her imprisoned fingers; "adieu now, soon to meet again! Adieu! My headache, I think, has disappeared."

La Peyrade picked up his hat, and seemed about to rush from the apartment; but at the door he turned and cast upon the handsome creature a look of tenderness. The countess made him, with her head, a graceful gesture of adieu; then, seeing that la Peyrade was inclined to return to her, she raised her forefinger as a warning to control himself and go.

La Peyrade turned and left the apartment.

CHAPTER VII. HOW TO SHUT THE DOOR IN PEOPLE'S FACES

On the staircase la Peyrade stopped to exhale, if we may so express it, the happiness of which his heart was full. The words of the countess, the ingenious preparation she had made to put him on the track of her sentiments, seemed to him the guarantee of her sincerity, and he left her full of faith.

Possessed by that intoxication of happy persons which shows itself in their gestures, their looks, their very gait, and sometimes in actions not authorized by their common-sense, after pausing a moment, as we have said, on the staircase, he ran up a few steps till he could see the door of the Thuilliers' apartment.

"At last!" he cried, "fame, fortune, happiness have come to me; but, above all, I can now give myself the joy of vengeance. After Dutocq and Cerizet, I will crush *you*, vile bourgeois brood!"

So saying, he shook his fist at the innocent door. Then he turned and ran out; the popular saying that the earth could not hold him, was true at that moment of his being.

The next day, for he could not restrain any longer the tempest that was swelling within him, la Peyrade went to see Thuillier in the bitterest and most hostile of moods. What was therefore his amazement when, before he had time to put himself on guard and stop the demonstration of union and oblivion, Thuillier flung himself into his arms.

"My friend," cried the municipal councillor, as he loosened his clasp, "my political fortune is made; this morning all the newspapers, without exception, have spoken of the seizure of my pamphlet; and you ought to see how the opposition sheets have mauled the government."

"Simple enough," said la Peyrade, not moved by this enthusiasm; "you are a topic for them, that's all. But this does not alter the situation; the prosecution will be only the more determined to have you condemned."

"Well, then," said Thuillier, proudly raising his head, "I will go to prison, like Beranger, like Lamennais, like Armand Carrel."

"My good fellow, persecution is charming at a distance; but when you hear the big bolts run upon you, you may be sure you won't like it as well."

"But," objected Thuillier, "prisoners condemned for political offences are always allowed to do their time in hospital if they like. Besides, I'm not yet

281

convicted. You said yourself you expected to get me acquitted."

"Yes, but since then I have heard things which make that result very doubtful; the same hand that withheld your cross has seized your pamphlet; you are being murdered with premeditation."

"If you know who that dangerous enemy is," said Thuillier, "you can't refuse to point him out to me."

"I don't know him," replied la Peyrade; "I only suspect him. This is what you get by playing too shrewd a game."

"Playing a shrewd game!" said Thuillier, with the curiosity of a man who is perfectly aware that he has nothing of that kind on his conscience.

"Yes," said la Peyrade, "you made a sort of decoy of Celeste to attract young bloods to your salon. All the world has not the forbearance of Monsieur Godeschal, who forgave his rejection and generously managed that affair about the house."

"Explain yourself better," said Thuillier, "for I don't see what you mean."

"Nothing is easier to understand. Without counting me, how many suitors have you had for Mademoiselle Colleville? Godeschal, Minard junior, Phellion junior, Olivier Vinet, the substitute judge,—all men who have been sent about their business, as I am."

"Olivier Vinet, the substitute judge!" cried Thuillier, struck with a flash of light. "Of course; the blow must have come from him. His father, they say, has a long arm. But it can't be truly said that we sent him about his business, —to use your expression, which strikes me as indecorous,—for he never came to the house but once, and made no offer; neither did Minard junior or Phellion junior, for that matter. Godeschal is the only one who risked a direct proposal, and he was refused at once, before he dipped his beak in the water."

"It is always so!" said la Peyrade, still looking for a ground of quarrel. "Straightforward and outspoken persons are always those that sly men boast of fooling."

"Ah ca! what's all this?" said Thuillier; "what are you insinuating? Didn't you settle everything with Brigitte the other day? You take a pretty time to come and talk to me about your love-affairs, when the sword of justice is hanging over my head."

"Oh!" said la Peyrade, ironically; "so now you are going to make the most of your interesting position of accused person! I knew very well how it would be; I was certain that as soon as your pamphlet appeared the old cry of not getting what you expected out of me would come up."

"Parbleu! your pamphlet!" cried Thuillier. "I think you are a fine fellow to boast of that when, on the contrary, it has caused the most deplorable complications."

"Deplorable? how so? you have just said your political fortune was made."

"Well, truly, my dear Theodose," said Thuillier, with feeling, "I should never have thought that you would choose the hour of adversity to come and put your pistol at our throats and make me the object of your sneers and innuendoes."

"Well done!" said la Peyrade; "now it is the hour of adversity! A minute ago you were flinging yourself into my arms as a man to whom some signal piece of luck had happened. You ought really to choose decidedly between being a man who needs pity and a glorious victor."

"It is all very well to be witty," returned Thuillier; "but you can't controvert what I say. I am logical, if I am not brilliant. It is very natural that I should console myself by seeing that public opinion decides in my favor, and by reading in its organs the most honorable assurances of sympathy; but do you suppose I wouldn't rather that things had taken their natural course? Besides, when I see myself the object of unworthy vengeance on the part of persons as influential as the Vinets, how can I help measuring the extent of the dangers to which I am exposed?"

"Well," said la Peyrade, with pitiless persistency, "I see that you prefer to play the part of Jeremiah."

"Yes," said Thuillier, in a solemn tone. "Jeremiah laments over a friendship I did think true and devoted, but which I find has only sarcasms to give me when I looked for services."

"What services?" asked la Peyrade. "Did you not tell me positively, no later than yesterday, that you would not accept my help under any form whatever? I offered to plead your case, and you answered that you would take a better lawyer."

"Yes; in the first shock of surprise at such an unexpected blow, I did say that foolish thing; but, on reflection, who can explain as well as you can the intention of the words you wrote with your own pen? Yesterday I was almost out of my mind; but you, with your wounded self-love, which can't forgive a momentary impatience, you are very caustic and cruel."

"So," said la Peyrade, "you formally request me to defend you before the jury?"

"Yes, my dear fellow; and I don't know any other hands in which I could

283

better place my case. I should have to pay a monstrous sum to some great legal luminary, and he wouldn't defend me as ably as you."

"Well, I refuse. Roles have changed, as you see, diametrically. Yesterday, I thought, as you do, that I was the man to defend you. To-day, I see that you had better take the legal luminary, because, with Vinet's antagonism against you the affair is taking such proportions that whoever defends it assumes a fearful responsibility."

"I understand," said Thuillier, sarcastically. "Monsieur has his eye on the magistracy, and he doesn't want to quarrel with a man who is already talked of for Keeper of the Seals. It is prudent, but I don't know that it is going to help on your marriage."

"You mean," said la Peyrade, seizing the ball in its bound, "that to get you out of the claws of that jury is a thirteenth labor of Hercules, imposed upon me to earn the hand of Mademoiselle Colleville? I expected that demands would multiply in proportion to the proofs of my devotion. But that is the very thing that has worn me out, and I have come here to-day to put an end to this slave labor by giving back to you your pledges. You may dispose of Celeste's hand; for my part, I am no longer a suitor for it."

The unexpectedness and squareness of this declaration left Thuillier without words or voice, all the more because at this moment entered Brigitte. The temper of the old maid had also greatly moderated since the previous evening, and her greeting was full of the most amicable familiarity.

"Ah! so here you are, you good old barrister," she said.

"Mademoiselle, your servant," he replied, gravely.

"Well," she continued, paying no attention to the stiffness of his manner, "the government has got itself into a pretty mess by seizing your pamphlet. You ought to see how the morning papers lash it! Here," she added, giving Thuillier a small sheet printed on sugar-paper, in coarse type, and almost illegible,—"here's another, you didn't read; the porter has just brought it up. It is a paper from our old quarter, 'L'Echo de la Bievre.' I don't know, gentlemen, if you'll be of my opinion, but I think nothing could be better written. It is droll, though, how inattentive these journalists are! most of them write your name without the H; I think you ought to complain of it."

Thuillier took the paper, and read the article inspired to the reviewer of the tanner's organ by stomach gratitude. Never in her life had Brigitte paid the slightest attention to a newspaper, except to know if it was the right size for the packages she wrapped up in it; but now, suddenly, converted to a worship of the press by the ardor of her sisterly love, she stood behind Thuillier and re-read, over his shoulder, the more striking passages of the page she thought so eloquent, pointing her finger to them.

"Yes," said Thuillier, folding up the paper, "that's warm, and very flattering to me. But here's another matter! Monsieur has come to tell me that he refuses to plead for me, and renounces all claim to Celeste's hand."

"That is to say," said Brigitte, "he renounces her if, after having pleaded, the marriage does not take place 'subito.' Well, poor fellow, I think that's a reasonable demand. When he has done that for us there ought to be no further delay; and whether Mademoiselle Celeste likes it or not, she must accept him, because, you know, there's an end to all things."

"Do you hear that, my good fellow?" said la Peyrade, seizing upon Brigitte's speech. "When I have pleaded, the marriage is to take place. Your sister is frankness itself; she, at least, doesn't practise diplomacy."

"Diplomacy!" echoed Brigitte. "I'd like to see myself creeping underground in matters. I say things as I think them. The workman has worked, and he ought to have his pay."

"Do be silent," cried Thuillier, stamping his foot; "you don't say a word that doesn't turn the knife in the wound."

"The knife in the wound?" said Brigitte, inquiringly. "Ah ca! are you two quarrelling?"

"I told you," said Thuillier, "that la Peyrade had returned our promises; and the reason he gives is that we are asking him another service for Celeste's hand. He thinks he has done us enough without it."

"He has done us some services, no doubt," said Brigitte; "but it seems to me that we have not been ungrateful to him. Besides, it was he who made the blunder, and I think it rather odd he should now wish to leave us in the lurch."

"Your reasoning, mademoiselle," said la Peyrade, "might have some appearance of justice if I were the only barrister in Paris; but as the streets are black with them, and as, only yesterday, Thuillier himself spoke of engaging some more important lawyer than myself, I have not the slightest scruple in refusing to defend him. Now, as to the marriage, in order that it may not be made the object of another brutal and forcible demand upon me, I here renounce it in the most formal manner, and nothing now prevents Mademoiselle Colleville from accepting Monsieur Felix Phellion and all his advantages."

"As you please, my dear monsieur," said Brigitte, "if that's your last word. We shall not be at a loss to find a husband for Celeste,—Felix Phellion or another. But you must permit me to tell you that the reason you give is not the true one. We can't go faster than the fiddles. If the marriage were settled to-day, there are the banns to publish; you have sense enough to know that Monsieur le maire can't marry you before the formalities are complied with, and before then Thuillier's case will have been tried."

"Yes," said la Peyrade, "and if I lose the case it will be I who have sent him to prison,—just as yesterday it was I who brought about the seizure."

"As for that, it seems to me that if you had written nothing the police would have found nothing to bite."

"My dear Brigitte," said Thuillier, seeing la Peyrade shrug his shoulders, "your argument is vicious in the sense that the writing was not incriminating on any side. It is not la Peyrade's fault if persons of high station have organized a persecution against me. You remember that little substitute, Monsieur Olivier Vinet, whom Cardot brought to one of our receptions. It seems that he and his father are furious that we didn't want him for Celeste, and they've sworn my destruction."

"Well, why did we refuse him," said Brigitte, "if it wasn't for the fine eyes of monsieur here? For, after all, a substitute in Paris is a very suitable match."

"No doubt," said la Peyrade, nonchalantly. "Only, he did not happen to bring you a million."

"Ah!" cried Brigitte, firing up. "If you are going to talk any more about that house you helped us to buy, I shall tell you plainly that if you had had the money to trick the notary you never would have come after us. You needn't think I have been altogether your dupe. You spoke just now of a bargain, but you proposed that bargain yourself. 'Give me Celeste and I'll get you that house,'—that's what you said to us in so many words. Besides which, we had to pay large sums on which we never counted."

"Come, come, Brigitte," said Thuillier, "you are making a great deal out of nothing."

"Nothing! nothing!" exclaimed Brigitte. "Did we, or did we not, have to pay much more than we expected?"

"My dear Thuillier," said la Peyrade, "I think, with you, that the matter is now settled, and it can only be embittered by discussing it further. My course was decided on before I came here; all that I have now heard can only confirm it. I shall not be the husband of Celeste, but you and I can remain good friends."

He rose to leave the room.

"One moment, monsieur," said Brigitte, barring his way; "there is one matter which I do not consider settled; and now that we are no longer to have interests in common, I should not be sorry if you would be so good as to tell me what has become of a sum of ten thousand francs which Thuillier gave you to bribe those rascally government offices in order to get the cross we have never got."

"Brigitte!" cried Thuillier, in anguish, "you have a devil of a tongue! You ought to be silent about that; I told it to you in a moment of ill-temper, and you promised me faithfully never to open your lips about it to any one, no matter who."

"So I did; but," replied the implacable Brigitte, "we are parting. When people part they settle up; they pay their debts. Ten thousand francs! For my part, I thought the cross itself dear at that; but for a cross that has melted away, monsieur himself will allow the price is too high."

"Come, la Peyrade, my friend, don't listen to her," said Thuillier, going up to the barrister, who was pale with anger. "The affection she has for me blinds her; I know very well what government offices are, and I shouldn't be surprised if you had had to pay out money of your own."

"Monsieur," said la Peyrade, "I am, unfortunately, not in a position to return to you, instantly, that money, an accounting for which is so insolently demanded. Grant me a short delay; and have the goodness to accept my note, which I am ready to sign, if that will give you patience."

"To the devil with your note!" cried Thuillier; "you owe me nothing; on the contrary, it is we who owe you; for Cardot told me I ought to give you at least ten thousand francs for enabling us to buy this magnificent property."

"Cardot! Cardot!" said Brigitte; "he is very generous with other people's money. We were giving monsieur Celeste, and that's a good deal more than ten thousand francs."

La Peyrade was too great a comedian not to turn the humiliation he had just endured into a scene finale. With tears in his voice, which presently fell from his eyes, he turned to Brigitte.

"Mademoiselle," he said, "when I had the honor to be received by you I was poor; you long saw me suffering and ill at ease, knowing, alas! too well, the indignities that poverty must bear. From the day that I was able to give you a fortune which I never thought of for myself I have felt, it is true, more assurance; and your own kindness encouraged me to rise out of my timidity and depression. To-day, when I, by frank and loyal conduct, release you from anxiety,—for, if you chose to be honest, you would acknowledge that you have been thinking of another husband for Celeste,—we might still remain friends, even though I renounce a marriage which my delicacy forbids me to pursue. But you have not chosen to restrain yourself with the limits of social politeness, of which you have a model beside you in Madame de Godollo, who, I am persuaded, although she is not at all friendly to me, would never have approved of your odious behavior. Thank Heaven! I have in my heart some religious sentiment at least; the Gospel is not to me a mere dead-letter, and—understand me well, mademoiselle—*I forgive you.* It is not to Thuillier, who would refuse them, but to you that I shall, before long, pay the ten thousand francs which you insinuate I have applied to my own purposes. If, by the time they are returned to you, you feel regret for your unjust suspicions, and are unwilling to accept the money, I request that you will turn it over to the bureau of Benevolence to the poor—"

"To the bureau of Benevolence!" cried Brigitte, interrupting him. "No, I thank you! the idea of all that money being distributed among a crowd of do-nothings and devotes, who'll spend it in junketing! I've been poor too, my lad; I made bags for the money of others long before I had any money of my own; I have some now, and I take care of it. So, whenever you will, I am ready to receive that ten thousand francs and keep it. If you didn't know how to do what you undertook to do, and spent that money in trying to put salt on a sparrow's tail, so much the worse for you."

Seeing that he had missed his effect, and had made not the slightest impression on Brigitte's granite, la Peyrade cast a disdainful look upon her and left the room majestically. As he did so he noticed a movement made by Thuillier to follow him, and also the imperious gesture of Brigitte, always queen and mistress, which nailed her brother to his chair.

CHAPTER VIII

At the moment when la Peyrade was preparing to lay at the feet of the countess the liberty he had recovered in so brutal a manner, he received a perfumed note, which made his heart beat, for on the seal was that momentous "All or Nothing" which she had given him as the rule of the relation now to be inaugurated between them. The contents of the note were as follows:—

```
Dear Monsieur,—I have heard of the step you have taken; thank
you! But I must now prepare to take my own. I cannot, as you may
well think, continue to live in this house, and among these people
who are so little of our own class and with whom we have nothing
in common. To arrange this transaction, and to avoid explanations
of the fact that the entresol welcomes the voluntary exile from
the first-floor, I need to-day and to-morrow to myself. Do not
therefore come to see me until the day after. By that time I shall
have executed Brigitte, as they say at the Bourse, and have much
to tell you.
```

Tua tota,

Torna de Godollo.

That "Wholly thine" in Latin seemed charming to la Peyrade, who was not, however, astonished, for Latin is a second national language to the Hungarians. The two days' waiting to which he was thus condemned only fanned the flame of the ardent passion which possessed him, and on the third day when reached the house by the Madeleine his love had risen to a degree of incandescence of which only a few days earlier he would scarcely have supposed himself capable.

This time the porter's wife perceived him; but he was now quite indifferent as to whether or not the object of his visit should be known. The ice was broken, his happiness was soon to be official, and he was more disposed to cry it aloud in the streets than to make a mystery of it.

Running lightly up the stairs, he prepared to ring the bell, when, on putting out his hand to reach the silken bell-cord he perceived that the bell-cord had disappeared. La Peyrade's first thought was that one of those serious illnesses which make all noises intolerable to a patient would explain its absence; but with the thought came other observations that weakened it, and which, moreover, were not in themselves comforting.

From the vestibule to the countess's door a stair carpet, held at each step by a brass rod, made a soft ascent to the feet of visitors; this, too, had been removed. A screen-door covered with green velvet and studded with brass nails had hitherto protected the entrance to the apartment; of that no sign, except the injury to the wall done by the workmen in taking it away. For a moment the barrister thought, in his agitation, that he must have mistaken the floor, but, casting his eye over the baluster he saw that he had not passed the entresol. Madame de Godollo must, therefore, be in the act of moving away.

He then resigned himself to make known his presence at the great lady's door as he would have done at that of a grisette. He rapped with his knuckles, but a hollow sonority revealing the void, "intonuere cavernae," echoed beyond the door which he vainly appealed to with his fist. He also perceived from beneath that door a ray of vivid light, the sure sign of an uninhabited apartment where curtains and carpets and furniture no longer dim the light or deaden sound. Compelled to believe in a total removal, la Peyrade now supposed that in the rupture with Brigitte, mentioned as probable by Madame de Godollo, some brutal insolence of the old maid had necessitated this abrupt departure. But why had he not been told of it? And what an idea, to expose him to this ridiculous meeting with what the common people call, in their picturesque language, "the wooden face"!

Before leaving the door finally, and as if some doubt still remained in his mind, la Peyrade made a last and most thundering assault upon it.

"Who's knocking like that, as if they'd bring the house down?" said the porter, attracted by the noise to the foot of the staircase.

"Doesn't Madame de Godollo still live here?" asked la Peyrade.

"Of course she doesn't live here now; she has moved away. If monsieur had told me he was going to her apartment I would have spared him the trouble of battering down the door."

"I knew that she was going to leave the apartment," said la Peyrade, not wishing to seem ignorant of the project of departure, "but I had no idea she was going so soon."

"I suppose it was something sudden," said the porter, "for she went off early this morning with post-horses."

"Post-horses!" echoed la Peyrade, stupefied. "Then she has left Paris?"

"That's to be supposed," said the porter; "people don't usually take post-horses and a postilion to change from one quarter of Paris to another."

"And she did not tell you where she was going?"

"Ah! monsieur, what an idea! Do people account to us porters for what they do?"

"No, but her letters—those that come after her departure?"

"Her letters? I am ordered to deliver them to Monsieur le commandeur, the little old gentlemen who came to see her so often; monsieur must have met him."

"Yes, yes, certainly," said la Peyrade, keeping his presence of mind in the midst of the successive shocks which came upon him,—"the powered little man who was here every day."

"I couldn't say every day; but he came often. Well, I am told to give the countess's letters to him."

"And for other persons of her acquaintance," said la Peyrade, carelessly, "did she leave no message?"

"None, monsieur."

"Very well," said la Peyrade, "good-morning." And he turned to go out.

"But I think," said the porter, "that Mademoiselle Thuillier knows more about it than I do. Won't monsieur go up? She is at home; and so is Monsieur Thuillier."

"No, never mind," said la Peyrade, "I only came to tell Madame de Godollo about a commission she asked me to execute; I haven't time to stop now."

"Well, as I told you, she left with post-horses this morning. Two hours earlier monsieur might still have found her; but now, with post-horses, she must by this time have gone a good distance."

La Peyrade departed, with a sense of despair in his heart. Added to the anxiety caused by this hasty departure, jealousy entered his soul, and in this agonizing moment of disappointment the most distressing explanations crowded on his mind.

Then, after further reflection, he said to himself:—

"These clever diplomatic women are often sent on secret missions which require the most absolute silence, and extreme rapidity of movement."

But here a sudden revulsion of thought overcame him:—

"Suppose she were one of those intriguing adventurers whom foreign governments employ as agents? Suppose the tale, more or less probable, of that Russian princess forced to sell her furniture to Brigitte were also that of this Hungarian countess? And yet," he continued, as his brain made a third evolution in this frightful anarchy of ideas and feelings, "her education, her manners, her language, all bespoke a woman of the best position. Besides, if she were only a bird of passage, why have given herself so much trouble to win me over?"

La Peyrade might have continued to plead thus for and against for a long time had he not been suddenly grasped round the shoulders by a strong arm and addressed in a well-known voice.

"Take care! my dear barrister; a frightful danger threatens you; you are running right into it."

La Peyrade, thus arrested, looked round and found himself in the arms of Phellion.

The scene took place in front of a house which was being pulled down at the corner of the rues Duphot and Saint-Honore. Posted on the pavement of the other side of the street, Phellion, whose taste for watching the process of building our readers may remember, had been witnessing for the last fifteen minutes the drama of a wall about to fall beneath the united efforts of a squadron of workmen. Watch in hand, the great citizen was estimating the length of the resistance which that mass of freestone would present to the destructive labor of which it was the object. Precisely at the crucial moment of the impending catastrophe la Peyrade, lost in the tumult of his thoughts, was entering, heedless of the shouts addressed to him on all sides, the radius within which the stones would fall. Seen by Phellion (who, it must be said, would have done the same for a total stranger) la Peyrade undoubtedly owed his life to him; for, at the moment when he was violently flung back by the vigorous grasp of the worthy citizen, the wall fell with the noise of a cannon-shot, and the stones rolled in clouds of dust almost to his very feet.

"Are you blind and deaf?" said the workman whose business it was to warn the passers, in a tone of amenity it is easy to imagine.

"Thank you, my dear friend," said la Peyrade, recalled to earth. "I should certainly have been crushed like an idiot if it hadn't been for you."

And he pressed Phellion's hand.

"My reward," replied the latter, "lies in the satisfaction of knowing that you are saved from an imminent peril. And I may say that that satisfaction is mingled, for me, with a certain pride; for I was not mistaken by a single second in the calculation which enabled me to foresee the exact moment when that formidable mass would be displaced from its centre of gravity. But what were you thinking of, my dear monsieur? Probably of the plea you are about to make in the Thuillier affair. The public prints have informed me of the danger of prosecution by the authorities which hangs above the head of our estimable friend. You have a noble cause to defend, monsieur. Habituated as I am, through my labors as a member of the reading committee of the

Odeon, to judge of works of intellect, and with my hand upon my conscience, I declare that after reading the incriminated passages, I can find nothing in the tone of that pamphlet which justifies the severe measures of which it is the object. Between ourselves," added the great citizen, lowering his voice, "I think the government has shown itself petty."

"So I think," said la Peyrade, "but I am not employed for the defence. I have advised Thuillier to engage some noted lawyer."

"It may be good advice," said Phellion; "at any rate, it speaks well for your modesty. Poor man! I went to him at once when the blow fell, but I did not see him; I saw only Brigitte, who was having a discussion with Madame de Godollo. There is a woman with strong political views; it seems she predicted that the seizure would be made."

"Did you know that the countess had left Paris?" said la Peyrade, rushing at the chance of speaking on the subject of his present monomania.

"Ah! left Paris, has she?" said Phellion. "Well, monsieur, I must tell you that, although there was not much sympathy between us, I regard her departure as a misfortune. She will leave a serious void in the salon of our friends. I say this, because it is my belief, and I am not in the habit of disguising my convictions."

"Yes," said la Peyrade, "she is certainly a very distinguished woman, with whom in spite of her prejudice against me, I think I should have come to an understanding. But this morning, without leaving any word as to where she was going, she started suddenly with post-horses."

"Post-horses!" said Phellion. "I don't know whether you will agree with me, monsieur, but I think that travelling by post is a most agreeable method of conveyance. Certainly Louis XI., to whom we owe the institution, had a fortunate inspiration in the matter; although, on the other hand, his sanguinary and despotic government was not, to my humble thinking, entirely devoid of reproach. Once only in my life have I used that method of locomotion, and I can truly say I found it far superior, in spite of its inferior relative rapidity, to the headlong course of what in England are called *railways*; where speed is attained only at the price of safety."

La Peyrade paid but little attention to Phellion's phraseology. "Where can she have gone?"—round that idea he dug and delved in every direction, an occupation that would have made him indifferent to a far more interesting topic. However, once started, like the locomotive he objected to, the great citizen went on:—

"I made that journey at the period of Madame Phellion's last confinement.

She was in Perche, with her mother, when I learned that serious complications were feared from the milk-fever. Overcome with terror at the danger which threatened my wife, I went instantly to the post-office to obtain a seat in the mail-coach, but all were taken; I found they had been engaged for more than a week. Upon that, I came to a decision; I went to the rue Pigalle, and, for a very large sum in gold a post-chaise and three horses were placed at my disposal, when unfortunately the formality of a passport, with which I had neglected to supply myself, and without which, in virtue of the decrees of the consulate of 17 Nivose, year VII., the post agents were not permitted to deliver horses to travellers—"

The last few words were like a flash of light to la Peyrade, and without waiting for the end of the postal odyssey of the great citizen, he darted away in the direction of the rue Pigalle, before Phellion, in the middle of his sentence, perceived his departure.

Reaching the Royal postal establishment, la Peyrade was puzzled as to whom to address himself in order to obtain the information he wanted. He began by explaining to the porter that he had a letter to send to a lady of his acquaintance that morning by post, neglecting, very thoughtlessly, to send him her address, and that he thought he might discover it by means of the passport which she must have presented in order to obtain horses.

"Was it a lady accompanied by a maid whom I took up on the boulevard de la Madeleine?" asked a postilion sitting in the corner of the room where la Peyrade was making his preliminary inquiry.

"Exactly," said la Peyrade, going eagerly up to the providential being, and slipping a five-franc piece into his hand.

"Ah! well, she's a queer traveller!" said the man, "she told me to take her to the Bois de Boulogne, and there she made me drive round and round for an hour. After that, we came back to the Barriere de l'Etoile, where she gave me a good 'pourboire' and got into a hackney coach, telling me to take the travelling carriage back to the man who lets such carriages in the Cour des Coches, Faubourg Saint-Honore."

"Give me the name of that man?" said la Peyrade, eagerly.

"Simonin," replied the postilion.

Furnished with that information la Peyrade resumed his course, and fifteen minutes later he was questioning the livery-stable keeper; but that individual knew only that a lady residing on the Boulevard de la Madeleine had hired, without horses, a travelling-carriage for half a day; that he had sent out the said carriage at nine that morning, and it was brought back at twelve by a postilion of the Royal Post house.

"Never mind," thought la Peyrade, "I am certain now she has not left Paris, and is not avoiding me. Most probably, she wants to break utterly with the Thuilliers, and so has invented this journey. Fool that I am! no doubt there's a letter waiting for me at home, explaining the whole thing."

Worn out with emotion and fatigue, and in order to verify as quickly as possible this new supposition, la Peyrade flung himself into a street cab, and in less than a quarter of an hour, having promised the driver a good pourboire, he was deposited at the house in the rue Saint-Dominique d'Enfer. There he was compelled to endure still longer the tortures of waiting. Since Brigitte's departure, the duty of the porter, Coffinet, had been very negligently performed, and when la Peyrade rushed to the lodge to inquire for his letter, which he thought he saw in the case that belonged to him, the porter and his wife were both absent and their door was locked. The wife was doing some household work in the building, and Coffinet himself, taking advantage of that circumstance, had allowed a friend to entice him into a neighboring wine-shop, where, between two glasses, he was supporting, against a republican who was talking disrespectfully against it, the cause of the owners of property.

It was twenty minutes before the worthy porter, remembering the "property" entrusted to his charge, decided to return to his post. It is easy to imagine the reproaches with which la Peyrade overwhelmed him. He excused himself by saying that he had gone to do a commission for Mademoiselle, and that he couldn't be at the door and where his masters chose to send him at the same time. At last, however, he gave the lawyer a letter bearing the Paris postmark.

With his heart rather than his eyes la Peyrade recognized the handwriting, and, turning over the missive, the arms and motto confirmed the hope that he had reached the end of the cruellest emotion he had ever in his life experienced. To read that letter before that odious porter seemed to him a profanation. With a refinement of feeling which all lovers will understand, he gave himself the pleasure of pausing before his happiness; he would not even unseal that blissful note until the moment when, with closed doors and no interruptions to distract him, he could enjoy at his ease the delicious sensation of which his heart had a foretaste.

Rushing up the staircase two steps at a time, the now joyous lover committed the childish absurdity of locking himself in; then, having settled himself at his ease before his desk, and having broken the seal with religious care, he was forced to press his hand on his heart, which seemed to burst from his bosom, before he could summon calmness to read the following letter:—

Dear Monsieur,—I disappear forever, because my play is played
out. I thank you for having made it both attractive and easy. By
setting against you the Thuilliers and Collevilles (who are fully
informed of your sentiments towards them), and by relating in a
manner most mortifying to their bourgeois self-love the true
reason of your sudden and pitiless rupture with them, I am proud
and happy to believe that I have done you a signal service. The
girl does not love you, and you love nothing but the eyes of her
"dot"; I have therefore saved you both from a species of hell.
But, in exchange for the bride you have so curtly rejected,
another charming girl is proposed to you; she is richer and more
beautiful than Mademoiselle Colleville, and—to speak of myself
—more at liberty than

Your unworthy servant,

Torna "Comtesse de Godollo."

P.S. For further information apply, without delay, to Monsieur du
Portail, householder, rue Honore-Chevalier, near the rue de la
Cassette, quartier Saint-Sulpice, by whom you are expected.

When he had read this letter the advocate of the poor took his head in his
hands; he saw nothing, heard nothing, thought nothing; he was annihilated.

Several days were necessary to la Peyrade before he could even begin to
recover from the crushing blow which had struck him down. The shock was
terrible. Coming out of that golden dream which had shown him a perspective
of the future in so smiling an aspect, he found himself fooled under conditions
most cruel to his self-love, and to his pretensions to depth and cleverness;
irrevocably parted from the Thuilliers; saddled with a hopeless debt of
twenty-five thousand francs to Madame Lambert, together with another of ten
thousand to Brigitte, which his dignity required him to pay with the least
delay possible; and, worst of all,—to complete his humiliation and his sense
of failure,—he felt that he was not cured of the passionate emotion he had felt
for this woman, the author of his great disaster, and the instrument of his ruin.

Either this Delilah was a very great lady, sufficiently high in station to
allow herself such compromising caprices,—but even so, she would scarcely
have cared to play the role of a coquette in a vaudeville where he himself
played the part of ninny,—or she was some noted adventuress who was in the
pay of this du Portail and the agent of his singular matrimonial designs. Evil
life or evil heart, these were the only two verdicts to be pronounced on this
dangerous siren, and in either case, it would seem, she was not very deserving
of the regrets of her victim; nevertheless, he was conscious of feeling them.
We must put ourselves in the place of this son of Provence, this region of hot
blood and ardent heads, who, for the first time in his life finding himself face
to face with jewelled love in laces, believed he was to drink that passion from
a wrought-gold cup. Just as our minds on waking keep the impression of a
vivid dream and continue in love with what we know was but a shadow, la
Peyrade had need of all his mental energy to drive away the memory of that
treacherous countess. We might go further and say that he never ceased to

297

long for her, though he was careful to drape with an honest pretext the intense desire that he had to find her. That desire he called curiosity, ardor for revenge; and here follow the ingenious deductions which he drew for himself:—

"Cerizet talked to me about a rich heiress; the countess, in her letter, intimates that the whole intrigue she wound about me was to lead to a rich marriage; rich marriages flung at a man's head are not so plentiful that two such chances should come to me within a few weeks; therefore the match offered by Cerizet and that proposed by the countess must be the crazy girl they are so frantic to make me marry; therefore Cerizet, being in the plot, must know the countess; therefore, through him I shall get upon her traces. In any case, I am sure of information about this extraordinary choice that has fallen upon me; evidently, these people, whoever they are, who can pull the wires of such puppets to reach their ends must be persons of considerable position; therefore, I'll go and see Cerizet."

And he went to see Cerizet.

Since the dinner at the Rocher de Cancale, the pair had not met. Once or twice la Peyrade had asked Dutocq at the Thuilliers' (where the latter seldom went now, on account of the distance to their new abode) what had become of his copying clerk.

"He never speaks of you," Dutocq had answered.

Hence it might be inferred that resentment, the "manet alta mente repostum" was still living in the breast of the vindictive usurer. La Peyrade, however, was not stopped by that consideration. After all, he was not going to ask for anything; he went under the pretext of renewing an affair in which Cerizet had taken part, and Cerizet never took part in anything unless he had a personal interest in it. The chances were, therefore, that he would be received with affectionate eagerness rather than unpleasant acerbity. Moreover, he decided to go and see the copying clerk at Dutocq's office; it would look, he thought, less like a visit than if he went to his den in the rue des Poules. It was nearly two o'clock when la Peyrade made his entrance into the precincts of the justice-of-peace of the 12th arrondissement. He crossed the first room, in which were a crowd of persons whom civil suits of one kind or another summoned before the magistrate. Without pausing in that waiting-room, la Peyrade pushed on to the office adjoining that of Dutocq. There he found Cerizet at a shabby desk of blackened wood, at which another clerk, then absent, occupied the opposite seat.

Seeing his visitor, Cerizet cast a savage look at him and said, without rising, or suspending the copy of the judgment he was then engrossing:—

"You here, Sieur la Peyrade? You have been doing fine things for your friend Thuillier!"

"How are you?" asked la Peyrade, in a tone both resolute and friendly.

"I?" replied Cerizet. "As you see, still rowing my galley; and, to follow out the nautical metaphor, allow me to ask what wind has blown you hither; is it, perchance, the wind of adversity?"

La Peyrade, without replying, took a chair beside his questioner, after which he said in a grave tone:—

"My dear fellow, we have something to say to each other."

"I suppose," said Cerizet, spitefully, "the Thuilliers have grown cold since the seizure of the pamphlet."

"The Thuilliers are ungrateful people; I have broken with them," replied la Peyrade.

"Rupture or dismissal," said Cerizet, "their door is shut against you; and from what Dutocq tells me, I judge that Brigitte is handling you without gloves. You see, my friend, what it is to try and manage affairs alone; complications come, and there's no one to smooth the angles. If you had got me that lease, I should have had a footing at the Thuilliers', Dutocq would not have abandoned you, and together we could have brought you gently into port."

"But suppose I don't want to re-enter that port?" said la Peyrade, with some sharpness. "I tell you I've had enough of those Thuilliers, and I broke with them myself; I warned them to get out of my sun; and if Dutocq told you anything else you may tell him from me that he lies. Is that clear enough? It seems to me I've made it plain."

"Well, exactly, my good fellow, if you are so savage against your Thuilliers you ought to have put me among them, and then you'd have seen me avenge you."

"There you are right," said la Peyrade; "I wish I could have set you at their legs—but as for that matter of the lease I tell you again, I was not master of it."

"Of course," said Cerizet, "it was your conscience which obliged you to tell Brigitte that the twelve thousand francs a year I expected to make out of it were better in her pocket than in mine."

"It seems that Dutocq continues the honorable profession of spy which he formerly practised at the ministry of finance," said la Peyrade, "and, like others who do that dirty business, he makes his reports more witty than truthful—"

"Take care!" said Cerizet; "you are talking of my patron in his own lair."

"Look here!" said la Peyrade. "I have come to talk to you on serious matters. Will you do me the favor to drop the Thuilliers and all their belongings, and give me your attention?"

"Say on, my friend," said Cerizet, laying down his pen, which had never ceased to run, up to this moment, "I am listening."

"You talked to me some time ago," said la Peyrade, "about marrying a girl who was rich, fully of age, and slightly hysterical, as you were pleased to put it euphemistically."

"Well done!" cried Cerizet. "I expected this; but you've been some time coming to it."

"In offering me this heiress, what did you have in your mind?" asked la Peyrade.

"Parbleu! to help you to a splendid stroke of business. You had only to stoop and take it. I was formally charged to propose it to you; and, as there wasn't any brokerage, I should have relied wholly on your generosity."

"But you are not the only person who was commissioned to make me that offer. A woman had the same order."

"A woman!" cried Cerizet in a perfectly natural tone of surprise. "Not that I know of."

"Yes, a foreigner, young and pretty, whom you must have met in the family of the bride, to whom she seems to be ardently devoted."

"Never," said Cerizet, "never has there been the slightest question of a woman in this negotiation. I have every reason to believe that I am exclusively charged with it."

"What!" said la Peyrade, fixing upon Cerizet a scrutinizing eye, "did you never hear of the Comtesse Torna de Godollo?"

"Never, in all my life; this is the first time I ever heard that name."

"Then," said la Peyrade, "it must really have been another match; for that woman, after many singular preliminaries, too long to explain to you, made me a formal offer of the hand of a young woman much richer than Mademoiselle Colleville—"

"And hysterical?" asked Cerizet.

"No, she did not embellish the proposal with that accessory; but there's another detail which may put you on the track of her. Madame de Godollo exhorted me, if I wished to push the matter, to go and see a certain Monsieur du Portail—"

"Rue Honore-Chevalier?" exclaimed Cerizet, quickly.

"Precisely."

"Then it is the same marriage which is offered to you through two different mediums. It is strange I was not informed of this collaboration!"

"In short," said la Peyrade, "you not only didn't have wind of the countess's intervention, but you don't know her, and you can't give me any information about her—is that so?"

"At present I can't," replied Cerizet, "but I'll find out about her; for the whole proceeding is rather cavalier towards me; but this employment of two agents only shows you how desirable you are to the family."

At this moment the door of the room was opened cautiously, a woman's head appeared, and a voice, which was instantly recognized by la Peyrade, said, addressing the copying-clerk:—

"Ah! excuse me! I see monsieur is busy. Could I say a word to monsieur when he is alone?"

Cerizet, who had an eye as nimble as a hand, instantly noticed a certain fact. La Peyrade, who was so placed as to be plainly seen by the new-comer, no sooner heard that drawling, honeyed voice, than he turned his head in a manner to conceal his features. Instead therefore of being roughly sent away, as usually happened to petitioners who addressed the most surly of official clerks, the modest visitor heard herself greeted in a very surprising manner.

"Come in, come in, Madame Lambert," said Cerizet; "you won't be kept waiting long; come in."

The visitor advanced, and then came face to face with la Peyrade.

"Ah! monsieur!" cried his creditor, whom the reader has no doubt recognized, "how fortunate I am to meet monsieur! I have been several times to his office to ask if he had had time to attend to my little affair."

"I have had many engagements which have kept me away from my office lately; but I attended to that matter; everything has been done right, and is now in the hands of the secretary."

"Oh! how good monsieur is! I pray God to bless him," said the pious woman, clasping her hands.

"Bless me! do you have business with Madame Lambert?" said Cerizet;

"you never told me that. Are you Pere Picot's counsel?"

"No, unfortunately," said Madame Lambert, "my master won't take any counsel; he is so self-willed, so obstinate! But, my good monsieur, what I came to ask is whether the family council is to meet."

"Of course," said Cerizet, "and not later than to-morrow."

"But monsieur, I hear those gentlemen of the Royal court said the family had no rights—"

"Yes, that's so," said the clerk; "the lower court and the Royal court have both, on the petition of the relatives, rejected their demand for a commission."

"I should hope so!" said the woman; "to think of making him out a lunatic! him so full of wisdom and learning!"

"But the relations don't mean to give up; they are going to try the matter again under a new form, and ask for the appointment of a judicial counsel. That's what the family council meets for to-morrow; and I think, this time, my dear Madame Lambert, your old Picot will find himself restrained. There are serious allegations, I can tell you. It was all very well to take the eggs, but to pluck the hen was another thing."

"Is it possible that monsieur can suppose—" began the devote, clasping her hands under her chin.

"I suppose nothing," said Cerizet; "I am not the judge of this affair. But the relations declare that you have pocketed considerable sums, and made investments about which they demand inquiry."

"Oh! heavens!" said the woman, casting up her eyes; "they can inquire; I am poor; I have not a deed, nor a note, nor a share; not the slightest security of any kind in my possession."

"I dare say not," said Cerizet, glancing at la Peyrade out of the corner of his eye; "but there are always friends to take care of such things. However, that is none of my business; every one must settle his own affairs in his own way. Now, then, say what you have to say, distinctly."

"I came, monsieur," she replied, "to implore you, monsieur, to implore Monsieur the judge's clerk, to speak in our favor to Monsieur the justice-of-peace. Monsieur the vicar of Saint-Jacques is also to speak to him. That poor Monsieur Picot!" she went on, weeping, "they'll kill him if they continue to worry him in this way."

"I sha'n't conceal from you," said Cerizet, "that the justice-of-peace is very ill-disposed to your cause. You must have seen that the other day, when he refused to receive you. As for Monsieur Dutocq and myself, our assistance won't help you much; and besides, my good woman, you are too close-mouthed."

"Monsieur asked me if I had laid by a few little savings; and I couldn't tell him that I had, be—because they have gone to keep the h—house of that poor Monsieur Pi—i—cot; and now they accuse me of r—robbing him!"

Madame Lambert sobbed.

"My opinion is," said Cerizet, "that you are making yourself out much poorer than you are; and if friend Peyrade here, who seems to be more in your confidence, hadn't his tongue tied by the rules of his profession—"

"I!" said la Peyrade, hastily, "I don't know anything of madame's affairs. She asked me to draw up a petition on a matter in which there was nothing judicial or financial."

"Ah! that's it, is it?" said Cerizet. "Madame had doubtless gone to see you about this petition the day Dutocq met her at your office, the morning after our dinner at the Rocher de Cancale—when you were such a Roman, you know."

Then, without seeming to attach any importance to the reminiscence, he added:—

"Well, my good Madame Lambert, I'll ask my patron to speak to the justice-of-peace, and, if I get a chance, I'll speak to him myself; but, I repeat it, he is very much prejudiced against you."

Madame Lambert retired with many curtseys and protestations of gratitude. When she was fairly gone la Peyrade remarked:—

"You don't seem to believe that that woman came to me about a petition; and yet nothing was ever truer. She is thought a saint in the street she lives in, and that old man they accuse her of robbing is actually kept alive by her devotion, so I'm told. Consequently, the neighbors have put it into the good woman's head to apply for the Montyon prize; and it was for the purpose of putting her claims in legal shape that she applied to me."

"Dear! dear! the Montyon prize!" cried Cerizet; "well, that's an idea! My good fellow, we ought to have cultivated it before,—I, especially, as banker of the poor, and you, their advocate. As for this client of yours, it is lucky for her Monsieur Picot's relatives are not members of the French academy; it is in the correctional police-court, sixth chamber, where they mean to give her the reward of virtue. However, to come back to what we were talking about. I tell you that after all your tergiversations you had better settle down peaceably; and I advise you, as your countess did, to go and see du Portail."

303

"Who and what is he?" asked la Peyrade.

"He is a little old man," replied Cerizet, "as shrewd as a weasel. He gives me the idea of having dealings with the devil. Go and see him! Sight, as they say, costs nothing."

"Yes," said la Peyrade, "perhaps I will; but, first of all, I want you to find out for me about this Comtesse de Godollo."

"What do you care about her? She is nothing but a supernumerary, that countess."

"I have my reasons," said la Peyrade; "you can certainly get some information about her in three days; I'll come and see you then."

"My good fellow," said Cerizet, "you seem to me to be amusing yourself with things that don't pay; you haven't fallen in love with that go-between, have you?"

"Plague take him!" thought la Peyrade; "he spies everything; there's no hiding anything from him! No," he said, aloud, "I am not in love; on the contrary, I am very cautious. I must admit that this marriage with a crazy girl doesn't attract me, and before I go a step into it I want to know where I put my feet. These crooked proceedings are not reassuring, and as so many influences are being brought to bear, I choose to control one by another. Therefore don't play sly, but give me all the information you get into your pouch about Madame la Comtesse Torna de Godollo. I warn you I know enough to test the veracity of your report; and if I see you are trying to overreach me I'll break off short with your du Portail."

"Trying to overreach you, monseigneur!" replied Cerizet, in the tone and manner of Frederic Lemaitre. "Who would dare attempt it?"

As he pronounced those words in a slightly mocking tone, Dutocq appeared, accompanied by his little clerk.

"Bless me!" he exclaimed, seeing la Peyrade and Cerizet together; "here's the trinity reconstituted! but the object of the alliance, the 'casus foederis,' has floated off. What have you done to that good Brigitte, la Peyrade? She is after your blood."

"What about Thuillier?" asked la Peyrade.

Moliere was reversed; here was Tartuffe inquiring for Orgon.

"Thuillier began by not being very hostile to you; but it now seems that the seizure business has taken a good turn, and having less need of you he is getting drawn into his sister's waters; and if the tendency continues, I haven't a doubt that he'll soon come to think you deserving of hanging."

"Well, I'm out of it all," said la Peyrade, "and if anybody ever catches me in such a mess again!—Well, adieu, my friends," he added. "And you, Cerizet, as to what we were speaking about, activity, safety, and discretion!"

When la Peyrade reached the courtyard of the municipal building, he was accosted by Madame Lambert, who was lying in wait for him.

"Monsieur wouldn't believe, I am sure," she said, in a deprecating tone, "the villainous things that Monsieur Cerizet said about me; monsieur knows it was the little property I received from my uncle in England that I placed in his hands."

"Yes, yes," said la Peyrade, "but you must understand that with all these rumors set about by your master's relatives the prize of virtue is desperately endangered."

"If it is God's will that I am not to have it—"

"You ought also to understand how important it is for your interests to keep secret the other service which I did for you. At the first appearance of any indiscretion on your part that money, as I told you, will be peremptorily returned to you."

"Oh! monsieur may be easy about that."

"Very well; then good-bye to you, my dear," said la Peyrade, in a friendly tone.

As he turned to leave her, a nasal voice was heard from a window on the staircase.

"Madame Lambert!" cried Cerizet, who, suspecting the colloquy, had gone to the staircase window to make sure of it. "Madame Lambert! Monsieur Dutocq has returned; you may come up and see him, if you like."

Impossible for la Peyrade to prevent the conference, although he knew the secret of that twenty-five thousand francs ran the greatest danger.

"Certainly," he said to himself as he walked away, "I'm in a run of ill-luck; and I don't know where it will end."

In Brigitte's nature there was such an all-devouring instinct of domination, that it was without regret, and, we may even say, with a sort of secret joy that she saw the disappearance of Madame de Godollo. That woman, she felt, had a crushing superiority over her; and this, while it had given a higher order to the Thuillier establishment, made her ill at ease. When therefore the separation took place, which was done, let us here say, on good terms, and under fair and honorable pretexts, Mademoiselle Thuillier breathed more

305

freely. She felt like those kings long swayed by imperious and necessary ministers, who celebrate within their hearts the day when death delivers them from a master whose services and rival influence they impatiently endured.

Thuillier was not far from having the same sentiment about la Peyrade. But Madame de Godollo was only the elegance, whereas la Peyrade was the utility of the house they had now simultaneously abandoned; and after the lapse of a few days, a terrible need of Theodose made itself felt in the literary and political existence of his dear, good friend. The municipal councillor found himself suddenly appointed to draft an important report. He was unable to decline the task, saddled as he was with the reputation, derived from his pamphlet, of being a man of letters and an able writer; therefore, in presence of the perilous honor conferred upon him by his colleagues of the general Council, he sat down terrified by his solitude and his insufficiency.

In vain did he lock himself into his study, gorge himself with black coffee, mend innumerable pens, and write a score of times at the head of his paper (which he was careful to cut of the exact dimensions as that used by la Peyrade) the solemn words: "Report to the Members of the Municipal Council of the City of Paris," followed, on a line by itself, by a magnificent *Messieurs*—nothing came of it! He was fain to issue furious from his study, complaining of the horrible household racket which "cut the thread of his ideas"; though really no greater noise than the closing of a door or the opening of a closet or the moving of a chair had made itself heard. All this, however, did not help the advancement of the work, which remained, as before—simply begun.

Most fortunately, it happened that Rabourdin, wanting to make some change in his apartment, came, as was proper, to submit his plan to the owner of the house. Thuillier granted cordially the request that was made to him, and then discoursed to his tenant about the report with which he was charged,— being desirous, he said, to obtain his ideas on the subject.

Rabourdin, to whom no administrative question was foreign, very readily threw upon the subject a number of very clear and lucid ideas. He was one of those men to whom the quality of the intellect to which they address themselves is more or less indifferent; a fool, or a man of talent who will listen to them, serves equally well to think aloud to, and they are, as a stimulant, about the same thing. After Rabourdin had said his say, he observed that Thuillier had not understood him; but he had listened to himself with pleasure, and he was, moreover, grateful for the attention, obtuse as it was, of his hearer, and also for the kindliness of the landlord in receiving his request.

"I must have among my papers," he said as he went away, "something on this subject; I will look it up and send it to you."

Accordingly, that same evening Thuillier received a voluminous manuscript; and he spent the entire night in delving into that precious repository of ideas, from which he extracted enough to make a really remarkable report, clumsily as the pillage was managed. When read before the council it obtained a very great success, and Thuillier returned home radiant and much elated by the congratulations he had received. From that moment—a moment that was marked in his life, for even to advanced old age he still talked of the "report he had had the honor of making to the Council-general of the Seine"—la Peyrade went down considerably in his estimation; he felt then that he could do very well without the barrister, and this thought of emancipation was strengthened by another happiness which came to him at almost the same time.

A parliamentary crisis was imminent,—a fact that caused the ministry to think about depriving its adversaries of a theme of opposition which always has great influence on public opinion. It resolved therefore to relax its rigor, which of late had been much increased against the press. Being included in this species of hypocritical amnesty, Thuillier received one morning a letter from the barrister whom he had chosen in place of la Peyrade. This letter announced that the Council of State had dismissed the complaint, and ordered the release of the pamphlet.

Then Dutocq's prediction was realized. That weight the less within his bosom, Thuillier took a swing toward insolence; he chorused Brigitte, and came at last to speak of la Peyrade as a sort of adventurer whom he had fed and clothed, a tricky fellow who had *extracted* much money from him, and had finally behaved with such ingratitude that he was thankful not to count him any longer among his friends. Orgon, in short, was in full revolt, and like Dorine, he was ready to cry out: "A beggar! who, when he came, had neither shoes nor coat worth a brass farthing."

Cerizet, to whom these indignities were reported by Dutocq, would gladly have served them up hot to la Peyrade; but the interview in which the copying clerk was to furnish information about Madame de Godollo did not take place at the time fixed. La Peyrade made his own discoveries in this wise:

Pursued by the thought of the beautiful Hungarian, and awaiting, or rather not awaiting the result of Cerizet's inquiry, he scoured Paris in every direction, and might have been seen, like the idlest of loungers, in the most frequented places, his heart telling him that sooner or later he must meet the object of his ardent search.

One evening—it was towards the middle of October—the autumn, as frequently happens in Paris, was magnificent, and along the boulevards, where the Provencal was airing his love and his melancholy, the out-door life and gaiety were as animated as in summer. On the boulevard des Italiens, formerly known as the boulevard de Gand, as he lounged past the long line of chairs before the Cafe de Paris, where, mingled with a few women of the Chaussee d'Antin accompanied by their husbands and children, may be seen toward evening a cordon of nocturnal beauties waiting only a gloved hand to gather them, la Peyrade's heart received a cruel shock. From afar, he thought he saw his adored countess.

She was alone, in a dazzling toilet scarcely authorized by the place and her isolation; before her, mounted on a chair, trembled a tiny lap-dog, which she stroked from time to time with her beautiful hands. After convincing himself that he was not mistaken, la Peyrade was about to dart upon that celestial vision, when he was forestalled by a dandy of the most triumphant type. Without throwing aside his cigar, without even touching his hat, this handsome young man began to converse with the barrister's ideal; but when she saw la Peyrade making towards her the siren must have felt afraid, for she rose quickly, and taking the arm of the man who was talking to her, she said aloud:—

"Is your carriage here, Emile? Mabille closes to-night, and I should like to go there."

The name of that disreputable place thus thrown in the face of the unhappy barrister, was a charity, for it saved him from a foolish action, that of addressing, on the arm of the man who had suddenly made himself her cavalier, the unworthy creature of whom he was thinking a few seconds earlier with so much tenderness.

"She is not worth insulting," he said to himself.

But, as lovers are beings who will not allow their foothold to be taken from them easily, the Provencal was neither convinced nor resigned as yet. Not far from the place which his countess had left, sat another woman, also alone; but this one was ripe with years, with feathers on her head, and beneath the folds of a cashmere shawl she concealed the plaintive remains of tarnished elegance and long past luxury. There was nothing imposing about this sight, nor did it command respect, but the contrary. La Peyrade went up to the woman without ceremony and addressed her.

"Madame," he said, "do you know that woman who has just gone away on the arm of a gentleman?"

"Certainly, monsieur; I know nearly all the women who come here."

"And her name is?—"

"Madame Komorn."

"Is she as impregnable as the fortress of that name?"

Our readers will doubtless remember that at the time of the insurrection in Hungary our ears were battered by the press and by novelists about the famous citadel of Komorn; and la Peyrade knew that by assuming a tone of indifference or flippancy he was more likely to succeed with his inquiries.

"Has monsieur any idea of making her acquaintance?"

"I don't know," replied la Peyrade, "but she is a woman who makes people think of her."

"And a very dangerous woman, monsieur," added his companion; "a fearful spendthrift, but with no inclination to return generously what is done for her. I can speak knowingly of that; when she first arrived here from Berlin, six months ago, she was very warmly recommended to me."

"Ah!" exclaimed la Peyrade.

"Yes, at that time I had in the environs of Ville d'Avray a very beautiful place, with park and coverts and a stream for fishing; but as I was alone I found it dull, and several of these ladies and gentlemen said to me, 'Madame Louchard, why don't you organize parties in the style of picnics?'"

"Madame Louchard!" repeated la Peyrade, "are you any relation to Monsieur Louchard of the commercial police?"

"His wife, monsieur, but legally separated from him. A horrid man who wants me to go back to him; but I, though I'm ready to forgive most things, I can't forgive a want of respect; just imagine that he dared to raise his hand against me!"

"Well," said la Peyrade, trying to bring her back to the matter in hand; "you organized those picnics, and Madame de Godo—I mean Madame Komorn—"

"Was one of my first lodgers. It was there she made acquaintance with an Italian, a handsome man, and rich, a political refugee, but one of the lofty kind. You understand it didn't suit my purposes to have intrigues going on in my house; still the man was so lovable, and so unhappy because he couldn't make Madame Komorn like him, that at last I took an interest in this particular love affair; which produced a pot of money for madame, for she managed to get immense sums out of that Italian. Well, would you believe that when—being just then in great need—I asked her to assist me with a trifling little sum, she refused me point-blank, and left my house, taking her lover with her, who, poor man, can't be thankful for the acquaintance now."

"Why not? What happened to him?" asked la Peyrade.

"It happened to him that this serpent knows every language in Europe; she is witty and clever to the tips of her fingers, but more manoeuvring than either; so, being, as it appears, in close relations to the police, she gave the government a lot of papers the Italian left about carelessly, on which they expelled him from France."

"Well, after his departure, Madame Komorn—"

"Since then, she has had a good many adventures and upset several fortunes, and I thought she had left Paris. For the last two months she was nowhere to be seen, but three days ago she reappeared, more brilliant than ever. My advice to monsieur is not to trust himself in that direction; and yet, monsieur looks to me a Southerner, and Southerners have passions; perhaps what I have told him will only serve to spur them up. However, being warned, there's not so much danger, and she is a most fascinating creature—oh! very fascinating. She used to love me very much, though we parted such ill-friends; and just now, seeing me here, she came over and asked my address, and said she should come and see me."

"Well, madame, I'll think about it," said la Peyrade, rising and bowing to her.

The bow was returned with extreme coldness; his abrupt departure did not show him to be a man of *serious* intentions.

It might be supposed from the lively manner in which la Peyrade made these inquiries that his cure though sudden was complete; but this surface of indifference and cool self-possession was only the stillness of the atmosphere that precedes a storm. On leaving Madame Louchard, la Peyrade flung himself into a street-cab and there gave way to a passion of tears like that Madame Colleville had witnessed on the day he believed that Cerizet had got the better of him in the sale of the house.

What was his position now? The investment of the Thuilliers, prepared with so much care, all useless; Flavie well avenged for the odious comedy he had played with her; his affairs in a worse state than they were when Cerizet and Dutocq had sent him, like a devouring wolf, into the sheepfold from which he had allowed the stupid sheep to drive him; his heart full of revengeful projects against the woman who had so easily got the better of what he thought his cleverness; and the memory, still vivid, of the seductions to which he had succumbed,—such were the thoughts and emotions of his sleepless night, sleepless except for moments shaken by agitated dreams.

The next day la Peyrade could think no more; he was a prey to fever, the violence of which became sufficiently alarming for the physician who attended him to take all precautions against the symptoms now appearing of brain fever: bleeding, cupping, leeches, and ice to his head; these were the agreeable finale to his dream of love. We must hasten to add, however, that this violent crisis in the physical led to a perfect cure of the mental being. The barrister came out of his illness with no other sentiment than cold contempt for the treacherous Hungarian, a sentiment which did not even rise to a desire for vengeance.

CHAPTER IX. GIVE AND TAKE

Once more afoot, and reckoning with his future, on which he had lost so much ground, la Peyrade asked himself if he had not better try to renew his relations with the Thuilliers, or whether he should be compelled to fall back on the rich crazy woman who had bullion where others have brains. But everything that reminded him of his disastrous campaign was repulsive to him; besides, what safety was there in dealing with this du Portail, a man who could use such instruments for his means of action?

Great commotions of the soul are like those storms which purify the atmosphere; they induce reflection, they counsel good and strong resolutions. La Peyrade, as the result of the cruel disappointment he had just endured, examined his own soul. He asked himself what sort of existence was this, of base and ignoble intrigue, which he had led for the past year? Was there for him no better, no nobler use to make of the faculties he felt within him? The bar was open to him as to others; that was a broad, straight path which could lead him to all the satisfaction of legitimate ambition. Like Figaro, who displayed more science and calculation in merely getting a living than statesmen had shown in governing Spain for a hundred years, he, la Peyrade, in order to install and maintain himself in the Thuillier household and marry the daughter of a clarionet and a smirched coquette, had spent more mind, more art, and—it should also be said, because in a corrupt society it is an element that must be reckoned—more dishonesty than was needed to advance him in some fine career.

"Enough of such connections as Dutocq and Cerizet," he said to himself; "enough of the nauseating atmosphere of the Minards and Phellions and Collevilles and Barniols and all the rest of them. I'll shake off this province 'intra muros,' a thousand times more absurd and petty than the true provinces; they at least, side by side with their pettiness, have habits and customs that are characteristic, a 'sui generis' dignity; they are frankly what they are, the antipodes of Parisian life; this other is but a parody of it. I will fling myself upon Paris."

In consequence of these reflections, la Peyrade went to see two or three barristers who had offered to introduce him at the Palais in secondary cases. He accepted those that presented themselves at once, and three weeks after his rupture with the Thuilliers he was no longer the "advocate of the poor," but a barrister pleading before the Royal court.

He had already pleaded several cases successfully when he received, one morning, a letter which greatly disturbed him. The president of the order of barristers requested him to come to his office at the Palais in the course of the day, as he had something of importance to say to him. La Peyrade instantly thought of the transaction relating to the purchase of the house on the boulevard de la Madeleine; it must have come, he thought, to the ears of the Council of Discipline; if so he was accountable to that tribunal and he knew its severity.

Now this du Portail, whom he had never yet been to see, in spite of his conditional promise to Cerizet, was likely to have heard the whole story of that transaction from Cerizet himself. Evidently all means were thought good by that man, judging by the use he had made of the Hungarian woman. In his savage determination to bring about the marriage with the crazy girl, had this virulent old man denounced him? On seeing him courageously and with some appearance of success entering a career in which he might find fame and independence, had his persecutor taken a step to make that career impossible? Certainly there was enough likelihood in this suggestion to make the barrister wait in cruel anxiety for the hour when he might learn the true nature of the alarming summons.

While breakfasting rather meagrely, his mind full of these painful conjectures, Madame Coffinet, who had the honor to take charge of his housekeeping, came up to ask if he would see Monsieur Etienne Lousteau. [See "The Great Man of the Provinces in Paris."]

Etienne Lousteau! la Peyrade had an idea that he had heard the name before.

"Show him into my office," he said to the portress.

A moment later he met his visitor, whose face did not seem utterly unknown to him.

"Monsieur," said this new-comer, "I had the honor of breakfasting with you not long ago at Vefour's; I was invited to that meeting, afterwards rather disturbed, by Monsieur Thuillier."

"Ah, very good!" said the barrister, offering a chair; "you are attached to the staff of a newspaper?"

"Editor-in-chief of the 'Echo de la Bievre,' and it is on the subject of that paper that I have now called to see you. You know what has happened?"

"No," said la Peyrade.

"Is it possible you are not aware that the ministry met with terrible defeat last night? But instead of resigning, as every one expected, they have dissolved the Chamber and appeal to the people."

"I knew nothing of all that," said la Peyrade. "I have not read the morning papers."

"So," continued Lousteau, "all parliamentary ambitions will take the field, and, if I am well informed, Monsieur Thuillier, already member of the Council-general, intends to present himself as candidate for election in the 12th arrondissement."

"Yes," said la Peyrade, "that is likely to be his intention."

"Well, monsieur, I desire to place at his disposition an instrument the value of which I am confident you will not underestimate. The 'Echo de la Bievre,' a specialist paper, can have a decisive influence on the election in that quarter."

"And you would be disposed," asked la Peyrade, "to make that paper support Monsieur Thuillier's candidacy?"

"Better than that," replied Lousteau. "I have come to propose to Monsieur Thuillier that he purchase the paper itself. Once the proprietor of it he can use it as he pleases."

"But in the first place," said la Peyrade, "what is the present condition of the enterprise? In its character as a specialist journal—as you called it just now—it is a sheet I have seldom met with; in fact, it would be entirely unknown to me were it not for the remarkable article you were so good as to devote to Thuillier's defence at the time his pamphlet was seized."

Etienne Lousteau bowed his thanks, and then said:

"The position of the paper is excellent; we can give it to you on easy terms, for we were intending shortly to stop the publication."

"That is strange for a prosperous journal."

"On the contrary, it happens to be quite natural. The founders, who were all representatives of the great leather interest, started this paper for a special object. That object has been attained. The 'Echo de la Bievre' has therefore become an effect without a cause. In such a case, stockholders who don't like the tail end of matters, and are not eager after small profits, very naturally prefer to sell out."

"But," asked la Peyrade, "does the paper pay its costs?"

"That," replied Lousteau, "is a point we did not consider; we were not very anxious to have subscribers; the mainspring of the whole affair was direct and immediate action on the ministry of commerce to obtain a higher duty on the introduction of foreign leathers. You understand that outside of the tannery circle, this interest was not very exciting to the general reader."

"I should have thought, however," persisted la Peyrade, "that a newspaper, however circumscribed its action, would be a lever which depended for its force on the number of its subscribers."

"Not for journals which aim for a single definite thing," replied Lousteau, dogmatically. "In that case, subscribers are, on the contrary, an embarrassment, for you have to please and amuse them, and in so doing, the real object has to be neglected. A newspaper which has a definite and circumscribed object ought to be like the stroke of that pendulum which, striking steadily on one spot, fires at a given hour the cannon of the Palais-Royal."

"At any rate," said la Peyrade, "what price do you put upon a publication which has no subscribers, does not pay its expenses, and has until now been devoted to a purpose totally different from that you propose for it?"

"Before answering," returned Lousteau, "I shall ask you another question. Have you any intention of buying it?"

"That's according to circumstances," replied la Peyrade. "Of course I must see Thuillier; but I may here remark to you that he knows absolutely nothing about newspaper business. With his rather bourgeois ideas, the ownership of a newspaper will seem to him a ruinous speculation. Therefore, if, in addition to an idea that will scare him, you suggest an alarming price, it is useless for me to speak to him. I am certain he would never go into the affair."

"No," replied Lousteau. "I have told you we should be reasonable; these gentlemen have left the whole matter in my hands. Only, I beg to remark that we have had propositions from other parties, and in giving Monsieur Thuillier this option, we intended to pay him a particular courtesy. When can I have your answer?"

"To-morrow, I think; shall I have the honor of seeing you at your own house, or at the office of the journal?"

"No," said Lousteau, "to-morrow I will come here, at the same hour, if that is convenient to you."

"Perfectly," replied la Peyrade, bowing out his visitor, whom he was inclined to think more consequential than able.

By the manner in which the barrister had received the proposition to become an intermediary to Thuillier, the reader must have seen that a rapid revolution had taken place in his ideas. Even if he had not received that extremely disquieting letter from the president of the order of barristers, the new situation in which Thuillier would be placed if elected to the Chamber gave him enough to think about. Evidently his dear good friend would have to come back to him, and Thuillier's eagerness for election would deliver him over, bound hand and foot. Was it not the right moment to attempt to renew his marriage with Celeste? Far from being an obstacle to the good resolutions inspired by his amorous disappointment and his incipient brain fever, such a finale would ensure their continuance and success. Moreover, if he received, as he feared, one of those censures which would ruin his dawning prospects at the bar, it was with the Thuilliers, the accomplices and beneficiaries of the cause of his fall, that his instinct led him to claim an asylum.

With these thoughts stirring in his mind la Peyrade obeyed the summons and went to see the president of the order of barristers.

He was not mistaken; a very circumstantial statement of his whole proceeding in the matter of the house had been laid before his brethren of the bar; and the highest dignitary of the order, after stating that an anonymous denunciation ought always to be received with great distrust, told him that he was ready to receive and welcome an explanation. La Peyrade dared not entrench himself in absolute denial; the hand from which he believed the blow had come seemed to him too resolute and too able not to hold the proofs as well. But, while admitting the facts in general, he endeavored to give them an acceptable coloring. In this, he saw that he had failed, when the president said to him:—

"After the vacation which is now beginning I shall report to the Council of the order the charges made against you, and the statements by which you have defended yourself. The Council alone has the right to decide on a matter of such importance."

Thus dismissed, la Peyrade felt that his whole future at the bar was imperilled; but at least he had a respite, and in case of condemnation a new project on which to rest his head. Accordingly, he put on his gown, which he had never worn till now, and went to the fifth court-room, where he was employed upon a case.

As he left the court-room, carrying one of those bundles of legal papers held together by a strip of cotton which, being too voluminous to hold under the arm, are carried by the hand and the forearm pressed against the chest, la Peyrade began to pace about the Salle des Pas perdus with that harassed look of business which denotes a lawyer overwhelmed with work. Whether he had really excited himself in pleading, or whether he was pretending to be exhausted to prove that his gown was not a dignity for show, as it was with many of his legal brethren, but an armor buckled on for the fight, it is certain

317

that, handkerchief in hand, he was mopping his forehead as he walked, when, in the distance, he spied Thuillier, who had evidently just caught sight of him, and was beginning on his side to manoeuvre.

La Peyrade was not surprised by the encounter. On leaving home he had told Madame Coffinet he was going to the Palais, and should be there till three o'clock, and she might send to him any persons who called on business. Not wishing to let Thuillier accost him too easily, he turned abruptly, as if some thought had changed his purpose, and went and seated himself on one of the benches which surround the walls of that great antechamber of Justice. There he undid his bundle, took out a paper, and buried himself in it with the air of a man who had not had time to examine in his study a case he was about to plead. It is not necessary to say that while doing this the Provencal was watching the manoeuvres of Thuillier out of the corner of his eye. Thuillier, believing that la Peyrade was really occupied in some serious business, hesitated to approach him.

However, after sundry backings and fillings the municipal councillor made up his mind, and sailing straight before the wind he headed for the spot he had been reconnoitring for the last ten minutes.

"Bless me, Theodose!" he cried as soon as he had got within hailing distance. "Do you come to the Palais now?"

"It seems to me," replied Theodose, "that barristers at the Palais are like Turks at Constantinople, where a friend of mine affirmed you could see a good many. It is YOU whom it is rather surprising to see here."

"Not at all," said Thuillier, carelessly. "I've come about that cursed pamphlet. Is there ever any end to your legal bothers? I was summoned here this morning, but I don't regret it, as it gives me the happy chance of meeting you."

"I, too," said la Peyrade, tying up his bundle. "I am very glad to see you, but I must leave you now; I have an appointment, and I suppose you want to do your business at once."

"I have done it," said Thuillier.

"Did you speak to Olivier Vinet, that mortal enemy of yours? he sits in that court," asked la Peyrade.

"No," said Thuillier, naming another official.

"Well, that's queer!" said the barrister; "that fellow must have the gift of ubiquity; he has been all the morning in the fifth court-room, and has just this minute given a judgment on a case I pleaded."

Thuillier colored, and got out of his hobble as best he could. "Oh, hang it!" he said; "those men in gowns are all alike, I don't know one from another."

La Peyrade shrugged his shoulders and said aloud, but as if to himself: "Always the same; crafty, crooked, never straightforward."

"Whom are you talking about?" asked Thuillier, rather nonplussed.

"Why, of you, my dear fellow, who take me for an imbecile, as if I and the whole world didn't know that your pamphlet business came to an end two weeks ago. Why, then, summon you to court?"

"Well, I was sent for," said Thuillier, with embarrassment; "something about registry fees,—it is all Greek to me, I can't comprehend their scrawls."

"And they chose," said la Peyrade, "precisely the very day when the Moniteur, announcing the dissolution of the Chamber, made you think about being a candidate for the 12th arrondissement."

"Why not?" asked Thuillier, "what has my candidacy to do with the fees I owe to the court?"

"I'll tell you," said la Peyrade, dryly. "The court is a thing essentially amiable and complaisant. 'Tiens!' it said to itself, 'here's this good Monsieur Thuillier going to be a candidate for the Chamber; how hampered he'll be by his attitude to his ex-friend Monsieur de la Peyrade, with whom he wishes now he hadn't quarrelled. I'll summon him for fees he doesn't owe; that will bring him to the Palais where la Peyrade comes daily; and in that way he can meet him by chance, and so avoid taking a step which would hurt his self-love.'"

"Well, there you are mistaken!" cried Thuillier, breaking the ice. "I used so little craft, as you call it, that I've just come from your house, there! and your portress told me where to find you."

"Well done!" said la Peyrade, "I like this frankness; I can get on with men who play above-board. Well, what do you want of me? Have you come to talk about your election? I have already begun to work for it."

"No, really?" said Thuillier, "how?"

"Here," replied la Peyrade, feeling under his gown for his pocket and bringing out a paper, "here's what I scribbled just now in the court-room while the lawyer on the other side rambled on like an expert."

"What is it about?" asked Thuillier.

"Read and you'll see."

The paper read as follows:—

```
Estimate for a newspaper, small size, at thirty francs a year.

Calculating the editions at 5,000 the costs are:—

    Paper, 5 reams at 12 francs  … … … .  1,860 francs.
    Composition   … … … … … … 2,400     "
     Printing … … … … … … … . .    450     "
    One administrator   … … … … … …   250"
    One clerk   … … … … … … … .   100     "
    One editor (also cashier)   … … … . .    200      "
    One despatcher … … … … … … . .   100"
    Folders   … … … … … … . .   120     "
    One office boy  … … … … … … . .  80  "
    Office expenses  … … … … … … .   150   "
    Rent … … … … … … … … . 100  "
    License and postage   … … … … . . 7,500      "
    Reporting and stenographic news   … … . . 1,800      "
                                                 ‾‾‾‾‾

                          Total monthly,  15,110  "
                          "  yearly,       181,320  "
```

"Do you want to set up a paper?" asked Thuillier, in dread.

"I?" asked la Peyrade, "I want nothing at all; you are the one to be asked if you want to be a deputy."

"Undoubtedly I do; because, when you urged me to become a municipal councillor, you put the idea into my head. But reflect, my dear Theodose, one hundred and eighty one thousand three hundred and twenty francs to put out! Have I a fortune large enough to meet such a demand?"

"Yes," said la Peyrade, "you could very well support that expense, for considering the end you want to obtain there is nothing exorbitant in it. In England they make much greater sacrifices to get a seat in Parliament; but in any case, I beg you to observe that the costs are very high on that estimate, and some could be cut off altogether. For instance, you would not want an administrator. You, yourself, an old accountant, and I, an old journalist, can very well manage the affair between us. Also rent, we needn't count that; you have your old apartment in the rue Saint-Dominique which is not yet leased; that will make a fine newspaper office."

"All that costs off two thousand four hundred francs a year," said Thuillier.

"Well, that's something; but your error consists in calculating on the yearly cost. When do the elections takeplace?"

"In two months," said Thuillier.

"Very good; two months will cost you thirty thousand francs, even supposing the paper had no subscribers."

"True," said Thuillier, "the expense is certainly less than I thought at first. But does a newspaper really seem to you essential?"

"So essential that without that power in our hands, I won't have anything to do with the election. You don't seem to see, my poor fellow, that in going to live in the other quarter you have lost, electorally speaking, an immense amount of ground. You are no longer the man of the place, and your election could be balked by the cry of what the English call 'absenteeism.' This makes your game very hard to play."

"I admit that," said Thuillier; "but there are so many things wanted besides money,—a name for one thing, a manager, editorial staff, and so forth."

"A name, we have one made to hand; editors, they are you and I and a few young fellows who grow on every bush in Paris. As for the manager, I have a man in view."

"What name is it?" asked Thuillier.

"L'Echo de la Bievre."

"But there is already a paper of that name."

"Precisely, and that's why I give my approval to the affair. Do you think I should be fool enough to advise you to start an entirely new paper? 'Echo de la Bievre!' that title is a treasure to a man who wants support for his candidacy in the 12th arrondissement. Say the word only, and I put that treasure into your hands."

"How?" asked Thuillier, with curiosity.

"Parbleu! by buying it; it can be had for a song."

"There now, you see," said Thuillier in a discouraged tone; "you never counted in the cost of purchase."

"How you dwell on nothings!" said la Peyrade, hunching his shoulders; "we have other and more important difficulties to solve."

"Other difficulties?" echoed Thuillier.

"Parbleu!" exclaimed la Peyrade; "do you suppose that after all that has taken place between us I should boldly harness myself to your election without knowing exactly what benefit I am to get for it?"

"But," said Thuillier, rather astonished, "I thought that friendship was a good exchange for such services."

"Yes; but when the exchange consists in one side giving all and the other side nothing, friendship gets tired of that sort of sharing, and asks for something a little better balanced."

"But, my dear Theodose, what have I to offer you that you have not already rejected?"

"I rejected it, because it was offered without heartiness, and seasoned with Mademoiselle Brigitte's vinegar; every self-respecting man would have acted as I did. Give and keep don't pass, as the old legal saying is; but that is precisely what you persist in doing."

"I!—I think you took offence very unreasonably; but the engagement might be renewed."

"So be it," replied la Peyrade; "but I will not put myself at the mercy of either the success of the election or Mademoiselle Celeste's caprices. I claim the right to something positive and certain. Give and take; short accounts make good friends."

"I perfectly agree with you," said Thuillier, "and I have always treated you with too much good faith to fear any of these precautions you now want to take. But what guarantees do you want?"

"I want that the husband of Celeste should manage your election, and not Theodose de la Peyrade."

"By hurrying things as much as possible, so Brigitte said, it would still take fifteen days; and just think, with the elections only eight weeks off, to lose two of them doing nothing!"

"Day after to-morrow," replied la Peyrade, "the banns can be published for the first time at the mayor's office, in the intervals of publication some things could be done, for though the publishing of the banns is not a step from which there is no retreat, it is at least a public pledge and a long step taken; after that we can get your notary to draw the contract at once. Moreover, if you decide on buying this newspaper, I shouldn't be afraid that you would go back on me, for you don't want a useless horse in your stable, and without me I am certain you can't manage him."

"But, my dear fellow," said Thuillier, going back to his objections, "suppose that affair proves too onerous?"

"There's no need to say that you are the sole judge of the conditions of the purchase. I don't wish any more than you do to buy a pig in a poke. If to-morrow you authorize me, I won't say to buy, but to let these people know that you may possibly make the purchase, I'll confer with one of them on your behalf, and you may be certain that I'll stand up for your interests as if they were my own."

"Very good, my dear fellow," said Thuillier, "go ahead!"

"And as soon as the paper is purchased we are to fix the day for signing the contract?"

"Yes," replied Thuillier; "but will you bind yourself to use your utmost influence on the election?"

"As if it were my own," replied la Peyrade, "which, by the bye, is not altogether an hypothesis. I have already received suggestions about my own candidacy, and if I were vindictive—"

"Certainly," said Thuillier, with humility, "you would make a better deputy than I; but you are not of the required age, I think."

"There's a better reason than that," said la Peyrade; "you are my friend; I find you again what you once were, and I shall keep the pledges I have given you. As for the election, I prefer that people say of me, 'He makes deputies, but will be none himself.' Now I must leave you and keep my appointment. To-morrow in my own rooms, come and see me; I shall have something to announce."

Whoso has ever been a newspaper man will ever be one; that horoscope is as sure and certain as that of drunkards. Whoever has tasted that feverishly busy and relatively lazy and independent life; whoever has exercised that sovereignty which criticises intellect, art, talent, fame, virtue, absurdity, and even truth; whoever has occupied that tribune erected by his own hands, fulfilled the functions of that magistracy to which he is self-appointed,—in short, whosoever has been, for however brief a span, that proxy of public opinion, looks upon himself when remanded to private life as an exile, and the moment a chance is offered to him puts out an eager hand to snatch back his crown.

For this reason when Etienne Lousteau went to la Peyrade, a former journalist, with an offer of the weapon entitled the "Echo de la Bievre," all the latter's instincts as a newspaper man were aroused, in spite of the very inferior quality of the blade. The paper had failed; la Peyrade believed he could revive it. The subscribers, on the vendor's own showing, were few and far between, but he would exercise upon them a "compelle intrare" both powerful and irresistible. In the circumstances under which the affair was presented to him it might surely be considered provincial. Threatened with the loss of his position at the bar, he was thus acquiring, as we said before, a new position and that of a "detached fort"; compelled, as he might be, to defend himself, he could from that vantage-ground take the offensive and oblige his enemies to reckon with him.

On the Thuillier side, the newspaper would undoubtedly make him a personage of considerable importance; he would have more power on the election; and by involving their capital in an enterprise which, without him, they would feel a gulf and a snare, he bound them to him by self-interests so firmly that there was nothing to fear from their caprice or ingratitude.

This horizon, rapidly taken in during Etienne Lousteau's visit, had fairly dazzled the Provencal, and we have seen the peremptory manner in which Thuillier was forced into accepting with some enthusiasm the discovery of this philosopher's-stone.

The cost of the purchase was ridiculously insignificant. A bank-note for five hundred francs, for which Etienne Lousteau never clearly accounted to the share-holders, put Thuillier in possession of the name, property, furniture, and good-will of the newspaper, which he and la Peyrade at once busied themselves in reorganizing.

CHAPTER X. IN WHICH CERIZET PRACTISES THE HEALING ART AND

THE ART OF POISONING ON THE SAME DAY

While this regeneration was going on, Cerizet went one morning to see du Portail, with whom la Peyrade was now more than ever determined to hold no communication.

"Well," said the little old man to the poor man's banker, "what effect did the news we gave to the president of the bar produce on our man? Did the affair get wind at the Palais?"

"Phew!" said Cerizet, whose intercourse, no doubt pretty frequent, with du Portail had put him on a footing of some familiarity with the old man, "there's no question of that now. The eel has wriggled out of our hands; neither softness nor violence has any effect upon that devil of a man. He has quarrelled with the bar, and is in better odor than ever with Thuillier. 'Necessity,' says Figaro, 'obliterates distance.' Thuillier needs him to push his candidacy in the quartier Saint-Jacques, so they kissed and made up."

"And no doubt," said du Portail, without much appearance of feeling, "the marriage is fixed for an early day?"

"Yes," replied Cerizet, "but there's another piece of work on hand. That crazy fellow has persuaded Thuillier to buy a newspaper, and he'll make him sink forty thousand francs in it. Thuillier, once involved, will want to get his money back, and in my opinion they are bound together for the rest of their days."

"What paper is it?"

"Oh, a cabbage-leaf that calls itself the 'Echo de la Bievre'!" replied Cerizet with great scorn; "a paper which an old hack of a journalist on his last legs managed to set up in the Mouffetard quarter by the help of a lot of tanners—that, you know, is the industry of the quarter. From a political and literary point of view the affair is nothing at all, but Thuillier has been made to think it a masterly stroke."

"Well, for local service to the election the instrument isn't so bad," remarked du Portail. "La Peyrade has talent, activity, and much resource of mind; he may make something out of that 'Echo.' Under what political banner will Thuillier present himself?"

"Thuillier," replied the beggars' banker, "is an oyster; he hasn't any opinions. Until the publication of his pamphlet he was, like all those bourgeois, a rabid conservative; but since the seizure he has gone over to the Opposition. His first stage will probably be the Left-centre; but if the election wind should blow from another quarter, he'll go straight before it to the extreme left. Self-interest, for those bourgeois, that's the measure of their convictions."

"Dear, dear!" said du Portail, "this new combination of la Peyrade's may assume the importance of a political danger from the point of view of my opinions, which are extremely conservative and governmental." Then, after a moment's reflection, he added, "I think you did newspaper work once upon a time; I remember 'the courageous Cerizet.'"

"Yes," replied the usurer, "I even managed one with la Peyrade,—an evening paper; and a pretty piece of work we did, for which we were finely recompensed."

"Well," said du Portail, "why don't you do it again,—journalism, I mean,— with la Peyrade."

Cerizet looked at du Portail in amazement.

"Ah ca!" he cried, "are you the devil, monsieur? Can nothing ever be hidden from you?"

"Yes," said du Portail, "I know a good many things. But what has been settled between you and la Peyrade?"

"Well, remembering my experience in the business, and not knowing whom else to get, he offered to make me manager of the paper."

"I did not know that," said du Portail, "but it was quite probable. Did you accept?"

"Conditionally; I asked time for reflection. I wanted to know what you thought of the offer."

"Parbleu! I think that out of an evil that can't be remedied we should get, as the proverb says, wing or foot. I had rather see you inside than outside of that enterprise."

"Very good; but in order to get into it there's a difficulty. La Peyrade knows I have debts, and he won't help me with the thirty-three-thousand francs' security which must be paid down in my name. I haven't got them, and if I had, I wouldn't show them and expose myself to the insults of creditors."

"You must have a good deal left of that twenty-five thousand francs la Peyrade paid you not more than two months ago," remarked du Portail.

"Only two thousand two hundred francs and fifty centimes," replied Cerizet. "I was adding it up last night; the rest has all gone to pay off pressing debts."

"But if you have paid your debts you haven't any creditors."

"Yes, those I've paid, but those I haven't paid I still owe."

"Do you mean to tell me that your liabilities were more than twenty-five thousand francs?" said du Portail, in a tone of incredulity.

"Does a man go into bankruptcy for less?" replied Cerizet, as though he were enunciating a maxim.

"Well, I see I am expected to pay that sum myself," said du Portail, crossly; "but the question is whether the utility of your presence in this enterprise is worth to me the interest on one hundred and thirty-three thousand, three hundred and thirty-three francs, thirty-three centimes."

"Hang it!" said Cerizet, "if I were once installed near Thuillier, I shouldn't despair of soon putting him and la Peyrade at loggerheads. In the management of a newspaper there are lots of inevitable disagreements, and by always taking the side of the fool against the clever man, I can increase the conceit of one and wound the conceit of the other until life together becomes impossible. Besides, you spoke just now of political danger; now the manager of a newspaper, as you ought to know, when he has the intellect to be something better than a man of straw, can quietly give his sheet a push in the direction wanted.

"There's a good deal of truth in that," said du Portail, "but defeat to la Peyrade, that's what I am thinking about."

"Well," said Cerizet, "I think I have another nice little insidious means of demolishing him with Thuillier."

"Say what it is, then!" exclaimed du Portail, impatiently; "you go round and round the pot as if I were a man it would do you some good to finesse with."

"You remember," said Cerizet, coming out with it, "that some time ago Dutocq and I were much puzzled to know how la Peyrade was, all of a sudden, able to make that payment of twenty-five thousand francs?"

"Ha!" said the old man quickly, "have you discovered the origin of that very improbable sum in our friend's hands; and is that origin shady?"

"You shall judge," said Cerizet.

And he related in all its details the affair of Madame Lambert,—adding, however, that on questioning the woman closely at the office of the justice-of-peace, after the meeting with la Peyrade, he had been unable to extract from her any confession, although by her whole bearing she had amply confirmed the suspicions of Dutocq and himself.

"Madame Lambert, rue du Val-de-Grace, No. 9; at the house of Monsieur Picot, professor of mathematics," said du Portail, as he made a note of the information. "Very good," he added; "come back and see me to-morrow, my dear Monsieur Cerizet."

"But please remark," said the usurer, "that I must give an answer to la Peyrade in the course of to-day. He is in a great hurry to start the business."

"Very well; you must accept, asking a delay of twenty-four hours to obtain your security. If, after making certain inquiries I see it is more to my interests not to meddle in the affair, you can get out of it by merely breaking your word; you can't be sent to the court of assizes for that."

Independently of a sort of inexplicable fascination which du Portail exercised over his agent, he never lost an opportunity to remind him of the very questionable point of departure of their intercourse.

The next day Cerizet returned.

"You guessed right," said du Portail. "That woman Lambert, being obliged to conceal the existence of her booty, and wanting to draw interest on her stolen property, must have taken it into her head to consult la Peyrade; his devout exterior may have recommended him to her. She probably gave him that money without taking a receipt. In what kind of money was Dutocq paid?"

"In nineteen thousand-franc notes, and twelve of five-hundred francs."

"That's precisely it," said du Portail. "There can't be the slightest doubt left. Now, what use do you expect to make of this information bearing upon Thuillier."

"I expect to put it into his head that la Peyrade, to whom he is going to give his goddaughter and heiress, is over head and ears in debt; that he makes enormous secret loans; and that in order to get out of his difficulties he means to gnaw the newspaper to the bone; and I shall insinuate that the position of a man so much in debt must be known to the public before long, and become a fatal blow to the candidate whose right hand he is."

"That's not bad," said du Portail; "but there's another and even more conclusive use to be made of the discovery."

"Tell me, master; I'm listening," said Cerizet.

329

"Thuillier has not yet been able, has he, to explain to himself the reason of the seizure of the pamphlet?"

"Yes, he has," replied Cerizet. "La Peyrade was telling me only yesterday, by way of explaining Thuillier's idiotic simplicity, that he had believed a most ridiculous bit of humbug. The 'honest bourgeois' is persuaded that the seizure was instigated by Monsieur Olivier Vinet, substitute to the procureur-general. The young man aspired for a moment to the hand of Mademoiselle Colleville, and the worthy Thuillier has been made to imagine that the seizure of his pamphlet was a revenge for the refusal."

"Good!" said du Portail; "to-morrow, as a preparation for the other version of which you are to be the organ, Thuillier shall receive from Monsieur Vinet a very sharp and decided denial of the abuse of power he foolishly gave ear to."

"Will he?" said Cerizet, with curiosity.

"But another explanation must take its place," continued du Portail; "you must assure Thuillier that he is the victim of police machinations. That is all the police is good for, you know,—machinations."

"I know that very well; I've made that affirmation scores of times when I was working for the republican newspapers and—"

"When you were 'the courageous Cerizet,'" interrupted du Portail. "Well, the present machination, here it is. The government was much displeased at seeing Thuillier elected without its influence to the Council-general of the Seine; it was angry with an independent and patriotic citizen who showed by his candidacy that he could do without it; and it learned, moreover, that this excellent citizen was preparing a pamphlet on the subject, always a delicate one, of the finances, as to which this dangerous adversary had great experience. So, what did this essentially corrupt government do? It suborned a man in whom, as it learned, Thuillier placed confidence, and for a sum of twenty-five thousand francs (a mere trifle to the police), this treacherous friend agreed to insert into the pamphlet three or four phrases which exposed it to seizure and caused its author to be summoned before the court of assizes. Now the way to make the explanation clinch the doubt in Thuillier's mind is to let him know that the next day la Peyrade, who, as Thuillier knew, hadn't a sou, paid Dutocq precisely that very sum of twenty-five thousand francs."

"The devil!" cried Cerizet, "it isn't a bad trick. Fellows of the Thuillier species will believe anything against the police."

"We shall see, then," continued du Portail, "whether Thuillier will want to keep such a collaborator beside him, and above all, whether he will be so eager to give him his goddaughter."

"You are a strong man, monsieur," said Cerizet, again expressing his approbation; "but I must own that I feel some scruples at the part assigned me. La Peyrade came and offered me the management of the paper, and, you see, I should be working to evict him."

"And that lease he knocked you out of in spite of his promises, have you forgotten that?" asked the little old man. "Besides, are we not aiming for his happiness, though the obstinate fellow persists in thwarting our benevolent intentions?"

"It is true," said Cerizet, "that the result will absolve me. Yes, I'll go resolutely along the ingenious path you've traced out for me. But there's one thing more: I can't fling my revelation at Thuillier's head at the very first; I must have time to prepare the way for it, but that security will have to be paid in immediately."

"Listen to me, Monsieur Cerizet," said du Portail, in a tone of authority; "if the marriage of la Peyrade to my ward takes place it is my intention to reward your services, and the sum of thirty thousand francs will be your perquisite. Now, thirty thousand from one side and twenty-five thousand from the other makes precisely fifty-five thousand francs that the matrimonial vicissitudes of your friend la Peyrade will have put into your pocket. But, as country people do at the shows of a fair, I shall not pay till I come out. If you take that money out of your own hoard I shall feel no anxiety; you will know how to keep it from the clutches of your creditors. If, on the contrary, my money is at stake, you will have neither the same eagerness nor the same intelligence in keeping it out of danger. Therefore arrange your affairs so that you can pay down your own thirty-three thousand; in case of success, that sum will bring you in pretty nearly a hundred per cent. That's my last word, and I shall not listen to any objections."

Cerizet had no time to make any, for at that moment the door of du Portail's study opened abruptly, and a fair, slender woman, whose face expressed angelic sweetness, entered the room eagerly. On her arm, wrapped in handsome long clothes, lay what seemed to be the form of an infant.

"There!" she said, "that naughty Katte insisted that the doctor was not here. I knew perfectly well that I had seen him enter. Well, doctor," she continued, addressing Cerizet, "I am not satisfied with the condition of my little one, not satisfied at all; she is very pallid, and has grown so thin. I think she must be teething."

Du Portail made Cerizet a sign to accept the role so abruptly thrust upon him.

"Yes, evidently," he said, "it is the teeth; children always turn pale at that crisis; but there's nothing in that, my dear lady, that need make you anxious."

"Do you really think so, doctor," said the poor crazed girl, whom our readers have recognized as du Portail's ward, Lydie de la Peyrade; "but see her dear little arms, how thin they are getting."

Then taking out the pins that fastened the swathings, she exhibited to Cerizet a bundle of linen which to her poor distracted mind represented a baby.

"Why, no, no," said Cerizet, "she is a trifle thin, it is true, but the flesh is firm and her color excellent."

"Poor darling!" said Lydie, kissing her dream lovingly. "I do think she is better since morning. What had I better give her, doctor? Broth disgusts her, and she won't take soup."

"Well," said Cerizet, "try panada. Does she like sweet things?"

"Oh, yes!" cried the poor girl, her face brightening, "she adores them. Would chocolate be good for her?"

"Certainly," replied Cerizet, "but without vanilla; vanilla is very heating."

"Then I'll get what they call health-chocolate," said Lydie, with all the intonations of a mother, listening to the doctor as to a god who reassured her. "Uncle," she added, "please ring for Bruneau, and tell him to go to Marquis at once and get some pounds of that chocolate."

"Bruneau has just gone out," said her guardian; "but there's no hurry, he shall go in the course of the day."

"There, she is going to sleep," said Cerizet, anxious to put an end to the scene, which, in spite of his hardened nature, he felt to be painful.

"True," said the girl, replacing the bandages and rising; "I'll put her to bed. Adieu, doctor; it is very kind of you to come sometimes without being sent for. If you knew how anxious we poor mothers are, and how, with a word or two, you can do us such good. Ah, there she is crying!"

"She is so sleepy," said Cerizet; "she'll be much better in her cradle."

"Yes, and I'll play her that sonata of Beethoven that dear papa was so fond of; it is wonderful how calming it is. Adieu, doctor," she said again, pausing on the threshold of the door. "Adieu, kind doctor!" And she sent him a kiss.

Cerizet was quite overcome.

"You see," said du Portail, "that she is an angel,—never the least ill-humor, never a sharp word; sad sometimes, but always caused by a feeling of motherly solicitude. That is what first gave the doctors the idea that if reality could take the place of her constant hallucination she might recover her reason. Well, this is the girl that fool of a Peyrade refuses, with the accompaniment of a magnificent 'dot.' But he must come to it, or I'll forswear my name. Listen," he added as the sound of a piano came to them; "hear! what talent! Thousands of sane women can't compare with her; they are not as reasonable as she is, except on the surface."

When Beethoven's sonata, played from the soul with a perfection of shades and tones that filled her hardened hearer with admiration, had ceased to sound, Cerizet said:—

"I agree with you, monsieur; la Peyrade refuses an angel, a treasure, a pearl, and if I were in his place—But we shall bring him round to your purpose. Now I shall serve you not only with zeal, but with enthusiasm, I may say fanaticism."

As Cerizet was concluding this oath of fidelity at the door of the study, he heard a woman's voice which was not that of Lydie.

"Is he in his study, the dear commander?" said that voice, with a slightly foreign accent.

"Yes, madame, but please come into the salon. Monsieur is not alone; I will tell him you are here."

This was the voice of Katte, the old Dutch maid.

"Stop, go this way," said du Portail quickly to Cerizet.

And he opened a hidden door which led through a dark corridor directly to the staircase, whence Cerizet betook himself to the office of the "Echo de la Bievre," where a heated discussion was going on.

The article by which the new editors of every newspaper lay before the public their "profession of faith," as the technical saying is, always produces a laborious and difficult parturition. In this particular case it was necessary, if not openly to declare Thuillier's candidacy, to at least make it felt and foreseen. The terms of the manifesto, after la Peyrade had made a rough draft of it, were discussed at great length. This discussion took place in Cerizet's presence, who, acting on du Portail's advice, accepted the management, but postponed the payment of the security till the next day, through the latitude allowed in all administrations for the accomplishment of that formality.

Cleverly egged on by this master-knave, who, from the start, made himself Thuillier's flatterer, the discussion became stormy, and presently bitter; but as, by the deed of partnership the deciding word was left to la Peyrade in all matters concerning the editorship, he finally closed it by sending the manifesto, precisely as he had written it, to the printing office.

Thuillier was incensed at what he called an abuse of power, and finding himself alone with Cerizet later in the day, he hastened to pour his griefs and resentments into the bosom of his faithful manager, thus affording the latter a ready-made and natural opportunity to insinuate the calumnious revelation agreed upon with du Portail. Leaving the knife in the wound, Cerizet went out to make certain arrangements to obtain the money necessary for his bond.

Tortured by the terrible revelation, Thuillier could not keep it to himself; he felt the need of confiding it, and of talking over the course he would be compelled to take by this infernal discovery. Sending for a carriage he drove home, and half an hour later he had told the whole story to his Egeria.

Brigitte had from the first very vehemently declared against all the determinations made by Thuillier during the last few days. For no purpose whatever, not even for the sake of her brother's election, would she agree to a renewal of the relation to la Peyrade. In the first place, she had treated him badly, and that was a strong reason for disliking him; then, in case that adventurer, as she now called him, married Celeste, the fear of her authority being lessened gave her a species of second-sight; she had ended by having an intuitive sense of the dark profundities of the man's nature, and now declared that under no circumstances and for no possible price would she make one household with him.

"Ruin yourself if you choose," she said, "you are the master of that, and you can do as you like; a fool and his money are soon parted."

When, therefore, she listened to her brother's confidences it was not with reproaches, but, on the contrary, with a crow of triumph, celebrating the probable return of her power, that she welcomed them.

"So much the better!" she cried; "it is well to know at last that the man is a spy. I always thought so, the canting bigot! Turn him out of doors without an explanation. WE don't want him to work that newspaper. This Monsieur Cerizet seems, from what you tell me, the right sort of man, and we can get another manager. Besides, when Madame de Godollo went away she promised to write to me; and she can easily put us in the way of finding some one. Poor, dear Celeste! what a fate we were going to give her!"

"How you run on!" said Thuillier. "La Peyrade, my dear, is so far only accused. He must be heard in his defence. And besides, there's a deed that binds us."

"Ah, very good!" said Brigitte; "I see how it will be; you'll let that man twist you round his finger again. A deed with a spy! As if there could be deeds with such fellows."

"Come, come, be calm, my good Brigitte," returned Thuillier. "We mustn't do anything hastily. Certainly, if la Peyrade cannot furnish a justification, clear, categorical, and convincing, I shall decide to break with him, and I'll prove to you that I am no milksop. But Cerizet himself is not certain; these are mere inductions, and I only came to consult you as to whether I ought, or ought not, to demand an explanation outright."

"Not a doubt about it," replied Brigitte. "You ought to demand an explanation and go to the bottom of this thing; if you don't, I cast you off as my brother."

"That suffices," said Thuillier, leaving the room with solemnity; "you shall see that we will come to an understanding."

CHAPTER XI. EXPLANATIONS AND WHAT CAME OF THEM

On his return to the office after his conference with Brigitte, Thuillier found la Peyrade at his post as editor-in-chief, and in a position of much embarrassment, caused by the high hand he had reserved for himself as the sole selector of articles and contributors. At this moment, Phellion, instigated by his family, and deeply conscious of his position on the reading-committee of the Odeon, had come to offer his services as dramatic critic.

"My dear monsieur," he said, continuing his remarks to la Peyrade, after inquiring of Thuillier about his health, "I was a great student of the theatre in my youth; the stage and its scenic effects continue to have for me peculiar attractions; and the white hairs which crown my brow to-day seem to me no obstacle to my allowing your interesting publication to profit by the fruit of my studies and my experience. As member of the reading-committee of the Odeon theatre, I am conversant with the modern drama, and—if I may be quite sure of your discretion—I will even confide to you that among my papers it would not be impossible for me to find a certain tragedy entitled 'Sapor,' which in my young days won me some fame when read in salons."

"Ah!" said la Peyrade, endeavoring to gild the refusal he should be forced to give, "why not try to have it put upon the stage? We might be able to help you in that direction."

"Certainly," said Thuillier, "the director of any theatre to whom we should recommend—"

"No," replied Phellion. "In the first place, as member of the reading-committee of the Odeon, having to sit in judgment upon others, it would not become me to descend into the arena myself. I am an old athlete, whose business it is to judge of blows he can no longer give. In this sense, criticism is altogether within my sphere, and all the more because I have certain views on the proper method of composing dramatic feuilletons which I think novel. The 'castigat ridendo mores' ought to be, according to my humble lights, the great law, I may say the only law of the stage. I should therefore show myself pitiless for those works, bred of imagination, in which morality has no part, and to which mothers of families—"

"Excuse me," said la Peyrade, "for interrupting you; but before allowing you to take the trouble to develop your poetical ideas, I ought to tell you that we have already made arrangements for our dramatic criticism."

"Ah! that's another thing," said Phellion; "an honest man must keep his word."

"Yes," said Thuillier, "we have our dramatic critic, little thinking that you would offer us your valuable assistance."

"Well," said Phellion, suddenly becoming crafty,—for there is something in the newspaper atmosphere, impossible to say what, which flies to the head, the bourgeois head especially,—"since you are good enough to consider my pen capable of doing you some service, perhaps a series of detached thoughts on different subjects, to which I should venture to give the name of 'Diversities,' might be of a nature to interest your readers."

"Yes," said la Peyrade, with a maliciousness that was quite lost upon Phellion, "thoughts, especially in the style of la Rochefoucauld or la Bruyere, might do. What do you think yourself, Thuillier?"

He reserved to himself the right to leave the responsibility of refusals, as far as he could, to the proprietor of the paper.

"But I imagine that thoughts, especially if detached, cannot be very consecutive," said Thuillier.

"Evidently not," replied Phellion; "detached thoughts imply the idea of a very great number of subjects on which the author lets his pen stray without the pretension of presenting a whole."

"You will of course sign them?" said la Peyrade.

"Oh, no!" replied Phellion, alarmed. "I could not put myself on exhibition in that way."

"Your modesty, which by the bye I understand and approve, settles the matter," said la Peyrade. "Thoughts are a subject altogether individual, which imperatively require to be personified by a name. You must be conscious of this yourself. 'Divers Thoughts by Monsieur Three-Stars' says nothing to the public."

Seeing that Phellion was about to make objections, Thuillier, who was in a hurry to begin his fight with la Peyrade, cut the matter short rather sharply.

"My dear Phellion," he said, "I beg your pardon for not being able to enjoy the pleasure of your conversation any longer, but we have to talk, la Peyrade and I, over a matter of much importance, and in newspaper offices this devilish time runs away so fast. If you are willing, we will postpone the question to another day. Madame Phellion is well, I trust?"

"Perfectly well," said the great citizen, rising, and not appearing to resent his dismissal. "When does your first number appear?" he added; "it is eagerly

338

awaited in the arrondissement."

"To-morrow I think our confession of faith will make its appearance," replied Thuillier, accompanying him to the door. "You will receive a copy, my dear friend. We shall meet again soon, I hope. Come and see us, and bring that manuscript; la Peyrade's point of view may be a little arbitrary."

With this balm shed upon his wound, Phellion departed, and Thuillier rang the bell for the porter.

"Could you recognize the gentlemen who has just gone out the next time you see him?" asked Thuillier.

"Oh, yes, m'sieu, his round ball of a head is too funny to forget; besides, it is Monsieur Phellion; haven't I opened the door to him hundreds of times?"

"Well, whenever he comes again neither I nor Monsieur de la Peyrade will be here. Remember that's a positive rule. Now leave us."

"The devil!" cried la Peyrade, when the two partners were alone, "how you manage bores. But take care; among the number there may be electors. You did right to tell Phellion you would send him a copy of the paper; he has a certain importance in the quarter."

"Well," said Thuillier, "we can't allow our time to be taken up by all the dull-heads who come and offer their services. But now you and I have to talk, and talk very seriously. Be seated and listen."

"Do you know, my dear fellow," said la Peyrade, laughing, "that journalism is making you into something very solemn? 'Be seated, Cinna,'—Caesar Augustus couldn't have said it otherwise."

"Cinnas, unfortunately, are more plentiful than people think," replied Thuillier.

He was still under the goad of the promise he had made to Brigitte, and he meant to fulfil it with cutting sarcasm. The top continued the whirling motion imparted to it by the old maid's lash.

La Peyrade took a seat at the round table. As he was puzzled to know what was coming, he endeavored to seem unconcerned, and picking up the large scissors used for the loans which all papers make from the columns of their brethren of the press, he began to snip up a sheet of paper, on which, in Thuillier's handwriting, was an attempt at a leading article, never completed.

Though la Peyrade was seated and expectant, Thuillier did not begin immediately; he rose and went toward the door which stood ajar, with the intention of closing it. But suddenly it was flung wide open, and Coffinet appeared.

"Will monsieur," said Coffinet to la Peyrade, "receive two ladies? They are very well-dressed, and the young one ain't to be despised."

"Shall I let them in?" said la Peyrade to Thuillier.

"Yes, since they are here," growled Thuillier; "but get rid of them as soon as possible."

Coffinet's judgment on the toilet of the two visitors needs revision. A woman is well-dressed, not when she wears rich clothes, but when her clothes present a certain harmony of shapes and colors which form an appropriate and graceful envelope to her person. Now a bonnet with a flaring brim, surmounted by nodding plumes, an immense French cashmere shawl, worn with the awkward inexperience of a young bride, a plaid silk gown with enormous checks and a triple tier of flounces with far too many chains and trinkets (though to be just, the boots and gloves were irreproachable), constituted the apparel of the younger of these ladies. As for the other, who seemed to be in the tow of her dressy companion, she was short, squat, and high-colored, and wore a bonnet, shawl, and gown which a practised eye would at once have recognized as second hand. Mothers of actresses are always clothed by this very economical process. Their garments, condemned to the service of two generations, reverse the order of things, and go from descendants to ancestors.

Advancing two chairs, la Peyrade inquired, "To whom have I the honor of speaking?"

"Monsieur," said the younger visitor, "I am a dramatic artist, and as I am about to make my first appearance in this quarter, I allow myself to hope that a journal of this locality will favor me."

"At what theatre?" asked la Peyrade.

"The Folies, where I am engaged for the Dejazets."

"The Folies?" echoed la Peyrade, in a tone that demanded an explanation.

"Folies-Dramatiques," interposed the agreeable Madame Cardinal, whom the reader has doubtless recognized.

"When do you appear?" asked la Peyrade.

"Next week, monsieur,—a fairy piece in which I play five parts."

"You'll encourage her, monsieur, won't you?" said Madame Cardinal, in a coaxing voice; "she's so young, and I can certify she works day and night."

"Mother!" said Olympe, with authority, "the public will judge me; all I want is that monsieur will kindly promise to notice my debut."

"Very good, mademoiselle," said la Peyrade in a tone of dismissal, beginning to edge the pair to the door.

Olympe Cardinal went first, leaving her mother to hurry after her as best she could.

"At home to no one!" cried Thuillier to the office-boy as he closed the door and slipped the bolt. "Now," he said, addressing la Peyrade, "we will talk. My dear fellow," he went on, starting with irony, for he remembered to have heard that nothing was more confusing to an adversary, "I have heard something that will give you pleasure. I know now why MY pamphlet was seized."

So saying, he looked fixedly at la Peyrade.

"Parbleu!" said the latter in a natural tone of voice, "it was seized because they chose to seize it. They wanted to find, and they found, because they always find the things they want, what the king's adherents call 'subversive doctrine.'"

"No, you are wrong," said Thuillier; "the seizure was planned, concocted, and agreed upon before publication."

"Between whom?" asked la Peyrade.

"Between those who wanted to kill the pamphlet, and the wretches who were paid to betray it."

"Well, in any case, those who paid," said la Peyrade, "got mighty little for their money; for, persecuted though it was, I don't see that your pamphlet made much of a stir."

"Those who sold may have done better?" said Thuillier with redoubled irony.

"Those who sold," returned la Peyrade, "were the cleverer of the two."

"Ah, I know," said Thuillier, "that you think a great deal of cleverness; but allow me to tell you that the police, whose hand I see in all this, doesn't usually throw its money away."

And again he looked fixedly at la Peyrade.

"So," said the barrister, without winking, "you have discovered that the police had plotted in advance the smothering of your pamphlet?"

"Yes, my dear fellow; and what is more, I know the actual sum paid to the person who agreed to carry out this honorable plot."

"The person," said la Peyrade, thinking a moment,—"perhaps I know the person; but as for the money, I don't know a word about that."

"Well, I can tell you the amount. It was twenty-five—thousand—francs," said Thuillier, dwelling on each word; "that was the sum paid to Judas."

"Oh! excuse me, my dear fellow, but twenty-five thousand francs is a good deal of money. I don't deny that you have become an important man; but you are not such a bugbear to the government as to lead it to make such sacrifices. Twenty-five thousand francs is as much as would ever be given for the suppression of one of those annoying pamphlets about the Civil list. But our financial lucubrations didn't annoy in that way; and such a sum borrowed from the secret-service money for the mere pleasure of plaguing you, seems to me rather fabulous."

"Apparently," said Thuillier, acrimoniously, "this honest go-between had some interest in exaggerating my value. One thing is very sure; this monsieur had a debt of twenty-five thousand francs which harassed him much; and a short time before the seizure this same monsieur, who had no means of his own, paid off that debt; and unless you can tell me where else he got the money, the inference I think is not difficult to draw."

It was la Peyrade's turn to look fixedly at Thuillier.

"Monsieur Thuillier," he said, raising his voice, "let us get out of enigmas and generalities; will you do me the favor to name that person?"

"Well, no," replied Thuillier, striking his hand upon the table, "I shall not name him, because of the sentiments of esteem and affection which formerly united us; but you have understood me, Monsieur la Peyrade."

"I ought to have known," said the Provencal, in a voice changed by emotion, "that in bringing a serpent to this place I should soon be soiled by his venom. Poor fool! do you not see that you have made yourself the echo of Cerizet's calumny?"

"Cerizet has nothing to do with it; on the contrary, he has told me the highest good of you. How was it, not having a penny the night before,—and I had reason to know it,—that you were able to pay Dutocq the round sum of twenty-five thousand francs the next day?"

La Peyrade reflected for a moment.

"No," he said, "it was not Dutocq who told you that. He is not a man to wrestle with an enemy of my strength without a strong interest in it. It was Cerizet; he's the infamous calumniator, from whose hands I wrenched the lease of your house near the Madeleine,—Cerizet, whom in kindness, I went to seek on his dunghill that I might give him the chance of honorable employment; that is the wretch, to whom a benefit is only an encouragement to treachery. Tiens! if I were to tell you what that man is I should turn you sick with disgust; in the sphere of infamy he has discovered worlds."

This time Thuillier made an able reply.

"I don't know anything about Cerizet except through you," he said; "you introduced him to me as a manager, offering every guarantee; but, allowing him to be blacker than the devil, and supposing that this communication comes from him, I don't see, my friend, that all that makes YOU any the whiter."

"No doubt I was to blame," said la Peyrade, "for putting such a man into relations with you; but we wanted some one who understood journalism, and that value he really had for us. But who can ever sound the depths of souls like his? I thought him reformed. A manager, I said to myself, is only a machine; he can do no harm. I expected to find him a man of straw; well, I was mistaken, he will never be anything but a man of mud."

"All that is very fine," said Thuillier, "but those twenty-five thousand francs found so conveniently in your possession, where did you get them? That is the point you are forgetting to explain."

"But to reason about it," said la Peyrade; "a man of my character in the pay of the police and yet so poor that I could not pay the ten thousand francs your harpy of a sister demanded with an insolence which you yourself witnessed —"

"But," said Thuillier, "if the origin of this money is honest, as I sincerely desire it may be, what hinders you from telling me how you got it?"

"I cannot," said la Peyrade; "the history of that money is a secret entrusted to me professionally."

"Come, come, you told me yourself that the statutes of your order forbid all barristers from doing business of any kind."

"Let us suppose," said la Peyrade, "that I have done something not absolutely regular; it would be strange indeed after what I risked, as you know, for you, if you should have the face to reproach me with it."

"My poor friend, you are trying to shake off the hounds; but you can't make me lose the scent. You wish to keep your secret; then keep it. I am master of my own confidence and my own esteem; by paying you the forfeit stipulated in our deed I take the newspaper into my own hands."

"Do you mean that you dismiss me?" cried la Peyrade. "The money that you have put into the affair, all your chances of election, sacrificed to the calumnies of such a being as Cerizet!"

"In the first place," said Thuillier, "another editor-in-chief can be found; it is a true saying that no man is indispensable. As for election to the Chamber I would rather never receive it than owe it to the help of one who—"

"Go on," said la Peyrade, seeing that Thuillier hesitated, "or rather, no, be silent, for you will presently blush for your suspicions and ask my pardon humbly."

By this time la Peyrade saw that without a confession to which he must compel himself, the influence and the future he had just recovered would be cut from under his feet. Resuming his speech he said, solemnly:—

"You will remember, my friend, that you were pitiless, and, by subjecting me to a species of moral torture, you have forced me to reveal to you a secret that is not mine."

"Go on," said Thuillier, "I take the whole responsibility upon myself. Make me see the truth clearly in this darkness, and if I have done wrong I will be the first to say so."

"Well," said la Peyrade, "those twenty-five thousand francs are the savings of a servant-woman who came to me and asked me to take them and to pay her interest."

"A servant with twenty-five thousand francs of savings! Nonsense; she must serve in monstrously rich households."

"On the contrary, she is the one servant of an infirm old savant; and it was on account of the discrepancy which strikes your mind that she wanted to put her money in my hands as a sort of trustee."

"Bless me! my friend," said Thuillier, flippantly, "you said we were in want of a romance-feuilletonist; but really, after this, I sha'n't be uneasy. Here's imagination for you!"

"What?" said la Peyrade, angrily, "you don't believe me?"

"No, I do not believe you. Twenty-five thousand francs savings in the service of an old savant! that is about as believable as the officer of La Dame Blanche buying a chateau with his pay."

"But if I prove to you the truth of my words; if I let you put your finger upon it?"

"In that case, like Saint Thomas, I shall lower my flag before the evidence. Meanwhile you must permit me, my noble friend, to wait until you offer me that proof."

Thuillier felt really superb.

"I'd give a hundred francs," he said to himself, "if Brigitte could have been here and heard me impeach him."

"Well," said la Peyrade, "suppose that without leaving this office, and by means of a note which you shall read, I bring into your presence the person from whom I received the money; if she confirms what I say will you believe me?"

This proposal and the assurance with which it was made rather staggered Thuillier.

"I shall know what to do when the time comes," he replied, changing his tone. "But this must be done at once, now, here."

"I said, without leaving this office. I should think that was clear enough."

"And who will carry the note you write?" asked Thuillier, believing that by thus examining every detail he was giving proofs of amazing perspicacity.

"Carry the note! why, your own porter of course," replied la Peyrade; "you can send him yourself."

"Then write it," said Thuillier, determined to push him to the wall.

La Peyrade took a sheet of paper with the new heading and wrote as follows, reading the note aloud:—

```
Madame Lambert is requested to call at once, on urgent business,
at the office of the "Echo de la Bievre," rue Saint-Dominique
d'Enfer. The bearer of this note will conduct her. She is awaited
impatiently by her devoted servant,
```

Theodose de la Peyrade.

"There, will that suit you?" said the barrister, passing the paper to Thuillier.

"Perfectly," replied Thuillier, taking the precaution to fold the letter himself and seal it. "Put the address," he added.

Then he rang the bell for the porter.

"You will carry this letter to its address," he said to the man, "and bring back with you the person named. But will she be there?" he asked, on reflection.

"It is more than probable," replied la Peyrade; "in any case, neither you nor I will leave this room until she comes. This matter must be cleared up."

"Then go!" said Thuillier to the porter, in a theatrical tone.

When they were alone, la Peyrade took up a newspaper and appeared to be absorbed in its perusal.

Thuillier, beginning to get uneasy as to the upshot of the affair, regretted that he had not done something the idea of which had come to him just too late.

"Yes, I ought," he said to himself, "to have torn up that letter, and not driven him to prove his words."

Wishing to do something that might look like retaining la Peyrade in the position of which he had threatened to deprive him, he remarked presently:—

"By the bye, I have just come from the printing-office; the new type has arrived, and I think we might make our first appearance to-morrow."

La Peyrade did not answer; but he got up and took his paper nearer to the window.

"He is sulky," thought Thuillier, "and if he is innocent, he may well be. But, after all, why did he ever bring a man like that Cerizet here?"

Then to hide his embarrassment and the preoccupation of his mind, he sat down before the editor's table, took a sheet of the head-lined paper and made himself write a letter.

Presently la Peyrade returned to the table and sitting down, took another sheet and with the feverish rapidity of a man stirred by some emotion he drove his pen over the paper.

From the corner of his eye, Thuillier tried hard to see what la Peyrade was writing, and noticing that his sentences were separated by numbers placed between brackets, he said:—

"Tiens! are you drawing up a parliamentary law?"

"Yes," replied la Peyrade, "the law of the vanquished."

Soon after this, the porter opened the door and introduced Madame Lambert, whom he had found at home, and who arrived looking rather frightened.

"You are Madame Lambert?" asked Thuillier, magisterially.

"Yes, monsieur," said the woman, in an anxious voice.

After requesting her to be seated and noticing that the porter was still there as if awaiting further orders he said to the man:—

"That will do; you may go; and don't let any one disturb us."

The gravity and the lordly tone assumed by Thuillier only increased Madame Lambert's uneasiness. She came expecting to see only la Peyrade, and she found herself received by an unknown man with a haughty manner, while the barrister, who had merely bowed to her, said not a word; moreover, the scene took place in a newspaper office, and it is a well-known fact that to pious persons especially all that relates to the press is infernal and diabolical.

"Well," said Thuillier to the barrister, "it seems to me that nothing hinders you from explaining to madame why you have sent for her."

In order to leave no loophole for suspicion in Thuillier's mind la Peyrade knew that he must put his question bluntly and without the slightest preparation; he therefore said to her "ex abrupto":—

"We wish to ask you, madame, if it is not true that about two and a half months ago you placed in my hands, subject to interest, the sum, in round numbers, of twenty-five thousand francs."

Though she felt the eyes of Thuillier and those of la Peyrade upon her, Madame Lambert, under the shock of this question fired at her point-blank, could not restrain a start.

"Heavens!" she exclaimed, "twenty-five thousand francs! and where should I get such a sum as that?"

La Peyrade gave no sign on his face of the vexation he might be supposed to feel. As for Thuillier, who now looked at him with sorrowful commiseration, he merely said:—

"You see, my friend!"

"So," resumed la Peyrade, "you are very certain that you did not place in my hands the sum of twenty-five thousand francs; you declare this, you affirm it?"

"Why, monsieur! did you ever hear of such a sum as that in the pocket of a poor woman like me? The little that I had, as everybody knows, has gone to eke out the housekeeping of that poor dear gentleman whose servant I have been for more than twenty years."

"This," said Thuillier, pompously, "seems to me categorical."

La Peyrade still did not show the slightest sign of annoyance; on the contrary, he seemed to be playing into Thuillier's hand.

"You hear, my dear Thuillier," he said, "and if necessary I shall call for your testimony, that madame here declares that she did not possess twenty-five thousand francs and could not therefore have placed them in my hands. Now, as the notary Dupuis, in whose hands I fancied I had placed them, left Paris this morning for Brussels carrying with him the money of all his clients, I have no account with madame, by her own showing, and the absconding of the notary—"

"Has the notary Dupuis absconded?" screamed Madame Lambert, driven by this dreadful news entirely out of her usual tones of dulcet sweetness and Christian resignation. "Ah, the villain! it was only this morning that he was taking the sacrament at Saint-Jacques du Haut-Pas."

"To pray for a safe journey, probably," said la Peyrade.

"Monsieur talks lightly enough," continued Madame Lambert, "though that brigand has carried off my savings. But I gave them to monsieur, and monsieur is answerable to me for them; he is the only one I know in this transaction."

"Hey?" said la Peyrade to Thuillier, pointing to Madame Lambert, whose whole demeanor had something of the mother-wolf suddenly bereft of her cubs; "is that nature? tell me! Do you think now that madame and I are playing a comedy for your benefit?"

"I am thunderstruck at Cerizet's audacity," said Thuillier. "I am overwhelmed with my own stupidity; there is nothing for me to do but to submit myself entirely to your discretion."

"Madame," said la Peyrade, gaily, "excuse me for thus frightening you; the notary Dupuis is still a very saintly man, and quite incapable of doing an injury to his clients. As for monsieur here, it was necessary that I should prove to him that you had really placed that money in my hands; he is, however, another myself, and your secret, though known to him, is as safe as it is with me."

"Oh, very good, monsieur!" said Madame Lambert. "I suppose these gentlemen have no further need of me?"

"No, my dear madame, and I beg you to pardon me for the little terror I was compelled to occasion you."

Madame Lambert turned to leave the room with all the appearance of respectful humility, but when she reached the door, she retraced her steps, and coming close to la Peyrade said, in her smoothest tones:—

"When does monsieur expect to be able to refund me that money?"

"But I told you," said la Peyrade, stiffly, "that notaries never return on demand the money placed in their hands."

"Does monsieur think that if I went to see Monsieur Dupuis himself and asked him—"

"I think," said la Peyrade, interrupting her, "that you would do a most ridiculous thing. He received the money from me in my own name, as you requested, and he knows only me in the matter."

"Then monsieur will be so kind, will he not, as to get back that money for me as soon as possible? I am sure I would not wish to press monsieur, but in two or three months from now I may want it; I have heard of a little property it would suit me to buy."

"Very good, Madame Lambert," said la Peyrade, with well-concealed irritation, "it shall be done as you wish; and in less time, perhaps, than you have stated I shall hope to return your money to you."

"That won't inconvenience monsieur, I trust," said the woman; "he told me that at the first indiscretion I committed—"

"Yes, yes, that is all understood," said la Peyrade, interrupting her.

"Then I have the honor to be the very humble servant of these gentlemen," said Madame Lambert, now departing definitively.

"You see, my friend, the trouble you have got me into," said la Peyrade to Thuillier as soon as they were alone, "and to what I am exposed by my kindness in satisfying your diseased mind. That debt was dormant; it was in a chronic state; and you have waked it up and made it acute. The woman brought me the money and insisted on my keeping it, at a good rate of interest. I refused at first; then I agreed to place it in Dupuis's hands, explaining to her that it couldn't be withdrawn at once; but subsequently, when Dutocq pressed me, I decided, after all, to keep it myself."

"I am dreadfully sorry, dear friend, for my silly credulity. But don't be uneasy about the exactions of that woman; we will manage to arrange all that, even if I have to make you an advance upon Celeste's 'dot.'"

"My excellent friend," said la Peyrade, "it is absolutely necessary that we should talk over our private arrangements; to tell you the truth, I have no fancy for being hauled up every morning and questioned as to my conduct. Just now, while waiting for that woman, I drew up a little agreement, which you and I will discuss and sign, if you please, before the first number of the paper is issued."

"But," said Thuillier, "our deed of partnership seems to me to settle—" "—

that by a paltry forfeit of five thousand francs, as stated in Article 14," interrupted Theodose, "you can put me, when you choose, out of doors. No, I thank you! After my experience to-day, I want some better security than that."

At this moment Cerizet with a lively and all-conquering air, entered the room.

"My masters!" he exclaimed, "I've brought the money; and we can now sign the bond."

Then, remarking that his news was received with extreme coldness, he added:—

"Well? what is it?"

"It is this," replied Thuillier: "I refuse to be associated with double-face men and calumniators. We have no need of you or your money; and I request you not to honor these precincts any longer with your presence."

"Dear! dear! dear!" said Cerizet; "so papa Thuillier has let the wool be pulled over his eyes again!"

"Leave the room!" said Thuillier; "you have nothing more to do here."

"Hey, my boy!" said Cerizet, turning to la Peyrade, "so you've twisted the old bourgeois round your finger again? Well, well, no matter! I think you are making a mistake not to go and see du Portail, and I shall tell him—"

"Leave this house!" cried Thuillier, in a threatening tone.

"Please remember, my dear monsieur, that I never asked you to employ me; I was well enough off before you sent for me, and I shall be after. But I'll give you a piece of advice: don't pay the twenty-five thousand francs out of your own pocket, for that's hanging to your nose."

So saying, Cerizet put his thirty-three thousand francs in banknotes back into his wallet, took his hat from the table, carefully smoothed the nap with his forearm and departed.

Thuillier had been led by Cerizet into what proved to be a most disastrous campaign. Now become the humble servant of la Peyrade, he was forced to accept his conditions, which were as follows: five hundred francs a month for la Peyrade's services in general; his editorship of the paper to be paid at the rate of fifty francs a column,—which was simply enormous, considering the small size of the sheet; a binding pledge to continue the publication of the paper for six months, under pain of the forfeiture of fifteen thousand francs; an absolute omnipotence in the duties of editor-in-chief,—that is to say, the sovereign right of inserting, controlling, and rejecting all articles without being called to explain the reasons of his actions,—such were the stipulations of a treaty in duplicate made openly, "in good faith," between the contracting parties. *But*, in virtue of another and secret agreement, Thuillier gave security for the payment of the twenty-five thousand francs for which la Peyrade was accountable to Madame Lambert, binding the said Sieur de la Peyrade, in case the payment were required before his marriage with Celeste Colleville could take place, to acknowledge the receipt of said sum advanced upon the dowry.

Matters being thus arranged and accepted by the candidate, who saw no chance of election if he lost la Peyrade, Thuillier was seized with a happy thought. He went to the Cirque-Olympique, where he remembered to have seen in the ticket-office a former employee in his office at the ministry of Finance,—a man named Fleury; to whom he proposed the post of manager. Fleury, being an old soldier, a good shot, and a skilful fencer, would certainly make himself an object of respect in a newspaper office. The working-staff of the paper being thus reconstituted, with the exception of a few co-editors or reporters to be added later, but whom la Peyrade, thanks to the facility of his pen, was able for the present to do without, the first number of the new paper was launched upon the world.

Thuillier now recommenced the explorations about Paris which we saw him make on the publication of his pamphlet. Entering all reading-rooms and cafes, he asked for the "Echo de la Bievre," and when informed, alas, very frequently, that the paper was unknown in this or that establishment, "It is incredible!" he would exclaim, "that a house which respects itself does not take such a widely known paper."

On that, he departed disdainfully, not observing that in many places, where this ancient trick of commercial travellers was well understood, they were laughing behind his back.

The evening of the day when the inauguration number containing the "profession of faith" appeared, Brigitte's salon, although the day was not Sunday, was filled with visitors. Reconciled to la Peyrade, whom her brother had brought home to dinner, the old maid went so far as to tell him that, without flattery, she thought his leading article was a famous HIT. For that matter, all the guests as they arrived, reported that the public seemed enchanted with the first number of the new journal.

The public! everybody knows what that is. To every man who launches a bit of writing into the world, the public consists of five or six intimates who cannot, without offending the author, avoid knowing something more or less of his lucubrations.

"As for me!" cried Colleville, "I can truthfully declare that it is the first political article I ever read that didn't send me to sleep."

"It is certain," said Phellion, "that the leading article seems to me to be stamped with vigor joined to an atticism which we may seek in vain in the columns of the other public prints."

"Yes," said Dutocq, "the matter is very well presented; and besides, there's a turn of phrase, a clever diction, that doesn't belong to everybody. However, we must wait and see how it keeps on. I fancy that to-morrow the 'Echo de la Bievre' will be strongly attacked by the other papers."

"Parbleu!" cried Thuillier, "that's what we are hoping for; and if the government would only do us the favor to seize us—"

"No, thank you," said Fleury, whom Thuillier had also brought home to dinner, "I don't want to enter upon those functions at first."

"Seized!" said Dutocq, "oh, you won't be seized; but I think the ministerial journals will fire a broadside at you."

The next day Thuillier was at the office as early as eight o'clock, in order to be the first to receive that formidable salvo. After looking through every morning paper he was forced to admit that there was no more mention of the "Echo de la Bievre" than if it didn't exist. When la Peyrade arrived he found his unhappy friend in a state of consternation.

"Does that surprise you?" said the Provencal, tranquilly. "I let you enjoy yesterday your hopes of a hot engagement with the press; but I knew myself that in all probability there wouldn't be the slightest mention of us in to-day's papers. Against every paper which makes its debut with some distinction, there's always a two weeks', sometimes a two months' conspiracy of silence."

"Conspiracy of silence!" echoed Thuillier, with admiration.

He did not know what it meant, but the words had a grandeur and a *something* that appealed to his imagination. After la Peyrade had explained to him that by "conspiracy of silence" was meant the agreement of existing journals to make no mention of new-comers lest such notice should serve to advertise them, Thuillier's mind was hardly better satisfied than it had been by the pompous flow of the words. The bourgeois is born so; words are coins which he takes and passes without question. For a word, he will excite himself or calm down, insult or applaud. With a word, he can be brought to make a revolution and overturn a government of his own choice.

The paper, however, was only a means; the object was Thuillier's election. This was insinuated rather than stated in the first numbers. But one morning, in the columns of the "Echo," appeared a letter from several electors thanking their delegate to the municipal council for the firm and frankly liberal attitude in which he had taken on all questions of local interests. "This firmness," said the letter, "had brought down upon him the persecution of the government, which, towed at the heels of foreigners, had sacrificed Poland and sold itself to England. The arrondissement needed a man of such tried convictions to represent it in the Chamber,—a man holding high and firm the banner of dynastic opposition, a man who would be, by the mere signification of his name, a stern lesson given to the authorities."

Enforced by an able commentary from la Peyrade, this letter was signed by

Barbet and Metivier and all Brigitte's tradesmen (whom, in view of the election she had continued to employ since her emigration); also by the family doctor and apothecary, and by Thuillier's builder, and Barniol, Phellion's son-in-law, who professed to hold rather "advanced" political opinions. As for Phellion himself, he thought the wording of the letter not altogether circumspect, and—always without fear as without reproach—however much he might expect that this refusal would injure his son in his dearest interests, he bravely refrained from signing it.

This trial kite had the happiest effect. The ten or a dozen names thus put forward were considered to express the will of the electors and were called "the voice of the quarter." Thus Thuillier's candidacy made from the start such rapid progress that Minard hesitated to put his own claims in opposition.

Delighted now with the course of events, Brigitte was the first to say that the time had come to attend to the marriage, and Thuillier was all the more ready to agree because, from day to day, he feared he might be called upon to pay the twenty-five thousand francs to Madame Lambert for which he had pledged himself. A thorough explanation now took place between la Peyrade and the old maid. She told him honestly of the fear she felt as to the maintenance of her sovereign authority when a *son-in-law* of his mind and character was established in the household.

"If we," she ended by saying, "are to oppose each other for the rest of our days, it would be much better, from the beginning, to make two households; we shouldn't be the less friends for that."

La Peyrade replied that nothing under the sun would induce him to consent to such a plan; on the contrary, he regarded as amongst his happiest prospects for the future the security he should feel about the wise management of the material affairs of the home in such hands as hers. He should have enough to do in the management of outside interests, and he could not comprehend, for his part, how she could suppose he had ever had the thought of interfering in matters that were absolutely out of his province. In short, he reassured her so completely that she urged him to take immediate steps for the publication of the banns and the signature of the marriage contract,—declaring that she reserved to herself all the preparations relating to Celeste, whose acceptance of this sudden conclusion she pledged herself to secure.

"My dear child," she said to Celeste the next morning, "I think you have given up all idea of being Felix Phellion's wife. In the first place, he is more of an atheist than ever, and, besides, you must have noticed yourself that his mind is quite shaky. You have seen at Madame Minard's that Madame Marmus, who married a savant, officer of the Legion of honor, and member of the Institute. There's not a more unhappy woman; her husband has taken her to live behind the Luxembourg, in the rue Duguay-Trouin, a street that is neither paved nor lighted. When he goes out, he doesn't know where he is going; he gets to the Champ de Mars when he wants to go to the Faubourg Poissoniere; he isn't even capable of giving his address to the driver of a street cab; and he is so absent-minded he couldn't tell if it were before dinner or after. You can imagine what sort of time a woman must have with a man whose nose is always at a telescope snuffing stars."

"But Felix," said Celeste, "is not as absent-minded as that."

"Of course not, because he is younger; but with years his absent-mindedness and his atheism will both increase. We have therefore decided that he is not the husband you want, and we all, your mother, father, Thuillier and myself, have determined that you shall take la Peyrade, a man of the world, who will make his way, and one who has done us great services in the past, and who will, moreover, make your godfather deputy. We are disposed to give you, in consideration of him, a much larger 'dot' than we should give to any other husband. So, my dear, it is settled; the banns are to be published immediately, and this day week we sign the contract. There's to be a great dinner for the family and intimates, and after that a reception, at which the contract will be signed and your trousseau and corbeille exhibited. As I take all that into my own hands I'll answer for it that everything shall be of the best kind; especially if you are not babyish, and give in pleasantly to our ideas."

"But, aunt Brigitte," began Celeste, timidly.

"There's no 'but,' in the matter," said the old maid, imperiously; "it is all arranged, and will be carried out, unless, mademoiselle, you pretend to have more wisdom than your elders."

"I will do as you choose, aunt," replied Celeste, feeling as if a thunder-cloud had burst upon her head, and knowing but too well that she had no power to struggle against the iron will which had just pronounced her doom.

She went at once to pour her sorrows into Madame Thuillier's soul; but when she heard her godmother advising patience and resignation the poor child felt that from that feeble quarter she could get no help for even the slightest effort of resistance, and that her sacrifice was virtually accomplished.

Precipitating herself with a sort of frenzy into the new element of activity thus introduced into her life, Brigitte took the field in the making of the trousseau and the purchase of the corbeille. Like many misers, who on great occasions come out of their habits and their nature, the old maid now thought nothing too good for her purpose; and she flung her money about so lavishly that until the day appointed for the signing of the contract, the jeweller, dressmaker, milliner, lingere, etc. (all chosen from the best establishments in Paris), seemed to occupy the house.

"It is like a procession," said Josephine, the cook, admiringly, to Francoise, the Minards' maid; "the bell never stops ringing from morning till night."

CHAPTER XII. A STAR

The dinner on the great occasion was ordered from Chabot and Potel, and not from Chevet, by which act Brigitte intended to prove her initiative and her emancipation from the late Madame de Godollo. The invited guests were as follows: three Collevilles, including the bride, la Peyrade the groom, Dutocq and Fleury, whom he had asked to be his witnesses, the extremely limited number of his relatives leaving him no choice, Minard and Rabourdin, chosen as witnesses for Celeste, Madame and Mademoiselle Minard and Minard junior, two of Thuillier's colleagues in the Council-general; the notary Dupuis, charged with the duty of drawing up the contract, and lastly, the Abbe Gondrin, director of the consciences of Madame Thuillier and Celeste, who was to give the nuptial blessing.

The latter was the former vicar of Saint-Jacques du Haut-Pas, whose great refinement of manner and gift of preaching had induced the archbishop to remove him from the humble parish where his career had begun to the aristocratic church of the Madeleine. Since Madame Thuillier and Celeste had again become his parishioners, the young abbe visited them occasionally, and Thuillier, who had gone to him to explain, after his own fashion, the suitableness of the choice made for Celeste in the person of la Peyrade (taking pains as he did so to cast reflections on the religious opinions of Felix Phellion), had easily led him to contribute by his persuasive words to the resignation of the victim.

When the time came to sit down to table three guests were missing,—two Minards, father and son, and the notary Dupuis. The latter had written a note to Thuillier in the morning, excusing himself from the dinner, but saying that at nine o'clock precisely he would bring the contract and place himself at the orders of Mademoiselle Thuillier. As for Julien Minard, his mother excused him as being confined to his room with a sore-throat. The absence of Minard senior remained unexplained, but Madame Minard insisted that they should sit down to table without him; which was done, Brigitte ordering that the soup be kept hot for him, because in the bourgeois code of manners and customs a dinner without soup is no dinner at all.

The repast was far from gay, and though the fare was better, the vivacity and the warmth of the conversation was far, indeed, from that of the famous improvised banquet at the time of the election to the Council-general. The gaps occasioned by the absence of three guests may have been one reason; then Flavie was glum; she had had an interview with la Peyrade in the afternoon which ended in tears; Celeste, even if she had been content with the

357

choice imposed on her, would scarcely, as a matter of propriety, have seemed joyful; in fact, she made no effort to brighten a sad face, and dared not look at her godmother, whose own countenance gave the impression, if we may so express it, of the long bleating of a sheep. The poor girl seeing this feared to exchange a look with her lest she might drive her to tears. Thuillier now felt himself, on all sides, of such importance that he was pompous and consequential; while Brigitte, uneasy out of her own world, where she could lord it over every one without competition, seemed constrained and embarrassed.

Colleville tried by a few jovialities to raise the temperature of the assemblage; but the coarse salt of his witticisms had an effect, in the atmosphere in which he produced them, of a loud laugh in a sick-chamber; and a mute intimation from his wife, Thuillier, and la Peyrade to *behave himself* put a stopper on his liveliness and turbulent expansion. It was somewhat remarkable that the gravest member of the party, aided by Rabourdin, was the person who finally warmed up the atmosphere. The Abbe Gondrin, a man of a most refined and cultivated mind, had, like every pure and well-ordered soul, a fund of gentle gaiety which he was well able to communicate, and liveliness was beginning to dawn upon the party when Minard entered the room.

After making his excuses on the ground of important duties, the mayor of the eleventh arrondissement, who was in the habit of taking the lead in the conversation wherever he went, said, having swallowed a few hasty mouthfuls:—

"Messieurs and mesdames, have you heard the great news?"

"No, what is it?" cried several voices at once.

"The Academy of Sciences received, to-day, at its afternoon session, the announcement of a vast discovery: the heavens possess a new star!"

"Tiens!" said Colleville; "that will help to replace the one that Beranger thought was lost when he grieved (to that air of 'Octavie') over Chateaubriand's departure: 'Chateaubriand, why fly thy land?'"

This quotation, which he sang, exasperated Flavie, and if the custom had been for wives to sit next to their husbands, the former clarionet of the Opera-Comique would not have escaped with a mere "Colleville!" imperiously calling him to order.

"The point which gives this great astronomical event a special interest on this occasion," continued Minard, "is that the author of the discovery is a denizen of the twelfth arrondissement, which many of you still inhabit, or have inhabited. But other points are striking in this great scientific fact. The Academy, on the reading of the communication which announced it, was so convinced of the existence of this star that a deputation was appointed to visit the domicile of the modern Galileo and compliment him in the name of the whole body. And yet this star is not visible to either the eye or the telescope! It is only by the power of calculation and induction that its existence and the place it occupies in the heavens have been proved in the most irrefutable manner: 'There *must* be *there* a hitherto unknown star; I cannot see it, but I am sure of it,'—that is what this man of science said to the Academy, whom he instantly convinced by his deductions. And do you know, messieurs, who is this Christopher Columbus of a new celestial world? An old man, two-thirds blind, who has scarcely eyes enough to walk in the street."

"Wonderful! Marvellous! Admirable!" came from all sides.

"What is the name of this learned man?" asked several voices.

"Monsieur Picot, or, if you prefer it, pere Picot, for that is how they call him in the rue du Val-de-Grace, where he lives. He is simply an old professor of mathematics, who has turned out several very fine pupils,—by the bye, Felix Phellion, whom we all know, studied under him, and it was he who read, on behalf of his blind old master, the communication to the Academy this afternoon."

Hearing that name, and remembering the promise Felix had made her to lift her to the skies, which, as he said it, she had fancied a sign of madness, Celeste looked at Madame Thuillier, whose face had taken a sudden glow of animation, and seemed to say to her, "Courage, my child! all is not lost."

"My dear Theodose," said Thuillier, "Felix is coming here to-night; you must take him aside and get him to give you a copy of that communication; it would be a fine stroke of fortune for the 'Echo' to be the first to publish it."

"Yes," said Minard, assuming the answer, "that would do good service to the public, for the affair is going to make a great noise. The committee, not finding Monsieur Picot at home, went straight to the Minister of Public Instruction; and the minister flew to the Tuileries and saw the King; and the 'Messager' came out this evening—strange to say, so early that I could read it in my carriage as I drove along—with an announcement that Monsieur Picot is named Chevalier of the Legion of honor, with a pension of eighteen hundred francs from the fund devoted to the encouragement of science and letters."

"Well," said Thuillier, "there's one cross at least well bestowed."

"But eighteen hundred francs for the pension seems to me rather paltry," said Dutocq.

"So it does," said Thuillier, "and all the more because that money comes from the tax-payers; and, when one sees the taxes, as we do, frittered away on court favorites—"

"Eighteen hundred francs a year," interrupted Minard, "is certainly something, especially for savants, a class of people who are accustomed to live on very little."

"I think I have heard," said la Peyrade, "that this very Monsieur Picot leads a strange life, and that his family, who at first wanted to shut him up as a lunatic, are now trying to have guardians appointed over him. They say he allows a servant-woman who keeps his house to rob him of all he has. Parbleu! Thuillier, you know her; it is that woman who came to the office the other day about some money in Dupuis's hands."

"Yes, yes, true," said Thuillier, significantly; "you are right, I do know her."

"It is queer," said Brigitte, seeing a chance to enforce the argument she had used to Celeste, "that all these learned men are good for nothing outside of their science; in their homes they have to be treated like children."

"That proves," said the Abbe Gondrin, "the great absorption which their studies give to their minds, and, at the same time, a simplicity of nature which is very touching."

"When they are not as obstinate as mules," said Brigitte, hastily. "For myself, monsieur l'abbe, I must say that if I had had any idea of marriage, a savant wouldn't have suited me at all. What do they do, these savants, anyhow? Useless things most of the time. You are all admiring one who has discovered a star; but as long as we are in this world what good is that to us? For all the use we make of stars it seems to me we have got enough of them as it is."

"Bravo, Brigitte!" said Colleville, getting loose again; "you are right, my girl, and I think, as you do, that the man who discovers a new dish deserves better of humanity."

"Colleville," said Flavie, "I must say that your style of behavior is in the worst taste."

"My dear lady," said the Abbe Gondrin, addressing Brigitte, "you might be right if we were formed of matter only; and if, bound to our body, there were not a soul with instincts and appetites that must be satisfied. Well, I think that this sense of the infinite which is within us, and which we all try to satisfy each in our own way, is marvellously well helped by the labors of astronomy, that reveal to us from time to time new worlds which the hand of the Creator has put into space. The infinite in you has taken another course; this passion for the comfort of those about you, this warm, devoted, ardent affection which you feel for your brother, are equally the manifestation of aspirations which have nothing material about them, and which, in seeking their end and object, never think of asking, 'What good does that do? what is the use of this?' Besides, I must assure you that the stars are not as useless as you seem to think. Without them how would navigators cross the sea? They would be puzzled to get you the vanilla with which you have flavored the delicious cream I am now eating. So, as Monsieur Colleville has perceived, there is more affinity than you think between a dish and a star; no one should be despised,—neither an astronomer nor a good housekeeper—"

The abbe was here interrupted by the noise of a lively altercation in the antechamber.

"I tell you that I will go in," said a loud voice.

"No, monsieur, you shall not go in," said another voice, that of the man-servant. "The company are at table, I tell you, and nobody has the right to force himself in."

Thuillier turned pale; ever since the seizure of his pamphlet, he fancied all sudden arrivals meant the coming of the police.

Among the various social rules imparted to Brigitte by Madame de Godollo, the one that most needed repeating was the injunction never, as mistress of the house, to rise from the table until she gave the signal for retiring. But present circumstances appeared to warrant the infraction of the rule.

"I'll go and see what it is," she said to Thuillier, whose anxiety she noticed at once. "What *is* the matter?" she said to the servant as soon as she reached the scene of action.

"Here's a gentleman who wants to come in, and says that no one is ever dining at eight o'clock at night."

"But who are you, monsieur?" said Brigitte, addressing an old man very oddly dressed, whose eyes were protected by a green shade.

"Madame, I am neither a beggar nor a vagabond," replied the old man, in stentorian tones; "my name is Picot, professor of mathematics."

"Rue du Val-de-Grace?" asked Brigitte.

"Yes, madame,—No. 9, next to the print-shop."

"Come in, monsieur, come in; we shall be only too happy to receive you," cried Thuillier, who, on hearing the name, had hurried out to meet the savant.

"Hein! you scamp," said the learned man, turning upon the man-servant, who had retired, seeing that the matter was being settled amicably, "I told you I should get in."

Pere Picot was a tall old man, with an angular, stern face, who, despite the corrective of a blond wig with heavy curls, and that of the pacific green shade we have already mentioned, expressed on his large features, upon which the fury of study had produced a surface of leaden pallor, a snappish and quarrelsome disposition. Of this he had already given proof before entering the dining-room, where every one now rose to receive him.

His costume consisted of a huge frock-coat, something between a paletot and a dressing-gown, between which an immense waistcoat of iron-gray cloth, fastened from the throat to the pit of the stomach with two rows of buttons, hussar fashion, formed a sort of buckler. The trousers, though October was nearing its close, were made of black lasting, and gave testimony to long service by the projection of a darn on the otherwise polished surface covering the knees, the polish being produced by the rubbing of the hands upon those parts. But, in broad daylight, the feature of the old savant's appearance which struck the eye most vividly was a pair of Patagonian feet, imprisoned in slippers of beaver cloth, the which, moulded upon the mountainous elevations of gigantic bunions, made the spectator think, involuntarily, of the back of a dromedary or an advanced case of elephantiasis.

Once installed in a chair which was hastily brought for him, and the company having returned to their places at table, the old man suddenly burst out in thundering tones, amid the silence created by curiosity:—

"Where is he,—that rogue, that scamp? Let him show himself; let him dare to speak to me!"

"Who is it that offends you, my dear monsieur?" said Thuillier, in conciliating accents, in which there was a slight tone of patronage.

"A scamp whom I couldn't find in his own home, and they told me he was here, in this house. I'm in the apartment, I think, of Monsieur Thuillier of the Council-general, place de la Madeleine, first story above the entresol?"

"Precisely," said Thuillier; "and allow me to add, monsieur, that you are surrounded with the respect and sympathy of all."

"And you will doubtless permit me to add," said Minard, "that the mayor of the arrondissement adjoining that which you inhabit congratulates himself on being here in presence of Monsieur Picot,—*the* Monsieur Picot, no doubt, who has just immortalized his name by the discovery of a star!"

"Yes, monsieur," replied the professor, elevating to a still higher pitch the stentorian diapason of his voice, "I am Picot (Nepomucene), but I have not discovered a star; I don't concern myself with any such fiddle-faddle; besides, my eyes are very weak; and that insolent young fellow I have come here to find is making me ridiculous with such talk. I don't see him here; he is hiding himself, I know; he dares not look me in the face."

"Who is this person who annoys you?" asked several voices at once.

"An unnatural pupil of mine," replied the old mathematician; "a scamp, but full of ideas; his name is Felix Phellion."

The name was received, as may well be imagined, with amazement. Finding the situation amusing, Colleville and la Peyrade went off into fits of laughter.

"You laugh, fools!" cried the irate old man, rising. "Yes, come and laugh within reach of my arm."

So saying, he brandished a thick stick with a white china handle, which he used to guide himself, thereby nearly knocking over a candelabrum on the dinner-table upon Madame Minard's head.

"You are mistaken, monsieur," cried Brigitte, springing forward and seizing his arm. "Monsieur Felix is not here. He will probably come later to a reception we are about to give; but at present he has not arrived."

"They don't begin early, your receptions," said the old man; "it is past eight o'clock. Well, as Monsieur Felix is coming later, you must allow me to wait for him. I believe you were eating your dinners; don't let me disturb you."

And he went back peaceably to his chair.

"As you permit it, monsieur," said Brigitte, "we will continue, or, I should say, finish dinner, for we are now at the dessert. May I offer you anything,—a glass of champagne and a biscuit?"

"I am very willing, madame," replied the intruder. "No one ever refuses champagne, and I am always ready to eat between my meals; but you dine very late."

A place was made for him at table between Colleville and Mademoiselle Minard, and the former made it his business to fill the glass of his new neighbor, before whom was placed a dish of small cakes.

"Monsieur," said la Peyrade in a cajoling tone, "you saw how surprised we were to hear you complain of Monsieur Felix Phellion,—so amiable, so inoffensive a young man. What has he done to you, that you should feel so angry with him?"

With his mouth full of cakes, which he was engulfing in quantities that made Brigitte uneasy, the professor made a sign that he would soon answer; then, having mistaken his glass and swallowed the contents of Colleville's, he replied:—

"You ask what that insolent young man had done to me? A rascally thing; and not the first, either. He knows that I cannot abide stars, having very good reason to hate them, as you shall hear: In 1807, being attached to the Bureau of Longitudes, I was part of the scientific expedition sent to Spain, under the direction of my friend and colleague, Jean-Baptiste Biot, to determine the arc of the terrestrial meridian from Barcelona to the Balearic isles. I was just in the act of observing a star (perhaps the very one my rascally pupil has discovered), when suddenly, war having broken out between France and Spain, the peasants, seeing me perched with a telescope on Monte Galazzo, took it into their heads that I was making signals to the enemy. A mob of savages broke my instruments, and talked of stringing me up. They were just going to do it, when the captain of a vessel took me prisoner and thrust me into the citadel of Belver, where I spent three years in the harshest captivity. Since them, as you may well believe, I loathe the whole celestial system; though I was, without knowing it, the first to observe the famous comet of 1811; but I should have taken care not to say a word about it if it had not been for Monsieur Flauguergues, who announced it. Like all my pupils, Phellion knows my aversion to stars, and he knew very well the worst trick he could play me would be to saddle one on my back; and that deputation that came to play the farce of congratulating me was mighty lucky not to find me at home, for if they had, I can assure those gentlemen of the Academy, they would have had a hot reception."

Everybody present thought the old mathematician's monomania quite delightful, except la Peyrade, who now, in perceiving Felix Phellion's part in the affair, regretted deeply having caused the explanation.

"And yet, Monsieur Picot," said Minard, "if Felix Phellion is only guilty of attributing his discovery to you, it seems to me that his indiscreet behavior has resulted in a certain compensation to you: the cross of the Legion of honor, a pension, and the glory attached to your name are not to be despised."

"The cross and the pension I take," said the old man, emptying his glass, which, to Brigitte's terror, he set down upon the table with a force that threatened to smash it. "The government has owed them to me these twenty years; not for the discovery of stars,—things that I have always despised,—but for my famous 'Treatise on Differential Logarithms' (Kepler thought proper to call them monologarithms), which is a sequel to the tables of Napier; also for my 'Postulatum' of Euclid, of which I was the first to discover the solution; but above all, for my 'Theory of Perpetual Motion,'— four volumes in quarto with plates; Paris, 1825. You see, therefore, monsieur, that to give me glory is bringing water to the Seine. I had so little need of Monsieur Felix Phellion to make me a position in the scientific world that I turned him out of my house long ago."

"Then it isn't the first star," said Colleville, flippantly, "that he dared to put upon you?"

"He did worse than that," roared the old man; "he ruined my reputation, he tarnished my name. My 'Theory of Perpetual Motion,' the printing of which cost me every penny I owned, though it ought to have been printed gratis at the Royal Printing-office, was calculated to make my fortune and render me immortal. Well, that miserable Felix prevented it. From time to time, pretending to bring messages from my editor, he would say, the young sycophant, 'Papa Picot, your book is selling finely; here's five hundred francs —two hundred francs—and once it was two thousand—which your publisher charged me to give you.' This thing went on for years, and my publisher, who had the baseness to enter into the plot, would say to me, when I went to the shop: 'Yes, yes, it doesn't do badly, it *bubbles*, that book; we shall soon be at the end of this edition.' I, who didn't suggest anything, I pocketed my money, and thought to myself: 'My book is liked, little by little its ideas are making their way; I may now expect, from day to day, that some great capitalist will come to me and propose to apply my system—'"

"—of 'Absorption of Liquids'?" asked Colleville, who had been steadily filling the old fellow's glass.

"No, monsieur, my 'Theory of Perpetual Motion,' 4 vols. in quarto with plates. But no! days, weeks went by and nobody came; so, thinking that my publisher did not put all the energy he should into the matter, I tried to sell the second edition to another man. It was that, monsieur, that enabled me to discover the whole plot, on which, as I said before, I turned that serpent out of my house. In six years only nine copies had been sold! Kept quiet in false security I had done nothing for the propagation of my book, which had been left to take care of itself; and thus it was that I, victim of black and wicked jealousy, was shamefully despoiled of the value of my labors."

"But," said Minard, making himself the mouthpiece of the thoughts of the company, "may we not see in that act a manner as ingenious as it was delicate to—"

"To give me alms! is that what you mean?" interrupted the old man, with a roar that made Mademoiselle Minard jump in her chair; "to humiliate me, dishonor me—me, his old professor! Am I in need of charity? Has Picot (Nepomucene), to whom his wife brought a dowry of one hundred thousand francs, ever stretched out his palm to any one? But in these days nothing is respected. Old fellows, as they call us, our religion and our good faith is taken advantage of so that these youths may say to the public: 'Old drivellers, don't you see now they are good for nothing? It needs *us*, the young generation, *us*, the moderns, *us*, Young France, to bring them up on a bottle.' Young greenhorn! let me see *you* try to feed *me*! Old drivellers know more in their little finger than you in your whole brain, and you'll never be worth us, paltry little intriguer that you are! However, I know my day of vengeance will come; that young Phellion can't help ending badly; what he did to-day, reading a statement to the Academy, under my name, was forgery, forgery! and the law will send him to the galleys for that."

"True," said Colleville, "forgery of a public star."

Brigitte, who quaked for her glasses, and whose nerves were exacerbated by the monstrous consumption of cakes and wine, now gave the signal to return to the salon. Besides, she had heard the door-bell ring several times, announcing the arrival of guests for the evening. The question then was how to transplant the professor, and Colleville politely offered him his arm.

"No, monsieur," he said, "you must allow me to stay where I am. I am not dressed for a party, and besides, a strong light hurts my eyes. Moreover, I don't choose to give myself as a spectacle; it will be best that my interview with Felix Phellion should take place between 'four-eyes,' as they say."

"Well, let him alone, then," said Brigitte to Colleville.

No one insisted,—the old man having, unconsciously, pretty nigh discrowned himself in the opinion of the company. But before leaving, the careful housewife removed everything that was at all fragile from his reach; then, by way of a slight attention, she said:—

"Shall I send you some coffee?"

"I'll take it, madame," responded pere Picot, "and some cognac with it."

"Oh! parbleu! he takes everything," said Brigitte to the male domestic, and she told the latter to keep an eye on the old madman.

When Brigitte returned to the salon she found that the Abbe Gondrin had become the centre of a great circle formed by nearly the whole company, and as she approached, she heard him say:—

"I thank Heaven for bestowing upon me such a pleasure. I have never felt an emotion like that aroused by the scene we have just witnessed; even the rather burlesque form of this confidence, which was certainly very artless, for it was quite involuntary, only adds to the honor of the surprising generosity it revealed. Placed as I am by my ministry in the way of knowing of many charities, and often either the witness or intermediary of good actions, I think I never in my life have met with a more touching or a more ingenious devotion. To keep the left hand ignorant of what the right hand does is a great step in Christianity; but to go so far as to rob one's self of one's own fame to benefit another under such conditions is the gospel applied in its highest precepts; it is being more than a Sister of Charity; it is doing the work of an apostle of beneficence. How I should like to know that noble young man, and shake him by the hand."

With her arm slipped through that of her godmother, Celeste was standing very near the priest, her ears intent upon his words, her arm pressing tighter and tighter that of Madame Thuillier, as the abbe analyzed the generous action of Felix Phellion, until at last she whispered under her breath:—

"You hear, godmother, you hear!"

To destroy the inevitable effect which this hearty praise would surely have on Celeste, Thuillier hastened to say:—

"Unfortunately, Monsieur l'abbe, the young man of whom you speak so warmly is not altogether unknown to you. I have had occasion to tell you about him, and to regret that it was not possible to follow out certain plans which we once entertained for him; I allude to the very compromising independence he affects in his religious opinions."

"Ah! is that the young man?" said the abbe; "you surprise me much; I must say such an idea would never have crossed my mind."

"You will see him presently, Monsieur l'abbe," said la Peyrade, joining in the conversation, "and if you question him on certain grounds you will have no difficulty in discovering the ravages that a love of science can commit in the most gifted souls."

"I am afraid I shall not see him," said the abbe, "as my black gown would be out of place in the midst of the more earthly gaiety that will soon fill this salon. But I know, Monsieur de la Peyrade, that you are a man of sincerely pious convictions, and as, without any doubt, you feel as much interest in the young man's welfare as I do myself, I shall say to you in parting: Do not be uneasy about him; sooner or later, such choice souls come back to us, and if the return of these prodigals should be long delayed I should not fear, on seeing them go to God, that His infinite mercy would fail them."

So saying, the abbe looked about to find his hat, and proceeded to slip quietly away.

Suddenly a fearful uproar was heard. Rushing into the dining-room, whence came a sound of furniture overturned and glasses breaking, Brigitte found Colleville occupied in adjusting his cravat and looking himself over to be sure that his coat, cruelly pulled awry, bore no signs of being actually torn.

"What is the matter?" cried Brigitte.

"It is that old idiot," replied Colleville, "who is in a fury. I came to take my coffee with him, just to keep him company, and he took a joke amiss, and collared me, and knocked over two chairs and a tray of glasses because Josephine didn't get out of his way in time."

"It is all because you've been teasing him," said Brigitte, crossly; "why couldn't you stay in the salon instead of coming here to play your jokes, as you call them? You think you are still in the orchestra of the Opera-Comique."

This sharp rebuke delivered, Brigitte, like the resolute woman that she was, saw that she absolutely must get rid of the ferocious old man who threatened her household with flames and blood. Accordingly, she approached pere Picot, who was tranquilly engaged in burning brandy in his saucer.

"Monsieur," she said, at the top of her lungs, as if she were speaking to a deaf person (evidently thinking that a blind one ought to be treated in the same manner), "I have come to tell you something that may annoy you. Monsieur and Madame Phellion have just arrived, and they inform me that their son, Monsieur Felix, is not coming. He has a cold and a sore-throat."

"Then he got it this afternoon reading that lecture," cried the professor, joyfully. "That's justice!—Madame, where do you get your brandy?"

"Why, at my grocer's," replied Brigitte, taken aback by the question.

"Well, madame, I ought to tell you that in a house where one can drink such excellent champagne, which reminds me of that we used to quaff at the table of Monsieur de Fontanes, grand-master of the University, it is shameful to keep such brandy. I tell you, with the frankness I put into everything, that it is good only to wash your horses' feet, and if I had not the resource of burning it—"

"He is the devil in person," thought Brigitte; "not a word of excuse about all that glass, but he must needs fall foul of my brandy too!—Monsieur," she resumed, in the same raised diapason, "as Monsieur Felix is not coming, don't you think your family will be uneasy at your absence?"

"Family? I haven't any, madame, owing to the fact that they want to make me out a lunatic. But I have a housekeeper, Madame Lambert, and I dare say she will be surprised not to see me home by this time. I think I had better go now; if I stay later, the scene might be more violent. But I must own that in this strange quarter I am not sure if I can find my way."

"Then take a carriage."

"Carriage here, carriage there, indeed! my spiteful relations wouldn't lose the chance of calling me a spendthrift."

"I have an important message to send into your quarter," said Brigitte, seeing she must resolve to make the sacrifice, "and I have just told my porter to take a cab and attend to it. If you would like to take advantage of that convenience—"

"I accept it, madame," said the old professor, rising; "and, if it comes to the worst, I hope you will testify before the judge that I was niggardly about a cab."

"Henri," said Brigitte to the man-servant, "take monsieur down to the porter and tell him to do the errand I told him about just now, and to take monsieur to his own door, and be very careful of him."

"Careful of him!" echoed the old man. "Do you take me for a trunk, madame, or a bit of cracked china?"

Seeing that she had got her man fairly to the door, Brigitte allowed herself to turn upon him.

"What I say, monsieur, is for your good. You must allow me to observe that you have not an agreeable nature."

"Careful of him! careful of him!" repeated the old man. "Don't you know, madame, that by the use of such words you may get people put into lunatic asylums? However, I will not reply rudely to the polite hospitality I have received,—all the more because, I think, I have put Monsieur Felix, who missed me intentionally, in his right place."

"Go, go, go, you old brute!" cried Brigitte, slamming the door behind him.

Before returning to the salon she was obliged to drink a whole glassful of water, the restraint she had been forced to put upon herself in order to get rid of this troublesome guest having, to use her own expression, "put her all about."

CHAPTER XIII. THE MAN WHO THINKS THE STAR TOO BRIGHT

The next morning Minard paid a visit to Phellion in his study. The great citizen and his son Felix were at that moment engaged in a conversation which seemed to have some unusual interest for them.

"My dear Felix," cried the mayor of the eleventh arrondissement, offering his hand warmly to the young professor, "it is you who bring me here this morning; I have come to offer you my congratulations."

"What has occurred?" asked Phellion. "Have the Thuilliers—"

"It has nothing to do with the Thuilliers," interrupted the mayor. "But," he added, looking hard at Felix, "can that sly fellow have concealed the thing even from you?"

"I do not think," said Phellion, "that ever, in his life, has my son concealed a thing from me."

"Then you know about the sublime astronomical discovery which he communicated to the Academy of Sciences yesterday?"

"Your kindness for me, Monsieur le maire," said Felix, hastily, "has led you astray; I was only the reader of the communication."

"Oh! let me alone!" said Minard; "reader, indeed! I know all about it."

"But see," said Felix, offering Minard the "Constitutionnel," "here's the paper; not only does it announce that Monsieur Picot is the maker of the discovery, but it mentions the rewards which, without losing a moment, the government has bestowed upon him."

"Felix is right," said Phellion; "that journal is to be trusted. On this occasion I think the government has acted very properly."

"But, my dear commander, I repeat to you that the truth of the affair has got wind, and your son is shown to be a most admirable fellow. To put his own discovery to the credit of his old professor so as to obtain for him the recognition and favor of the authorities—upon my word, in all antiquity I don't know a finer trait!"

"Felix!" said Phellion, beginning to show some emotion, "these immense labors to which you have devoted so much time of late, these continual visits to the Observatory—"

372

"But, father," interrupted Felix, "Monsieur Minard has been misinformed."

"Misinformed!" cried Minard, "when I know the whole affair from Monsieur Picot himself!"

At this argument, stated in a way to leave no possible doubt, the truth began to dawn upon Phellion.

"Felix, my son!" he said, rising to embrace him.

But he was obliged to sit down again; his legs refused to bear his weight; he turned pale; and that nature, ordinarily so impassible, seemed about to give way under the shock of this happiness.

"My God!" said Felix, terrified, "he is ill; ring the bell, I entreat you, Monsieur Minard."

And he ran to the old man, loosened his cravat and unfastened the collar of his shirt, striking him in the palms of his hands. But the sudden faintness was but momentary; almost immediately himself again, Phellion gathered his son to his heart, and holding him long in his embrace, he said, in a voice broken by the tears that came to put an end to this shock of joy:—

"Felix, my noble son! so great in heart, so great in mind!"

The bell had been rung by Minard with magisterial force, and with such an accent that the whole household was alarmed, and came running in.

"It is nothing, it is nothing," said Phellion to the servants, sending them away. But almost at the same moment, seeing his wife, who now entered the room, he resumed his habitual solemnity.

"Madame Phellion," he said, pointing to Felix, "how many years is it since you brought that young man into the world?"

Madame Phellion, bewildered by the question, hesitated a moment, and then said:—

"Twenty-five years next January."

"Have you not thought, until now, that God had amply granted your maternal desires by making this child of your womb an honest man, a pious son, and by gifting him for mathematics, that Science of sciences, with an aptitude sufficiently remarkable?"

"I have," said Madame Phellion, understanding less and less what her husband was coming to.

"Well," continued Phellion, "you owe to God an additional thanksgiving, for He has granted that you be the mother of a man of genius; his toil, which

373

lately we rebuked, and which made us fear for the reason of our child, was the way—the rough and jagged way—by which men come to fame."

"Ah ca!" cried Madame Phellion, "can't you stop coming yourself to an explanation of what you mean, and get there?"

"Your son," said Minard, cautious this time in measuring the joy he was about to bestow, fearing another fainting-fit of happiness, "has just made a very important scientific discovery."

"Is it true?" said Madame Phellion, going up to Felix, and taking him by both hands as she looked at him lovingly.

"When I say important," continued Minard, "I am only sparing your maternal emotions; it is, in truth, a sublime, a dazzling discovery. He is only twenty-five years old, but his name, from henceforth, is immortal."

"And this is the man," said Madame Phellion, half beside herself, and kissing Felix with effusion, "to whom that la Peyrade is preferred!"

"No, not preferred, madame," said Minard, "for the Thuilliers are not the dupes of that adventurer. But he has made himself necessary to them. Thuillier fancies that without la Peyrade he could not be elected; the election is still doubtful, and they are sacrificing everything to it."

"But isn't it odious," cried Madame Phellion, "to consider such interests before the happiness of their child!"

"Ah!" said Minard, "but Celeste is not their child, only their adopted daughter."

"Brigitte's, if you like," said Madame Phellion; "but as for Thuillier—"

"My good wife," said Phellion, "no censoriousness. The good God has just sent us a great consolation; and, indeed, though certainly far advanced, this marriage, about which I regret to say Felix does not behave with all the philosophy I could desire, may still not take place."

Seeing that Felix shook his head with a look of incredulity, Minard hastened to say:—

"Yes, yes, the commander is quite right. Last night there was a hitch about signing the contract, and it was not signed. You were not there, by the bye, and your absence was much remarked upon."

"We were invited," said Phellion, "and up to the last moment we hesitated whether to go or not. But, as you will readily see, our position was a false one; besides, Felix—and I see now it must have been in consequence of his lecture at the Academy—was completely worn out with fatigue and emotion.

To present ourselves without him would have seemed very singular; therefore we decided that it would be wisest and best to absent ourselves."

The presence of the man whom he had just declared immortal did not deter Minard, when the occasion was thus made for him, from plunging eagerly into one of the most precious joys of bourgeois existence, namely, the retailing of gossip.

"Just imagine!" he began; "last night at the Thuilliers' the most extraordinary things took place, one after another."

First he related the curious episode of pere Picot. Then he told of the hearty approbation given to Felix's conduct by the Abbe Gondrin, and the desire the young preacher had expressed to meet him.

"I'll go and see him," said Felix; "do you know where he lives?"

"Rue de la Madeleine, No. 8," replied Minard. "But the great event of the evening was the spectacle of that fine company assembled to listen to the marriage-contract, and waiting in expectation a whole hour for the notary, who—never came!"

"Then the contract is not signed?" said Felix, eagerly.

"Not even read, my friend. Suddenly some one came in and told Brigitte that the notary had started for Brussels."

"Ah! no doubt," said Phellion, naively; "some very important business."

"Most important," replied Minard; "a little bankruptcy of five hundred thousand francs which the gentleman leaves behind him."

"But who is this public officer," demanded Phellion, "so recreant, in this scandalous manner, to the sacred duties of his calling?"

"Parbleu! your neighbor in the rue Saint-Jacques, the notary Dupuis."

"What!" said Madame Phellion, "that pious man? Why, he is churchwarden of the parish!"

"Eh! madame, those are the very ones," said Minard, "to run off—there are many precedents for that."

"But," said Phellion, "such news cast suddenly among the company must have fallen like a thunderbolt."

"Especially," said Minard, "as it was brought in the most unexpected and singular manner."

"Tell us all about it," said Madame Phellion, with animation.

"Well, it seems," continued Minard, "that this canting swindler had charge of the savings of a number of servants, and that Monsieur de la Peyrade—because, you see, they are all of a clique, these pious people—was in the habit of recruiting clients for him in that walk of life—"

"I always said so!" interrupted Madame Phellion. "I knew that Provencal was no good at all."

"It seems," continued the mayor, "that he had placed in Dupuis's hands all the savings of an old housekeeper, pious herself, amounting to a pretty little sum. Faith! I think myself it was worth some trouble. How much do you suppose it was? Twenty-five thousand francs, if you please! This housekeeper, whose name is Madame Lambert—"

"Madame Lambert!" cried Felix; "why, that's Monsieur Picot's housekeeper; close cap, pale, thin face, speaks always with her eyes lowered, shows no hair?"

"That's she," said Minard,—"a regular hypocrite!"

"Twenty-five thousand francs of savings!" said Felix. "I don't wonder that poor pere Picot is always out of money."

"And that someone had to meddle with the sale of his book," said Minard, slyly. "However that may be, you can imagine that the woman was in a fine state of mind on hearing of the flight of the notary. Off she went to la Peyrade's lodgings; there she was told he was dining at the Thuilliers'; to the Thuilliers' she came, after running about the streets—for they didn't give her quite the right address—till ten o'clock; but she got there while the company were still sitting round waiting for the notary, and gaping at each other, no one knowing what to say and do, for neither Brigitte nor Thuillier have faculty enough to get out of such a scrape with credit; and we all missed the voice of Madame de Godollo and the talent of Madame Phellion."

"Oh! you are too polite, Monsieur le maire," said Madame Phellion, bridling.

"Well, as I said," continued Minard, "at ten o'clock Madame Lambert reached the antechamber of Monsieur the general-councillor, and there she asked, in great excitement, to see la Peyrade."

"That was natural," said Phellion; "he being the intermediary of the investment, this woman had a right to question him."

"You should just have seen that Tartuffe!" continued Minard. "He had no sooner gone out than he returned, bringing the news. As everybody was longing to get away, there followed a general helter-skelter. And then what

376

does our man do? He goes back to Madame Lambert, who was crying that she was ruined! she was lost!—which might very well be true, but it might also be only a scene arranged between them in presence of the company, whom the woman's outcries detained in the antechamber. 'Don't be anxious, my good woman,' said la Peyrade; 'the investment was made at your request, consequently, I owe you nothing; BUT it is enough that the money passed through my hands to make my conscience tell me I am responsible. If the notary's assets are not enough to pay you I will do so.'"

"Yes," said Phellion, "that was my idea as you told it; the intermediary is or ought to be responsible. I should not have hesitated to do as Monsieur de la Peyrade did, and I do not think that after such conduct as that he ought to be taxed with Jesuitism."

"Yes, you would have done so," said Minard, "and so should I, but we shouldn't have done it with a brass band; we should have paid our money quietly, like gentlemen. But this electoral manager, how is he going to pay it? Out of the 'dot'?"

At this moment the little page entered the room and gave a letter to Felix Phellion. It came from pere Picot, and was written at his dictation by Madame Lambert, for which reason we will not reproduce the orthography. The writing of Madame Lambert was of those that can never be forgotten when once seen. Recognizing it instantly, Felix hastened to say:—

"A letter from the professor"; then, before breaking the seal, he added, "Will you permit me, Monsieur le maire."

"He'll rate you finely," said Minard, laughing. "I never saw anything so comical as his wrath last night."

Felix, as he read the letter, smiled to himself. When he had finished it, he passed it to his father, saying:—

"Read it aloud if you like."

Whereupon, with his solemn voice and manner, Phellion read as follows:—

My dear Felix,—I have just received your note; it came in the
nick of time, for I was, as they say, in a fury with you. You tell
me that you were guilty of that abuse of confidence (about which I
intended to write you a piece of my mind) in order to give a knock-
down blow to my relations by proving that a man capable of making
such complicated calculations as your discovery required was not a
man to put in a lunatic asylum or drag before a judiciary council.
That argument pleases me, and it makes such a good answer to the
infamous proceedings of my relations that I praise you for having
had the idea. But you sold it to me, that argument, pretty dear
when you put me in company with a star, for you know very well *that*
propinquity wouldn't please me at all. It is not at my age, and
after solving the great problem of perpetual motion, that a man
could take up with such rubbish as that,—good only for boys and
greenhorns like you; and that is what I have taken the liberty this
morning to go and tell the minister of public instruction, by whom
I must say I was received with the most perfect urbanity. I asked
him to see whether, as he had made a mistake and sent them to the
wrong address, he could not take back his cross and his pension,—
though to be sure, as I told him, I deserved them for other
things.

"The government," he replied, "is not in the habit of making
mistakes; what it does is always properly done, and it never
annuls an ordinance signed by the hand of his Majesty. Your great
labors have deserved the two favors the King has granted you; it
is a long-standing debt, which I am happy to pay off in his name."

"But Felix?" I said; "because after all for a young man it is not
such a bad discovery."

"Monsieur Felix Phellion," replied the minister, "will receive in
the course of the day his appointment to the rank of Chevalier of
the Legion of honor; I will have it signed this morning by the
king. Moreover, there is a vacant place at the Academy of
Sciences, and if you are not a candidate for it—"

"I, in the Academy!" I interrupted, with the frankness of speech
you know I always use; "I execrate academies; they are stiflers,
extinguishers, assemblages of sloths, idlers, shops with big signs
and nothing to sell inside—"

"Well, then," said the minister, smiling, "I think that at the
next election Monsieur Felix Phellion will have every chance, and
among those chances I count the influence of the government which
is secured to him."

There, my poor boy, is all that I have been able to do to reward
your good intentions and to prove to you that I am no longer
angry. I think the relations are going to pull a long face. Come
and talk about it to-day at four o'clock,—for I don't dine after
bedtime, as I saw some people doing last night in a house where I
had occasion to mention your talents in a manner that was very
advantageous to you. Madame Lambert, who does better with a
saucepan than with pen and ink, shall distinguish herself, though
it is Friday, and she never lets me off a fast day. But she has
promised us a fish dinner worthy of an archbishop, with a fine
half-bottle of champagne (doubled if need be) to wash it down.

Your old professor and friend,

Picot (Nepomucene),

Chevalier of the Legion of honor.

P.S.—Do you think you could obtain from your respectable mother a
little flask of that old and excellent cognac you once gave me?
Not a drop remains, and yesterday I was forced to drink some stuff

only fit to bathe horses' feet, as I did not hesitate to say to
the beautiful Hebe who served it to me.

"Of course he shall have some," said Madame Phellion; "not a flask, but a gallon."

"And I," said Minard, "who pique myself on mine, which didn't come from Brigitte's grocer either, I'll send him several bottles; but don't tell him who sent them, Monsieur le chevalier, for you never can tell how that singular being will take things."

"Wife," said Phellion, suddenly, "get me my black coat and a white cravat."

"Where are you going?" asked Madame Phellion. "To the minister, to thank him?"

"Bring me, I say, those articles of habiliment. I have an important visit to make; and Monsieur le maire will, I know, excuse me."

"I myself must be off," said Minard. "I, too, have important business, though it isn't about a star."

Questioned in vain by Felix and his wife, Phellion completed his attire with a pair of white gloves, sent for a carriage, and, at the end of half an hour, entered the presence of Brigitte, whom he found presiding over the careful putting away of the china, glass, and silver which had performed their several functions the night before. Leaving these housekeeping details, she received her visitor.

"Well, papa Phellion," she said, when they were both seated in the salon, "you broke your word yesterday; you were luckier than the rest. Do you know what a trick that notary played us?"

"I know all," said Phellion; "and it is the check thus unexpectedly given to the execution of your plans that I shall take for the text of an important conversation which I desire to have with you. Sometimes Providence would seem to take pleasure in counteracting our best-laid schemes; sometimes, also, by means of the obstacles it raises in our path, it seems to intend to indicate that we are bearing too far to the right or to the left, and should pause to reflect upon our way."

"Providence!" said Brigitte the strong-minded,—"Providence has something else to do than to look after us."

"That is one opinion," said Phellion; "but I myself am accustomed to see its decrees in the little as well as the great things of life; and certainly, if it had allowed the fulfilment of your engagements with Monsieur de la Peyrade to be even partially begun yesterday, you would not have seen me here to-day."

"Then," said Brigitte, "do you think that by default of a notary the marriage will not take place? They do say that for want of a monk the abbey won't come to a standstill."

"Dear lady," said the great citizen, "you will do me the justice to feel that neither I, nor my wife, have ever attempted to influence your decision; we have allowed our young people to love each other without much consideration as to where that attachment would lead—"

"It led to upsetting their minds," said Brigitte; "that's what love is, and that's why I deprived myself of it."

"What you say is, indeed, true of my unfortunate son," resumed Phellion; "for, notwithstanding the noble distractions he has endeavored to give to his sorrow, he is to-day so miserably overcome by it that this morning, in spite of the glorious success he has just obtained, he was speaking to me of undertaking a voyage of circumnavigation around the globe,—a rash enterprise which would detain him from his native land at least three years, if, indeed, he escaped the dangers of so prolonged a journey."

"Well," said Brigitte, "it isn't a bad idea; he'll return consoled, having discovered three or four more new stars."

"His present discovery suffices," said Phellion, with double his ordinary gravity, "and it is under the auspices of that triumph, which has placed his name at so great a height in the scientific world, that I have the assurance to say to you, point-blank: Mademoiselle, I have come to ask you, on behalf of my son, who loves as he is beloved, for the hand in marriage of Mademoiselle Celeste Colleville."

"But, my dear man," replied Brigitte, "it is too late; remember that we are *diametrically* engaged to la Peyrade."

"It is never, they say, too late to do well, and yesterday it would have been in my judgment too early. My son, having to offer an equivalent for a fortune, could not say to you until to-day: 'Though Celeste, by your generosity has a "dot" which mine is far from equalling, yet I have the honor to be a member of the Royal order of the Legion of honor, and shortly, according to appearance, I shall be a member of the Royal Academy of Sciences, one of the five branches of the Institute.'"

"Certainly," said Brigitte; "Felix is getting to be a very pretty match, but we have passed our word to la Peyrade; the banns are published at the mayor's office, and unless something extraordinary happens the contract will be signed. La Peyrade is very busy about Thuillier's election, which he has now got into good shape; we have capital engaged with him in the affair of this newspaper; and it would be impossible to go back on our promise, even if we wished to do so."

"So," said Phellion, "in one of the rare occasions of life when reason and inclination blend together, you think you must be guided solely by the question of material interests. Celeste, as we know, has no inclination for Monsieur de la Peyrade. Brought up with Felix—"

"Brought up with Felix!" interrupted Brigitte. "She was given a period of time to choose between Monsieur de la Peyrade and your son,—that's how we coerce her, if you please,—and she would not take Monsieur Felix, whose atheism is too well known."

"You are mistaken, mademoiselle, my son is not an atheist; for Voltaire himself doubted if there could be atheists; and no later than yesterday, in this house, an ecclesiastic, as admirable for his talents as for his virtues, after making a magnificent eulogy of my son, expressed the desire to know him."

"Parbleu! yes, to convert him," said Brigitte. "But as for this marriage, I am sorry to tell you that the mustard is made too late for the dinner; Thuillier will never renounce his la Peyrade."

"Mademoiselle," said Phellion, rising, "I feel no humiliation for the useless step I have this day taken; I do not even ask you to keep it secret, for I shall myself mention it to our friends and acquaintances."

"Tell it to whom you like, my good man," replied Brigitte, acrimoniously. "Because your son has discovered a star,—if, indeed, he did discover it, and not that old fool the government decorated—do you expect him to marry a daughter of the King of the French?"

"Enough," said Phellion, "we will say no more. I might answer that, without depreciating the Thuilliers, the Orleans family seems to me more distinguished; but I do not like to introduce acerbity into the conversation, and therefore, begging you to receive the assurance of my humble respects, I retire."

So saying, he made his exit majestically, and left Brigitte with the arrow of his comparison, discharged after the manner of the Parthian "in extremis," sticking in her mind, and she herself in a temper all the more savage because already, the evening before, Madame Thuillier, after the guests were gone, had the incredible audacity to say something in favor of Felix. Needless to relate that the poor helot was roughly put down and told to mind her own business. But this attempt at a will of her own in her sister-in-law had already put the old maid in a vile humor, and Phellion, coming to reopen the subject, exasperated her. Josephine, the cook, and the "male domestic," received the after-clap of the scene which had just taken place. Brigitte found that in her absence everything had been done wrong, and putting her own hand to the work, she hoisted herself on a chair, at the risk of her neck, to reach the upper shelves of the closet, where her choicest china, for gala days, was carefully kept under lock and key.

This day, which for Brigitte began so ill, was, beyond all gainsaying, one of the stormiest and most portentous of this narrative.

CHAPTER XIV. A STORMY DAY

As an exact historian, we must go back and begin the day at six in the morning, when we can see Madame Thuillier going to the Madeleine to hear the mass that the Abbe Gondrin was in the habit of saying at that hour, and afterwards approaching the holy table,—a viaticum which pious souls never fail to give themselves when it is in their minds to accomplish some great resolution.

About mid-day the abbe received a visit in his own home from Madame Thuillier and Celeste. The poor child wanted a little development of the words by which the priest had given security, the evening before, in Brigitte's salon, for the eternal welfare of Felix Phellion. It seemed strange to the mind of this girl-theologian that, without practising religion, a soul could be received into grace by the divine justice; for surely the anathema is clear: Out of the Church there is no salvation.

"My dear child," said the Abbe Gondrin, "learn to understand that saying which seems to you so inexplicable. It is more a saying of thanksgiving for those who have the happiness to live within the pale of our holy mother the Church than a malediction upon those who have the misfortune to live apart from her. God sees to the depths of all hearts; He knows His elect; and so great is the treasure of His goodness that to none is it given to limit its riches and its munificence. Who shall dare to say to God: Thou wilt be generous and munificent so far and no farther. Jesus Christ forgave the woman in adultery, and on the cross He promised heaven to a thief, in order to prove to us that He deals with men, not according to human sentiments, but according to *his* wisdom and *his* mercy. He who thinks himself a Christian may be in the eyes of God an idolator; and another who is thought a pagan may, by his feelings and his actions be, without his own knowledge, a Christian. Our holy religion has this that is divine about it; all grandeur, all heroism are but the practice of its precepts. I was saying yesterday to Monsieur de la Peyrade that pure souls must be, in course of time, its inevitable conquest. It is all-important to give them their just credit; that is a confidence which returns great dividends; and, besides, charity commands it."

"Ah! my God!" cried Celeste, "to learn that too late! I, who could have chosen between Felix and Monsieur de la Peyrade, and did not dare to follow the ideas of my heart! Oh! Monsieur l'abbe, couldn't you speak to my mother? Your advice is always listened to."

"Impossible, my dear child," replied the vicar. "If I had the direction of

Madame Colleville's conscience I might perhaps say a word, but we are so often accused of meddling imprudently in family matters! Be sure that my intervention here, without authority or right, would do you more harm than good. It is for you and for those who love you," he added, giving a look to Madame Thuillier, "to see if these arrangements, already so far advanced, could be changed in the direction of your wishes."

It was written that the poor child was to drink to the dregs the cup she had herself prepared by her intolerance. As the abbe finished speaking, his housekeeper came in to ask if he would receive Monsieur Felix Phellion. Thus, like the Charter of 1830, Madame de Godollo's officious falsehood was turned into truth.

"Go this way," he said hastily, showing his two penitents out by a private corridor.

Life has such strange encounters that it does sometimes happen that the same form of proceeding must be used by courtesans and by the men of God.

"Monsieur l'abbe," said Felix to the young vicar as soon as they met, "I have heard of the kind manner in which you were so very good as to speak of me in Monsieur Thuillier's salon last night, and I should have hastened to express my gratitude if another interest had not drawn me to you."

The Abbe Gondrin passed hastily over the compliments, eager to know in what way he could be useful to his fellow-man.

"With an intention that I wish to think kindly," replied Felix, "you were spoken to yesterday about the state of my soul. Those who read it so fluently know more than I do about my inner being, for, during the last few days I have felt strange, inexplicable feelings within me. Never have I doubted God, but, in contact with that infinitude where he has permitted my thought to follow the traces of his work I seem to have gathered a sense of him less vague, more immediate; and this has led me to ask myself whether an honest and upright life is the only homage which his omnipotence expects of me. Nevertheless, there are numberless objections rising in my mind against the worship of which you are the minister; while sensible of the beauty of its external form in many of its precepts and practices, I find myself deterred by my reason. I shall have paid dearly, perhaps by the happiness of my whole life, for the slowness and want of vigor which I have shown in seeking the solution of my doubts. I have now decided to search to the bottom of them. No one so well as you, Monsieur l'abbe, can help me to solve them. I have come with confidence to lay them before you, to ask you to listen to me, to answer me, and to tell me by what studies I can pursue the search for light. It is a cruelly afflicted soul that appeals to you. Is not that a good ground for the seed of your word?"

The Abbe Gondrin eagerly protested the joy with which, notwithstanding his own insufficiency, he would undertake to reply to the scruples of conscience in the young savant. After asking him for a place in his friendship, and telling him to come at certain hours for conversation, he asked him to read, as a first step, the "Thoughts" of Pascal. A natural affinity, on the side of science, would, he believed, be established between the spirit of Pascal and that of the young mathematician.

While this scene was passing, a scene to which the greatness of the interests in question and the moral and intellectual elevation of the personages concerned in it gave a character of grandeur which, like all reposeful, tranquil aspects, is easier far to comprehend than to reproduce, another scene, of sharp and bitter discord, that chronic malady of bourgeois households, where the pettiness of minds and passions gives open way to it, was taking place in the Thuillier home.

Mounted upon her chair, her hair in disorder and her face and fingers dirty, Brigitte, duster in hand, was cleaning the shelves of the closet, where she was replacing her library of plates, dishes, and sauce-boats, when Flavie came in and accosted her.

"Brigitte," she said, "when you have finished what you are about you had better come down to our apartment, or else I'll send Celeste to you; she seems to me to be inclined to make trouble."

"In what way?" asked Brigitte, continuing to dust.

"I think she and Madame Thuillier went to see the Abbe Gondrin this morning, and she has been attacking me about Felix Phellion, and talks of him as if he were a god; from that to refusing to marry la Peyrade is but a step."

"Those cursed skull-caps!" said Brigitte; "they meddle in everything! I didn't want to invite him, but you would insist."

"Yes," said Flavie, "it was proper."

"Proper! I despise proprieties!" cried the old maid. "He's a maker of speeches; he said nothing last night that wasn't objectionable. Send Celeste to me; I'll settle her."

At this instant a servant announced to Brigitte the arrival of a clerk from the office of the new notary chosen, in default of Dupuis, to draw up the contract. Without considering her disorderly appearance, Brigitte ordered him to be shown in, but she made him the condescension of descending from her perch instead of talking from the height of it.

"Monsieur Thuillier," said the clerk, "came to our office this morning to explain to the master the clauses of the contract he has been so good as to entrust to us. But before writing down the stipulations, we are in the habit of obtaining from the lips of each donor a direct expression of his or her intentions. In accordance with this rule, Monsieur Thuillier told us that he gives to the bride the reversion, at his death, of the house he inhabits, which I presume to be this one?"

"Yes," said Brigitte, "that is the understanding. As for me, I give three hundred thousand francs a year in the Three-per-cents, capital and interest; but the bride is married under the dotal system."

"That is so," said the clerk, consulting his notes. "Mademoiselle Brigitte, three thousand francs a year. Now, there is Madame Celeste Thuillier, wife of Louis-Jerome Thuillier, who gives six thousand in the Three-per-cents, capital and interest, and six thousand more at her death."

"All that is just as if the notary had written it down," said Brigitte; "but if it is your custom you can see my sister-in-law; they will show you the way."

So saying, the old maid ordered the "male domestic" to take the clerk to Madame Thuillier.

A moment later the clerk returned, saying there was certainly some misunderstanding, and that Madame Thuillier declared she had no intention of making any agreement in favor of the marriage.

"That's a pretty thing!" cried Brigitte. "Come with me, monsieur."

Then, like a hurricane, she rushed into Madame Thuillier's chamber; the latter was pale and trembling.

"What's this you have told monsieur?—that you give nothing to Celeste's 'dot'?"

"Yes," said the slave, declaring insurrection, although in a shaking voice; "my intention is to do nothing."

"Your intention," said Brigitte, scarlet with anger, "is something new."

"That is my intention," was all the rebel replied.

"At least you will give your reasons?"

"The marriage does not please me."

"Ha! and since when?"

"It is not necessary that monsieur should listen to our discussion," said Madame Thuillier; "it will not appear in the contract."

"No wonder you are ashamed of it," said Brigitte; "the appearance you are making is not very flattering to you—Monsieur," she continued, addressing the clerk, "it is easier, is it not, to mark out passages in a contract than to add them?"

The clerk made an affirmative sign.

"Then put in what you were told to write; later, if madame persists, the clause can be stricken out."

The clerk bowed and left the room.

When the two sisters-in-law were alone together, Brigitte began.

"Ah ca!" she cried, "have you lost your head? What is this crotchet you've taken into it?"

"It is not a crotchet; it is a fixed idea."

"Which you got from the Abbe Gondrin; you dare not deny that you went to see him with Celeste."

"It is true that Celeste and I saw our director this morning, but I did not open my lips to him about what I intended to do."

"So, then, it is in your own empty head that this notion sprouted?"

"Yes. As I told you yesterday, I think Celeste can be more suitably married, and my intention is not to rob myself for a marriage of which I disapprove."

"*You* disapprove! Upon my word! are we all to take madame's advice?"

"I know well," replied Madame Thuillier, "that I count for nothing in this house. So far as I am concerned, I have long accepted my position; but, when the matter concerns the happiness of a child I regard as my own—"

"Parbleu!" cried Brigitte, "you never knew how to have one; for, certainly, Thuillier—"

"Sister," said Madame Thuillier, with dignity, "I took the sacrament this morning, and there are some things I cannot listen to."

"There's a canting hypocrite for you!" cried Brigitte; "playing the saint, and bringing trouble into families! And you think to succeed, do you? Wait till Thuillier comes home, and he'll shake this out of you."

By calling in the marital authority in support of her own, Brigitte showed weakness before the unexpected resistance thus made to her inveterate tyranny. Madame Thuillier's calm words, which became every moment more resolute, baffled her completely, and she found no resource but insolence.

"A drone!" she cried; "a helpless good-for-nothing! who can't even pick up her own handkerchief! that thing wants to be mistress of this house!"

"I wish so little to be its mistress," said Madame Thuillier, "that last night I allowed you to silence me after the first words I said in behalf of Celeste. But I am mistress of my own property, and as I believe that Celeste will be wretched in this marriage, I keep it to use as may seem best to me."

"Your property, indeed!" said Brigitte, with a sneer.

"Yes, that which I received from my father and my mother, and which I brought as my 'dot' to Monsieur Thuillier."

"And pray who invested it, this property, and made it give you twelve thousand francs a year?"

"I have never asked you for any account of it," said Madame Thuillier, gently. "If it had been lost in the uses you made of it, you would never have heard a single word from me; but it has prospered, and it is just that I should have the benefit. It is not for myself that I reserve it."

"Perhaps not; if this is the course you take, it is not at all sure that you and I will go out of the same door long."

"Do you mean that Monsieur Thuillier will send me away? He must have reasons for doing that, and, thank God! I have been a wife above reproach."

"Viper! hypocrite! heartless creature!" cried Brigitte, coming to an end of her arguments.

"Sister," said Madame Thuillier, "you are in my apartment—"

"Am I, you imbecile?" cried the old maid, in a paroxysm of anger. "If I didn't restrain myself—"

And she made a gesture both insulting and threatening.

Madame Thuillier rose to leave the room.

"No! you shall not go out," cried Brigitte, pushing her down into her chair; "and till Thuillier comes home and decides what he will do with you you'll stay locked up here."

Just as Brigitte, her face on fire, returned to the room where she had left Madame Colleville, her brother came in. He was radiant.

"My dear," he said to the Megaera, not observing her fury, "everything is going on finely; the conspiracy of silence is broken; two papers, the 'National' and a Carlist journal, have copied articles from us, and there's a little attack in a ministerial paper."

"Well, all is not going on finely here," said Brigitte, "and if it continues, I shall leave the barrack."

"Whom are you angry with now?" asked Thuillier.

"With your insolent wife, who has made me a scene; I am trembling all over."

"Celeste make you a scene!" said Thuillier; "then it is the very first time in her life."

"There's a beginning to everything, and if you don't bring her to order—"

"But what was it about—this scene?"

"About madame's not choosing that la Peyrade should marry her goddaughter; and out of spite, to prevent the marriage, she refused to give anything in the contract."

"Come, be calm," said Thuillier, not disturbed himself, the admission of the "Echo" into the polemic making another Pangloss of him. "I'll settle all that."

"You, Flavie," said Brigitte, when Thuillier had departed to his wife, "you will do me the pleasure to go down to your own apartment, and tell Mademoiselle Celeste that I don't choose to see her now, because if she made me any irritating answer I might box her ears. You'll tell her that I don't like conspiracies; that she was left at liberty to choose Monsieur Phellion junior if she wanted him, and she did not want him; that the matter is now all arranged, and that if she does not wish to see her 'dot' reduced to what you are able to give her, which isn't as much as a bank-messenger could carry in his waistcoat pocket—"

"But, my dear Brigitte," interrupted Flavie, turning upon her at this impertinence, "you may dispense with reminding us in this harsh way of our poverty; for, after all, we have never asked you for anything, and we pay our rent punctually; and as for the 'dot,' Monsieur Felix Phellion is quite ready to take Celeste with no more than a bank-messenger could carry in his *bag*."

And she emphasized the last word by her way of pronouncing it.

"Ha! so you too are going to meddle in this, are you?" cried Brigitte. "Very good; go and fetch him, your Felix. I know, my little woman, that this marriage has never suited you; it IS disagreeable to be nothing more than a mother to your son-in-law."

Flavie had recovered the coolness she had lost for an instant, and without replying to this speech she merely shrugged her shoulders.

At this moment Thuillier returned; his air of beatitude had deserted him.

"My dear Brigitte," he said to his sister, "you have a most excellent heart, but at times you are so violent—"

"Ho!" said the old maid, "am I to be arraigned on this side too?"

"I certainly do not blame you for the cause of the trouble, and I have just rebuked Celeste for her assumption; but there are proper forms that must be kept."

"Forms! what are you talking about? What forms have I neglected?"

"But, my dear friend, to raise your hand against your sister!"

"I, raise my hand against that imbecile? What nonsense you talk!"

"And besides," continued Thuillier, "a woman of Celeste's age can't be kept in prison."

"Your wife!—have I put her in prison?"

"You can't deny it, for I found the door of her room double-locked."

"Parbleu! all this because in my anger at the infamous things she was spitting at me I may have turned the key of the door without intending it."

"Come, come," said Thuillier, "these are not proper actions for people of our class."

"Oh! so it is I who am to blame, is it? Well, my lad, some day you'll remember this, and we shall see how your household will get along when I have stopped taking care of it."

"You'll always take care of it," said Thuillier. "Housekeeping is your very life; you will be the first to get over this affair."

"We'll see about that," said Brigitte; "after twenty years of devotion, to be treated like the lowest of the low!"

And rushing to the door, which she slammed after her with violence, she went away.

Thuillier was not disturbed by this exit.

"Were you there, Flavie," he asked, "when the scene took place?"

"No, it happened in Celeste's room. What did she do to her?"

"What I said,—raised her hand to her and locked her in like a child. Celeste may certainly be rather dull-minded, but there are limits that must not be passed."

"She is not always pleasant, that good Brigitte," said Flavie; "she and I

391

have just had a little set-to."

"Oh, well," said Thuillier, "it will all pass off. I want to tell you, my dear Flavie, what fine success we have had this morning. The 'National' quotes two whole paragraphs of an article in which there were several sentences of mine."

Thuillier was again interrupted in the tale of his great political and literary success,—this time by the entrance of Josephine the cook.

"Can monsieur tell me where to find the key of the great trunk?" she said.

"What do you want with it?" asked Thuillier.

"Mademoiselle told me to take it to her room."

"What for?"

"Mademoiselle must be going to make a journey. She is getting her linen out of the drawers, and her gowns are on the bed."

"Another piece of nonsense!" said Thuillier. "Flavie, go and see what she has in her head."

"Not I," said Madame Colleville; "go yourself. In her present state of exasperation she might beat me."

"And my stupid wife, who must needs raise a fuss about the contract!" cried Thuillier. "She really must have said something pretty sharp to turn Brigitte off her hinges like this."

"Monsieur has not told me where to find the key," persisted Josephine.

"I don't know anything about it," said Thuillier, crossly; "go and look for it, or else tell her it is lost."

"Oh, yes!" said Josephine, "it is likely I'd dare to go and tell her that."

Just then the outer door-bell rang.

"No doubt that's la Peyrade," said Thuillier, in a tone of satisfaction.

The Provencal appeared a moment later.

"Faith, my dear friend," cried Thuillier, "it is high time you came; the house is in revolution, all about you, and it needs your silvery tongue to bring it back to peace and quietness."

Then he related to his assistant editor the circumstances of the civil war which had broken out.

La Peyrade turned to Madame Colleville.

"I think," he said, "that under the circumstances in which we now stand there is no impropriety in my asking for an interview of a few moments with Mademoiselle Colleville."

In this the Provencal showed his usual shrewd ability; he saw that in the mission of pacification thus given to him Celeste Colleville was the key of the situation.

"I will send for her, and we will leave you alone together," said Flavie.

"My dear Thuillier," said la Peyrade, "you must, without any violence, let Mademoiselle Celeste know that her consent must be given without further delay; make her think that this was the purpose for which you have sent for her; then leave us; I will do the rest."

The man-servant was sent down to the entresol with orders to tell Celeste that her godfather wished to speak to her. As soon as she appeared, Thuillier said, to carry out the programme which had been dictated to him:—

"My dear, your mother has told us things that astonish us. Can it be true that with your contract almost signed, you have not yet decided to accept the marriage we have arranged for you?"

"Godfather," said Celeste, rather surprised at this abrupt summons, "I think I did not say that to mamma."

"Did you not just now," said Flavie, "praise Monsieur Felix Phellion to me in the most extravagant manner?"

"I spoke of Monsieur Phellion as all the world is speaking of him."

"Come, come," said Thuillier, with authority, "let us have no equivocation; do you refuse, yes or no, to marry Monsieur de la Peyrade?"

"Dear, good friend," said la Peyrade, intervening, "your way of putting the question is rather too abrupt, and, in my presence, especially, it seems to me out of place. In my position as the most interested person, will you allow me to have an interview with mademoiselle, which, indeed, has now become necessary? This favor I am sure will not be refused by Madame Colleville. Under present circumstances, there can surely be nothing in my request to alarm her maternal prudence."

"I would certainly yield to it," said Flavie, "if I did not fear that these discussions might seem to open a question which is irrevocably decided."

"But, my dear madame, I have the strongest desire that Mademoiselle Celeste shall remain, until the very last moment, the mistress of her own choice. I beg you, therefore, to grant my request."

"So be it!" said Madame Colleville; "you think yourself very clever, but if you let that girl twist you round her finger, so much the worse for you. Come, Thuillier, since we are 'de trop' here."

As soon as the pair were alone together, la Peyrade drew up a chair for Celeste, and took one himself, saying:—

"You will, I venture to believe, do me the justice to say that until to-day I have never annoyed you with the expression of my sentiments. I was aware of the inclinations of your heart, and also of the warnings of your conscience. I hoped, after a time, to make myself acceptable as a refuge from those two currents of feeling; but, at the point which we have now reached, I think it is not either indiscreet or impatient to ask you to let me know plainly what course you have decided upon."

"Monsieur," replied Celeste, "as you speak to me so kindly and frankly, I will tell you, what indeed you know already, that, brought up as I was with Monsieur Felix Phellion, knowing him far longer than I have known you, the idea of marrying alarmed me less in regard to him than it would in regard to others."

"At one time, I believe," remarked la Peyrade, "you were permitted to choose him if you wished."

"Yes, but at that time difficulties grew up between us on religious ideas."

"And to-day those difficulties have disappeared?"

"Nearly," replied Celeste. "I am accustomed to submit to the judgment of those who are wiser than myself, monsieur, and you heard yesterday the manner in which the Abbe Gondrin spoke of Monsieur Phellion."

"God forbid," said la Peyrade, "that I should seek to invalidate the judgment of so excellent a man; but I venture to say to you, mademoiselle, that there are great differences among the clergy; some are thought too stern, some far too indulgent; moreover, the Abbe Gondrin is more of a preacher than a casuist."

"But, Monsieur Felix," said Celeste, eagerly, "seems to wish to fulfil Monsieur l'abbe's hopes of him, for I know that he went to see him this morning."

"Ah!" said la Peyrade, with a touch of irony, "so he really decided to go to Pere Anselme! But, admitting that on the religious side Monsieur Phellion may now become all that you expect of him, have you reflected, mademoiselle, on the great event which has just taken place in his life?"

"Undoubtedly; and that is not a reason to think less of him."

"No, but it is a reason why he should think more of himself. For the modesty which was once the chief charm of his nature, he is likely to substitute great assumption, and you must remember, mademoiselle, that he who has discovered one world will want to discover two; you will have the whole firmament for rival; in short, could you ever be happy with a man so entirely devoted to science?"

"You plead your cause with such adroitness," said Celeste, smiling, "that I think you might be as a lawyer more disquieting than an astronomer."

"Mademoiselle," said la Peyrade, "let us speak seriously; there is another and far more serious aspect to the situation. Do you know that, at this moment, in this house, and without, I am sure, desiring it, you are the cause of most distressing and regrettable scenes?"

"I, monsieur!" said Celeste, in a tone of surprise that was mingled with fear.

"Yes, concerning your godmother. Through the extreme affection that she has for you she seems to have become another woman; for the first time in her life she has shown a mind of her own. With an energy of will which comes at times to those who have never expended any, she declares that she will not make her proposed liberal gift to you in the contract; and I need not tell you who is the person aimed at in this unexpected refusal."

"But, monsieur, I entreat you to believe that I knew nothing of this idea of my godmother."

"I know that," said la Peyrade, "and the matter itself would be of small importance if Mademoiselle Brigitte had not taken this attitude of your godmother, whom she has always found supple to her will, as a personal insult to herself. Very painful explanations, approaching at last to violence, have taken place. Thuillier, placed between the hammer and the anvil, has been unable to stop the affair; on the contrary, he has, without intending it, made matters worse, till they have now arrived at such a point that Mademoiselle Brigitte is packing her trunks to leave the house."

"Monsieur! what are you telling me?" cried Celeste, horrified.

"The truth; and the servants will confirm it to you—for I feel that my revelations are scarcely believable."

"But it is impossible! impossible!" said the poor child, whose agitation increased with every word of the adroit Provencal. "I cannot be the cause of such dreadful harm."

"That is, you did not intend to be, for the harm is done; and I pray Heaven it may not be irremediable."

"But what am I to do, good God!" cried Celeste, wringing her hands.

"I should answer, without hesitation, sacrifice yourself, mademoiselle, if it were not that I should then be forced to play the painful part of victimizer."

"Monsieur," said Celeste, "you interpret ill the resistance that I have made, though, in fact, I have scarcely expressed it. I have certainly had a preference, but I have never considered myself in the light of a victim; and whatever it is necessary to do to restore peace in this house to which I have brought trouble, I shall do it without repugnance, and even willingly."

"That would be for me," said la Peyrade, humbly, "more than I could dare ask for myself; but, for the result which we both seek, I must tell you frankly that something more is needed. Madame Thuillier has not changed her nature to instantly change back again on the mere assurance by others of your compliance. It is necessary that she should hear from your own lips that you accede to my suit, and that you do so with eagerness,—assumed, indeed, but sufficiently well assumed to induce her to believe in it."

"So be it," said Celeste. "I shall know how to seem smiling and happy. My godmother, monsieur, has been a mother to me; and for such a mother, what is there that I would not endure?"

The position was such, and Celeste betrayed so artlessly the depth and, at the same time, the absolute determination of her sacrifice, that with any heart at all la Peyrade would have loathed the part he was playing; but Celeste, to him, was a means of ascent, and provided the ladder can hold you and hoist you, who would ever ask if it cared to or not? It was therefore decided that Celeste should go to her godmother and convince her of the mistake she had made in supposing an objection to la Peyrade which Celeste had never intended to make. Madame Thuillier's opposition overcome, all was once more easy. La Peyrade took upon himself the duty of making peace between the two sisters-in-law, and we can well imagine that he was not at a loss for fine phrases with which to assure the artless girl of the devotion and love which would take from her all regret for the moral compulsion she had now undergone.

When Celeste went to her godmother she found her by no means as difficult to convince as she had expected. To go to the point of rebellion which Madame Thuillier had actually reached, the poor woman, who was acting against her instincts and against her nature, had needed a tension of will that, in her, was almost superhuman. No sooner had she received the false confidences of her goddaughter than the reaction set in; the strength failed her to continue in the path she had taken. She was therefore easily the dupe of the comedy which Celeste's tender heart was made to play for la Peyrade's benefit.

The tempest calmed on this side, the barrister found no difficulty in making Brigitte understand that in quelling the rebellion against her authority she had gone a little farther than was proper. This authority being no longer in danger, Brigitte ceased to be incensed with the sister-in-law she had been on the point of beating, and the quarrel was settled with a few kind words and a kiss, poor Celeste paying the costs of war.

After dinner, which was only a family meal, the notary, to whose office they were to go on the following day to sign the contract (it being impossible to give a second edition of the abortive party), made his appearance. He came, he said, to submit the contract to the parties interested before engrossing it. This attention was not surprising in a man who was just entering into business relations with so important a person as the municipal councillor, whom it was his interest to firmly secure for a client.

La Peyrade was far too shrewd to make any objections to the terms of the contract, which was now read. A few changes requested by Brigitte, which gave the new notary a high idea of the old maid's business capacity, showed la Peyrade plainly that more precautions were being taken against him than were altogether becoming; but he was anxious not to raise difficulties, and he knew that the meshes of a contract are never so close that a determined and clever man cannot get through them. The appointment was then made for the signing of the contract the next day, at two o'clock, in the notary's office, the family only being present.

During the rest of the evening, taking advantage of Celeste's pledge to seem smiling and happy, la Peyrade played, as it were, upon the poor child, forced her, by a specious exhibition of gratitude and love, to respond to him on a key that was far, indeed, from the true state of a heart now wholly filled by Felix. Flavie, seeing the manner in which la Peyrade put forth his seductions, was reminded of the pains he had formerly taken to fascinate herself. "The monster!" she said, beneath her breath. But she was forced to bear the torture with a good grace; la Peyrade was evidently approved by all, and in the course of the evening a circumstance came to light, showing a past service done by him to the house of Thuillier, which brought his influence and his credit to the highest point.

Minard was announced.

"My dear friends," he said, "I have come to make a little revelation which will greatly surprise you, and will, I think, prove a lesson to all of us when a question arises as to receiving foreigners in our homes."

"What is it?" cried Brigitte, with curiosity.

"That Hungarian woman you were so delighted with, that Madame Torna, Comtesse de Godollo—"

"Well?" exclaimed the old maid.

"Well," continued Minard, "she was no better than she should be; you were petting in your house for two months the most impudent of kept women."

"Who told you that tale?" asked Brigitte, not willing to admit that she had fallen into such a snare.

"Oh, it isn't a tale," said the mayor, eagerly. "I know the thing myself, 'de visu.'"

"Dear me! do you frequent such women?" said Brigitte, resuming the offensive. "That's a pretty thing! what would Zelie say if she knew it?"

"In the discharge of my duties," said Minard, stiffly, provoked at this reception of his news, "I have seen *your friend*, Madame de Godollo, in company with others of her class."

"How do you know it was she if you only saw her?" demanded Brigitte.

The wily Provencal was not the man to lose an occasion that fell to him ready-made.

"Monsieur le maire is not mistaken," he said, with decision.

"Tiens! so you know her, too," said Brigitte; "and you let us consort with such vermin?"

"No," said la Peyrade, "on the contrary. Without scandal, without saying a word to any one, I removed her from your house. You remember how suddenly the woman left it? It was I who compelled her to do so; having discovered what she was, I gave her two days to leave the premises; threatening her, in case she hesitated, to tell you all."

"My dear Theodose," said Thuillier, pressing his hand, "you acted with as much prudence as decision. This is one more obligation that we owe to you."

"You see, mademoiselle," said la Peyrade, addressing Celeste, "the strange protectress whom a friend of yours selected."

"Thank God," said Madame Thuillier. "Felix Phellion is above such vile things."

"Ah ca! papa Minard, we'll keep quiet about all this; silence is the word. Will you take a cup of tea?"

"Willingly," replied Minard.

"Celeste," said the old maid, "ring for Henri, and tell him to put the large kettle on the fire."

Though the visit to the notary was not to be made till two in the afternoon, Brigitte began early in the morning of the next day what Thuillier called her *rampage*, a popular term which expresses that turbulent, nagging, irritating activity which La Fontaine has described so well in his fable of "The Old Woman and her Servants." Brigitte declared that if you didn't take time by the forelock no one would be ready. She prevented Thuillier from going to his office, insisting that if he once got off she never should see him again; she plagued Josephine, the cook, about hurrying the breakfast, and in spite of what had happened the day before she scarcely restrained herself from nagging at Madame Thuillier, who did not enter, as she thought she should have done, into her favorite maxim, "Better be early than late."

Presently down she went to the Collevilles' to make the same disturbance; and there she put her veto on the costume, far too elegant, which Flavie meditated wearing, and told Celeste the hat and gown she wished her to appear in. As for Colleville, who could not, he declared, stay away all the morning from his official duties, she compelled him to put on his dress-suit before he went out, made him set his watch by hers, and warned him that if he was late no one would wait for him.

The amusing part of it was that Brigitte herself, after driving every one at the point of the bayonet, came very near being late herself. Under pretext of aiding others, independently of minding her own business, which, for worlds, she would never have spared herself, she had put her fingers and eyes into so many things that they ended by overwhelming her. However, she ascribed the delay in which she was almost caught to the hairdresser, whom she had sent for to make, on this extraordinary occasion, what she called her "part." That artist having, unadvisedly, dressed her hair in the fashion, he was compelled, after she had looked at herself in the glass, to do his work over again, and conform to the usual style of his client, which consisted chiefly in never being "done" at all, a method that gave her head a general air of what is vulgarly called "a cross cat."

About half-past one o'clock la Peyrade, Thuillier, Colleville, Madame Thuillier, and Celeste were assembled in the salon. Flavie joined them soon after, fastening her bracelets as she came along to avoid a rebuff, and having the satisfaction of knowing that she was ready before Brigitte. As for the latter, already furious at finding herself late, she had another cause for exasperation. The event of the day seemed to require a corset, a refinement which she usually discarded. The unfortunate maid, whose duty it was to lace her and to discover the exact point to which she was willing to be drawn in, alone knew the terrors and storms of a corset day.

"I'd rather," said the girl, "lace the obelisk; I know it would lend itself to being laced better than she does; and, anyhow, it couldn't be bad-tongued."

While the party in the salon were amusing themselves, under their breaths, at the "flagrante delicto" of unpunctuality in which Queen Elizabeth was caught, the porter entered, and gave to Thuillier a sealed package, addressed to "Monsieur Thuillier, director of the 'Echo de la Bievre.' *In haste.*"

Thuillier opened the envelope, and found within a copy of a ministerial journal which had hitherto shown itself discourteous to the new paper by refusing the *exchange* which all periodicals usually make very willingly with one another.

Puzzled by the fact of this missive being sent to his own house and not to the office of the "Echo," Thuillier hastily opened the sheet, and read, with what emotion the reader may conceive, the following article, commended to his notice by a circle in red ink:—

An obscure organ was about to expire in its native shade when an
ambitious person of recent date bethought himself of galvanizing
it. His object was to make it a foothold by which to climb from
municipal functions to the coveted position of deputy. Happily
this object, having come to the surface, will end in failure.
Electors will certainly not be inveigled by so wily a manner of
advancing self-interests; and when the proper time arrives, if
ridicule has not already done justice on this absurd candidacy, we
shall ourselves prove to the pretender that to aspire to the
distinguished honor of representing the nation something more is
required than the money to buy a paper and pay an underling to put
into good French the horrible diction of his articles and
pamphlets. We confine ourselves to-day to this limited notice, but
our readers may be sure that we shall keep them informed about
this electoral comedy, if indeed the parties concerned have the
melancholy courage to go on with it.

Thuillier read twice over this sudden declaration of war, which was far from leaving him calm and impassible; then, taking la Peyrade aside, he said to him:—

"Read that; it is serious."

"Well?" said la Peyrade, after reading the article.

"Well? how well?" exclaimed Thuillier.

"I mean, what do you find so serious in that?"

"What do I find so serious?" repeated Thuillier. "I don't think anything could be more insulting to me."

"You can't doubt," said la Peyrade, "that the virtuous Cerizet is at the bottom of it; he has thrown this firecracker between your legs by way of revenge."

"Cerizet, or anybody else who wrote that diatribe is an insolent fellow," cried Thuillier, getting angry, "and the matter shall not rest there."

"For my part," said la Peyrade, "I advise you to make no reply. You are not named; though, of course, the attack is aimed at you. But you ought to let our adversary commit himself farther; when the right moment comes, we'll rap him over the knuckles."

"No!" said Thuillier, "I won't stay quiet one minute under such an insult."

"The devil!" said the barrister; "what a sensitive epidermis! Do reflect, my dear fellow, that you have made yourself a candidate and a journalist, and therefore you really must harden yourself better than that."

"My good friend, it is a principle of mine not to let anybody step on my toes. Besides, they say themselves they are going on with this thing. Therefore, it is absolutely necessary to cut short such impertinence."

"But do consider," said la Peyrade. "Certainly in journalism, as in candidacy, a hot temper has its uses; a man makes himself respected, and stops attacks—"

"Just so," said Thuillier, "'principiis obsta.' Not to-day, because we haven't the time, but to-morrow I shall carry that paper into court."

"Into court!" echoed la Peyrade; "you surely wouldn't go to law in such a matter as this? In the first place, there is nothing to proceed upon; you are not named nor the paper either, and, besides, it is a pitiable business, going to law; you'll look like a boy who has been fighting, and got the worst of it, and runs to complain to his mamma. Now if you had said that you meant to make Fleury intervene in the matter, I could understand that—though the affair is rather personal to you, and it might be difficult to make it seem—"

"Ah ca!" said Thuillier, "do you suppose I am going to commit myself with a Cerizet or any other newspaper bully? I pique myself, my dear fellow, on possessing civic courage, which does not give in to prejudices, and which, instead of taking justice into its own hands, has recourse to the means of defence that are provided by law. Besides, with the legal authority the Court of Cassation now has over duelling, I have no desire to put myself in the way of being expatriated, or spending two or three years in prison."

"Well," said la Peyrade, "we'll talk it over later; here's your sister, and she would think everything lost if this little matter reached her ears."

When Brigitte appeared Colleville shouted "Full!" and proceeded to sing the chorus of "La Parisienne."

"Heavens! Colleville, how vulgar you are!" cried the tardy one, hastening to cast a stone in the other's garden to avoid the throwing of one into hers. "Well, are you all ready?" she added, arranging her mantle before a mirror. "What o'clock is it? it won't do to get there before the time, like provincials."

"Ten minutes to two," said Colleville; "I go by the Tuileries."

"Well, then we are just right," said Brigitte; "it will take about that time to get to the rue Caumartin. Josephine," she cried, going to the door of the salon, "we'll dine at six, therefore be sure you put the turkey to roast at the right time, and mind you don't burn it, as you did the other day. Bless me! who's that?" and with a hasty motion she shut the door, which she had been holding open. "What a nuisance! I hope Henri will have the sense to tell him we are out."

Not at all; Henri came in to say that an old gentleman, with a very genteel air, had asked to be received on urgent business.

"Why didn't you say we were all out?"

"That's what I should have done if mademoiselle had not opened the door of the salon so that the gentleman could see the whole family assembled."

"Oh, yes!" said Brigitte, "you are never in the wrong, are you?"

"What am I to say to him?" asked the man.

"Say," replied Thuillier, "that I am very sorry not to be able to receive him, but I am expected at a notary's office about a marriage contract; but that if he could return two hours hence—"

"I have told him all that," said Henri, "and he answered that that contract was precisely what he had come about, and that his business concerned you more than himself."

"You had better go and see him, Thuillier, and get rid of him in double-quick," said Brigitte; "that's shorter than talking to Henri, who is always an orator."

If la Peyrade had been consulted he might not have joined in that advice, for he had had more than one specimen of the spokes some occult influence was putting into the wheels of his marriage, and the present visit seemed to him ominous.

"Show him into my study," said Thuillier, following his sister's advice; and, opening the door which led from the salon to the study, he went to receive his importunate visitor.

Brigitte immediately applied her eye to the keyhole.

"Goodness!" she exclaimed, "there's my imbecile of a Thuillier offering him a chair! and away in a corner, too, where I can't hear a word they say!"

La Peyrade was walking about the room with an inward agitation covered by an appearance of great indifference. He even went up to the three women, and made a few lover-like speeches to Celeste, who received them with a smiling, happy air in keeping with the role she was playing. As for Colleville, he was killing the time by composing an anagram on the six words of "le journal 'l'Echo de la Bievre,'" for which he had found the following version, little reassuring (as far as it went) for the prospects of that newspaper: "O d'Echo, jarni! la bevue reell"—but as the final "e" was lacking to complete the last word, the work was not altogether as satisfactory as it should have been.

"He's taking snuff!" said Brigitte, her eye still glued to the keyhole; "his gold snuff-box beats Minard's—though, perhaps, it is only silver-gilt," she added, reflectively. "He's doing the talking, and Thuillier is sitting there listening to him like a buzzard. I shall go in and tell them they can't keep ladies waiting that way."

But just as she put her hand on the lock she heard Thuillier's visitor raise his voice, and that made her look through the keyhole again.

"He is standing up; he's going," she said with satisfaction.

But a moment later she saw she had made a mistake; the little old man had only left his chair to walk up and down the room and continue the conversation with greater freedom.

"My gracious! I shall certainly go in," she said, "and tell Thuillier we are going without him, and he can follow us."

So saying, the old maid gave two little sharp and very imperious raps on the door, after which she resolutely entered the study.

La Peyrade, goaded by anxiety, had the bad taste to look through the keyhole himself at what was happening. Instantly he thought he recognized the small old man he had seen under the name of "the commander" on that memorable morning when he had waited for Madame de Godollo. Then he saw Thuillier addressing his sister with impatience and with gestures of authority altogether out of his usual habits of deference and submission.

"It seems," said Brigitte, re-entering the salon, "that Thuillier finds some great interest in that creature's talk, for he ordered me bluntly to leave them, though the little old fellow did say, rather civilly, that they would soon be through. But Jerome added: '*Mind*, you are to wait for me.' Really, since he has taken to making newspapers I don't know him; he has set up an air as if he were leading the world with his wand."

"I am very much afraid he is being entangled by some adventurer," said la Peyrade. "I am pretty sure I saw that old man at Madame de Godollo's the day I went to warn her off the premises; he must be of the same stripe."

"Why didn't you tell me?" cried Brigitte. "I'd have asked him for news of the countess, and let him see we knew what we knew of his Hungarian."

Just then the sound of moving chairs was heard, and Brigitte darted back to the keyhole.

"Yes," she said, "he is really going, and Thuillier is bowing him out respectfully!"

As Thuillier did not immediately return, Colleville had time to go to the window and exclaim at seeing the little old gentleman driving away in an elegant coupe, of which the reader has already heard.

"The deuce!" cried Colleville; "what an ornate livery! If he is an adventurer he is a number one."

At last Thuillier re-entered the room, his face full of care, his manner extremely grave.

"My dear la Peyrade," he said, "you did not tell us that another proposal of marriage had been seriously considered by you."

"Yes, I did; I told you that a very rich heiress had been offered to me, but that my inclinations were here, and that I had not given any encouragement to the affair; consequently, of course, there was no serious engagement."

"Well, I think you do wrong to treat that proposal so lightly."

"What! do you mean to say, in presence of these ladies, that you blame me for remaining faithful to my first desires and our old engagement?"

"My friend, the conversation that I have just had has been a most instructive one to me; and when you know what I know, with other details personal to yourself, which will be confided to you, I think that you will enter into my ideas. One thing is certain; we shall not go to the notary to-day; and as for you, the best thing that you can do is to go, without delay, to Monsieur du Portail."

"That name again! it pursues me like a remorse," exclaimed la Peyrade.

"Yes; go at once; he is awaiting you. It is an indispensable preliminary before we can go any farther. When you have seen that excellent man and heard what he has to say to you—well, *then* if you persist in claiming Celeste's hand, we might perhaps carry out our plans. Until then we shall take no steps in the matter."

"But, my poor Thuillier," said Brigitte, "you have let yourself be gammoned by a rascal; that man belongs to the Godollo set."

"Madame de Godollo," replied Thuillier, "is not at all what you suppose her to be, and the best thing this house can do is never to say one word about her, either good or evil. As for la Peyrade, as this is not the first time he has been requested to go and see Monsieur du Portail, I am surprised that he hesitates to do so."

"Ah ca!" said Brigitte, "that little old man has completely befooled you."

"I tell you that that little old man is all that he appears to be. He wears seven crosses, he drives in a splendid equipage, and he has told me things that have overwhelmed me with astonishment."

"Well, perhaps he's a fortune-teller like Madame Fontaine, who managed once upon a time to upset me when Madame Minard and I, just to amuse ourselves, went to consult her."

"Well, if he is not a sorcerer he certainly has a very long arm," said Thuillier, "and I think a man would suffer for it if he didn't respect his advice. As for you, Brigitte, he saw you only for a minute, but he told me your whole character; he said you were a masterful woman, born to command."

"The fact is," said Brigitte, licking her chops at this compliment, like a cat drinking cream, "he has a very well-bred air, that little old fellow. You take my advice, my dear," she said, turning to la Peyrade; "if such a very big-wig as that wants you to do so, go and see this du Portail, whoever he is. That, it seems to me, won't bind you to anything."

"You are right, Brigitte," said Colleville; "as for me, I'd follow up all the Portails, or Porters, or Portents for the matter of that, if they asked me to."

The scene was beginning to resemble that in the "Barber of Seville," where everybody tells Basil to go to bed, for he certainly has a fever. La Peyrade, thus prodded, picked up his hat in some ill-humor, and went where his destiny called him,—"quo sua fata vocabant."

CHAPTER XV. AT DU PORTAIL'S

On reaching the rue Honore-Chevalier la Peyrade felt a doubt; the dilapidated appearance of the house to which he was summoned made him think he had mistaken the number. It seemed to him that a person of Monsieur du Portail's evident importance could not inhabit such a place. It was therefore with some hesitation that he accosted Sieur Perrache, the porter. But no sooner had he entered the antechamber of the apartment pointed out to him than the excellent deportment of Bruneau, the old valet, and the extremely comfortable appearance of the furniture and other appointments made him see that he was probably in the right place. Introduced at once, as soon as he had given his name, into the study of the master of the house, his surprise was great when he found himself in presence of the commander, so called, the friend of Madame de Godollo, and the little old man he had seen half an hour earlier with Thuillier.

"At last!" said du Portail, rising, and offering la Peyrade a chair, "at last we meet, my refractory friend; it has taken a good deal to bring you here."

"May I know, monsieur," said la Peyrade, haughtily, not taking the chair which was offered to him, "what interest you have in meddling with my affairs? I do not know you, and I may add that the place where I once saw you did not create an unconquerable desire in me to make your acquaintance."

"Where have you seen me?" asked du Portail.

"In the apartment of a strumpet who called herself Madame de Godollo."

"Where monsieur, consequently, went himself," said the little old man, "and for a purpose much less disinterested than mine."

"I have not come here," said la Peyrade, "to bandy words with any one. I have the right, monsieur, to a full explanation as to the meaning of your proceedings towards me. I therefore request you not to delay them by a facetiousness to which, I assure you, I am not in the humor to listen."

"Then, my dear fellow," said du Portail, "sit down, for I am not in the humor to twist my neck by talking up at you."

The words were reasonable, and they were said in a tone that showed the old gentleman was not likely to be frightened by grand airs. La Peyrade therefore deferred to the wishes of his host, but he took care to do so with the worst grace possible.

"Monsieur Cerizet," said du Portail, "a man of excellent standing in the world, and who has the honor to be one of your friends—"

"I have nothing to do with that man now," said la Peyrade, sharply, understanding the malicious meaning of the old man's speech.

"Well, the time has been," said du Portail, "when you saw him, at least, occasionally: for instance, when you paid for his dinner at the Rocher de Cancale. As I was saying, I charged the virtuous Monsieur Cerizet to sound you as to a marriage—"

"Which I refused," interrupted la Peyrade, "and which I now refuse again, more vehemently than ever."

"That's the question," said the old man. "I think, on the contrary, that you will accept it; and it is to talk over this affair with you that I have so long desired a meeting."

"But this crazy girl that you are flinging at my head," said la Peyrade, "what is she to you? She can't be your daughter, or you would put more decency into your hunt for a husband."

"This young girl," replied du Portail, "is the daughter of one of my friends who died about ten years ago; at his death I took her to live with me, and have given her all the care her sad condition needed. Her fortune, which I have greatly increased, added to my own, which I intend to leave to her, will make her a very rich heiress. I know that you are no enemy to handsome 'dots,' for you have sought them in various places,—Thuillier's house, for instance, or, to use your own expression, that of a strumpet whom you scarcely knew. I have therefore supposed you would accept at my hands a very rich young woman, especially as her infirmity is declared by the best physicians to be curable; whereas you can never cure Monsieur and Mademoiselle Thuillier, the one of being a fool, the other of being a fury, any more than you could cure Madame Komorn of being a woman of very medium virtue and extremely giddy."

"It may suit me," replied la Peyrade, "to marry the daughter of a fool and a fury if I choose her, or I might become the husband of a clever coquette, if passion seized me, but the Queen of Sheba herself, if imposed upon me, neither you, monsieur, nor the ablest and most powerful man living could force me to accept."

"Precisely; therefore it is to your own good sense and intelligence that I now address myself; but we have to come face to face with people in order to speak to them, you know. Now, then, let us look into your present situation, and don't get angry if, like a surgeon who wants to cure his patient, I lay my hand mercilessly on wounds which have long tormented and harassed you.

The first point to state is that the Celeste Colleville affair is at an end for you."

"Why so?" demanded la Peyrade.

"Because I have just seen Thuillier and terrified him with the history of the misfortunes he has incurred, and those he will incur if he persists in the idea of giving you his goddaughter in marriage. He knows now that it was I who paralyzed Madame du Bruel's kind offices in the matter of the cross; that I had his pamphlet seized; that I sent that Hungarian woman into his house to handle you all, as she did; and that my hand is opening fire in the ministerial journals, which will only increase from bad to worse,—not to speak of other machinations which will be directed against his candidacy. Therefore you see, my good friend, that not only have you no longer the credit in Thuillier's eyes of being his great helper to that election, but that you actually block the way to his ambition. That is enough to prove to you that the side by which you have imposed yourself on that family—who have never sincerely liked or desired you—is now completely battered down and dismantled."

"But to have done all that which you claim with such pretension, who are you?" demanded la Peyrade.

"I shall not say that you are very inquisitive, for I intend to answer your question later; but for the present let us continue, if you please, the autopsy of your existence, dead to-day, but which I propose to resuscitate gloriously. You are twenty-eight years old, and you have begun a career in which I shall not allow you to make another step. A few days hence the Council of the order of barristers will assemble and will censure, more or less severely, your conduct in the matter of the property you placed with such candor in Thuillier's hands. Do not deceive yourself; censure from that quarter (and I mention only your least danger) is as fatal to a barrister as being actually disbarred."

"And it is to your kind offices, no doubt," said la Peyrade, "that I shall owe that precious result?"

"Yes, I may boast of it," replied du Portail, "for, in order to tow you into port it has been necessary to strip you of your rigging; unless that were done, you would always have tried to navigate under your own sails the bourgeois shoals that you are now among."

Seeing that he, undoubtedly, had to do with a strong hand, la Peyrade thought best to modify his tone; and so, with a more circumspect air, he said:
—

"You will allow me, monsieur, to reserve my acknowledgments until I receive some fuller explanation."

"Here you are, then," continued du Portail, "at twenty-eight years of age, without a penny, virtually without a profession; with antecedents that are very —middling; with associates like Monsieur Dutocq and the courageous Cerizet; owing to Mademoiselle Thuillier ten thousand francs, and to Madame Lambert twenty-five thousand, which you are no doubt extremely desirous to return to her; and finally, this marriage, your last hope, your sheet-anchor, has just become an utter impossibility. Between ourselves, if I have something reasonable to propose to you, do you not think that you had much better place yourself at my disposal?"

"I have time enough to prove that your opinion is mistaken," returned la Peyrade; "and I shall not form any resolutions so long as the designs you choose to have upon me are not more fully explained."

"You were spoken to, at my instigation, about a marriage," resumed du Portail. "This marriage, as I think, is closely connected with a past existence from which a certain hereditary or family duty has devolved upon you. Do you know what that uncle of yours, to whom you applied in 1829, was doing in Paris? In your family he was thought to be a millionaire; and, dying suddenly, you remember, before you got to him, he did not leave enough for his burial; a pauper's grave was all that remained to him."

"Did you know him?" asked la Peyrade.

"He was my oldest and dearest friend," replied du Portail.

"If that is so," said la Peyrade, hastily, "a sum of two thousand francs, which I received on my arrival in Paris from some unknown source—"

"Came from me," replied du Portail. "Unfortunately, engaged at the time in a rush of important affairs, which you shall hear of later, I could not immediately follow up the benevolent interest I felt in you for your uncle's sake; this explains why I left you in the straw of a garret, where you came, like a medlar, to that maturity of ruin which brought you under the hand of a Dutocq and a Cerizet."

"I am none the less grateful to you, monsieur," said la Peyrade; "and if I had known you were that generous protector, whom I was never able to discover, I should have been the first to seek occasion to meet you and to thank you."

"A truce to compliments," said du Portail; "and, to come at once to the serious side of our present conference, what should you say if I told you that this uncle, whose protection and assistance you came to Paris to obtain, was an agent of that occult power which has always been the theme of feeble ridicule and the object of silly prejudice?"

411

"I do not seize your meaning," said la Peyrade, with uneasy curiosity; "may I ask you to be more precise?"

"For example, I will suppose," continued du Portail, "that your uncle, if still living, were to say to you to-day: 'You are seeking fortune and influence, my good nephew; you want to rise above the crowd and to play your part in all the great events of your time; you want employment for a keen, active mind, full of resources, and slightly inclined to intrigue; in short, you long to exert in some upper and elegant sphere that force of will and subtlety which at present you are wasting in the silly and useless manipulation of the most barren and tough-skinned animal on earth, to wit: a bourgeois. Well, then, lower your head, my fine nephew; enter with me through the little door which I will open to you; it gives admittance to a great house, often maligned, but better far than its reputation. That threshold once crossed, you can rise to the height of your natural genius, whatever its spark may be. Statesmen, kings even, will admit you to their most secret thoughts; you will be their occult collaborator, and none of the joys which money and the highest powers can bestow upon a man will be lacking to you."

"But, monsieur," objected la Peyrade, "without venturing to understand you, I must remark that my uncle died so poor, you tell me, that public charity buried him."

"Your uncle," replied du Portail, "was a man of rare talent, but he had a certain weak side in his nature which compromised his career. He was eager for pleasure, a spendthrift, thoughtless for the future; he wanted also to taste those joys that are meant for the common run of men, but which for great, exceptional vocations are the worst of snares and impediments: I mean the joys of family. He had a daughter whom he madly loved, and it was through her that his terrible enemies opened a breach in his life, and prepared the horrible catastrophe that ended it."

"Is that an encouragement to enter this shady path, where, you say, he might have asked me to follow him?"

"But if I myself," said du Portail, "should offer to guide you in it, what then?"

"You, monsieur!" said la Peyrade, in stupefaction.

"Yes, I—I who was your uncle's pupil at first, and later his protector and providence; I, whose influence the last half-century has daily increased; I, who am wealthy; I, to whom all governments, as they fall one on top of the others like houses of cards, come to ask for safety and for the power to rebuild their future; I, who am the manager of a great theatre of puppets (where I have Columbines in the style of Madame de Godollo); I, who to-

412

morrow, if it were necessary to the success of one of my vaudevilles or one of my dramas, might present myself to your eyes as the wearer of the grand cordon of the Legion of honor, of the Order of the Black Eagle, or that of the Golden Fleece. Do you wish to know why neither you nor I will die a violent death like your uncle, and also why, more fortunate than contemporaneous kings, I can transmit my sceptre to the successor whom I myself may choose? Because, like you, my young friend, in spite of your Southern appearance, I was cold, profoundly calculating, never tempted to lose my time on trifles at the outskirts; because heat, when I was led by force of circumstances to employ it, never went below the surface. It is more than probable that you have heard of me; well, for you I will open a window in my cloud; look at me, observe me well; have I a cloven hoof, or a tail at the end of my spine? On the contrary, am I not a model of the most inoffensive of householders in the Saint-Sulpice quarter? In that quarter, where I have enjoyed, I may say it, universal esteem for the last twenty-five years, I am called du Portail; but to you, if you will allow me, I shall now name myself *Corentin*."

"Corentin!" cried la Peyrade, with terrified astonishment.

"Yes, monsieur; and you see that in telling you that secret I lay my hand upon you, and enlist you. Corentin! 'the greatest man of the police in modern times,' as the author of an article in the 'Biographies of Living Men' has said of me—as to whom I ought in justice to remark that he doesn't know a thing about my life."

"Monsieur," said la Peyrade, "I can assure you that I shall keep that secret; but the place which you offer me near you—in your employ—"

"That frightens you, or, at least, it makes you uneasy," said Corentin, quickly. "Before you have even considered the thing the word scares you, does it? The police! *Police*! you are afraid to encounter the terrible prejudice that brands it on the brow."

"Certainly," said la Peyrade, "it is a necessary institution; but I do not think that it is always calumniated. If the business of those who manage it is honorable why do they conceal themselves so carefully?"

"Because all that threatens society, which it is the mission of the police to repress," replied Corentin, "is plotted and prepared in hiding. Do thieves and conspirators put upon their hats, 'I am Guillot, the shepherd of this flock'? And when we are after them must we ring a bell to let them know we are coming?"

"Monsieur," said la Peyrade, "when a sentiment is universal it ceases to be a prejudice, it becomes an opinion; and this opinion ought to be a law to every man who desires to keep his own esteem and that of others."

"And when you robbed that notary to enrich the Thuilliers for your own advantage," said Corentin, "did you keep your own esteem and that of the Council of barristers? And who knows, monsieur, if in your life there are not still blacker actions than that? I am a more honorable man than you, because, outside of my functions, I have not one doubtful act upon my conscience; and when the opportunity for *good* has been presented to me I have done it— always and everywhere. Do you think that the guardianship of that poor insane girl in my home has been all roses? But she was the daughter of my old friend, your uncle, and when, feeling the years creep on me, I propose to you, between sacks of money, to fit yourself to take my place—"

"What!" cried la Peyrade, "is that girl my uncle's daughter?"

"Yes; the girl I wish you to marry is the daughter of your uncle Peyrade,— for he democratized his name,—or, if you like it better, she was the daughter of Pere Canquoelle, a name he took from the little estate on which your father lived and starved with eleven children. You see, in spite of the secrecy your uncle always kept about his family, that I know all about it. Do you suppose that before selecting you as your cousin's husband I had not obtained every possible information about you? And what I have learned need not make you quite so supercilious to the police. Besides, as the vulgar saying is, the best of your nose is made of it. Your uncle belonged to the police, and, thanks to that, he became the confidant, I might almost say the friend, of Louis XVIII., who took the greatest pleasure in his companionship. And you, by nature and by mind, also by the foolish position into which you have got yourself, in short, by your whole being, have gravitated steadily to the conclusion I propose to you, namely, that of succeeding me,—of succeeding Corentin. That is the question between us, Monsieur. Do you really believe now that I have not a grasp or a 'seizin,' as you call it, upon you, and that you can manage to escape me for any foolish considerations of bourgeois vanity?"

La Peyrade could not have been at heart so violently opposed to this proposal as he seemed, for the vigorous language of the great master of the police and the species of appropriation which he made of his person brought a smile to the young man's lips.

Corentin had risen, and was walking up and down the room, speaking, apparently, to himself.

"The police!" he cried; "one may say of it, as Basile said of calumny to Batholo, 'The police, monsieur! you don't know what you despise!' And, after all," he continued, after a pause, "who are they who despise it? Imbeciles, who don't know any better than to insult their protectors. Suppress the police, and you destroy civilization. Do the police ask for the respect of such people? No, they want to inspire them with one sentiment only: fear, that great lever with which to govern mankind,—an impure race whose odious instincts God, hell, the executioner, and the gendarmes can scarcely restrain!"

Stopping short before la Peyrade, and looking at him with a disdainful smile, he continued:—

"So you are one of those ninnies who see in the police nothing more than a horde of spies and informers? Have you never suspected the statesmen, the diplomats, the Richelieus it produces? Mercury, monsieur,—Mercury, the cleverest of the gods of paganism,—what was he but the police incarnate? It is true that he was also the god of thieves. We are better than he, for we don't allow that junction of forces."

"And yet," said la Peyrade, "Vautrin, or, I should say, Jacques Collin, the famous chief of the detective police—"

"Yes, yes! but that's in the lower ranks," replied Corentin, resuming his walk; "there's always a muddy place somewhere. Still, don't be mistaken even in that. Vautrin is a man of genius, but his passions, like those of your uncle, dragged him down. But go up higher (for there lies the whole question, namely, the rung of the ladder on which a man has wits enough to perch). Take the prefect, for instance, that honored minister, flattered and respected, is he a spy? Well, I, monsieur, am the prefect of the secret police of diplomacy —of the highest statesmanship. And you hesitate to mount that throne!—to seem small and do great things; to live in a cave comfortably arranged like this, and command the light; to have at your orders an invisible army, always ready, always devoted, always submissive; to know the *other side* of everything; to be duped by no intrigue because you hold the threads of all within your fingers; to see through all partitions; to penetrate all secrets, search all hearts, all consciences,—these are the things you fear! And yet you were not afraid to go and wallow in a Thuillier bog; you, a thoroughbred, allowed yourself to be harnessed to a hackney-coach, to the ignoble business of electing that parvenu bourgeois."

"A man does what he can," said la Peyrade.

"Here's a very remarkable thing," pursued Corentin, replying to his own thought; "the French language, more just than public opinion, has given us our right place, for it has made the word police the synonym of civilization and the antipodes of savage life, when it said and wrote: 'l'Etat police,' from the Greek words state and city. So, I can assure you, we care little for the prejudice that tries to brand us; none know men as we do; and to know them brings contempt for their contempt as well as for their esteem."

"There is certainly much truth in what you say with such warmth," said la Peyrade, finally.

"Much truth!" exclaimed Corentin, going back to his chair, "say, rather, that it is all true, and nothing but the truth; yet it is not the whole truth. But enough for to-day, monsieur. To succeed me in my functions, and to marry your cousin with a 'dot' that will not be less than five hundred thousand francs, that is my offer. I do not ask you for an answer now. I should have no confidence in a determination not seriously reflected upon. To-morrow, I shall be at home all the morning. I trust that my conviction may then have formed yours."

Dismissing his visitor with a curt little bow, he added: "I do not bid you adieu, but au revoir, Monsieur de la Peyrade."

Whereupon Corentin went to a side-table, where he found all that he needed to prepare a glass of "eau sucree," which he had certainly earned, and, without looking at la Peyrade, who left the room rather stunned, he seemed to have no other interest on his mind than that prosaic preparation.

Was it, indeed, necessary that the morning after this meeting with Corentin a visit from Madame Lambert, now become an exacting and importunate creditor, should come to bear its weight on la Peyrade's determination? As the great chief had pointed out to him the night before, was there not in his nature, in his mind, in his aspirations, in the mistakes and imprudences of his past life, a sort of irresistible incline which drew him down toward the strange solution of existence thus suddenly offered to him?

Fatality, if we may so call it, was lavish of the inducements to which he was destined to succumb. This day was the 31st of October; the vacation of the Palais was just over. The 2nd of November was the day on which the courts reopened, and as Madame Lambert left his room he received a summons to appear on that day before the Council of his order.

To Madame Lambert, who pressed him sharply to repay her, under pretence that she was about to leave Monsieur Picot and return to her native place, he replied: "Come here the day after to-morrow, at the same hour, and your money will be ready for you."

To the summons to give account of his actions to his peers he replied that he did not recognize the right of the Council to question him on the facts of his private life. That was an answer of one sort, certainly. Inevitably it would result in his being stricken from the roll of the barristers of the Royal courts; but, at least, it had an air of dignity and protestation which saved, in a measure, his self-love.

Finally, he wrote a letter to Thuillier, in which he said that his visit to du Portail had resulted in his being obliged to accept another marriage. He therefore returned to Thuillier his promise, and took back his own. All this was curtly said, without the slightest expression of regret for the marriage he renounced. In a postscript he added: "We shall be obliged to discuss my position on the newspaper,"—indicating that it might enter into his plans not to retain it.

He was careful to make a copy of this letter, and an hour later, when, in Corentin's study, he was questioned as to the result of his night's reflections, he gave that great general, for all answer, the matrimonial resignation he had just despatched.

"That will do," said Corentin. "But as for your position on the newspaper, you may perhaps have to keep it for a time. The candidacy of that fool interferes with the plans of the government, and we must manage in some way to trip up the heels of the municipal councillor. In your position as editor-in-chief you may find a chance to do it, and I think your conscience won't kick at the mission."

"No, indeed!" said la Peyrade, "the thought of the humiliations to which I have been so long subjected will make it a precious joy to lash that bourgeois brood."

"Take care!" said Corentin; "you are young, and you must watch against those revengeful emotions. In our austere profession we love nothing and we hate nothing. Men are to us mere pawns of wood or ivory, according to their quality—with which we play our game. We are like the blade that cuts what is given it to cut, but, careful only to be delicately sharpened, wishes neither harm nor good to any one. Now let us speak of your cousin, to whom, I suppose, you have some curiosity to be presented."

La Peyrade was not obliged to pretend to eagerness, that which he felt was genuine.

"Lydie de la Peyrade," said Corentin, "is nearly thirty, but her innocence, joined to a gentle form of insanity, has kept her apart from all those passions, ideas, and impressions which use up life, and has, if I may say so, embalmed her in a sort of eternal youth. You would not think her more than twenty. She is fair and slender; her face, which is very delicate, is especially remarkable for an expression of angelic sweetness. Deprived of her full reason by a terrible catastrophe, her monomania has something touching about it. She always carries in her arms or keeps beside her a bundle of linen which she nurses and cares for as though it were a sick child; and, excepting Bruneau and myself, whom she recognizes, she thinks all other men are doctors, whom she consults about the child, and to whom she listens as oracles. A crisis which lately happened in her malady has convinced Horace Bianchon, that prince of science, that if the reality could be substituted for this long delusion

417

of motherhood, her reason would assert itself. It is surely a worthy task to bring back light to a soul in which it is scarcely veiled; and the existing bond of relationship has seemed to me to point you out as specially designated to effect this cure, the success of which Bianchon and two other eminent doctors who have consulted with him declare to be beyond a doubt. Now, I will take you to Lydie's presence; remember to play the part of doctor; for the only thing that makes her lose her customary serenity is not to enter into her notion of medical consultation."

After crossing several rooms Corentin was on the point of taking la Peyrade into that usually occupied by Lydie when employed in cradling or dandling her imaginary child, when suddenly they were stopped by the sound of two or three chords struck by the hand of a master on a piano of the finest sonority.

"What is that?" asked la Peyrade.

"That is Lydie," replied Corentin, with what might be called an expression of paternal pride; "she is an admirable musician, and though she no longer writes down, as in the days when her mind was clear, her delightful melodies, she often improvises them in a way that moves me to the soul—the soul of Corentin!" added the old man, smiling. "Is not that the finest praise I can bestow upon her? But suppose we sit down here and listen to her. If we go in, the concert will cease and the medical consultation begin."

La Peyrade was amazed as he listened to an improvisation in which the rare union of inspiration and science opened to his impressionable nature a source of emotions as deep as they were unexpected. Corentin watched the surprise which from moment to moment the Provencal expressed by admiring exclamations.

"Hein! how she plays!" said the old man. "Liszt himself hasn't a firmer touch."

To a very quick "scherzo" the performer now added the first notes of an "adagio."

"She is going to sing," said Corentin, recognizing the air.

"Does she sing too?" asked la Peyrade.

"Like Pasta, like Malibran; but hush, listen to her!"

After a few opening bars in "arpeggio" a vibrant voice resounded, the tones of which appeared to stir the Provencal to the depths of his being.

"How the music moves you!" said Corentin; "you were undoubtedly made for each other."

"My God! the same air! the same voice!"

"Have you already met Lydie somewhere?" asked the great master of the police.

"I don't know—I think not," answered la Peyrade, in a stammering voice; "in any case, it was long ago—But that air—that voice—I think—"

"Let us go in," said Corentin.

Opening the door abruptly, he entered, pulling the young man after him.

Sitting with her back to the door, and prevented by the sound of the piano from hearing what happened behind her, Lydie did not notice their entrance.

"Now have you any remembrance of her?" said Corentin.

La Peyrade advanced a step, and no sooner had he caught a glimpse of the girl's profile than he threw up his hands above his head, striking them together.

"It is she!" he cried.

Hearing his cry, Lydie turned round, and fixing her attention on Corentin, she said:—

"How naughty and troublesome you are to come and disturb me; you know very well I don't like to be listened to. Ah! but—" she added, catching sight of la Peyrade's black coat, "you have brought the doctor; that is very kind of you; I was just going to ask you to send for him. The baby has done nothing but cry since morning; I was singing to put her to sleep, but nothing can do that."

And she ran to fetch what she called her child from a corner of the room, where with two chairs laid on their backs and the cushions of the sofa, she had constructed a sort of cradle.

As she went towards la Peyrade, carrying her precious bundle with one hand, with the other she was arranging the imaginary cap of her "little darling," having no eyes except for the sad creation of her disordered brain. Step by step, as she advanced, la Peyrade, pale, trembling, and with staring eyes, retreated backwards, until he struck against a seat, into which, losing his equilibrium, he fell.

A man of Corentin's power and experience, and who, moreover, knew to its slightest detail the horrible drama in which Lydie had lost her reason, had already, of course, taken in the situation, but it suited his purpose and his ideas to allow the clear light of evidence to pierce this darkness.

"Look, doctor," said Lydie, unfastening the bundle, and putting the pins in

419

her mouth as she did so, "don't you see that she is growing thinner every day?"

La Peyrade could not answer; he kept his handkerchief over his face, and his breath came so fast from his chest that he was totally unable to utter a word.

Then, with one of those gestures of feverish impatience, to which her mental state predisposed her, she exclaimed, hastily:—

"But look at her doctor, look!" taking his arm violently and forcing him to show his features. "My God!" she cried, when she had looked him in the face.

Letting fall the linen bundle in her arms, she threw herself hastily backwards, and her eyes grew haggard. Passing her white hands rapidly over her forehead and through her hair, tossing it into disorder, she seemed to be making an effort to obtain from her memory some dormant recollection. Then, like a frightened mare, which comes to smell an object that has given it a momentary terror, she approached la Peyrade slowly, stooping to look into his face, which he kept lowered, while, in the midst of a silence inexpressible, she examined him steadily for several seconds. Suddenly a terrible cry escaped her breast; she ran for refuge into the arms of Corentin, and pressing herself against him with all her force, she exclaimed:—

"Save me! save me! It is he! the wretch! It is he who did it!"

And, with her finger pointed at la Peyrade, she seemed to nail the miserable object of her terror to his place.

After this explosion, she muttered a few disconnected words, and her eyes closed; Corentin felt the relaxing of all the muscles by which she had held him as in a vice the moment before, and he took her in his arms and laid her on the sofa, insensible.

"Do not stay here, monsieur," said Corentin. "Go into my study; I will come to you presently."

A few minutes later, after giving Lydie into the care of Katte and Bruneau, and despatching Perrache for Doctor Bianchon, Corentin rejoined la Peyrade.

"You see now, monsieur," he said with solemnity, "that in pursuing with a sort of passion the idea of this marriage, I was following, in a sense, the ways of God."

"Monsieur," said la Peyrade, with compunction, "I will confess to you—"

"Useless," said Corentin; "you can tell me nothing that I do not know; I, on the contrary, have much to tell you. Old Peyrade, your uncle, in the hope of earning a POT for this daughter whom he idolized, entered into a dangerous private enterprise, the nature of which I need not explain. In it he made enemies; enemies who stopped at nothing,—murder, poison, rape. To paralyze your uncle's action by attacking him in his dearest spot, Lydie was, not abducted, but enticed from her home and taken to a house apparently respectable, where for ten days she was kept concealed. She was not much alarmed by this detention, being told that it was done at her father's wish, and she spent her time with her music—you remember, monsieur, how she sang?"

"Oh!" exclaimed la Peyrade, covering his face with his hands.

"I told you yesterday that you might perhaps have more upon your conscience than the Thuillier house. But you were young; you had just come from your province, with that brutality, that frenzy of Southern blood in your veins which flings itself upon such an occasion. Besides, your relationship became known to those who were preparing the ruin of this new Clarissa Harlowe, and I am willing to believe than an abler and better man than you might not have escaped the entanglement into which you fell. Happily, Providence has granted that there is nothing absolutely irreparable in this horrible history. The same poison, according to the use that is made of it, may give either death or health."

"But, monsieur," said la Peyrade, "shall I not always be to her an object of horror?"

"The doctor, monsieur," said Katte, opening the door.

"How is Mademoiselle Lydie?" asked la Peyrade, eagerly.

"Very calm," replied Katte. "Just now, when we put her to bed,—though she did not want to go, saying she felt well,—I took her the bundle of linen, but she told me to take it away, and asked what I meant her to do with it."

"You see," said Corentin, grasping the Provencal's hand, "you are the lance of Achilles."

And he left the room with Katte to receive Doctor Bianchon.

Left alone, Theodose was a prey to thoughts which may perhaps be imagined. After a while the door opened, and Bruneau, the old valet, ushered in Cerizet. Seeing la Peyrade, the latter exclaimed:—

"Ha! ha! I knew it! I knew you would end by seeing du Portail. And the marriage,—how does that come on?"

"What are you doing here?" asked la Peyrade.

"Something that concerns you; or rather, something that we must do together. Du Portail, who is too busy to attend to business just now, has sent me in here to see you, and consult as to the best means of putting a spoke in

Thuillier's election; it seems that the government is determined to prevent his winning it. Have you any ideas about it?"

"No," replied la Peyrade; "and I don't feel in the mood just now to be imaginative."

"Well, here's the situation," said Cerizet. "The government has another candidate, which it doesn't yet produce, because the ministerial negotiations with him have been rather difficult. During this time Thuillier's chances have been making headway. Minard, on whom they counted to create a diversion, sits, the stupid fool, in his corner; the seizure of that pamphlet has given your blockhead of a protege a certain perfume of popularity. In short, the ministry are afraid he'll be elected, and nothing could be more disagreeable to them. Pompous imbeciles, like Thuillier, are horribly embarrassing in the Opposition; they are pitchers without handles; you can't take hold of them anywhere."

"Monsieur Cerizet," said la Peyrade, beginning to assume a protecting tone, and wishing to discover his late associate's place in Corentin's confidence, "you seem to know a good deal about the secret intentions of the government; have you found your way to a certain desk in the rue de Grenelle?"

"No. All that I tell you," said Cerizet, "I get from du Portail."

"Ah ca!" said la Peyrade, lowering his voice, "who *is* du Portail? You seem to have known him for some time. A man of your force ought to have discovered the real character of a man who seems to me to be rather mysterious."

"My friend," replied Cerizet, "du Portail is a pretty strong man. He's an old slyboots, who has had some post, I fancy, in the administration of the national domain, or something of that kind, under government; in which, I think, he must have been employed in the departments suppressed under the Empire."

"Yes?" said la Peyrade.

"That's where I think he made his money," continued Cerizet; "and being a shrewd old fellow, and having a natural daughter to marry, he has concocted this philanthropic tale of her being the daughter of an old friend named Peyrade; and your name being the same may have given him the idea of fastening upon you—for, after all, he has to marry her to somebody."

"Yes, that's all very well; but his close relations with the government, and the interest he takes in elections, how do you explain all that?"

"Naturally enough," replied Cerizet. "Du Portail is a man who loves money, and likes to handle it; he has done Rastignac, that great manipulator of elections, who is, I think, his compatriot, several signal services as an amateur; Rastignac, in return, gives him information, obtained through Nucingen, which enables him to gamble at the Bourse."

"Did he himself tell you all this?" asked la Peyrade.

"What do you take me for?" returned Cerizet. "With that worthy old fellow, from whom I have already wormed a promise of thirty thousand francs, I play the ninny; I flatten myself to nothing. But I've made Bruneau talk, that old valet of his. You can safely ally yourself to his family, my dear fellow; du Portail is powerfully rich; he'll get you made sub-prefect somewhere; and thence to a prefecture and a fortune is but one step."

"Thanks for the information," said la Peyrade; "at least, I shall know on which foot to hop. But you yourself, how came you to know him?"

"Oh! that's quite a history; by my help he was able to get back a lot of diamonds which had been stolen from him."

At this moment Corentin entered the room.

"All is well," he said to la Peyrade. "There are signs of returning reason. Bianchon, to whom I have told all, wishes to confer with you; therefore, my dear Monsieur Cerizet, we will postpone until this evening, if you are willing, our little study over the Thuillier election."

"Well, so here you have him, at last!" said Cerizet, slapping la Peyrade's shoulder.

"Yes," said Corentin, "and you know what I promised; you may rely on that."

Cerizet departed joyful.

CHAPTER XVI. CHECKMATE TO THUILLIER

The day after that evening, when Corentin, la Peyrade, and Cerizet were to have had their consultation in reference to the attack on Thuillier's candidacy, the latter was discussing with his sister Brigitte the letter in which Theodose declined the hand of Celeste, and his mind seemed particularly to dwell on the postscript where it was intimated that la Peyrade might not continue the editor of the "Echo de la Bievre." At this moment Henri, the "male domestic," entered the room to ask if his master would receive Monsieur Cerizet.

Thuillier's first impulse was to deny himself to that unwelcome visitor. Then, thinking better of it, he reflected that if la Peyrade suddenly left him in the lurch, Cerizet might possibly prove a precious resource. Consequently, he ordered Henri to show him in. His manner, however, was extremely cold, and in some sort expectant. As for Cerizet, he presented himself without the slightest embarrassment and with the air of a man who had calculated all the consequences of the step he was taking.

"Well, my dear monsieur," he began, "I suppose by this time you have been posted as to the Sieur la Peyrade."

"What may you mean by that?" said Thuillier, stiffly.

"Well, the man," replied Cerizet, "who, after intriguing to marry your goddaughter, breaks off the marriage abruptly—as he will, before long, break that lion's-share contract he made you sign about his editorship—can't be, I should suppose, the object of the same blind confidence you formerly reposed in him."

"Ah!" said Thuillier, hastily, "then do you know anything about la Peyrade's intention of leaving the newspaper?"

"No," said the other; "on the terms I now am with him, you can readily believe we don't see each other; still less should I receive his confidences. But I draw the induction from the well-known character of the person, and you may be sure that when he finds it for his interest to leave you, he'll throw you away like an old coat—I've passed that way, and I speak from experience."

"Then you must have had some difficulties with him before you joined my paper?" said Thuillier, interrogatively.

"Parbleu!" replied Cerizet; "the affair of this house which he helped you to buy was mine; I started that hare. He was to put me in relation with you, and make me the principal tenant of the house. But the unfortunate affair of that bidding-in gave him a chance to knock me out of everything and get all the profits for himself."

"Profits!" exclaimed Thuillier. "I don't see that he got anything out of that transaction, except the marriage which he now refuses—"

"But," interrupted Cerizet, "there's the ten thousand francs he got out of you on pretence of the cross which you never received, and the twenty-five thousand he owes to Madame Lambert, for which you went security, and which you will soon have to pay like a good fellow."

"What's this I hear?" cried Brigitte, up in arms; "twenty-five thousand francs for which you have given security?"

"Yes, mademoiselle," interposed Cerizet; "behind that sum which this woman had lent him there was a mystery, and if I had not laid my hand on the true explanation, there would certainly have been a very dirty ending to it. La Peyrade was clever enough not only to whitewash himself in Monsieur Thuillier's eyes, but to get him to secure the debt."

"But," said Thuillier, "how do you know that I did give security for that debt, if you have not seen him since then?"

"I know it from the woman herself, who tells the whole story now she is certain of being paid."

"Well," said Brigitte to her brother, "a pretty business you are engaged in!"

"Mademoiselle," said Cerizet, "I only meant to warn Monsieur Thuillier a little. I think myself that you are sure to be paid. Without knowing the exact particulars of this new marriage, I am certain the family would never allow him to owe you to such mortifying debts; if necessary, I should be very glad to intervene."

"Monsieur," said Thuillier, stiffly, "thanking you for your officious intervention, permit me to say that it surprises me a little, for the manner in which we parted would not have allowed me to hope it."

"Ah ca!" said Cerizet; "you don't think I was angry with you for that, do you? I pitied you, that was all. I saw you under the spell, and I said to myself: 'Leave him to learn la Peyrade by experience.' I knew very well that the day of justice would dawn for me, and before long, too. La Peyrade is a man who doesn't make you wait for his questionable proceedings."

"Allow me to say," remarked Thuillier, "that I do not consider the rupture of the marriage we had proposed a questionable proceeding. The matter was arranged, I may say, by mutual consent."

"And the trick he is going to play you by leaving the paper in the lurch, and the debt he has saddled you with, what are they?"

"Monsieur Cerizet," continued Thuillier, still holding himself on the reserve, "as I have said more than once to la Peyrade, no man is indispensable; and if the editorship of my paper becomes vacant, I feel confident that I shall at once meet with persons very eager to offer me their services."

"Is it for me you say that?" asked Cerizet. "Well, you haven't hit the nail; if you did me the honor to want my services it would be impossible for me to grant them. I have long been disgusted with journalism. I let la Peyrade, I hardly know why, persuade me to make this campaign with you; it didn't turn out happily, and I have vowed to myself to have no more to do with newspapers. It was about another matter altogether than I came to speak to you."

"Ah!" said Thuillier.

"Yes," continued Cerizet, "remembering the business-like manner in which you managed the affair of this house in which you do me the honor to receive me, I thought I could not do better than to call your attention to a matter of the same kind which I have just now in hand. But I shall not do as la Peyrade did, —make a bargain for the hand of your goddaughter, and profess great friendship and devotion to you personally. This is purely business, and I expect to make my profit out of it. Now, as I still desire to become the principal tenant of this house,—the letting of which must be a care and a disappointment to mademoiselle, for I saw as I came along that the shops were still unrented,—I think that this lease to me, if you will make it, might be reckoned in to my share of the profits. You see, monsieur, that the object of my visit has nothing to do with the newspaper."

"What is this new affair?" said Brigitte; "that's the first thing to know."

"It relates to a farm in Beauce, which has just been sold for a song, and it is placed in my hands to resell, at an advance, but a small one; you could really buy it, as the saying is, for a bit of bread."

And Cerizet went on to explain the whole mechanism of the affair, which we need not relate here, as no one but Brigitte would take any interest in it. The statement was clear and precise, and it took close hold on the old maid's mind. Even Thuillier himself, in spite of his inward distrust, was obliged to own that the affair had all the appearance of a good speculation.

"Only," said Brigitte, "we must first see the farm ourselves."

This, the reader will remember, was her answer to la Peyrade when he first proposed the purchase of the house at the Madeleine.

"Nothing is easier than that," said Cerizet. "I myself want to see it, and I have been intending to make a little excursion there. If you like, I'll be at your door this afternoon with a post-chaise, and to-morrow morning, very early, we can examine the farm, breakfast at some inn near by, and be back in time for dinner."

"A post-chaise!" said Brigitte, "that's very lordly; why not take the diligence?"

"Diligences are so uncertain," replied Cerizet; "you never know at what time they will get to a place. But you need not think about the expense, for I should otherwise go alone, and I am only too happy to offer you two seats in my carriage."

To misers, small gains are often determining causes in great matters; after a little resistance "pro forma," Brigitte ended by accepting the proposal, and three hours later the trio were on the road to Chartres, Cerizet having advised Thuillier not to let la Peyrade know of his absence, lest he might take some unfair advantage of it.

The next day, by five o'clock, the party had returned, and the brother and sister, who kept their opinions to themselves in presence of Cerizet, were both agreed that the purchase was a good one. They had found the soil of the best quality, the buildings in perfect repair, the cattle looked sound and healthy; in short, this idea of becoming the mistress of rural property seemed to Brigitte the final consecration of opulence.

"Minard," she remarked, "has only a town-house and invested capital, whereas we shall have all that and a country-place besides; one can't be really rich without it."

Thuillier was not sufficiently under the charm of that dream—the realization of which was, in any case, quite distant—to forget, even for a moment, the "Echo de la Bievre" and his candidacy. No sooner had he reached home than he asked for the morning's paper.

"It has not come," said the "male domestic."

"That's a fine distribution, when even the owner of the paper is not served!" cried Thuillier, discontentedly.

Although it was nearly dinner-time, and after his journey he would much rather have taken a bath than rush to the rue Saint-Dominique, Thuillier ordered a cab and drove at once to the office of the "Echo."

There a fresh disappointment met him. The paper "was made," as they say, and all the employees had departed, even la Peyrade. As for Coffinet, who was not to be found at his post of office-boy, nor yet at his other post of porter, he had gone "of an errand," his wife said, taking the key of the closet in which the remaining copies of the paper were locked up. Impossible, therefore, to procure the number which the unfortunate proprietor had come so far to fetch.

To describe Thuillier's indignation would be impossible. He marched up and down the room, talking aloud to himself, as people do in moments of excitement.

"I'll turn them all out!" he cried. And we are forced to omit the rest of the furious objurgation.

As he ended his anathema a rap was heard on the door.

"Come in!" said Thuillier, in a tone that depicted his wrath and his frantic impatience.

The door opened, and Minard rushed precipitately into his arms.

"My good, my excellent friend!" cried the mayor of the eleventh arrondissement, concluding his embrace with a hearty shake of the hand.

"Why! what is it?" said Thuillier, unable to comprehend the warmth of this demonstration.

"Ah! my dear friend," continued Minard, "such an admirable proceeding! really chivalrous! most disinterested! The effect, I assure you, is quite stupendous in the arrondissement."

"But what, I say?" cried Thuillier, impatiently.

"The article, the whole action," continued Minard, "so noble, so elevated!"

"But what article? what action?" said the proprietor of the "Echo," getting quite beside himself.

"The article of this morning," said Minard.

"The article of this morning?"

"Ah ca! did you write it when you were asleep; or, like Monsieur Jourdain doing prose, do you do heroism without knowing it?"

"I! I haven't written any article!" cried Thuillier. "I have been away from Paris for a day, and I don't even know what is in this morning's paper; and the office-boy is not here to give me a copy."

"I have one," said Minard, pulling the much desired paper from his pocket. "If the article is not years you have certainly inspired it; in any case, the deed is done."

Thuillier hurriedly unfolded the sheet Minard had given him, and devoured rather than read the following article:—

Long enough has the proprietor of this regenerated journal submitted without complaint and without reply to the cowardly insinuations with which a venal press insults all citizens who, strong in their convictions, refuse to pass beneath the Caudine Forks of power. Long enough has a man, who has already given proofs of devotion and abnegation in the important functions of the aedility of Paris, allowed these sheets to call him ambitious and self-seeking. Monsieur Jerome Thuillier, strong in his dignity, has suffered such coarse attacks to pass him with contempt. Encouraged by this disdainful silence, the stipendiaries of the press have dared to write that this journal, a work of conviction and of the most disinterested patriotism, was but the stepping-stone of a man, the speculation of a seeker for election. Monsieur Jerome Thuillier has held himself impassible before these shameful imputations because justice and truth are patient, and he bided his time to scotch the reptile. That time has come.

"That deuce of a Peyrade!" said Thuillier, stopping short; "how he does touch it off!"

"It is magnificent!" cried Minard.

Reading aloud, Thuillier continued:—

Every one, friends and enemies alike, can bear witness that Monsieur Jerome Thuillier has done nothing to seek a candidacy which was offered to him spontaneously.

"That's evident," said Thuillier, interrupting himself. Then he resumed:—

But, since his sentiments are so odiously misrepresented, and his intentions so falsely travestied, Monsieur Jerome Thuillier owes it to himself, and above all to the great national party of which he is the humblest soldier, to give an example which shall confound the vile sycophants of power.

"It is fine, the way la Peyrade poses me!" said Thuillier, pausing once more in his reading. "I see now why he didn't send me the paper; he wanted to enjoy my surprise—'confound the vile sycophants of power!' how fine that is!"

After which reflection, he continued:—

Monsieur Thuillier was so far from founding this journal of dynastic opposition to support and promote his election that, at the very moment when the prospects of that election seem most favorable to himself and most disastrous to his rivals, he here declares publicly, and in the most formal, absolute, and irrevocable manner that he *renounces his candidacy*.

"What?" cried Thuillier, thinking he had read wrong, or had misunderstood what he read.

"Go on! go on!" said the mayor of the eleventh.

Then, as Thuillier, with a bewildered air, seemed not disposed to continue his reading, Minard took the paper from his hands and read the rest of the article himself, beginning where the other had left off:—

430

Renounces his candidacy; and he strongly urges the electors to
transfer to Monsieur Minard, mayor of the eleventh arrondissement
and his friend and colleague in his municipal functions, all the
votes with which they seemed about to honor him.

"But this is infamous!" cried Thuillier, recovering his speech; "you have bought that Jesuit la Peyrade."

"So," said Minard, stupefied by Thuillier's attitude, "the article was not agreed upon between you?"

"The wretch has profited by my absence to slip it into the paper; I understand now why he prevented a copy from reaching me to-day."

"My dear friend," said Minard, "what you tell me will seem incredible to the public."

"I tell you it is treachery; it is an abominable trap. Renounce my candidacy! —why should I?"

"You understand, my dear friend," said Minard, "that I am truly sorry if your confidence has been abused, but I have just issued my circular manifesto; the die is cast, and luck to the lucky now."

"Leave me," said Thuillier; "it is a comedy for which you have paid."

"Monsieur Thuillier," said Minard, in a threatening voice, "I advise you not to repeat those words, unless you are ready to give me satisfaction for them."

Happily for Thuillier, who, we may remember, had made his profession of faith as to civic courage some time before, he was relieved from answering by Coffinet, who now opened the door of the editorial sanctum, and announced: —

"Messieurs the electors of the twelfth arrondissement."

The arrondissement was represented on this occasion by five persons. An apothecary, chairman of the deputation, proceeded to address Thuillier in the following terms:—

"We have come, monsieur, after taking cognizance of an article inserted this morning in the 'Echo de la Bievre,' to inquire of you what may be precisely the origin and bearing of that article; thinking it incredible that, having solicited our suffrages, you should, on the eve of this election, and from a most mistaken puritanism, have cast disorder and disunion into our ranks, and probably have caused the triumph of the ministerial candidate. A candidate does not belong to himself; he belongs to the electors who have promised to honor him with their votes. But," continued the orator, casting his eye at Minard, "the presence in these precincts of the candidate whom you have gone out of your way to recommend to us, indicates that between you

431

and him there is connivance; and I have no need to ask who is being here deceived."

"No, messieurs, no," said Thuillier; "I have not renounced my candidacy. That article was written and printed without my knowledge or consent. To-morrow you will see the denial of it in the same paper, and you will also learn that the infamous person who has betrayed my confidence is no longer the editor of this journal."

"Then," said the orator of the deputation, "in spite of your declaration to the contrary, you do continue to be the candidate of the Opposition?"

"Yes, messieurs, until death; and I beg you to use your utmost influence in the quarter to neutralize the effect of this deliberate falsehood until I am able to officially present the most formal disavowal."

"Hear! hear!" said the electors.

"And, as for the presence of Monsieur Minard, my competitor, in these precincts, I have not invited it; and at the moment when you entered this room, I was engaged in a very sharp and decided explanation with him."

"Hear! hear!" said the electors again.

Then, after cordially shaking the hand of the apothecary, Thuillier conducted the deputation to the outer door of the apartment; after which, returning to the editorial sanctum, he said:—

"My dear Minard, I withdraw the words which wounded you; but you can see now what justification I had for my indignation."

Here Coffinet again opened the door and announced:—

"Messieurs the electors of the eleventh arrondissement."

The arrondissement was represented this time by seven persons. A linen-draper, chairman of the delegation, addressed Thuillier in the following speech:—

"Monsieur, it is with sincere admiration that we have learned this morning from the columns of your paper, the great civic act by which you have touched all hearts. You have shown, in thus retiring, a most unusual disinterestedness, and the esteem of your fellow-citizens—"

"Excuse me," said Thuillier, interrupting him, "I cannot allow you to continue; the article about which you are so good as to congratulate me, was inserted by mistake."

"What!" said the linen-draper; "then do you not retire? Can you suppose that in opposition to the candidacy of Monsieur Minard (whose presence in these precincts seems to me rather singular) you have the slightest chance of success?"

"Monsieur," said Thuillier, "have the goodness to request the electors of your arrondissement to await the issue of to-morrow's paper, in which I shall furnish categorical explanations of the most distinct character. The article to-day is the result of a misunderstanding."

"It will be a sad pity, monsieur," said the linen-draper, "if you lose this occasion to place yourself in the eyes of your fellow-citizens beside the Washingtons and other great men of antiquity."

"I say again, *to-morrow*, messieurs," said Thuillier. "I am none the less sensible to the honor you do me, and I trust that when you know the whole truth, I shall not suffer in your esteem."

"A pretty queer mess this seems to be," said the voice of an elector.

"Yes," said another; "it looks as if they meant to bamboozle us."

"Messieurs, messieurs!" cried the chairman, putting a stop to the outbreak; "to-morrow—we will wait until to-morrow for the promised explanations."

Whereupon, the deputation retired.

It is not likely that Thuillier would have accompanied them beyond the door of the sanctum, but in any case he was prevented by the sudden entrance of la Peyrade.

"I have just come from your house, my dear fellow," said the Provencal; "they told me I should find you here."

"You have come, doubtless, for the purpose of explaining to me the strange article you allowed yourself to insert in my name."

"Precisely," said la Peyrade. "The remarkable man whom you know, and whose powerful influence you have already felt, confided to me yesterday, in your interests, the plans of the government, and I saw at once that your defeat was inevitable. I wished therefore to secure to you an honorable and dignified retreat. There was no time to lose; you were absent from Paris, and therefore —"

"Very good, monsieur," said Thuillier; "but you will take notice that from the present moment you are no longer the editor of this paper."

"That is what I came to tell you."

"Perhaps you also came to settle the little account we have together."

"Messieurs," said Minard, "I see that this is a business interview; I shall therefore take leave of you."

As soon as Minard had left the room, la Peyrade pulled out his pocket-book.

"Here are ten thousand francs," he said, "which I will beg you to remit to Mademoiselle Brigitte; and here, also, is the bond by which you secured the payment of twenty-five thousand francs to Madame Lambert; that sum I have now paid in full, and here is the receipt."

"Very good, monsieur," said Thuillier.

La Peyrade bowed and went away.

"Serpent!" said Thuillier as he watched him go.

"Cerizet said the right thing," thought la Peyrade,—"a pompous imbecile!"

The blow struck at Thuillier's candidacy was mortal, but Minard did not profit by it. While the pair were contending for votes, a government man, an aide-de-camp to the king, arrived with his hands full of tobacco licenses and other electoral small change, and, like the third thief, he slipped between the two who were thumping each other, and carried off the booty.

It is needless to say that Brigitte did not get her farm in Beauce. That was only a mirage, by help of which Thuillier was enticed out of Paris long enough for la Peyrade to deal his blow,—a service rendered to the government on the one hand, but also a precious vengeance for the many humiliations he had undergone.

Thuillier had certainly some suspicions as to the complicity of Cerizet, but that worthy managed to justify himself; and by manoeuvring the sale of the "Echo de la Bievre," now become a nightmare to the luckless owner, he ended by appearing as white as snow.

The paper was secretly bought up by Corentin, and the late opposition sheet became a "canard" sold on Sundays in the wine-shops and concocted in the dens of the police.

CHAPTER XVII. IN THE EXERCISE OF HIS FUNCTIONS

About two months after the scene in which la Peyrade had been convinced that through a crime of his past life his future was irrevocably settled, he (being now married to his victim, who was beginning to have lucid intervals, though the full return of her reason would not take place until the occasion indicated by the doctors) was sitting one morning with the head of the police in the latter's office. Taking part in the work of the department, the young man was serving an apprenticeship under that great master in the difficult and delicate functions to which he was henceforth riveted. But Corentin found that his pupil did not bring to this initiation all the ardor and amiability that he desired. It was plain that in la Peyrade's soul there was a sense of forfeiture and degradation; time would get the better of that impression, but the callus was not yet formed.

Opening a number of sealed envelopes enclosing the reports of his various agents, Corentin glanced over these documents, seldom as useful as the public suppose, casting them one after another contemptuously into a basket, whence they issued in a mass for a burning. But to one of them the great man evidently gave some particular attention; as he read it a smile flickered on his lips, and when he had finished, instead of adding it to the pile in the basket, he gave it to la Peyrade.

"Here," he said, "here's something that concerns you; it shows that in our profession, which just now seems to you unpleasantly serious, we do occasionally meet with comedies. Read it aloud; it will cheer me up."

Before la Peyrade began to read, Corentin added:—

"I ought to tell you that the report is from a man called Henri, whom Madame Komorn introduced as man-servant at the Thuilliers'; you probably remember him."

"So!" said la Peyrade, "servants placed in families! is that one of your methods?"

"Sometimes," replied Corentin; "in order to know all, we must use all means. But a great many lies are told about us on that subject. It is not true that the police, making a system of it, has, at certain periods, by a general enrolment of lacqueys and lady's-maids, established a vast network in private families. Nothing is fixed and absolute in our manner of proceeding; we act in accordance with the time and circumstances. I wanted an ear and an influence in the Thuillier household; accordingly, I let loose the Godollo upon it, and she, in turn, partly to assist herself, installed there one of our men, an intelligent fellow, as you will see for yourself. But for all that, if, at another time, a servant came and offered to sell me the secrets of his master, I should have him arrested, and let a warning reach the ears of the family to distrust the other servants. Now go on, and read that report."

Monsieur the Director of the Secret Police,

read la Peyrade aloud,—

I did not stay long with the little baron; he is a man wholly occupied in frivolous pleasures; and there was nothing to be gathered there that was worthy of a report to you. I have found another place, where I have already witnessed several thing which fit into the mission that Madame de Godollo gave me, and therefore, thinking them likely to interest you, I hasten to bring them to your knowledge. The household in which I am now employed is that of an old savant, named Monsieur Picot, who lives on a first floor, Place de la Madeleine, in the house and apartment formerly occupied by my late masters, the Thuilliers—

"What!" cried la Peyrade, interrupting his reading, "Pere Picot, that ruined old lunatic, occupying such an apartment as that?"

"Go on, go on!" said Corentin; "life is full of many strange things. You'll find the explanation farther along; for our correspondent—it is the defect of those fellows to waste themselves on details—is only too fond of dotting his i's."

La Peyrade read on:—

The Thuilliers left this apartment some weeks ago to return to their Latin quarter. Mademoiselle Brigitte never really liked our sphere; her total want of education made her ill at ease. Just because I speak correctly, she was always calling me 'the orator,' and she could not endure Monsieur Pascal, her porter, because, being beadle in the church of the Madeleine, he had manners; she even found something to say against the dealers in the great market behind the church, where, of course, she bought her provisions; she complained that they gave themselves *capable* airs, merely because they are not so coarse-tongued as those of the Halle, and only laughed at her when she tried to beat them down. She has leased the whole house to a certain Monsieur Cerizet (a very ugly man, with a nose all eaten away) for an annual rent of fifty-five thousand francs. This tenant seems to know what he is about. He has lately married an actress at one of the minor theatres, Mademoiselle Olympe Cardinal, and he was just about to occupy himself the first-floor apartment, where he proposed to establish his present business, namely, insurance for the "dots" of children, when Monsieur Picot, arriving from England with his wife, a very rich Englishwoman, saw the apartment and offered such a good price that Monsieur Cerizet felt constrained to take it. That was the time when, by the help of M. Pascal, the porter, with whom I have been careful to maintain good relations, I entered the household of Monsieur Picot.

"Monsieur Picot married to a rich Englishwoman!" exclaimed la Peyrade, interrupting himself again; "but it is incomprehensible."

"Go on, I tell you," said Corentin; "you'll comprehend it presently."

437

The fortune of my new master,

continued la Peyrade,

is quite a history; and I speak of it to Monsieur le directeur
because another person in whom Madame de Godollo was interested
has his marriage closely mixed up in it. That other person is
Monsieur Felix Phellion, the inventor of a star, who, in despair
at not being able to marry that demoiselle whom they wanted to
give to the Sieur la Peyrade whom Madame de Godollo made such a
fool of—

"Scoundrel!" said the Provencal, in a parenthesis. "Is that how he speaks of me? He doesn't know who I am."

Corentin laughed heartily and exhorted his pupil to read on.

—who, in despair at not being able to marry that demoiselle …
went to England in order to embark for a journey round the world
—a lover's notion! Learning of this departure, Monsieur Picot,
his former professor, who took great interest in his pupil, went
after him to prevent that nonsense, which turned out not to be
difficult. The English are naturally very jealous of discoveries,
and when they saw Monsieur Phellion coming to embark at the heels
of their own savants they asked him for his permit from the
Admiralty; which, not having been provided, he could not produce;
so then they laughed in his face and would not let him embark at
all, fearing that he should prove more learned than they.

"He is a fine hand at the 'entente cordiale,' your Monsieur Henri," said la Peyrade, gaily.

"Yes," replied Corentin; "you will be struck, in the reports of nearly all our agents, with this general and perpetual inclination to calumniate. But what's to be done? For the trade of spies we can't have angels."

Left upon the shore, Telemachus and his mentor—

"You see our men are lettered," commented Corentin.

—Telemachus and his mentor thought best to return to France, and
were about to do so when Monsieur Picot received a letter such as
none but an Englishwoman could write. It told him that the writer
had read his "Theory of Perpetual Motion," and had also heard of
his magnificent discovery of a star; that she regarded him as a
genius only second to Newton, and that if the hand of her who
addressed him, joined to eighty thousand pounds sterling—that is,
two millions—of "dot," was agreeable to him it was at his
disposal. The first thought of the good man was to make his pupil
marry her, but finding that impossible, he told her, before
accepting on his own account, that he was old and three-quarters
blind, and had never discovered a star, and did not own a penny.
The Englishwoman replied that Milton was not young either, and was
altogether blind; that Monsieur Picot seemed to her to have
nothing worse than a cataract, for she knew all about it, being
the daughter of a great oculist, and she would have him operated
upon; that as for the star, she did not care so very much about
that; it was the author of the "Theory of Perpetual Motion" who
was the man of her dreams, and to whom she again offered her hand
with eighty thousand pounds sterling (two millions) of "dot."
Monsieur Picot replied that if his sight were restored and she
would consent to live in Paris, for he hated England, he would let
himself be married. The operation was performed and was
successful, and, at the end of three weeks the newly married pair
arrived in the capital. These details I obtained from the lady's

maid, with whom I am on the warmest terms.

"Oh! the puppy!" said Corentin, laughing.

The above is therefore hearsay, but what remains to be told to
Monsieur le directeur are facts of which I can speak "de visu,"
and to which I am, consequently, in a position to certify. As
soon as Monsieur and Madame Picot had installed themselves, which
was done in the most sumptuous and comfortable manner, my master
gave me a number of invitations to dinner to carry to the
Thuillier family, the Colleville family, the Minard family, the
Abbe Gondrin, vicar of the Madeleine, and nearly all the guests
who were present at another dinner a few months earlier, when he
had an encounter with Mademoiselle Thuillier, and behaved, I must
say, in a rather singular manner. All the persons who received
these invitations were so astonished to learn that the old man
Picot had married a rich wife and was living in the Thuilliers'
old apartment that most of them came to inquire of Monsieur
Pascal, the porter, to see if they were hoaxed. The information
they obtained being honest and honorable, the whole society
arrived punctually on time; but Monsieur Picot did not appear.
The guests were received by Madame Picot, who does not speak
French and could only say, "My husband is coming soon"; after
which, not being able to make further conversation, the company
were dull and ill at ease. At last Monsieur Picot arrived, and all
present were stupefied on seeing, instead of an old blind man,
shabbily dressed, a handsome young elderly man, bearing his years
jauntily, like Monsieur Ferville of the Gymnase, who said with a
lively air:

"I beg your pardon, mesdames, for not being here at the moment of
your arrival; but I was at the Academy of Sciences, awaiting the
result of an election,—that of Monsieur Felix Phellion, who has
been elected unanimously less three votes."

This news seemed to have a great effect upon the company. So then
Monsieur Picot resumed:—

"I must also, mesdames, ask your pardon for the rather improper
manner in which I behaved a short time ago in the house where we
are now assembled. My excuse must be my late infirmity, the
annoyances of a family lawsuit, and of an old housekeeper who
robbed me and tormented me in a thousand ways, from whom I am
happily delivered. To-day you see me another man, rejuvenated and
rich with the blessings bestowed upon me by the amiable woman who
has given me her hand; and I should be in the happiest frame of
mind to receive you if the recollection of my young friend, whose
eminence as a man of science has just been consecrated by the
Academy, did not cast upon my mind a veil of sadness. All here
present," continued Monsieur Picot, raising his voice, which is
rather loud, "are guilty towards him: I, for ingratitude when he
gave me the glory of his discovery and the reward of his immortal
labors; that young lady, whom I see over there with tears in her
eyes, for having foolishly accused him of atheism; that other
lady, with the stern face, for having harshly replied to the
proposals of his noble father, whose white hairs she ought rather
to have honored; Monsieur Thuillier, for having sacrificed him to
ambition; Monsieur Colleville, for not performing his part of
father and choosing for his daughter the worthiest and most
honorable man; Monsieur Minard, for having tried to foist his son
into his place. There are but two persons in the room at this
moment who have done him full justice,—Madame Thuillier and
Monsieur l'Abbe Gondrin. Well, I shall now ask that man of God
whether we can help doubting the divine justice when this generous
young man, the victim of all of us, is, at the present hour, at
the mercy of waves and tempests, to which for three long years he
is consigned."

"Providence is very powerful, monsieur," replied the Abbe Gondrin.

"God will protect Monsieur Felix Phellion wherever he may be, and I have the firmest hope that three years hence he will be among his friends once more."

"But three years!" said Monsieur Picot. "Will it still be time? Will Mademoiselle Colleville have waited for him?"

"Yes, I swear it!" cried the young girl, carried away by an impulse she could not control.

Then she sat down again, quite ashamed, and burst into tears.

"And you, Mademoiselle Thuillier, and you, Madame Colleville, will you permit this young lady to reserve herself for one who is worthy of her?"

"Yes! Yes!" cried everybody; for Monsieur Picot's voice, which is very full and sonorous, seemed to have tears in it and affected everybody.

"Then it is time," he said, "to forgive Providence."

And rushing suddenly to the door, where my ear was glued to the keyhole, he very nearly caught me.

"Announce," he said to me, in a very loud tone of voice, "Monsieur Felix Phellion and his family."

And thereupon the door of a side room opened, and five or six persons came out, who were led by Monsieur Picot into the salon.

At the sight of her *lover*, Mademoiselle Colleville was taken ill, but the faint lasted only a minute; seeing Monsieur Felix at her feet she threw herself into Madame Thuillier's arms, crying out:—

"Godmother! you always told me to hope."

Mademoiselle Thuillier, who, in spite of her harsh nature and want of education, I have always myself thought a remarkable woman, now had a fine impulse. As the company were about to go into the dining-room,—

"One moment!" she said.

Then going up to Monsieur Phellion, senior, she said to him:

"Monsieur and old friend! I ask you for the hand of Monsieur Felix Phellion for our adopted daughter, Mademoiselle Colleville."

"Bravo! bravo!" they call cried in chorus.

"My God!" said Monsieur Phellion, with tears in his eyes; "what have I done to deserve such happiness?"

"You have been an honest man and a Christian without knowing it," replied the Abbe Gondrin.

Here la Peyrade flung down the manuscript.

"You did not finish it," said Corentin, taking back the paper. "However, there's not much more. Monsieur Henri confesses to me that the scene had *moved him*; he also says that, knowing the interest I had formerly taken in the marriage, he thought he ought to inform me of its conclusion; ending with a slightly veiled suggestion of a fee. No, stay," resumed Corentin, "here is a detail of some importance:—"

The English woman seems to have made it known during dinner that,
having no heirs, her fortune, after the lives of herself and her
husband, will go to Felix. That will make him powerfully rich one
of these days.

La Peyrade had risen and was striding about the room with rapid steps.

"Well," said Corentin, "what is the matter with you?"

"Nothing."

"That is not true," said the great detective. "I think you envy the happiness of that young man. My dear fellow, permit me to tell you that if such a conclusion were to your taste, you should have acted as he has done. When I sent you two thousand francs on which to study law, I did not intend you to succeed me; I expected you to row your galley laboriously, to have the needful courage for obscure and painful toil; your day would infallibly have come. But you chose to violate fortune—"

"Monsieur!"

"I mean hasten it, reap it before it ripened. You flung yourself into journalism; then into business, questionable business; you made acquaintance with Messieurs Dutocq and Cerizet. Frankly, I think you fortunate to have entered the port which harbors you to-day. In any case, you are not sufficiently simple of heart to have really valued the joys reserved for Felix Phellion. These bourgeois—"

"These bourgeois," said la Peyrade, quickly,—"I know them now. They have great absurdities, great vices even, but they have virtues, or, at the least, estimable qualities; in them lies the vital force of our corrupt society."

"*Your* society!" said Corentin, smiling; "you speak as if you were still in the ranks. You have another sphere, my dear fellow; and you must learn to be more content with your lot. Governments pass, societies perish or dwindle; but we—*we* dominate all things; the police is eternal."

TRANSLATOR'S NOTE

Note.—This volume ("Les Petits Bourgeois") was not published
until 1854, more than three years after Balzac's death; although
he says of it in March, 1844: "I must tell you that my work
entitled 'Les Petits Bourgeois,' owing to difficulties of
execution, requires still a month's labor, although the book is
entirely written." And again, in October, 1846, he says: "It is to
such scruples" (care in perfecting his work) "that delays which
have injured several of my works are due; for instance, 'Les
Paysans,' which has long been nearly finished, and 'Les Petits
Bourgeois,' which has been in type at the printing office for the
last eighteen months."

ADDENDUM

The following personages appear in other stories of the Human Comedy.

Barbet
    A Distinguished Provincial at Paris
    A Man of Business
    The Seamy Side of History
    The Middle Classes

Baudoyer, Isidore
    The Government Clerks
    The Middle Classes
    Cousin Pons

Beaumesnil, Mademoiselle
    The Middle Classes
    Scenes from a Courtesan's Life
    A Second Home

Bianchon, Horace
    Father Goriot
    The Atheist's Mass
    Cesar Birotteau
    The Commission in Lunacy
    Lost Illusions
    A Distinguished Provincial at Paris
    A Bachelor's Establishment
    The Secrets of a Princess
    The Government Clerks
    Pierrette
    A Study of Woman
    Scenes from a Courtesan's Life
    Honorine
    The Seamy Side of History
    The Magic Skin
    A Second Home
    A Prince of Bohemia
    Letters of Two Brides
    The Muse of the Department
    The Imaginary Mistress
    The Middle Classes
    Cousin Betty
    The Country Parson
In addition, M. Bianchon narrated the following:
    Another Study of Woman
    La Grande Breteche

Bousquier, Du (or Du Croisier or Du Bourguier)
    Jealousies of a Country Town
    The Middle Classes

Brisetout, Heloise
    Cousin Betty
    Cousin Pons
    The Middle Classes

Bruel, Jean Francois du
    A Bachelor's Establishment
    The Government Clerks
    A Start in Life

445

Lightning Source UK Ltd.
Milton Keynes UK
UKHW012016130123
415332UK00003B/140